Cursed with a poor sense of direction and a propensity to read, **Annie Claydon** spent much of her childhood lost in books. A degree in English Literature followed by a career in computing didn't lead directly to her perfect job—writing romance for Mills & Boon—but she has no regrets in taking the scenic route. She lives in London: a city where getting lost can be a joy.

**Louisa Heaton** lives on Hayling Island, Hampshire, with her husband, four children and a small zoo. She has worked in various roles in the health industry—most recently four years as a Community First Responder, answering 999 calls. When not writing Louisa enjoys other creative pursuits, including reading, quilting and patchwork—usually instead of the things she *ought* to be doing!

WITHDRAWN

# HEALED BY THE SINGLE DAD DOC

## ANNIE CLAYDON

# A CHILD TO HEAL THEM

## LOUISA HEATON

**MILLS & BOON**

Published in Great Britain 2018
by Mills & Boon, an imprint of HarperCollins*Publishers*
1 London Bridge Street, London, SE1 9GF

Healed by the Single Dad Doc © 2018 Annie Claydon

A Child to Heal Them © 2018 Louisa Heaton

ISBN: 978-0-263-93340-6

**MIX**
Paper from
responsible sources
FSC
www.fsc.org
**FSC** C007454

This book is produced from independently certified FSC™ paper
to ensure responsible forest management.
For more information visit www.harpercollins.co.uk/green.

Printed and bound in Spain
by CPI, Barcelona

# HEALED BY THE SINGLE DAD DOC

## ANNIE CLAYDON

# MILLS & BOON

To Kate.
Wishing you unicorns.

# CHAPTER ONE

DR ETHAN CONWAY WAS no stranger to the saving of lives. And also no stranger to the desolate feeling of having to accept that sometimes there is nothing that can be done.

And Jeff wasn't 'just' a dog. He was Ethan's dog. The gentle, giant Newfoundland would be over ninety now in human years. Old age was finally catching up with him and, if his gradual decline over the last three weeks hadn't come as any surprise, it had still been hard.

'All right, Jeff. She'll be here in a minute.' Ethan had parked the car in the empty forecourt of the veterinary surgery, and he twisted round in his seat. Jeff lifted his head slightly at the sound of his name and Ethan reached back, stroking the dog's head. Jeff had been with him for nine years, through love and loss, dreams and shattered hopes, and the thought of losing him now hurt.

*It's okay to be upset about this.*

The words of the pretty red-haired vet who'd seen Jeff last week sounded in Ethan's head. He'd explained to her that, in the scheme of things, this wasn't so bad and she'd cut through his bravado with one look.

Another car swung onto the forecourt, its headlights blinding him for a moment. It stopped at an interesting angle, taking up two parking spaces, and the driver's door opened. Kate Foster got out, hurrying across to where Ethan's car was parked.

'I'll straighten it up in a minute...' Ethan wound the driver's window down and she grinned at him. 'Have you been waiting long? I'm sorry, my last call took a bit longer than I anticipated.'

'I was early. And it's good of you to see us so late in the evening.'

She brushed the idea away with a wave of her hand, even though Ethan knew from his earlier conversation with the receptionist that Kate had been working all day. Despite that, she was all fresh-faced energy as she craned her neck through the window of his car, her gaze seeking Jeff out.

'Hello, Jeff. How are you doing, old boy?'

Jeff's tail thumped on the seat and he raised his head again. Kate smiled, and Ethan provided the answer to her question.

'He's been a lot more comfortable since you saw him last week. I've been giving him the medication regularly.'

She nodded. 'Good. Let's get him inside and I'll take a look at him.'

Kate unlocked the main door of the surgery and waited while Ethan unclipped the car safety-harness. Jeff lumbered slowly inside. The door slammed behind them and she squeezed past him in the narrow entranceway, leaving a scent of fresh air and flowers behind her as she walked through the darkened reception area and opened a door to the surgery at the back, flipping on the light.

'Bring him through...' She held the door open and Ethan bent, ready to lift the large dog up onto the examination couch. 'That's okay. Sit down there with him. He didn't much like it up on the couch last time, did he?'

She'd only seen Jeff once before but she remembered. Ethan sat down gratefully on the long vinyl-covered bench which ran along one wall of the surgery, and Jeff sprawled on the floor next to him, leaning against Ethan's legs.

'You'll be okay there for a moment? I've got to go and get my bag from the car.' She gave a smiling shrug that, for one moment, dispelled the weight in his heart. 'I should probably take another shot at that parking bay, too. I'm told the white lines are there for a reason.'

'We'll be fine. Call me if you need someone to wave you in to your space.'

She chuckled, and it occurred to Ethan that parking in a straight line wasn't much in Kate's nature. At work, she was thoughtful and methodical, but everything else she did betrayed a deliciously free spirit.

He heard the sound of the front door closing behind her. Then silence, broken only by the faint whisper of a car engine. A dull thud, and then silence again.

'Better go and see if she needs some help, Jeff.' Ethan shifted Jeff to one side a little and got to his feet. As he did so, the sound of a scream made the hairs on the back of his neck stand on end.

No... Not so much a scream as a battle cry—the incoherent noise of blind effort and determination. Ethan ran to the front door, cursing as he fumbled with the catch in the darkness.

His eyes strained against the shadows cast by the high hedge which ran around the forecourt. Kate's car had been backed into a parking space, and a few feet away she was struggling to escape from a dark form which was gripping her arm.

'Hey! Let go of her!' Ethan hollered at the top of his

lungs and the shadow froze for a moment. That moment was just enough for Kate to land a punch, and as the man's head snapped around his hood fell from across his face and Ethan saw him.

Young—early twenties, probably. Dark hair cut short. The details registered automatically in the back of Ethan's mind as he made a charge towards them, a roar escaping from his lips.

The more she fought, the greater danger there was of her being hurt. But instinct had taken over and Kate was fighting. She aimed another punch at the man and he threw her to the ground. Ethan heard Kate yelp as the man aimed a kick at her ribs, before running out of the forecourt and across the road.

'Kate…' She was halfway to her feet, scrambling backwards away from him as Ethan slowed his pace, walking towards her. 'Kate, it's all right.'

His words weren't registering. He'd seen this before, someone so frightened that they'd fight anyone off, even the people who came to help them. Ethan held his hands up in a gesture of surrender, his heart pounding.

She was stumbling towards her car, her eyes wide in the darkness, red corkscrew curls of hair escaping from the knot at the back of her head. Ethan tried to head her off, wondering whether she might be about to lock herself in her car and try to drive away, but she seemed more interested in the back of the vehicle than the driver's door.

'It's okay, Kate. He's gone now.'

'Gone?' The one word seemed to penetrate her panic. 'You're sure?'

'Yes, I saw him run across the road and get into a van. They've driven away.' He stepped forward and she practically fell into his arms, hugging him.

He could feel her body shaking against his. Ethan held her tight. This was...

It was almost...good. Almost the best thing he'd done in a long time. He smoothed the dishevelled curls on the back of her head, trying to focus on what he was supposed to be doing. Comfort. That was right.

'You've had a shock.' Ethan swallowed down the impulse to tell her that everything was all right now. However much he wanted to make it all right, that wasn't in his power. 'Are you hurt?'

'No, I...' He could feel her hands clutching at his sweater. 'I don't think so.'

'We'll get you inside and have a look.' He made to lead her towards the front door of the surgery, but she resisted, suddenly breaking free of him.

'Sorry...sorry, I'm okay. I have to get my bag.' Kate looked up at him apologetically, wiping the sleeve of her jacket across her tear-stained face. Flipping the car remote, she opened the boot, pushing a rug back to reveal a boot safe.

She sorted through her keys, pushing out a sharp breath as if to steady herself. But when she tried to open the safe, her hands were shaking too much.

'Let me.' Ethan held out his hand and for a moment panic flared in her eyes again and she gripped her keys tightly.

'Yes... Sorry. Thanks.' She handed the keys over and he opened the boot safe. Inside, he saw a small zipped bag which obviously held the drugs that she had been carrying.

He wished she'd stop apologising. And that she'd let him take her in his arms again so he could comfort her.

He should tackle the first, as the second was a more selfish impulse.

'This was why you fought him?' Ethan put the bag into her hands and she clutched it to her chest, nodding.

'I know I should have just let him take the car but I couldn't bear to think that these would get into the wrong hands.'

She was twisting her mouth wryly, probably about to apologise again. Ethan cut her short.

'You might have been a little too brave, but I can't say I would have done any different. I don't much like the thought of these getting onto the streets either.' He'd seen the results of that, more than once. And, if he couldn't entirely approve of a course of action that might result in Kate being hurt, he could understand her motives.

'And you shouted for help.' Ethan decided to concentrate on something that he could recommend entirely.

'I…was just making a noise. I didn't expect anyone to come. Thank you.' She looked up at him and smiled suddenly. *Really* smiled, as if he were some kind of hero, and not just a man who had a chequered and uncertain history of being there when he was needed.

'I'm just glad I was here to help.' Ethan took the risk of putting his arm loosely around her shoulders again, and she nestled against him as he shepherded her slowly towards the main door of the surgery.

He didn't seem to think anything of it. It was a big thing, running out of the surgery like that to help her. Ethan Conway was different from other men. Dependable, if ever she wanted to use that word again…

It was just the shock. The feeling that she wanted him to hold her and not let go would wear off, along with the tremor in her hands. He'd become just another guy, nicer to look at than most, but still easy to let go of.

But it seemed *he* wasn't letting go of her. He walked with her to the drugs cupboard, waiting while she negotiated the series of locks that kept it secure. Then back into the consulting room, where Jeff was dozing in exactly the same pose as when she'd left Ethan and him.

'I'll take a look at Jeff and then I should call the police.' Getting back to normal was what Kate needed to do now. She didn't want to think about Ethan's dark-blue eyes. Or the lilt of his accent, soft as the Yorkshire hills that could be seen from almost every part of this town.

'No. I'll make you a cup of tea. Then *I'll* call the police.'

His suggestion sounded a lot better. But she'd already spent too much time wanting to lean on him. She didn't want to compound the problem by showing him that she was hurt.

'That's okay, I'll…' Kate could feel her arm throbbing, from the elbow to the tip of her thumb. 'Actually, a cup of tea might be really nice. Thank you.'

He raised his eyebrows at her sudden *volte face*. 'Sure you're all right?'

'Yes, fine. I'd just really like a cup of tea. There's a tea station behind the reception area.' It would take him five minutes to make the tea and that would give Kate some time to inspect the damage. 'Milk and three sugars, please.'

He nodded. 'You feel dizzy?'

'No, I always take three sugars in my tea.' Kate looked up at him half-apologetically, and he nodded.

She waited until he'd closed the door to the surgery behind him and then carefully slipped her arm out of her jacket, rolling up the sleeve of her shirt. Her forearm was beginning to swell, and although the skin wasn't broken it was an angry red. Kate turned on the cold tap, wincing as she let the cool water pour over her arm.

She could move all of her fingers and her thumb. Kate might be more conversant with animal physiology but a fractured bone didn't look much different however many legs you had. This didn't look like a fracture, and the swelling would probably go down by morning.

'Don't tell anyone, right?' She whispered the words to Jeff as she carefully dabbed her arm dry with a tissue and rolled her sleeve back down. Sitting down next to him, she wriggled painfully into her jacket, and Jeff stretched, putting his head in her lap and drooling onto her trousers.

'Yes, I know. I just don't want any fuss.' She'd bet that Ethan *would* make a fuss, and she didn't want to feel how good it was to have him look after her.

He reappeared in the doorway, holding a cup of tea. Setting it down on her desk, he pulled the high-backed chair out. 'Sit here. Jeff will be all right for a moment.'

Kate stared at him. No doubt Jeff *would* be all right. It was her own reaction to Ethan's stubborn determination to look after her that she was worried about.

'I'm a doctor. You took a nasty fall just now, and when the guy ran he caught you in the ribs with his boot. I'd like to make sure you're okay.'

Damn it! When did doctors get to be blue-eyed, blond-haired handsome-hero material? Kate supposed that his profession must be in the notes that had been left on her desk somewhere, but at the moment she could barely think straight enough to remember her middle name.

'If you're thinking about telling me you're all right

again, then you should consider the possibility that adrenaline has a way of keeping the body going while you fight or fly.'

He had a point. Maybe she should have shown him her arm, to divert his attention from her ribs. But it was too late for that now, and mentioning any new aches and pains would only draw this out even further. Kate walked over to her desk, sitting down with a bump and wincing as pain shot up her back.

Ethan's expression softened, and she tried to ignore the fact that the smile on his face was inspiring both confidence and an inappropriate wish to touch him. He pulled up a chair, sitting down opposite her.

'What hurt you just then?'

'My side. Where he kicked me.' She brushed her hand across the spot, trying not to react to the pain that shot up her arm.

'Okay. May I take a look?'

'What kind of doctor are you?' She made one last attempt at resistance.

'The kind that knows the difference between a bruise and a cracked rib.' He grinned at her. 'Actually, I'm a trauma surgeon, so I've seen a fair number of both.'

'Oh. Sorry.' Kate felt herself redden.

'That's okay. Actually, everything's okay, just in case you were thinking of apologising about anything else.'

This guy was a bloody dream. Relaxed, good-humoured, handsome. Her hero...

She had to get a grip. If she just did what needed to be done, one thing at a time, she'd be okay. *Just draw the lines and stay within them. Forget about everything else.* She slipped off her jacket and Ethan reached around to the spot she'd indicated, pulling her shirt up a little so he could see.

'Lean forward a little more… That's right.'

She felt the brush of his hands against her side. It had been a while since she'd shivered at a man's touch against her skin and now wasn't a good time to get reacquainted with the feeling. She squeezed her eyes closed, trying to imagine herself somewhere else.

'Take a deep breath. In…' She felt his fingers around her ribs. Kate filled her lungs with air and her head began to swim.

'Out…' His fingers moved higher. 'Just relax.'

*Relax? Really?*

'Favourite place?'

'What?' Kate was dimly aware that his gentle examination had stopped.

'Your favourite place. Mine's at the top of Summer Hill. Do you know it?'

'Yes, I know it.' It was beautiful there, the hillside stretching gently down to woodlands and fields, small villages in the distance. It was a lovely spot, but not Kate's favourite. Despite the fact that London had chewed her up and spat her out, she still loved the place.

'Sitting by the river, in London. At dusk, watching the lights come on along the Embankment.'

'What part of the Embankment?'

'I like… You know the part by the statue of Boudicca?' Kate could almost hear the buzz of the traffic and the quiet sound of the water. She felt calmer now, just imagining it.

'Yes, I know it. I've always rather liked the cast-iron lamp stands they have there. The ones with dolphins at the base.'

'Yes, they're great. You know London?'

'I studied down there. Deep breath.'

Kate obeyed him without thinking. She was leaning against him now, his hands splayed around her back and sides. Relaxed, almost in an embrace...

She sat up abruptly, the picture of home that had been so real in her head suddenly dissolving. Ethan smiled slowly.

'Gotcha.'

'So you did. You're satisfied now?'

He nodded. 'Yes. I don't feel any sign of broken ribs. You may well hurt in the morning, though. May I see your face?'

He was going to do this face to face now? Kate fixed her gaze on the far corner of the room, so as not to meet his. She felt Ethan's thumb on her brow, smoothing back her hair. She must look such a mess...

'Just a graze. You might have a bruise there tomorrow.'

When he spoke, her concentration broke, and she looked at him. His face was a model of propriety, but his eyes... Those eyes would be wicked in any setting.

It was all in her own mind. A blue-eyed prince in shining armour. Someone who could chase away dragons and then gently inspect for any damage. It was beguiling.

'Okay...thanks.' Kate pulled the scrunchie out of her hair and coiled the mass of red curls back into a neat knot at the base of her neck. The everyday movement seemed to calm her a little.

'Anything else?'

'No. Thanks, there's nothing else.' Her arm hurt like crazy, but she needed this to end. Needed to get on to the next thing on her mental list of things to do after a mugging. 'We should call the police.'

'I'll go and call them now.' He stood up, pulling his phone from his pocket, easy and unhurried, as if there was nothing to worry about. Clearly he was planning to do it out of earshot.

'Thanks. I'll…drink my tea.'

Kate waited until he'd gone and stood, stretching her limbs, trying to shake off the feeling of numb dread that suddenly accompanied being alone. Jeff raised his head, his tail thumping on the floor, and Kate walked over to sit beside him and stroke his head.

'All right. Everything's all right, Jeff.'

But everything *wasn't* all right. She needed to stop being a victim and get back to doing her job.

'Kate… Run…' Mark had shouted the words and then taken off, running away from her down the deserted street.

One o'clock in the morning and she'd only had eyes for him, not noticing the two men lounging at the entrance to her local underground station.

But she hadn't been able to run. Her bag had been slung across her body and she'd felt it being pulled, the strap tightening around her. Someone had dragged at her arm, pulling her watch from her wrist.

She'd tried to scream then, but there had been a hand over her mouth. So frightened. She'd been so frightened.

'Be quiet.'

One of the men had held her from behind and the other had searched her, feeling her neck and hands for jewellery. Then he'd cut the strap of her bag and taken that.

That might have been the end of it. Kate had been praying they'd just take what they wanted and go. But they hadn't. She'd felt someone push her backwards, and in a moment of helpless terror she had known there was no way she could avert what was going to happen next.

She'd felt herself crash down the metal-edged stairs. Lying at the bottom, against the closed gates that led into the station, she'd sobbed for Mark—but he had already gone.

The sound of the door opening brought Kate back to the here and now, her heart thumping to the beat of memories that suddenly seemed new and raw again. Whatever had made her think that moving away would allow her to leave all that behind?

'Sorry. I didn't mean to make you jump.'

She wasn't aware that she *had* jumped. Just that the familiar feeling of dread was back again, threatening all she'd done to chase it away. Kate couldn't let it back in.

'I'm okay. Really. I just have to get back to normal.' She wasn't even sure what normal was at that moment. Her nerves were jangling with alarm, and she was acutely aware of every sound outside the window—even the cars, passing in the road outside, which normally went unnoticed.

'Sometimes *normal* doesn't quite hack it.' He spoke quietly and Kate realised that she must have snapped at him. She took a deep breath.

'I'm sorry. It's just a shock. I thought I'd be safe here...' Kate pressed her lips together. Something about Ethan made it all too easy to talk.

'Safe?'

'I moved up to Yorkshire from London a couple of years ago. I reckoned it couldn't happen...' Kate shrugged. Of course street crime happened here. It just

hadn't happened to her, and that had given her a false
sense of security.

'Something like this happened to you in London?
Were you hurt?' Not only did he make her want to talk,
he listened as well, reading between the lines. It was a
lethal combination.

'I... Look, I appreciate your concern, but I'm all right.'
Kate hung her head, squeezing her eyes shut. Maybe he
wouldn't see that she was crying. 'I know what to do next
and I really need to just get past this. I don't want to talk
about it any more.'

She felt the brush of something on her cheek. When
she opened her eyes, Ethan was wiping a tear away with
a tissue.

'Okay.' He gave her a smile. 'But I should warn you
that closing your eyes builds up the pressure.'

Despite everything, Kate choked with laughter. 'That's
your considered medical opinion, is it? That if I close my
eyes my head will explode?'

'Risk averted.' He gave her cheek another dab with
the tissue and handed her a fresh one.

She was trying so hard to get on top of this. And she
wasn't giving herself any time to be hurt or frightened—
just swallowing it all down, to a place where it could do
the most harm. Her free spirit seemed crushed under the
weight of it all.

But she clearly wanted him to back off, and she was
probably right. Ethan had no qualms about tending to her
injuries, but anything else... That was wandering into
the realms of emotional support, and Kate would be better off looking for that elsewhere.

'When did the police say they'd be coming?' She'd dried her eyes and seemed more composed now.

'About another half hour. I'll wait with you.' He held up his hand to quiet her protests. 'They said they wanted to speak with me as well. I saw the guy's face.'

She nodded, and Ethan wondered whether Kate had. If so, she seemed intent on burying that as well.

'If you don't mind, I'd like to take a look at Jeff now.'

Actually, he did mind. She'd just had a frightening experience and she should be concentrating on herself. But, if Ethan couldn't calm her, it seemed that Jeff could. When she stroked his head she stopped shaking and a little colour returned to her cheeks.

'When you've finished your tea...'

# CHAPTER TWO

ETHAN WOKE EARLY. There was something wrong about today and right from the start he felt off-balance.

His first thought wasn't for Jeff, sleeping peacefully in the dog basket in the conservatory. Nor was it for his son, Sam, who he could hear playing upstairs, driving his toy cars up and down the wall. It was for Kate.

She'd told him she was all right so many times, but he was pretty sure she wasn't. Perhaps she'd feel better this morning, but Ethan doubted it.

He picked up his phone and put it down again. If Kate had managed to get some sleep last night, she wouldn't welcome him waking her just to ask how she was. And Ethan doubted that he'd get any kind of meaningful answer. She'd just repeat the mantra she'd been using last night.

*I'm okay.*

For about fifteen minutes she *had* seemed okay. Ethan had let her examine Jeff and she'd suddenly snapped out of her shocked misery and into an easy, professional manner. For one moment, he'd envied Jeff her smile and then decided that whatever worked, worked.

Ethan could understand wanting to get on with life. When his wife had died eighteen months ago, his work had given him some relief. It was something that occupied his mind fully, temporarily driving away the pain and guilt.

*Kate's not your responsibility.*

That ought to be *his* mantra. Jenna's death had brought Ethan's own responsibilities into sharp focus. He'd let his wife down, too busy and too tired to notice that she was more than just a little under the weather, as she'd claimed. And now he had to concentrate all his energies on giving Sam the love he needed. If Kate's smile tempted him to forget that, then he had to turn away from it.

'Dad?'

Ethan turned to see Sam in the kitchen doorway. 'Hey, Sammy. Got my hug for me?'

Sam ran into his arms and Ethan hugged him tight. He'd promised his son this, during the dark days after Jenna had died. A hug every morning and one at night. Last night, he'd driven home as fast as he could, afraid that he wouldn't make it, but Sam had stayed awake, falling asleep in Ethan's arms almost as soon as he'd made good on his promise.

'Grandma said a lady was hurt by bad men. And you saved her.'

Ethan resisted the impulse to tell Sam that Grandma was exaggerating again. Didn't every kid need to know that his Dad was capable of chasing away the shadows?

'It was just one bad man. I shouted and he ran away.'

'But you saved her?' Sam gave him a deflated look.

'Yes, I saved her. What would you like for breakfast?' At the weekend, breakfast was their time, and Sam got to choose whatever he wanted.

'Bangers and mash!'

Ethan raised his eyebrows, and Sam cackled with

laughter. It seemed his son was turning into a practical joker, and the ache of having no one to share this with tugged at his heart.

'Waffles!'

'Okay, waffles it is.' Ethan set Sam down on his feet before he could change his mind again. His phone rang and he glanced at it. An unrecognised number ruled out Kate, the hospital and his parents, and anyone else could leave a message.

Two hours later, Ethan presented himself at the police station. He was half an hour early for the appointment he'd made with the police officer who'd called him and he intended to use that time wisely. The officer at the desk didn't recognise him, and he supposed that his absence had seen some changes here.

'I'm Dr Conway. Inspector Graham is expecting me.'

'You're the duty doctor?' The officer at the desk shot him a look that wasn't wholly welcoming.

*'No, worse luck.'*

Ethan heard Mags Graham's voice coming from behind the partition that divided the waiting area from the officers working behind the desk. Then the entrance door opened and Mags beckoned him through, closing the door behind him and shaking his hand warmly.

'Waiting for the duty doctor, are you?' Ethan looked around him. There were a few familiar faces who nodded a greeting in his direction.

Mags rolled her eyes. 'This guy's not as quick as you used to be.'

'Brave man. I was always far too afraid of you to keep you waiting.'

'Like hell you were.' Mags chuckled, leading him upstairs to her office and gesturing towards a group of chairs which were arranged around a small table to one side of her desk.

'So, what can I do for you, Ethan?'

'I witnessed an attempted mugging last night.'

Mags nodded. 'Yes, I pulled the file. Kate Foster. You dashed to the rescue.'

Ethan ignored the part about rescuing. He'd feel happier if everyone would stop saying that. 'I'm a little concerned.' Ethan frowned. He'd spent most of the morning telling himself that he shouldn't be concerned about Kate.

'On the record? Or off?' Mags was giving him that look—the one that told Ethan she knew full well that there was something he wasn't planning to say.

'Off the record. I think that this isn't the first time that Kate's been attacked. She wouldn't talk about it last night and she seemed very intent on telling everyone that she was all right. I'm not so sure she is, though.'

*That should do it. Keep a professional distance, report what you know and leave it at that.*

'Right.' Mags frowned. 'I see from the notes that you insisted she be driven home last night.'

'I thought that was sensible.'

'Yes, it was. We would do that normally anyway, and I imagine you haven't forgotten that. Is there anything we don't know about the scope of the attack last night? Something you're keeping quiet about?'

'No, I'm just concerned for her.' There it was again. *Concern.* Ethan knew that Mags was justifiably proud of the station's record for supporting victims of crime. Kate had needed him last night, but this morning he should back off.

Mags leaned back in her chair, her brow furrowed in thought. 'I'm going to say this as a friend...'

'Sure.' The signs were clear. He was in for a dose of Mags's straight talking.

'It's not unusual for witnesses of a crime to feel very protective towards people they've seen attacked. It's a perfectly natural reaction.'

'I'm aware of that.' Ethan's words sounded sharper than he'd meant them to. Mags was only trying to help, and the truth was that he *did* feel protective towards Kate. Perhaps Mags was right, and it was all down to the sudden rush of emotion he'd felt when he'd heard her scream.

Mags leaned forward in her chair. 'Look, Ethan. If someone I cared about was in the hospital, I'd be the first one sitting in your office, looking for a bit of...clarity. And you'd be telling me what I'm about to tell you.'

'To butt out and let you do your job?'

Mags laughed. 'I was thinking of putting it much more nicely than that. We're expecting Ms Foster any minute now, and she'll be seeing Laura, who's one of our best officers. My suggestion is that you wait and see her afterwards.'

Mags's perceptive gaze scanned his face for a moment, seeking out any clue that there was more to this than he'd told her already. Ethan was beginning to feel a little foolish.

'Thanks, I appreciate it. And I'm sorry if I'm overreacting.' He *was* overreacting. He'd seen senseless loss before and felt the tragedy of it. And somehow, when he'd least expected it, Kate's predicament had pushed all the wrong buttons.

'Nonsense. If everyone cared as much as you do, I'd be out of a job.' Mags smiled, seeming to consider the matter closed. 'Now, let's see the latest photo of Sam. I know there's one on your phone.'

And there were photos of Mags's two daughters in her desk drawer which Ethan wanted to see too. He should stop worrying about Kate and come to terms with the fact that what he felt was just a result of the circumstances they'd found themselves in last night.

The VIPER system meant that witnesses were protected from any contact with the person they were being asked to identify, using computer images instead of a traditional identification parade. Ethan had listened carefully to the instructions, as if this were the first time he was hearing them, and was sure of his choice. The young police officer who had been through the process with him left him in the interview room to wait, bringing him a cup of tea and the morning paper.

He drank the tea and pretended to read the paper. After ten minutes, the door of the interview room opened and Kate appeared, Mags standing behind her in the doorway.

She just hadn't been able to resist it. Mags had asked a couple of oblique questions about his love life over the photos of Sam, and Ethan had ignored the suggestion that it might be time to consider dating. Then she'd seen Kate, put two and two together and come up with five.

It was a perfectly reasonable mistake to make. If things had been different Ethan might well have asked Kate out for a coffee and seen where that led. But, if time had softened his grief over losing Jenna, it hadn't softened the feeling that he'd let her down. Or the resolve that his first and only priority had to be Sam now.

'They said you were waiting.' Kate's smile seemed brittle. And, even though the day was warm, she was wearing a thick sweater and jacket, as if to ward off some nameless chill. Ethan's heart bumped in his chest. Maybe his worries hadn't been so illogical after all.

'Yes. I wondered if you'd like a coffee. From somewhere other than the police canteen.'

Kate shrugged. 'Don't you have something to do?'

Mags's thoughtful gaze was fixed on Kate. 'I'm afraid maybe he does. I won't keep him too long.'

Ethan swallowed down the impulse to tell Mags that he could think of nothing more important right now than taking Kate by the arm and marching her outside into the fresh air.

'What, Mags?'

'I'm sorry about this, but the duty doctor hasn't come yet, and I have a man in the cells who was looking a little under the weather when he came in and is getting worse by the minute. He's just shown the custody sergeant a bite on his leg.'

'Bite?' Kate turned to her suddenly.

'Yes. It's not a human bite. We don't know what it is; it looks a few days old. Ethan, I wouldn't ask, but...'

He didn't have any choice. Ethan opened his mouth to ask whether Kate might wait somewhere for him but she spoke first.

'I'm a vet. I've seen practically every kind of bite there is. *Had* quite a few of them.'

'I'm sure that Ethan can deal with it.' Mags hadn't seemed to notice that some of the colour had suddenly returned to Kate's cheeks and she stood a little straighter.

'I'd appreciate Kate's opinion.' He was rewarded by a smile that didn't seem quite as strained as the last one.

'Fair enough.' Mags shot Ethan a questioning look but didn't argue. 'I'll get the medical kit brought down.'

* * *

This morning had been horrible. Before the taxi had arrived to take her to the police station, Kate had walked around her cottage checking everything. Locks. Dripping taps. She'd pulled all the plugs out of their sockets and then walked around the cottage a second time. She hated herself for doing it, but she couldn't help it.

The identification hadn't been much better. All she'd really wanted to do was to put this behind her, but the gentle voice of the woman police officer who'd showed her a set of short videos on a computer screen had screamed *victim*. She'd assured Kate that she wouldn't come face to face with her assailant, and Kate had wanted to scream back that she wasn't afraid.

She wasn't afraid, at least not of the man last night. She was afraid of herself. That she'd allow the bad dreams, the routines repeated over and over again, to take over her life the way they had last time. She'd been able to hide that from everyone but herself, but being unable to step out of her own flat had almost ruined her career and shown her that Mark's promises about sticking with her had been just empty words.

But, somehow, seeing Ethan had calmed her. Maybe because his final words to her last night were that he had to go in order to see his son before he went to sleep. A son meant a partner. And a partner meant that Ethan was unavailable. She could count him as a friend without any fear that she'd be tempted to step over the line.

'You've done this before?' Ethan seemed to know his way around the police station, walking ahead of the two police officers who were accompanying them.

'Yes, I used to be on the police surgeon's call roster.

I gave it up a couple of years ago, to spend more time with my son.'

'And you worked here?'

'Mostly.' He looked behind him, smiling at the woman police officer who'd popped her head around the door after Kate had finished her identification. 'Inspector Graham was so impressed by my abilities that she had me assigned here most of the time.'

'In your dreams. As a police officer, I have a duty to protect the public, and keeping you from bothering anyone else seemed like the way to go.'

Ethan chuckled. The easy respect between the two was clear. He must be good at his job, and perhaps Kate would get the opportunity to watch and learn a little.

The man was lying on the platform bed in his cell, a couple of blankets covering him, the custody sergeant standing at his side. Ethan glanced at the name on the custody record and leaned over him.

'Gary, I'm Dr Conway. I hear you're not feeling well.'

Gary opened his eyes, shading them from the light with his hand. 'My head's splitting.'

Probably a hangover—he stank of alcohol—but it was as well to make sure.

'You were drinking last night?'

'Yeah. It's what got me in here.'

He glanced up at Mags and she nodded. It probably wasn't entirely the drink that had got Gary locked up for the night, but whatever else he'd done wasn't Ethan's business. He preferred to be the cog in the system that didn't have to make judgements about others.

'All right. Have you hit your head at all, or fallen?'

'Dunno. Don't remember. My leg hurts.'

'I'll take a look then. Is that okay?'

'Knock yourself out, mate.' Gary closed his eyes again, and warning bells began to ring at the back of Ethan's head. He would have preferred it if Gary had been screaming for attention, because this lacklustre disinterest in what was happening around him didn't bode well.

A glance over his shoulder told him that the custody sergeant was ready to step in if Gary started to kick. Kate was out of range, standing quietly in the corner of the cell. Taking the blankets from Gary's legs, Ethan carefully rolled up the leg of his sweat pants.

Underneath was a haphazardly applied dressing of plaster and a bandage. Ethan cut off the dressings and saw the deep gash on the man's leg.

'This is a bite?'

He felt, rather than saw, Kate move closer, looking at the wound carefully. 'I think that's from a lizard. Lizard bites sometimes bleed very freely.'

'This is deep.' Ethan gently felt the skin around the wound. It was swollen and hot to the touch.

Kate turned her attention to Gary, poking his shoulder. He opened his eyes and kept them open, clearly liking Kate's smile a little better than he did Ethan's. Who could blame him?

'Was it a lizard that bit you?'

'Great, big ugly thing with sharp teeth.'

'About this long?' She held out her hands to indicate something of about three and a half feet in length. 'Brownish colour with a light belly? Scales?'

'Yeah, scales. Quick on its feet as well. My mate bought it from somewhere.' The man closed his eyes again.

'It could be a monitor lizard. Their bites often don't

hurt much at first, but give it twenty-four hours and they can become infected very quickly. If he's been drinking he probably didn't register the pain.' She turned to Ethan. It was a relief, but no particular surprise, to see that she was calm and collected. Almost welcoming the opportunity to do something which didn't revolve around last night.

'It's certainly infected.' Ethan took a surgical marker pen from the first-aid kit, drawing around the edge of the hard red lump that surrounded the bite, and noting the time so that any increase in the swelling could be monitored.

'You think we should call an ambulance?' Mags anticipated his next request.

'Yeah, this definitely needs to be looked at. I'll clean it and dress it to stop the bleeding.' He looked up as a young man appeared in the doorway, holding a medical bag.

'Sorry I'm late. If I could take a look at the patient now—'

'This is Dr Conway,' Mags broke in. 'He's worked with us before.'

'Oh.' The young doctor looked flustered and more than a little put out. Ethan stood, holding out his hand.

'If I can fill you in on the details, maybe you can take things from here.'

'His face… If looks could kill.' Kate smiled up at him as they walked out of the police station.

Ethan shrugged. 'If he'd got to the patient first, I don't imagine he could have done any better. I personally thought my diagnosis of a lizard bite was quite inspired. And I made it so quickly!'

The look of smiling outrage that Kate shot at him was exactly what he'd been aiming for. '*Your* diagnosis?'

'Yeah. It was me that said lizard first, wasn't it?'

'I don't think so. What kind of lizard was it you had in mind again?'

Ethan chuckled. 'Oh, you know. One of the ones with teeth.'

'They're the ones you really don't want to bite you.'

'My thoughts exactly. And whoever *did* say lizard did a very fine job.'

He hadn't planned on this. Before he'd seen Kate this morning Ethan had managed to convince himself that Mags was right and that the urge to see Kate, which had escalated into need, was just a result of his having witnessed the attack on her last night. But now laughter was buzzing between them and all he wanted to do was put his arm around her. To try and make her forget the things that had made her so hollow-eyed when he'd first set eyes on her this morning. It was confusing.

She looked up and down the high street as if she wasn't quite sure which way to go. Then she smiled up at him. 'I'm just looking for the bus stop. The police still have my car. Apparently there are some fingerprints and fibres on it.'

'Can I give you a lift home?' Somehow, making the decision to stay rather than go made him feel better. Sam was occupied and with his grandparents. Why shouldn't he spend some time with Kate?

'Thanks, but I'm not going home.'

'Where are you going, then?'

Kate hesitated, as if that wasn't something she really wanted him to know. Ethan raised his eyebrows in a signal that he wasn't going to accept silence for an answer.

'Actually, I'm going to the hospital. My arm really hurts, and I thought I'd go to the minor injuries clinic.'

Ethan rejected the urge to ask her why on earth she hadn't mentioned this last night. 'I'll give you a lift there, then. We can pick up a coffee on the way, if you like.'

'They gave me some tea.'

'Me too. I need something to wash the taste away.' He grinned at her. 'And coffee from the vending machine at the hospital isn't going to do it.'

She laughed suddenly. 'Yes, okay then. Thanks, coffee and a lift would be great.'

'I can walk from here. It's only down the road.' Ethan had gone to fetch the coffee, and that had given Kate some time to think. It felt safe in his car, but that was only a temporary relief, and she had to get used to functioning on her own.

'It's Saturday, and there are bound to be queues at the minor injuries clinic. If they're too long I can take a look at your arm myself.' He settled back into the driver's seat.

No. Feeling safe with Ethan was one thing. Relying on him was something very different. And she had the perfect excuse.

'I'm sure your partner won't thank me for keeping you away for so long. Didn't you say that you gave up working at weekends to spend more time with your family?'

'With my son. My wife died eighteen months ago and it's just me and Sam now—' He broke off as Kate's hand flew to her mouth.

'Oh. I'm so sorry.'

He nodded, seeming almost as lost for words as she was. 'It's… I didn't intend to be so blunt. I just can't think of a more tactful way of saying it.'

Kate swallowed hard, suddenly wanting to take a large swig of the coffee he still held in his hand. A sugar rush would be good right now.

'It's up to you to say it however you want. What you and your son are comfortable with is what matters.'

Ethan smiled suddenly, nodding. 'Sam's the one who really matters.'

'Of course. And I'm sure he wants you home on a Saturday morning, doesn't he?'

'Not this morning. I took him over to my parents when I knew I was coming down to the police station, and they've promised him a trip to the adventure park. I doubt he'll appreciate me coming home too soon.'

It would be wiser to turn his offer down nicely and get out of the car. But Kate couldn't do it, not now. She reached for the cardboard beaker in his hand.

'Thank you. It's very kind of you.'

He grinned, reaching for the ignition, and then thinking better of it and leaning back in his seat, taking a sip from his own drink. 'My pleasure. Anyway, I'm intrigued to know whether you're actually going to drink that.'

Kate peeled the plastic top from her beaker, squinting at her drink. 'Why, what have you put in it?'

'Only what you asked for—an extra shot of espresso, whipped cream and caramel. Just one sugar, this time. It sounds…interesting.'

'Ah. So you're a "don't put flavours in my coffee" type, are you?' His medium-sized cup, alongside her large one, indicated that he probably was. Kate took a sip from her beaker and rolled her eyes in an expression of defiant bliss.

Ethan chuckled and started the car.

* * *

It had been a relief to tell Kate where he stood. Letting her know that Sam was the single most important thing in his life now and hearing her obvious acceptance of that had cleared away his doubts and allowed him to concentrate on the matter at hand.

A and E was crowded and so was the minor injuries clinic. Kate seemed to be sticking close by his side, nursing her arm against her chest, and Ethan reckoned it must be really hurting her. He decided on a quieter place, away from the noise and activity, and steered her towards the lift.

'This is your office?' She looked around as he opened the door and ushered her inside. 'It's very tidy.'

'I don't spend much time in here. Not much chance to make a mess.' Ethan wondered what Kate thought of the straight lines and utilitarian order. Her own surgery was neat and comfortable but one wall broke the pattern, an exuberant mass of photographs, obviously added piecemeal as and when people provided pictures of the animals she'd treated.

It was a sobering thought. Last night, her free spirit seemed to have been crushed under the weight of shock and distress. This morning, it was as if she was undergoing some internal struggle. He'd seen flashes of that delicious exuberance, but she was still frightened and bemused, still trying to cope by putting everything back in its proper place.

'Is this your son Sam?' She was looking at the framed photograph on his desk, tucked neatly behind the phone.

'Yes, that's him. He's five now.' The framed photograph was just over a year and a half old, the last one that

Jenna had taken of him, and Ethan had stuck a more recent one of Sam in the corner of the frame.

'He's a beautiful little boy.' She was studying both photographs carefully. 'You must be very proud of him.'

'Yes, I am. He's got a great sense of humour, and he's kind.' Sam's dark hair and eyes were like Jenna's.

'Does he want to be a doctor when he grows up? Like his Dad?'

'No, he has bigger fish to fry. He wants to be a superhero and save the world.'

She gave a little laugh, putting the photograph back down again, tilting it carefully so that it was in the exact same place she'd found it. 'That's close enough to being a doctor, don't you think?'

Saving the world wasn't exactly Ethan's thing; he confined himself to doing the best he could. The photo on his desk was a reminder of that. Sam was smiling at his mother. They'd been a happy family. Two weeks later, Ethan had left for work, too hurried to do anything other than take Jenna's assurances that the urinary infection she had was a little better. That night he'd stayed at work and the following day Jenna had been taken into hospital. By that time, the sepsis had too tight a hold on her.

'Let's have a look at your arm, then.' He turned his mind to things that were still possible to change, watching as Kate pulled her jacket off painfully.

She got tangled in the sweater as she pulled it over her head, and he leaned forward to help. As he pulled it off her arm, she caught her breath in pain.

'That's really hurting you.'

She nodded, as if making a shameful admission. 'It does hurt a bit.'

'Let me see, then.' He gently rolled up the sleeve of

her shirt. The arm was swollen from wrist to elbow, the skin bruised and inflamed.

'And you didn't notice this last night?' Ethan couldn't help the gentle reproach.

'It hurt a bit then, too.'

And she'd pretended that it was nothing, the same as Jenna had. The thought clawed at his heart.

'All right. I'm going to want an X-ray.'

'It's not broken.'

'Let me be the judge of that. You're in *my* surgery now.'

'Okay, doctor.'

Ethan smiled. He wasn't going to allow her to go until he was sure that she was physically all right, and it seemed that Kate was finally coming to accept that.

'There's no fracture, which is always good.' Kate had craned over his shoulder while he reviewed the X-rays, and Ethan had been momentarily blinded by her scent. Now that she was back in her seat he could think more clearly. He paused for a moment to admire the fine structure of her bones, and then forced his mind back to the matter at hand.

'You have some bruising there. He grabbed your arm?' Ethan avoided the very obvious fact that the bruising was in the shape of a handprint.

'Yes.' Kate twisted her other hand around, trying to demonstrate, but her thumb was on the opposite side from the handprint. Slowly, shyly, she held her arm out towards him.

Ethan felt something block his throat. Gently, he laid his fingers on her arm over the bruises. 'Like this?'

'Yes. Just like that.'

Her gaze met his. An unspoken message that somehow tenderness might wipe away the violence. His hand, placed in the exact spot her attacker's had been, might somehow heal her.

'Well there's some trauma, and it'll be painful for a while, but with rest it should improve in the next week or so. The bruising will fade eventually.' If he could have erased the bruises now, Ethan would have given almost anything to do so.

She nodded. Ethan wondered whether kissing it better would make any difference, the way he did with Sam's bumps and scrapes, and decided that was way out of his medical remit.

'Use ice packs to relieve the swelling. And I'm going to give you a sling.'

'But my work...' Alarm registered in her eyes.

'Maybe you should take some time off work. Just a few days, to get over the shock.'

She shook her head, pulling her arm away from his fingers and cradling it in her lap. 'I don't want to take time off work. I want things back to normal as soon as possible.'

'Are you sure you're not pushing yourself too hard?'

'Yes, I'm sure. This is what I want.'

There was no disagreeing with her. And, even if he could, perhaps Kate was right about this and he was wrong. But he could at least attend to her medical needs.

'In that case, I'm going to insist you wear the sling for a week. You need to keep that arm rested to allow it to heal.'

Kate nodded. 'All right. I can get one of the veterinary nurses to help me at work.'

This was a victory of sorts. Ethan hid his smile, scribbling a note on his pad to send down to the dispensary. 'I'm going to prescribe some painkillers as well. Just enough for a few days. If you have significant pain after that, you should go and see your own doctor.'

'Thanks. I think I'll be wanting those.'

There was one more thing he had to ask. He didn't even want to think about it, but maybe it would be better coming from him.

'Have the police seen your injuries?' Ethan kept his eyes fixed on the pad in front of him, as if he were checking what he'd written and this was just an aside.

'No.'

When he glanced up at her, her cheeks were bright red. Ethan knew that the officer she'd seen would have asked about injuries, and Kate had probably repeated the mantra that she was okay. She'd probably turned down the offer of victim support as well.

'You know, don't you, that they've caught the man?' She nodded. 'And that they'll be wanting as much evidence against him as they can gather. It's up to you, of course.'

It was, technically, up to Kate. But Ethan had no doubt that there would be an attempt at persuasion. Maybe it was better coming from him.

'They'll want photographs, won't they? To show in court. They did that the last time.'

So she *had* been hurt before. It seemed to Ethan that Kate was fighting not just this incident but her memories of the last one.

'Yes, they will. As a medical practitioner, it's my duty to encourage you to report any injury that's the result of a crime. As a…friend, I'll tell you that this is a difficult process, but one that may well help you to feel better in the long run. It helps if you decide to do it on your own terms.'

She thought for a moment. Then that spark of resilience flashed in her eyes. 'Yes, you're right. Can you do it?'

The thought that she trusted *him* was almost overwhelming. Ethan could do it. He'd documented and photographed injuries many times before for police use. If there were any question about his personal involvement in the crime, then he'd take the flack that Mags would almost certainly dispense.

'You're sure?'

'Yes. Positive.' Now that Kate had made up her mind, she seemed impatient for action.

'All right. I'll go and get the forms and see if I can find a nurse.' An impartial observer would be good on two counts—first to countersign the forms. Mags would like that. And second to help Kate pull up her shirt at the back and position her arm. Because, if the first time he'd touched her had been intoxicating, now it was almost becoming a craving.

# CHAPTER THREE

THIS WAS NOT GOOD. A hero, someone who would appear out of nowhere and save the day... It was every girl's dream, which was absolutely fine, just as long as that hero didn't think he could remove himself from the imaginary world and infiltrate reality.

And Ethan Conway was more than six feet of solid reality. The kind that made her melt when she looked at him and shiver whenever he touched her. He'd stepped out of a dream, and was wreaking havoc with her waking world, and she'd let him do it. She'd given in and allowed him to help her.

He'd been in the right place at the right time. That was all it was. If she could just concentrate on not being so needy, then Ethan wouldn't seem so much of a hero.

Kate had learned her lesson, the last time she'd been mugged. It had been two days before Mark had come to see her. Looking around and declaring that he hated hospitals, he'd dumped an ostentatious bunch of flowers across her legs, making Kate wince in pain, and then had selected a chair, brushed it off with a handkerchief and sat down.

After the attack, as soon as she'd been able to get

someone to help her with the phone, Kate had made frantic calls, trying to find out whether Mark was all right. She'd heard that he was professing himself to be a bit shaken up, but that he was uninjured, and her friends had expressed surprise when they'd heard she was in hospital. Mark had never thought to mention that.

'It's every man for himself in these situations, Kate.' Mark had seemed keen to justify his actions, but suddenly guilt had cut into his air of nonchalance.

He couldn't have known. That was what Kate had been telling herself. He'd thought that she'd be able to run too, and that was why he hadn't come back. And afterwards…? Perhaps he'd felt guilty and that had kept him away.

Mark's mouth twisted suddenly. 'You need to keep your wits about you a bit more.'

'I… I couldn't get away…' Tears had blurred her vision and Kate had tried to blink them away. However needy she'd felt, however battered and bruised, it had been clear that Mark didn't want to see it.

'Like I said—if you'd been taking notice, then you would have been right behind me.'

Mark had shaken his head slowly, as if her slow-wittedness left him at a loss.

And that had been the end of it. Mark had talked about a film he'd gone to see—one that they'd been planning to see together—and had left exactly one hour after he'd arrived. He'd clearly been keeping his eye on the time.

She'd asked one of the nurses to give the flowers to a woman at the other end of the ward, who didn't seem to have any. Mark wasn't coming back.

And he'd been right in one thing. If Kate couldn't look after herself, then no one else would.

\* \* \*

Kate stubbornly refused to call Ethan, and he hadn't called her. For three weeks she'd worked solidly, trying to get her life back into some semblance of normality. And then his name showed up on her caller display.

This must be the call she'd made him promise to make. She tapped the answer button, smiling into the phone, trying to inject some of that smile into her tone.

'Hi, Ethan. How's everything?'

'It's Jeff. He's failing fast.' His voice was broken with emotion.

'Okay. Why don't I drop in and see you? I've just finished my Friday evening surgery, and I can be with you in half an hour.'

'Are you sure? That would be great.'

'That's fine. No point in having you come all the way here.' If Ethan *was* going to lose Jeff tonight, then it would be better for both he and his dog if they were at home. Then a thought struck her.

'What about Sam? Is he there?'

'I've explained everything to him. He seems to be taking it better than I am...'

Ethan's voice faltered and Kate wished she could hug him. This must be so hard for him. Not only dealing with his own feelings but also trying to decide what was best for Sam.

'I'll call my mother and ask her to pick him up. He can spend the night with my parents. Perhaps we can take things from there?' Ethan seemed to pull himself together suddenly.

'Okay, that's a good idea. I'll see you soon.'

Kate ended the call and pulled on her jacket. Then she hurried outside to her car.

* * *

Ethan had hoped that Sam would be gone by the time that Kate arrived. But his son was dawdling, obviously waiting for something before he went with his grandmother, and Ethan didn't have the heart to hurry him up.

The doorbell rang, and Sam ran to the door with him. 'Why don't you go upstairs and help Grandma?' Ethan tried to deflect Sam but Sam shook his head stubbornly.

'No!' Sam pressed his face against the glass in the front door, trying to see through the frosted panels. Ethan saw movement outside, a blur of red hair and the wave of an arm. Sam waved back.

'Out of the way, then.' Sam stepped back a little, allowing Ethan to open the door.

'Hello.' Sam greeted Kate before Ethan had a chance to.

'Hello. You must be Sam.' Kate smiled down at his son and Sam nodded.

'Are you the lady who might take Jeff to heaven?'

Sam had clearly taken everything that Ethan had told him and put it together in his own way. Ethan flashed a look of apology at Kate, gently trying to move Sam away from the doorway.

Both of them ignored him. Kate bent down and Sam escaped his grip, joining her on the front porch.

'Yes, I am.' She reached out, brushing the back of Sam's hand with one finger. 'Is it all right with you if I come in?'

Sam looked Kate up and down, obviously thinking about it. Kate was smiling, and any interruption was suddenly impossible, as the two sized each other up.

'Dad says that Jeff's very, very old.'

'Yes, he is.' Kate's tone was gentle.

'Will he see Mummy in heaven?' Sam's question delivered a knife to Ethan's heart. He saw Kate's gaze flip up towards him, in the way that most people's did when Sam asked questions about his mother, but she didn't back off or change the subject, leaving Sam to wonder what was going on.

'What do you think, Sam?'

'He will.'

'I think you're right.'

If Kate really was an angel, come to take Jeff to heaven, then she made a very good one. She almost shone in the evening sunshine, which slanted across the porch—red-haired, with soft, honey-coloured eyes, which were unafraid of Sam's questions. Sam seemed to see it too, stepping towards her and laying his hand on her knee. Then he leaned forward, whispering into Kate's ear, and Ethan strained unsuccessfully to hear what he was saying.

'Yes, of course I will.' Kate crooked her little finger, hooking it around Sam's. 'There. That makes it a promise.'

Sam nodded, clearly satisfied, and ran into the house and straight up the stairs to his grandmother. Kate got to her feet.

'How's your arm?'

'Fine. Gives me a twinge now and then, but it's okay.'

She was smiling. She was wearing a short-sleeved top, which allowed Ethan to see that the bruises on her arm had faded now. More than that, there was a lightness about her. Maybe she'd been right in getting straight back to work. It seemed that the last three weeks had lifted the burden that had rested on her shoulders.

'I'm sorry about Sam ambushing you.'

'That's okay. He's working it out for himself.'

Ethan thought about asking Kate what Sam had said to her and decided against it. If Sam had wanted him to know, he wouldn't have made such a show of whispering in Kate's ear. It seemed that Sam had grasped the concept of having secrets now, and Ethan supposed he should respect that.

She leaned forward, the evening sunlight tangling in her hair. For a moment, Ethan couldn't move. 'Can I come in, then?'

'Oh. Yes, of course. Thanks for coming.'

He showed her through to the conservatory, and she walked across to Jeff's basket, kneeling down. It looked as if Jeff was just sleeping, and Kate was stroking him gently, but Ethan knew that she was examining him.

'I think...' She looked up at him suddenly. 'Is Sam going now?'

'Yes, in a minute. As soon as my mother gets his things together. I think he's been waiting to see you.'

She pressed her lips together, in an unspoken understanding that this was hard. 'I think that if Sam has any goodbyes to say...'

'No, it's okay. I've been talking to him about this, and he's done what he wants to do.' Ethan indicated the drawing taped up by Jeff's basket. Sam had drawn himself, so that Jeff could show the picture to Jenna.

'That's nice.' Kate looked at the drawing and smiled, seeming to understand Sam's intentions.

'I'll go and see what he's doing.' Suddenly he wanted Sam away from here, so that he could keep what was left of his innocence of the realities of death for just a little longer. Ethan didn't want his son to see what he'd seen so often at the hospital.

'Okay. I'll stay here, with Jeff.'

*  *  *

Sam had gone, and Ethan no longer had to smile and pretend that everything was okay. He walked back into the conservatory and found Kate where he'd left her, kneeling on the floor next to Jeff's basket.

'Would you like to sit with him a while?'

This wasn't what Ethan had expected. He'd already said his goodbyes to Jeff, privately and out of Sam's earshot, anticipating that Kate would arrive and gently suggest that it was time to put Jeff to sleep. It would be over in a moment.

Suddenly he *did* want to spend a little more time with his old friend. But a little more time was what everyone always wanted, wasn't it?

'Don't you have to go?'

She shook her head. 'No, there's nowhere I have to be. Would you like me to make you a cup of tea?'

He was taking advantage of her time and her good nature. But Ethan couldn't resist. 'Thanks. I'd really like that.'

He picked up the large floor cushion that Sam liked to sprawl on from the corner of the room and sat down on it next to Jeff's basket, his hand straying to Jeff's head. Kate watched him, then nodded quickly, as if everything was going exactly as she wanted it to and disappeared into the kitchen.

He could hear her clattering quietly around, opening and closing cupboards. The temptation to get up and show her where the mugs and teabags were drifted away. Ethan was exactly where he was supposed to be at that moment.

The kettle took its time to boil, and Kate took her time making the tea. She walked back into the conservatory, holding two mugs, and put them down on the table next to him, pulling one of the wicker chairs across to the other side of Jeff's basket.

'Which one's yours?' Ethan reached for the mugs and she shrugged, so he picked up one and tasted it. 'Ugh. Too sweet...'

She grinned at him. 'That's because I'm not sweet enough.'

Ethan would take issue with that. Kate's sweetness wasn't like sugar, liable to melt at the first drop of adversity. It was like steel, unbending but true. He wanted her here, now, not just for Jeff but for himself.

She leaned back in her seat, sipping her tea. Clearly she wasn't going anywhere for a few precious minutes.

It didn't always happen like this. Sometimes an animal was in pain, and sometimes Kate didn't have the opportunity to wait with an owner while it drifted away. But now wasn't one of those times, and they could let nature take its course, secure in the knowledge that the drugs in Kate's bag could be used if they were needed.

Ethan wasn't ready to say goodbye yet, but he was getting there. She could see the small stress lines around his eyes begin to relax as the light grew dimmer. Kate lit one of the fat candles lined up along the low windowsill and they talked quietly in the flickering light. Waiting.

Jeff's sleep became deeper and his breathing slowed, stopping for long moments and then starting again. Ethan must have known that the time was coming, and he leaned over, his lips just inches away from Jeff's head.

'Go to sleep now, boy. Everything's all right.'

# CHAPTER FOUR

THE MOMENT THAT Ethan had dreaded became something peaceful that didn't feel as if something was tearing chunks out of his heart. Kate had waited a little while and then tucked Jeff's blanket over him, almost as if he really was just asleep.

This time Ethan made the tea, deciding at the last moment that as he wasn't driving he could have a glass of wine. Kate refused a half-glass for herself, and they sat on the steps which ran down from the open door of the conservatory onto the dark lawn.

'To Jeff.' She clinked her mug against his glass and Ethan smiled.

'Yeah, to Jeff.' He took a sip of the wine. 'Thanks for staying. I… I actually don't have the words to tell you how much I appreciate it.'

She nodded, staring straight ahead of her. 'You're welcome. We're not always lucky enough to be able to say goodbye to a friend like this but, when we can, it's something I want to try to make possible.'

'Well, thank you for making it possible this time. Can I ask you a question?' He'd tried to let go of the idea, but couldn't.

'Yes?' She turned to him, her eyes bright in the darkness. The thought that, if he reached for her, she might melt against him in the warmth of a summer evening's embrace almost made Ethan choke.

'What did Sam say to you?'

'Ah. I wondered when you'd get around to asking.'

'Is it a secret?' Ethan wasn't sure quite what he'd say if it was. He wouldn't blame Sam for wanting to share his secrets with Kate, but somehow it would seem like a rejection.

'No, it's not a secret. He said that I was to look after you.'

A tear pricked suddenly at the corner of Ethan's eye, and he rubbed his hand across his face, trying to cover the emotion. But it seemed that Kate wasn't fooled and she leaned towards him, bumping her shoulder gently against his arm.

'Growing up fast, is he?'

'Yeah. Very.'

'You said he was kind, and he is. That's a real credit to you.'

Ethan nodded. 'Yes he is. I'm not sure whether I taught him that, though, he seems to have come up with it all by himself.'

He heard Kate chuckle quietly beside him. 'I imagine that kindness is one of those things you get by example. You're worried about him?'

Ethan laughed. 'I'm *always* worried about him. That comes with the territory. Since Jenna died, I do the worrying for both of us.'

The words just slipped out. Maybe the darkness, and maybe the way that tonight had stripped away the boundaries. Or perhaps the way that Kate seemed to understand everything so well. Ethan tried to think of something to change the subject, and then he turned into her gaze.

She was wide-eyed and unflinching. When he talked about Jenna most people averted their gaze, but Kate didn't. 'I imagine that comes with the territory too. You must miss her very much.'

That wasn't an easy question to answer. Usually he would say, yes, he *did* miss Jenna, but tonight the simple response didn't seem enough.

'The first anniversary was hard. Sam and I... We're learning to move forward.' Ethan shrugged. 'Actually, he seems to have a momentum all of his own. I'm learning to keep up with him.'

Kate nodded. No questions. But, in the silence, Ethan felt that he could give whatever answer he wanted to.

'When Sam does something new, I miss not telling her about it.' Or just having *someone* to tell. Ethan wasn't sure which. But, since he'd promised himself he'd never let another woman down the way he had Jenna, he probably would never know.

'Jenna died very suddenly, and I'm not sure that she heard me when I told her I'd look after Sam...'

'I don't imagine she would have been in any doubt about that. It's obvious that Sam's your first priority.'

Ethan nodded. Here, now, it didn't seem so difficult to allow Kate in, even if it was just for a short time. If falling in love a second time would require a completely different skill set from any that he'd needed before, then perhaps Kate could teach him.

Ethan rejected the thought. They could be friends, without the complicating factor of his wanting to protect her all the time. Knowing that wasn't enough and that he should give all his energies to Sam.

'Time heals a lot of things.' He resorted to the familiar cliché and saw Kate nod.

It was getting darker, but Kate showed no signs of wanting to leave. Ethan didn't want her to go. He wanted these moments of quiet peace to last.

'Sam's been talking about a new puppy.' It seemed suddenly quite natural that Ethan should share it with Kate.

'Yes? What do you think?'

'I think…it's a really good idea. And it'll be good for Sam.'

'A little bit soon for you, though?' Kate wasn't afraid to voice Ethan's one reservation.

'Yes. But if it's what Sam wants, then that's fine with me. I wondered if you could recommend anyone.' The small hope that she couldn't still tugged at his heart.

Kate nodded, staring silently out into the darkness for a moment, her lips pursed in thought. 'Yes, I do know a couple of people who have litters of pups which are ready for new homes. Were you thinking of any particular breed?'

'Not another Newfoundland. Jeff was always so beautifully tempered, and he was great with kids, but he was a bit big for Sam to take for walks. Something a bit smaller would suit him better.'

'Yes, I'm sure it would. Can I suggest an alternative to taking a puppy home right away?'

'If you're going to tell me to wait, then that's not an option.' Ethan had already made that decision. Sam's wants and needs came first.

'I hear you. But one of our veterinary nurses is handrearing a litter. They're far too small to be rehomed just yet but Sam could choose one. You could visit every now and then, he'd see it grow, and then you could take the puppy when it's older.'

Ethan stared at her. He hadn't expected Kate to come up with a solution that would suit both him and Sam. 'That's… I think that Sam would really like that. What breed are they?'

'There's no pedigree certificate, but we know where they came from.' She grinned. 'They're definitely beagles. You can take my word on that.'

'Pretty good size for Sam, then.'

'I would think so, and generally speaking beagles are good with children. They need a lot of exercise, though, and you can't leave a beagle pup on its own all day while you're at work.'

'That wouldn't be a problem. My parents live in one of the villages about twenty minutes away from here. They look after Sam during the holidays and after school, and my dad's already said if Sam wants a puppy they'd take care of it while I'm at work. He's almost as keen on the idea as Sam is.'

Ethan made his decision, finding that it wasn't as difficult as he'd thought it would be.

'Would it be okay if we came to have a look at them?'

'Yes, of course. Give me a ring, whenever you're ready.' She shot him a mischievous grin. 'If one of the puppies chooses you, then Sam can visit any time he likes.'

'Thank you. That's very kind.' Ethan wanted to hug her, but that wouldn't be quite fair. She'd hug him back, thinking he needed comfort, but that wasn't his motive. He just wanted to feel her, soft in his arms.

'It's my pleasure.'

There were no words for this. Sitting here with Kate,

the light from the house casting warm shadows around them. If he could just make tonight something which stood by itself, which had no yesterday to sour it and no tomorrow to make it impossible, then he would have kissed her.

'I'm going to take Jeff now.' Her gentle words interrupted the dream of what Ethan knew couldn't happen. 'You can pop in over the next couple of days and see our receptionist to make arrangements.'

If he'd thought about it, Ethan would have known all along that Kate would take Jeff. He just hadn't been able to face it. Now he could. He tipped the contents of his glass into the flower bed next to the steps.

'I'll come with you.'

She hesitated, then shook her head firmly. 'No, that's okay. I'd appreciate it if you could give me a hand getting him into my car, but I'll be fine once I get to the surgery.'

Kate might feel okay about this, but he didn't. It was one thing to rationalise about lightning not striking twice, but quite another thing to leave her to negotiate the darkness outside the surgery.

'I'd like to just...see Jeff off. And, now I've thrown away three quarters of a glass of a very nice Chablis, it's the least you can do to let me tag along. I might go to my parents and spend the night there, so I'm around for Sam when he wakes up.'

'Okay. That sounds like a good idea.'

Ethan supressed a smile, wondering if he might add that he'd follow her home and see her inside. But there was an obvious flaw in the assertion that her place was on his way to his parents' house, which was that he didn't know where Kate lived. Maybe he'd work his way round to suggesting that later.

\* \* \*

Ethan seemed to want the company and Kate had to admit that she was very glad he was there. They'd carried Jeff into the surgery together, and Ethan hadn't left her side until she was safely back in her car. Then he'd bent down, tapping on the window.

'Which way are you going?'

'I live in Eadleigh. On the edge of the village.'

His face broke into a broad grin. 'It's on my way. I'll follow you and see you inside.'

The last time she'd negotiated the dark shadows which crowded in on her front path at night, she'd forced herself to walk and not run, but had still arrived inside the house breathless and pushing away the panic. Kate would certainly appreciate him being there, but she didn't want to admit it.

He turned suddenly, not waiting for her answer, and got into his car.

She parked in the lane outside her cottage, dimly aware that the lights of his car, which had shone reassuringly behind her all the way from the surgery, had just been extinguished. She looked in the rear-view mirror and saw him swing out of the driver's seat.

Okay. So he was a gentleman. The closeness that had tingled in the air between them this evening somehow made this a more obvious move than it otherwise might have been. Kate got out of her car, marching towards him.

'I'd ask you in but the place is a terrible mess. End of the week, you know? I do my housework on a Saturday...' She pressed her lips together. She was protesting too much and, if Ethan couldn't see the lie on her face in the darkness, he might well hear it in her voice.

He shrugged. 'Yeah, I know.'

'Well, goodnight, Ethan. I'm so sorry you lost Jeff this evening.'

He nodded. 'I think we both did our best for him and that means a lot. Thank you.'

Kate swallowed the impulse to hug him, and turned, hurrying up the front path. As she fumbled for her keys in her handbag, she saw Ethan leaning against his car, watching her inside, and breathed a word of thanks that she knew he couldn't hear.

Waving to him, she closed the front door, shooting the bolt on the new deadlock. Everything was quiet, undisturbed. Just the way she'd left it this morning. The back door was locked and the windows were secure.

She walked into the sitting room, slumping into a chair. The place was clean and rather relentlessly tidy, to the point that it looked a little starker than usual. During the hours when she wasn't either at work or trying to sleep she'd been keeping herself busy, finding that physical effort gave her some relief from the clamour of her thoughts.

She *could* have asked him in—offered him a cup of tea, given him the opportunity to talk a little more if he'd wanted to. But somehow, asking anyone into her home, her sanctuary, was a little more than she was able to do at the moment. Here she was safe.

Safe from the feeling that it would feel good just to curl up with Ethan and go to sleep, undisturbed by the nightmares. He'd taken on the role of hero in her imagination and this couldn't go on. His eyes were just eyes and they didn't need any adjectives to describe them.

She looked at her watch, stifling a yawn. She had an early call tomorrow and she hadn't had a great deal of sleep last night. Hopefully tonight would be different.

# CHAPTER FIVE

JOY. THE EMOTION came before Kate had the opportunity to temper it with reason. Her phone caught her unawares and when she saw Ethan's name on the caller display there was one moment of pure, heart-stopping joy.

'Hi, Ethan. How are things?' Her voice sounded strangely breathless and Kate looked around at the crowded waiting room full of patients for her evening surgery to see if anyone had noticed.

'Good, thanks. Are you okay?'

'Yes. I'm good.'

That got the denial over and done with. The last few days couldn't have been easy for Ethan, and they hadn't been easy for Kate either. But she was managing, and she couldn't imagine that Ethan was doing any differently.

'I was wondering if it would be okay for me and Sam to see the puppies you were talking about. Um, hold on a minute…'

Kate grinned. The shrill voice in the background told her that Sam was obviously getting excited at the prospect.

'Sorry about that. Sam! Holding your breath isn't going to make any difference.'

People were starting to look. Kate hurried into her

empty surgery to hide the stupid grin on her face. 'When do you want to come and see them?'

'Would the weekend be convenient for you?'

Kate was taking the puppies this weekend. She dismissed the feeling that it would be better to see Ethan again on neutral ground. She should look at it as seeing Sam. Letting *him* into her home, her safe place, was a great deal easier to contemplate.

'The weekend would be fine. Sue, the nurse who's looking after them, is going away, and I'm going to be taking them. How about Friday evening? I'm finishing work early.' From the sounds in the background, the sooner the better for Ethan. He obviously had a very excited child on his hands.

'Friday would be great.'

'That's good. Come to my place around seven. Do you remember where I live?'

'Yes. I remember.'

'Okay…' An awkward silence reminded Kate that really the only connection she had with Ethan was a professional one, even though it felt so very personal. 'I'll see you then. I'm in the middle of a surgery. I've got to run.'

'Of course. Thanks, I'll see you tomorrow.' The line abruptly cut out. Maybe the excitement was just too much for Sam and Ethan had to go and calm him down. Or maybe, that was really all they had to say to each other.

Settling the puppies into their home for the weekend had taken a while. Kate looked around the cottage and decided against vacuuming in favour of changing out of her work clothes. The top that she picked from the wardrobe was one that she rarely wore, but particularly liked.

'Stupid little…' Her fingers fumbled with the tiny

mother-of-pearl buttons. Ethan wasn't going to notice, and Sam almost certainly wouldn't. Maybe the pups would like it, but if they gnawed at the fine cotton she'd be sorry.

Pulling the scrunchie out, she brushed her hair. That was going to have to do. Any more and it might give the impression that she'd dressed up, and dressing up to spend Friday evening at home wasn't really her style any more.

There was a time when it had been. After the first mugging, she'd returned home from the hospital and locked herself in her flat. Locking out the hurt and the fear. Telling herself that she had to cope alone, because no one else would help her.

And she'd stayed there for six months, immobilised at first and struggling to get out to the hospital for her outpatient appointments. Her body had healed, but her heart hadn't, and she'd found herself alone, hardly ever going out and never letting anyone in.

As soon as she'd been able to, she'd dressed up on a Friday evening, marking the end of the week in the same way that ordinary people did, despite the fact that her weekends were pretty much the same as her weekdays. She'd cooked a nice meal and settled down to watch a film on the TV.

That wasn't her any more. She'd given in to the fear after she'd been mugged the first time, but this time it would be different. She would go out and invite people over just like any other normal human being. And Kate had to admit that she was looking forward to seeing Ethan, even if it meant letting him and his son into her home.

The sound of a car in the lane outside reached her.

Hers was the last cottage in the row and it was either
Ethan or someone who'd taken a wrong turn and got lost.
Kate approached the window, standing back from the net
curtains so that its occupants couldn't see her. Ethan's
dark-blue SUV was manoeuvring into a parking space.

She paced up and down the hallway impatiently. How
long did it take to get one child out of a car and up the
front path? Kate was just considering peeping through
the letter box to see what was going on when the doorbell rang.

'Hold the flowers, Sam.' Ethan retrieved the small bunch
of flowers from the footwell of his car and put them on
the back seat next to Sam.

'Dad!' Sam clearly wasn't in the mood for flowers.
He was in the mood for puppies and viewed anything
else as an obstacle.

The choosing and buying of flowers and their careful arrangement into the kind of posy that a child might
give had been a calculated time waster, intended to fill
the hour between picking up Sam from his parents' and
arriving at Kate's house. But, even though the urge to
give them to Kate himself had grown during the course
of the exercise, it was impossible.

'Come on, Sam. Kate's helping us, and this is our way
of saying thank you to her.'

'But she's not my girlfriend!' Sam protested.

'She doesn't have to be your girlfriend for us to give
her flowers. It's a way of saying thank you. Like when
we give Grandma flowers.'

'Is she going to kiss me?' When Sam presented Ethan's
mother with flowers, there was always a protracted phase

of hugging and kissing before the blooms were whisked off to the kitchen to be arranged.

'I wouldn't think so. Just give her the flowers and then she'll show you the puppies.'

'Oh.' Sam thought about it for a moment and then picked up the posy. 'Okay.'

Ethan breathed a sigh of relief and climbed out of the car, opening the back door to release Sam from his car seat. His son scarpered up the front path, almost dropping the flowers as he stretched for the doorbell. Ethan lifted him up so he could reach, putting him back down on his feet before Sam could jab his finger on the bell a second time.

Sam shuffled impatiently on the doorstep, looking as if he was about to kick the front door in an attempt to gain entry. Ethan laid his hand on his son's shoulder and the door opened. And then he forgot that he'd told himself that this visit was all about Sam, as his whole world suddenly upended.

Kate was wearing a thin, white cotton top with a green patterned border at the neck. It was practical and pretty, the kind of thing lots of women wore in the summer, but Kate made everything she wore seem special. Her hair curled around her shoulders, free of the pins and elastic bands that restrained it while she was at work. In the week since he'd seen her last, she seemed to have grown softer and prettier. Or maybe it was just that his memory wasn't up to recreating her perfectly.

Sam stepped forward, thrusting the flowers at her. 'From Dad.'

*Thanks, mate.* Kate flushed a little, the delicate red of her cheeks making Ethan wish for a moment that the arrangement of white roses and freesias *were* from him.

She took the posy, reading the tag which dangled from the raffia binding.

'It says here they're from you, Sam. Did you write that?'

'Yes. They're from me.' Sam seemed to think nothing of the abrupt *volte face*. 'Where are the puppies?'

'Come with me. They're through here.' Kate held out her hand and Sam took it, glancing back at Ethan as he followed them inside, closing the front door behind him.

She led the way through a small kitchen, neat and gleaming, the astringent smell of cleaning fluid still in the air despite the open window. An open door at the far end was barred by a child gate, and beyond that was a bright, airy room, the walls painted cream and the floor covered with newspaper and dog toys. In the corner was a high-sided wooden box.

Kate bent down to Sam. 'We have to be very quiet and gentle with them. They're only tiny and we don't want to frighten them.'

Sam nodded, leaning towards Kate to whisper to her. 'Can we go inside?'

'Yes, of course we can.' She swung open the child gate and led Sam into the room.

Ethan tried to ignore the four tiny forms curled up inside the box and lingered by the doorway, keeping his gaze on his son. Sam's eyes were as wide as saucers, and he was tiptoeing up to the box, trying very hard to be quiet.

'What do you think, Sam?' Kate bent down next to him, one hand resting lightly on his back. Just the right amount of reassurance, yet still allowing Sam the space to explore this new experience.

'They're little…' Sam was obviously considering the

practicalities of taking one of the tiny creatures for a walk and playing ball with it.

'Yes, they're very small now, but they're still growing. In a few weeks' time they'll be this big.' She held her hands out.

'That's the right size.'

'Yes, I think so too. Would you like to touch one of them?'

Sam twisted round, looking questioningly at Ethan, and he nodded. 'Yes, that's all right. Gently, so you don't hurt them.'

Sam reached into the box, his fingertips touching the puppy closest to him. It roused from its sleep and gave a little whelping bark, and Sam snatched his hand away.

'It's all right. He's just saying hello to you.' Kate dangled her hand inside the box and the puppy responded, licking her fingers. Sam caught his breath, holding his hand out, and Kate moved her fingers next to his so that the puppy moved across to lick Sam's hand.

'Dad, look, he's licking me.' Sam's face was shining with the kind of wonder that only a child had access to on a day-to-day basis.

'Yes, that's okay. Your dad can see.'

Kate was giving him a little space, allowing him to stand back, but suddenly Ethan didn't want to. If Jeff had been here, he probably would have ambled up to the puppies and tried to get into the box with them.

Ethan stepped forward, catching the scent of flowers as he bent down next to Kate—bright and clean, with an undertone of something sensual, like a summer's afternoon spent lying on a blanket in the middle of a meadow. And then she was gone, leaving him to talk to Sam and play with the puppies with him.

\* \* \*

Kate had given the puppies a bowl of food so that Sam could watch them eat, then ushered Ethan and him out onto the back garden, installing Sam in a child's garden chair next to the door which led from the utility room onto the patio.

Ethan's tall frame made the table and two chairs that sat on the paved area seem even smaller. He sat down, looking at the riot of spring colour that stretched twenty yards from the back of the cottage and spilled around each of its sides. Kate was pleased with the way her garden was coming along this year.

'You're a gardener, then.' Ethan laughed when she shrugged. 'It takes a lot of hard work to make a garden look this random and natural.'

He'd noticed. Kate suppressed a smile and set about arranging the teacups on the table. 'This is the second summer I've been here. I did a lot of planting last year, and I'm beginning to enjoy the results.'

'It's nice here. Quiet.'

That was one of the things that had attracted Kate to this place, away from the hustle of London. Away from the memories and the fears. But now it brought new fears. She realised that she hadn't sat out here in her garden for a few weeks, contenting herself with viewing it from behind the locked windows of the kitchen.

'We don't get a lot of through traffic.'

He nodded, his gaze following the trajectory of the lane that passed in front of her cottage and continued straight for another hundred yards. It then curled in an arc and stopped short.

'Where does the lane lead?'

Kate smiled. It wasn't the first time someone had

asked the question. 'This cottage used to be the second-to-last in the lane. There was another one further along, but I'm told it burned down about fifty years ago. You can still see the foundations if you walk down there.'

'You have a great view.' He nodded towards Summer Hill rising in the distance, and Kate remembered that he'd said it was his favourite place. 'I miss living in the countryside. My parents have a couple of acres out by Hambleton and I was brought up there.'

'I imagine living in the town's more convenient. With Sam…'

He shrugged. 'It has its pros and cons. It's further away from a community where everyone knows everyone else.'

'Yes, I've been learning all about that. I'm still the new girl here, but there's always something going on. I've managed to get on one of the teams for quiz night at the pub.'

Ethan chuckled. 'You're well on your way to becoming a local, then. I hope you take it seriously.'

'Very seriously. My grasp of anatomy came in useful last week.'

'What made you move up here?' He turned suddenly, as if this was a question that was more than just idle talk filling in the time while Sam stared at the puppies.

'I just wanted to make a new start. Have my own garden and a bit of fresh air. If this place was in London I wouldn't be able to even think about affording it.'

His gaze held hers for a moment, as if he knew that there was more to it than that. His dark-blue eyes were almost mesmerising, sucking her in and demanding the truth. And then he looked away.

'I think he's found a new friend.' One of the puppies

had finished eating and come to the doorway, pressing itself against the piece of wood that Kate had wedged across the threshold to stop the puppies from escaping.

She craned round to look at Sam, who was stroking the puppy and talking to it quietly. 'He doesn't need to make a decision yet.'

'I think I've made mine.' Ethan caught his son's attention. 'Sam, would you like it if we took one of these puppies home when it's a bit bigger?'

'Can we have them all?'

'I think one's enough.'

'Two?' Sam was obviously open to a bit of bargaining.

Kate giggled. 'But where are you going to get the time to play with two of them?'

Sam thought about it for a moment and nodded sagely. 'All right. Just one.'

Ethan's blue eyes were all she could see as he looked back at her. 'How old are they—six weeks?'

'Five and a half. As I said, they've no pedigree certificates, but they all come with a clean bill of health, and Sue's done a great job with socialising them. We're hoping to find homes for them to go to at eight weeks, but I can take the one you choose after that. Until you're ready.'

'Two and a half weeks will be fine.' Ethan nodded towards Sam, who had gone back to stroking the puppy. 'That's a very long time when you're five.'

'And when you're a bit older than five?' Kate didn't want to push Ethan.

'It's quite long enough to deal with a five-year-old who can't wait.' Ethan turned to Sam, catching his attention again. 'Is that the one, Sam?'

Sam turned his shining face up to him and nodded.

'You're sure?'

'Yes, Dad.'

Ethan chuckled. 'Good choice. We'd like to take that one, please, Kate.'

Suddenly her cottage became a home again. One where she might just think about opening the windows and allowing the perfumed breeze in, instead of locking it up like a fortress.

'He's yours.'

'Thank you. How much…?' Ethan reached into his jacket for his wallet.

'It'll cost you a good home and a lot of love. Nothing more.'

He nodded. 'Fair enough. Pick a charity, then.'

Kate thought about telling him no, but he obviously wanted to give something. 'The local mountain rescue? I'm a member. I help with the dog training exercises and give them their health checks. They're based over in Highbridge'

'I know it. That would be a pleasure.'

'Thank you.' Kate rose from her chair, trying to shake off the feeling that she wanted to reach across the table and touch Ethan's hand. When she picked up the puppy, Sam jumped to his feet, following her back to his father's side.

She caught a brief hint of Ethan's scent as she bent to deliver the puppy into his arms. Not enough to savour properly, but more than enough to want more. Kate straightened, turning to Sam.

'I'll let you and your Dad hold him for a while. So he can get to know you.'

'Yessss!' Sam looked as if he was about to burst from excitement, responding to Ethan's, 'What do you say?' with a hurried 'Thank you.'

Kate left them to it. Ethan's gentle hands and smouldering eyes. A little boy and his first puppy. Watching all that was more than she could bear, when there was no chance that she could have any of it. And she'd noticed a few weeds amongst the flowers which suddenly needed her urgent attention.

# CHAPTER SIX

ETHAN STARED AT his phone. His head told him that there was nothing wrong with the text. But his gut told him that everything was wrong with it.

Car broken down, on way back from Hallowes Common. Waiting for pick-up. Will be about half an hour late tonight, but will call when I am on my way. Sorry.

It all seemed perfectly straightforward. Kate was going to examine all the puppies at the surgery this evening, and she'd told Ethan that he could bring Sam over if he wanted. She was going to be half an hour late, that was all.

But he knew Kate better than that. Talking allowed more give and take than texting, and it conveyed more warmth. If Kate's first instinct was to text, then he'd be willing to bet that there was something wrong. He could feel a prickling sensation crawling along the back of his neck.

He was making something out of nothing. He was about to leave work, and it would take twenty minutes to get from the hospital to his parents' house, to pick up

Sam. He'd stay there, until Kate phoned to say that she was ready.

Or... Hallowes Common was twenty minutes in the other direction.

Kate was breathing so fast that her head was swimming. The hollow feeling in her chest felt as if it was about to swallow her. She put the paper bag over her mouth again, watching it inflate and deflate.

This wasn't happening. Okay, so it *was* happening, but she could deal with it. Her car had broken down, that was all. People's cars broke down all the time.

Squinting through her tears, she could see a car coming, appearing and disappearing as it negotiated the curves in the road ahead. Perhaps she should hide her keys. The chasm in her chest suddenly opened further and she let out a little cry of frustration at her own inability to cope.

Fixing her gaze on the steering wheel, she breathed into the bag. One... Two... Concentrate... She felt her heartbeat slow a little. And then the car that she'd seen in the distance rounded the corner.

Ethan. No. Not here. Not now.

She threw the paper bag into the footwell, trying to slow her breathing. Not daring to look him in the face as he walked towards her, she fixed her gaze on his left shoulder.

He reached the driver's door, squatting down next to it. He must have come straight from work. She hadn't seen Ethan in a white shirt and tie before. Even though the tie had been loosened and the shirt was open at the neck, he looked quite devastatingly reliable.

The 'R' word again. *Don't even think it. Don't think*

*the 'H' word, either.* It was difficult not to, because she didn't actually need to look at him to know he was handsome, she remembered all too well what he looked like.

Slowly, he raised his arm, circling his hand in an indication that she should put the window down. Kate complied with the instruction in a haze of misery.

'Hey, there.' He reached in, tipping her face gently towards him. 'Car's broken down, eh?'

'Yes.' Maybe he hadn't noticed the state she'd got herself into.

'Okay.' He lifted the tab on the inside of the door, and she heard the central locking disengage. Then he opened the door, bending down again next to her.

'Here.' He managed to retrieve the paper bag from the footwell without touching her. 'Just breathe.'

She couldn't resist his quiet, authoritative tone. It felt that, if she just did what Ethan said, everything would be all right.

'Better?'

She nodded wordlessly.

'All right. Keep going.'

She started to count again in her head, and then realised she was going too fast. Ethan was counting slower. When she followed his lead, the panic that was reverberating in her chest began to recede a little.

It seemed like an age but finally he stopped counting and her own rhythm took over. She felt surer now and stronger. She crumpled the paper bag in her lap, and Ethan nodded.

'Give me your keys. I'll go and get your bag from the back of your car and we'll go and sit in mine. Then we'll phone and find out where the tow truck is.'

He knew exactly what to do. Kate handed him her

keys, feeling the car rock slightly as he opened the boot. Then the sound of him unlocking the boot safe. He reappeared, carrying her veterinary bag in one hand and the smaller drugs bag in the other.

'Are you going to look at the engine?' That was what any self-respecting hero would do. He'd look under the bonnet and tell her to try the ignition. The engine would then choke reluctantly back to life.

Ethan raised one eyebrow. 'No. I'm a doctor, not a car mechanic. We'll wait for the tow truck.'

'Oh. Good.' The thought that Ethan had at least one chink in his armour was oddly reassuring. Kate got out of the car and followed him over to his, watching as he stowed her bags under the back seat and opened the passenger door for her.

'Are you on any medication?' When Kate got into the car, he bent down beside her again.

'No!'

He grinned suddenly. 'Fair enough. Have you changed the oil in your car recently?'

'So you *are* a mechanic, then.'

'No. I just thought you might like that line of questioning a little better. How quickly did you stop?'

'Slowly. I didn't need the brakes, but as far as I know they're okay as well.'

'Good to know. Look at my finger.' He held one finger up, moving it from side to side.

He could be forgiven for thinking she'd hit something, or bumped her head, after all the fuss she'd made. 'The engine just cut out and the car stopped. It's an old car and I've been thinking I should get a new one. I just…panicked a bit. Stupid.' She was feeling better now. Stronger. As if a smile wasn't totally out of the question.

'All right. Have you got the number of the garage? I'll give them a call and see where they are.'

A little of the colour had returned to her cheeks. Ethan swallowed the temptation to ask Kate why on earth she hadn't called and asked him to pick her up, and concentrated on the practicalities. Getting her out of the car and making sure she was all right.

The tow truck was out on another call, and he'd agreed that they'd leave the car and drop the keys in at the garage. Kate sat silently as he drove back into town and delivered her car keys to the mechanic.

'I'll take you home.' He got back into the driver's seat and started the engine.

'No—thank you, but I have to go to the surgery. And you need to pick up Sam. He'll be wanting to see his puppy.'

Her reaction was entirely expected. Ethan had his answer ready. 'He can see it another time. I called my parents to let them know, when I went to talk to the mechanic.'

'But he'll be disappointed.'

'Yes, he will. But it's not the end of the world, and he knows that he'll see the puppy soon. It's more important that you go home.'

'I can't, I have things to do. I just had a bit of a moment. It was stupid and I'm okay now.'

Ethan sighed. He'd expected that Kate would object, and she hadn't disappointed him. A garage forecourt probably wasn't the best place to do this, but at least the car afforded them some privacy.

'Look, I don't want to interfere—'

'Then don't.' She flashed a warning glare in his direction.

'All right, then, I *do* want to interfere. You're very clearly trying to pretend that nothing's wrong, and most of the time when you're with people, that's working pretty well. But for some of the time, probably when you're alone, I think you're suffering from symptoms of stress. Panic attacks…nightmares, maybe.'

The look in her eyes told him that his gamble had just paid off and that he was right. 'Some of the time isn't so bad, is it?'

'It's not so good, either. Did the police put you in touch with a victim support officer?'

'I'm *not* a victim!' The words were said with such vehemence that Ethan knew he'd touched a nerve. He pushed a little more.

'You're not afraid of allowing me a bit of time to process things, Kate. Why are you so afraid of doing the same for yourself? You'll heal if you just let yourself.'

That was it. She was suddenly white-faced and trembling. It was the healing, not the attack itself, that had the power to frighten her. And from what he knew of her, Kate didn't frighten easily.

'What happened—the last time you were attacked?'

'Does it matter?'

'Yes, I'm pretty sure that it does. Can you tell me?'

She stared at him, pressing her lips together as if she were trying to stop the words coming from her mouth.

'Kate, you're a strong woman. That's why I'm asking you to tell me.'

One tear escaped her eye and ran down her cheek. 'There were two of them. They grabbed me and took my bag. Searched me for jewellery.'

Ethan shivered. That small detail seemed like the

worst thing—unable to escape and being searched, none too gently he imagined. 'And then?'

'I was at the top of the steps which led down to the underground—it happened in London.'

Ethan nodded her on, almost afraid to hear what came next.

'They pushed me down the steps. I fell all the way.'

'And you were hurt badly?' The last time he'd asked that question she'd refused to answer. Ethan suspected she'd been hurt *very* badly, both physically and mentally.

'It wasn't as bad as it might have been. Concussion and a fractured ankle. Broken shoulder.' She tried to smile and Ethan felt his hand move across the seat towards her. Her injuries were bad enough that they would have left Kate immobile for a while. They would have taken away her only coping mechanisms…her independence and her ability to work.

'What then?' Something told him that there was more.

'I…' She heaved a sigh, but her gaze didn't leave his face. 'When I couldn't get out, because of my injuries, it wasn't so bad. But when I started to get back on my feet physically, the panic attacks began. I couldn't sleep and I'd constantly be checking the locks on the doors. I didn't go out of my flat for six months.'

If Ethan had ever doubted that she had the courage to tell him everything, now he didn't. The little tilt of her head, the defiance in her eyes, was unmistakeable.

'Were you alone? When you were attacked?'

She shook her head. 'No, I was… I was with a man. Someone I was going out with.'

'What happened to him?' Ethan wondered whether guilt over what had happened to her companion played a part in this.

'He ran away. He felt pretty bad about it afterwards, I suppose, but I only saw him once after that.'

It wasn't guilt, then, it was betrayal. Ethan took a breath.

'Kate, you know what's happening here, don't you.'

'Yes, I know. I lost everything—my job, my boyfriend. I nearly lost my flat because I couldn't keep the payments on the mortgage up. Then I made a new start and I thought that it was all behind me. Now I'm afraid it's going to happen again.' Her voice was expressionless, as if adding the emotion into the words was a little too much for her to bear.

'Then you'll know what you need to do.'

'I need to just stop it. By myself, the way I did last time.'

'No, you need to get some help.' Ethan could see now why that would be difficult for her. The one person who had been supposed to help her the last time hadn't just run away, he hadn't come back afterwards.

'My boss mustn't know. You can't tell anyone...' Alarm flashed in her eyes, and a sudden shard of warmth dispersed the chill that had settled over Ethan. She'd trusted him enough to tell him.

'You're in my car. I'll take that to mean that doctor-patient privilege applies.'

'You're not *my* doctor.'

Her sudden smile ripped away the last of his defences. Ethan had been trying to approach this professionally, as if she was a patient who could be cared *for*, but not *about*. Getting involved wasn't something he did any more, and he'd almost forgotten how that went.

'I'm *a* doctor. That probably covers it.' He attempted a grin, and she nodded.

'Okay then, doctor. What's your solution?'

He struggled momentarily with the urge to take her in his arms. To tell her that it was all going to be all right and that he'd stay with her through the darkest of nights. Kate didn't need reassurance, though, she needed action.

'I have a friend. She works at the hospital. I've referred people who are traumatised by surgery to her before and she's excellent at what she does. I can introduce you to her and she'll see you out of hours. The only way that anyone else will ever know about this is if you choose to tell them.'

'She must be expensive.' At least Kate was thinking about it. She hadn't turned the idea down out of hand.

'I think it would be an excellent investment to see her privately for a few sessions, if she can see you straight away.' Ethan wondered if Kate could afford it, and whether he could get away with speaking to Dr Usha Patel privately and paying for her sessions himself.

Kate shook her head suddenly. 'I don't want to jump the queue. There must be other people who need her much more than I do.'

Ethan sighed. 'That's Usha's problem. Leave her to sort her diary out for herself. If she can't do it, she'll say.'

The internal struggle—that need to talk that Kate was constantly pushing away—was written all over her face. Finally she made the right decision.

'You're right. I'll call her.'

When she got around to it, no doubt. Which might well be never. Ethan nodded, picking up his phone and consulting his contacts list. Kate almost jumped out of her seat.

'What are you doing? It's six o'clock.'

'Yes, that's fine. She often works in the evening. And

she owes me a favour.' He dialled Usha's number, hoping that she wasn't with a client.

He heard Usha's voice on the line and grinned. Kate was fidgeting in her seat. He explained quickly that a friend was experiencing some problems and it would be great if she could spare some time to talk with her.

'I'm sorry to hear that. Yes, I have some free time, I can fit her in.'

'Thanks, Usha.' He glanced at Kate. 'She says she can fit you in.'

'Wait…' Usha's voice held a trace of firmness in her tone. 'She's there? Are you railroading her into this, Ethan? Let me speak with her.'

He hadn't anticipated that it would be Usha who threw a spoke in the wheel of his plan. But Ethan had to admit that she was right.

'Um…right. Okay.' He handed the phone to Kate. 'She'd like to speak with you. I'll…go and get some coffee.' He could see a café across the road, and it was the only excuse he could think of to get out of the car and give Kate some privacy. He opened the door, hearing her tremulous, 'Hello?' behind him.

He spent five minutes hanging around in the window of the café, nursing a cup of coffee that would have been fresh brewed an hour ago. Finally he saw Kate take the phone from her ear.

Ethan got into the car and, at a loss for anything more to say, he proffered his polystyrene cup to her. She took it wordlessly, taking a sip from it.

'Ew! What are you trying to do, poison me? I suppose that's one way of making me feel no pain.' She wrinkled her nose, putting the cup back into his hand.

The ice broke. Ethan grinned, tipping the contents of

the cup out of the window and stowing it in the glove compartment, alongside a couple of empty cartons of Sam's favourite juice. 'Have you sorted things out with Usha?'

'It's all fixed. I'm going to see her tomorrow, after work.' Kate was obviously a lot happier about the idea now, and it occurred to Ethan that it was Usha who had put her mind at rest, not him.

'Good. I…um… I hope you didn't think I was rail-roading you.' He grinned stupidly. 'Actually, you'd be quite right if you did think that.'

Kate raised her eyebrows. 'Yes, I thought you were railroading me. It was what I needed, thank you.'

'It's my pleasure.' Ethan started the engine, and then realised he really should ask Kate where they were going next. 'Where to?'

'If you wouldn't mind giving me a lift to the surgery, I really do just need to pop in.'

'And then home?'

'Yes, thank you. Then home.'

Ethan nodded. It was time for him to back off and leave Usha and Kate to sort things out now. He'd won a victory, but somehow it had a bitter aftertaste.

# CHAPTER SEVEN

USHA WAS NICE, dressed in soft shades of grey and purple, with dangly earrings and a down-to-earth attitude. She'd listened to what Kate had to say, nodding her on as if none of this was anything to be ashamed of.

Then, five minutes before the end of the session, she'd issued Kate a challenge. Maybe this therapy thing wasn't as easy as she'd thought. But Usha had smiled and shrugged, adding a proviso. 'Give it a try.'

'I'll do it.' If Usha thought that she couldn't, then Kate would prove her wrong.

'We'll make another appointment for early next week, then.' Usha smiled serenely, and Kate left the comfortable consulting room wondering what on earth she'd let herself in for.

Or what Ethan had let her in for. He knew Usha, and he must also know that this wasn't going to be easy. But he must think that she could do it.

The one thing she hadn't shared was the struggle to put Ethan into context and think of him as if he were just any other friend. She'd deal with that one on her own. It was far too embarrassing to talk to Usha about it. A little common sense would have to do.

And common sense told her that Ethan would lose

some of his super-human powers if she concentrated on the Ethan who lived in the real world and not her imagination. Talking to him, instead of wishing he'd phone, would be a good idea. As she waited for the bus home, she dialled his number.

'Hello, Kate.' His tone was studiedly neutral, obviously waiting to see whether she'd kept the appointment she had with Usha before he said anything.

'Hi. I was thinking, since Sam didn't get to see the puppies yesterday, he might like to come to the working dog show we're holding at the weekend. It's not a very big one, just a local thing, but that could be nicer for him as he'll get to meet the dogs and their owners.'

There was a pause. Clearly he wasn't going to ask. 'That could be really nice. He'll be able to see what dogs can do when they're trained.'

'Well, it's on Saturday afternoon. In a little village called Hambleton. Do you know it?'

'Yes, I know it well. It's where my parents' house is, remember? And it's pronounced "Hampton".'

'Really? Is that a concerted effort to confuse anyone who doesn't come from around here?'

'Yes, we do our best. Where is it, in the church hall?'

'Yes, that's right. Spelled St Thomas's, and you can pronounce it however you like.'

She heard Ethan chuckle quietly. 'What time?'

'Two o'clock. I'll be there from one-thirty onwards with the mountain rescue team.'

'Right. Should be interesting. Thanks for letting me know about it.'

'Great. See you then, perhaps.'

Silence crackled down the line. Kate couldn't help smiling, because she knew what Ethan wanted to ask, and this time she had an answer that didn't make her feel as if she wanted to disappear.

'For goodness' sake… Okay, you win. How did this evening go?' There was a note of exasperated humour in his tone.

'It went well, thank you. Usha's given me some homework.'

'What was that, then—phoning me up and giving me a hard time?'

'No, that might be next week's assignment, though.' It was a dream diary. Kate didn't feel quite comfortable about telling him that, because her nightmares were often the dreams where she was helpless and Ethan wasn't there to save her.

She heard him chuckle quietly. 'All right. I'm not going to ask, that's between you and Usha. As long as you feel it's been positive.'

'Yes, I do. Thanks for putting me in touch with her.'

'No problem. I'm going to go now, before you do my nervous system any more damage. Oh, hang on a minute.' She could hear Sam's voice in the background, and smiled. 'Sam says hello.'

'Tell him hello back. I'll see him on Saturday, if you're able to come.'

'We'll be there.'

Ethan joined the small crowd that had gathered outside the church, and found that its main topic of conversation consisted of whether it was one minute to two or one minute past. Events such as these were usually attended by the stalwarts of the surrounding villages, most of whom were retired. They arrived on time, all knew each other and departed after half an hour, which was when the younger families would start to arrive.

'Hello, Ethan.' He'd known Mrs Sweetman since he was a child, and had thought her very old then. 'You're very early, dear.'

'Yes, I…' Couldn't wait to see Kate? If he were to voice that, then it would be old news by sundown. 'I happened to be passing.'

'With Sam, I see.' Mrs Sweetman smiled down at his son. 'How you've grown, dear.'

'Hello. I'm five now.' Sam responded with the same courtesy towards the elders of the village that Ethan had been taught.

'Are you, now? Doesn't time fly? I wonder when they're going to open the doors?'

'You can sync your phone, Mrs Sweetman. Then you'll know the right time.'

A little burst of pride made Ethan smile. He'd shown Sam how he synched the time display on his phone last week and his son had clearly been listening far more closely than it had appeared at the time.

'My telephone?' Mrs Sweetman was clearly thinking of an apparatus connected to the wall by a wire. 'That sounds rather clever.'

'Dad will show you. He showed me on his phone.' Sam seemed eager to help and Ethan breathed a small sigh of relief as the doors of the church hall opened. Offering Mrs Sweetman his arm, he walked slowly inside.

Kate was nowhere to be seen. Display boards with photographs were laid out on one side of the hall and a tea table on the other. The crowd migrated as one to the tea table.

'Where are the dogs, Dad?' Sam was looking a little disappointed.

'They'll be outside. We'll go and see them after we've got Mrs Sweetman a cup of tea.'

'Oh, thank you, dear. I could do with one after all that waiting.'

Sam carefully carried a plate of biscuits over to Mrs Sweetman and offered her one. He was duly thanked, and then they were free. Ethan hurried Sam through the hall and out of the fire doors at the side before anyone else could buttonhole them. The village had known his every move practically since he had been born. Now that he was a young widower with a child, its elders seemed intent on engaging him in conversation whenever they saw him to fend off any possibility of loneliness. It was kind, and a gesture that Ethan had appreciated when Jenna had first died. But he'd come to terms with being alone now, and this afternoon there was somewhere else he needed to be.

On the grass in a semi-circle, large, open-sided tents shaded the dogs and their owners from the sun. The police were there, along with a stand for hearing dogs and one for guide dogs. The mountain rescue dogs were at the far end, and Ethan wondered whether he would have to work through all the rest before he got to see Kate.

Sam saved him the trouble, running across the grass towards her. She was wearing a red T-shirt, with the mountain rescue insignia, and when she saw Sam she stretched her arms out in an expression of joy that made Ethan's heart thump in his chest.

He saw Sam hug her. He didn't often do that, saving his hugs for people he really liked. A little quiver of foreboding—the thought that he shouldn't let Sam become dependent on her hugs—was forgotten as he saw Sam's face when one of the men Kate was with issued a command to his dog and the animal trotted over to Sam, holding out its paw. Ethan saw Kate nod to Sam and he took the dog's paw and shook hands.

She looked up and saw Ethan. This time she didn't stretch her arms out, but her smile was no less broad.

'You made it, then.'

'Yes. We made it.'

He knew that Kate was perfectly capable of smiling through the most challenging problems. He'd fallen for her cover-up himself, believing that she was coping well with the after-effects of the attack, but he fancied that he was beginning to see a little more clearly now. And this afternoon, she had a lightness about her that convinced him her joy was genuine.

'Looks as if we have a budding dog trainer here.' She grinned over at Sam who was being introduced to each of the dogs in turn.

'I'm hoping so. We'll need to commit to some classes when the puppy's old enough.'

Ethan smiled across at one of Kate's companions and Mike strode over to shake his hand.

'Ethan. How are you doing? I haven't see you in a while.'

'I'm good. I've been busy.' It occurred to Ethan that he'd slowly withdrawn from village life over the last year, intent on proving to himself that he could manage alone. Maybe he *was* lonely.

'Sam told me all about his puppy when I saw him the other day with your father. Where *is* George?' Mike looked around.

'He'll be along later. He's taking Mum over to her

tailoring class first.' The tailoring class was actually an excuse to sit around, drink tea and talk. His mother had been attending it for ten years now, which meant she'd probably learned just about all she needed to know about the sewing part of the afternoon.

'Well, I'll let you have a look around. Kate, you've got the leaflets?'

'Yes.' Kate picked up a pile of leaflets from the table behind her and handed one to Ethan. 'Here you are.'

'Thanks.' Ethan knew all about the activities of the mountain rescuers, but he took the leaflet anyway, its value growing in inverse proportion to its usefulness, because Kate had given it to him.

'I'm in there...' She grinned and pointed out a small figure, standing with a group of others. 'I'll mention that because you wouldn't be able to recognise me otherwise.'

Maybe not. Maybe it was just his imagination that he'd recognise the way she held herself anywhere. 'Do you go out with the team?'

'Yes, I've completed my training and I'm a fully fledged mountain rescuer now. Even got the T-shirt.' She pointed at the logo on her shirt, and Ethan tried not to stare. The thin material draped over her curves looked great.

'But you don't handle any of the dogs?' Each dog responded only to the commands of one of the men.

'No, the dogs live with their handlers, and I didn't want to leave an animal alone while I was at work. I decided it was best to just help with them. And be a part of the team when we go out, of course.'

This meant a lot to Kate. She was all about the challenge, and the more he saw that the more he knew she could challenge her own demons if she just had the right tools to do it with. And, even though he'd decided to leave that to Usha, he couldn't help wanting to be a part of it.

'Come and say hello.' She turned to the men, who were now showing Sam the different commands that the dogs would respond to. 'I'm going to do some leafleting in a moment. That police sniffer-spaniel may be gorgeous, but he's getting all the attention.'

The afternoon seemed to go well. The sun shone and the old church hadn't seen so many people pass its doors in years. The mountain rescue team was busy, talking to people and showing them how they worked with the dogs. Sam had been sniffed by the spaniel and had watched a hearing-assistance dog nudge at its owner's hand when a bell was rung. Then, when Ethan's father had arrived, keen to see the display, he'd done it all again with him.

Ethan couldn't take his eyes off Kate. She was bright, smiling, always in the midst of people. In the end, he gave in to temptation, walked back to the mountain rescue stand and was promptly pressed into handing out leaflets.

'So where's mine, then?' His father's voice sounded behind him.

'Here you are.' Ethan handed him a leaflet. 'Make sure you read it carefully. Lots of good information.'

'Will do.' His father's eyes twinkled with quiet humour.

'Hello. Welcome!' Kate appeared, holding her hand out towards his father. This was the routine they'd fallen into. Leaflet first and then a greeting from Kate, who introduced visitors to the other members of the team so they could talk and ask questions.

'Hello. I'm George.' His father grinned, shaking her hand. 'I know your friend here.'

Ethan rolled his eyes. 'He's my father. Dad, this is Kate... Where's Sam?'

'Over there.' His father pointed to the next stand, which was taking kids in groups of six to show them how guide dogs negotiated a busy road. Ethan looked and counted only five heads.

He looked around but couldn't see Sam. Suddenly the safety of the village crumbled and panic tore at his heart. Sam *had* to be here somewhere. His father and Kate were looking too, Kate climbing up on a chair so that she could see over the heads of the people.

'There!' Ethan felt Kate's hand nudge his shoulder. 'There he is.'

Sam was walking towards them around the perimeter of the church hall. He seemed a little distracted, as if he didn't quite know where he was going. Then Ethan heard Kate catch her breath and she jumped down from the chair and started to run towards Sam. He'd just wiped his hands down the front of his white T-shirt, leaving a trail of blood.

Ethan reached Sam first, coming to a halt in front of his son and kneeling down. 'Sam? Show me your hands, mate.'

Sam held out his hands palms upwards. 'There's a man, Dad.'

'Did he hurt you?' The fear was like nothing he'd ever felt before.

'It's not his blood, Ethan.' Kate's voice beside him was calm and quiet. She was right. Sam's hands were smeared with blood, but there was no injury.

He had to get the T-shirt off him. If he pulled it over Sam's head it would smear blood all over his face, and Ethan had no idea where the blood had come from. He pulled his keys from his pocket, pushing them into the material to make a hole, then tearing the T-shirt all the way up the front so that Kate could slip it from his shoulders.

His own shirt was open over a T-shirt, and Ethan pulled it off his shoulders and wrapped it around Sam. The boy snuggled into it.

'There's a man, Dad.'

'What man? Is he bleeding?' Ethan had quickly examined Sam's chest and arms and there wasn't a mark on him. Just the blood on his hands, most of which had been smeared on the front of his T-shirt.

'He's over there…' Sam pointed behind him to the corner of the church hall. Then he wound his arms around Ethan's neck, clinging to him. His only two options were leaving Sam here on his own, or taking him with him to go and see, and both tore at him.

'I'll go.' Kate must have seen his hesitation and was already on her feet, jogging towards the spot that Sam had indicated. Fearless as always. Ethan hugged Sam tight, watching her go.

## CHAPTER EIGHT

THE CORNER OF the church hall was shaded by trees and the strip of land which lay beyond that, between the back of the building and the fence, felt secluded from the noise and bustle around the stands. Three feet in front of her, a man's body lay motionless, blood pooling around his shoulders onto the hard-baked ground.

Ethan obviously carried a great deal of guilt over not having been there when his wife needed him and he couldn't bring himself to leave Sam now. But he'd never forgive himself if he didn't tend to the injured man. She ran back to them.

'Ethan. Let your father take Sam. You have to come.'

He hesitated for one more agonising moment. 'Now, Ethan!' Kate issued the command, hoping that it gave him no choice. If she was wrong, then he could challenge her over it later.

Ethan shouted for his father, then transferred Sam into George's arms, telling him quickly to make sure all the blood was cleaned off him. As Ethan ran back towards her, she called to Mike, asking him to send someone from the police stand over with a first-aid kit, and then followed Ethan.

He dropped to his knees next to the man, all his attention now focussed on him. 'He's alive. I have a pulse.' Ethan's voice was quiet, concentrated, as he examined the man for injuries.

Kate looked up, trying to see what might have happened, in case that could help. 'He must have fallen from the roof. The gutter's broken and the fence has been smashed.'

Ethan nodded, his face grave. 'Call an ambulance. Tell them that a doctor's in attendance and we need them as soon as possible.'

'I'll get my phone.' She'd left it in her jacket pocket, back on the stand.

'Take mine.' Ethan handed her his phone and continued his examination, moving the man as little as possible so as not to further injure him.

'He's unconscious, probably fallen from a height of thirty feet. One of the fence palings has gone almost all the way through his leg below the knee. His airways are clear, pulse is very weak. His chest seems uninjured but…stomach's hard and distended.'

Kate knew that wasn't good. She relayed the details on to the ambulance controller. 'Anything else?'

'Can you pass me the phone, please?'

Ethan was very calm, very cool. That was more worrying than anything, because Kate knew full well that this was his reaction to the seriousness of the situation. He spoke quickly into the phone and she stared at the man's face. He was young, maybe not even twenty. Kate hoped that Ethan was receiving the assurances that he needed and that help would come soon.

She bent, laying her fingers gently on the man's brow, murmuring into his ear. 'Hold on. We're here for you.'

'That's right.' Ethan's voice beside her. 'Keep talking to him.'

The realisation that this was all she could do hit Kate and she blinked back her tears. If the man seemed unresponsive then maybe something she said might register. If that was the case, then she had to choose her words carefully.

She spoke as clearly as she could, telling the man that he was loved. That a doctor was here, and he had to hold on. Then again, there was no way of knowing when and if he might drift back into consciousness.

'Give me your hand.' She stretched her hand out, and Ethan guided it to a spot on the man's leg just above the knee. 'Press hard…harder. Good. That's right. Keep that up, you're doing just fine.'

She was so frightened of making a mistake that could cost a life. But Ethan would tell her what to do. The police dog-handler arrived back with the first-aid kit, kneeling down next to them and opening it, following Ethan's calm, quiet instructions.

Scissors, to cut the leg of the man's jeans. Dressings. The policeman handed over what Ethan needed and he started to pack around the wound, taping it tightly to stop the bleeding.

'Okay, I think we have it. Kate, release the pressure… good. Clean your hands and put a pair of gloves on.'

There was no blood on her hands but she cleaned them anyway. She heard Ethan ask if there was a cervical collar in the first-aid kit, and the policeman looked helplessly through its contents.

'There.' She picked up the collar, tearing the wrappings, and gave it to Ethan.

'Thanks. Can you find his pulse?'

'Yes.' She felt the man's wrist, feeling the faint rhythm of his heart under her fingers. 'Got it.'

'Okay, tell me if it weakens.'

She couldn't. She didn't know enough. But Ethan had no one else here to help him, and she had to. She knew how to do this, even if she'd only done it with animals before.

Ethan was working quickly and carefully, his attention now centred on the man's stomach and chest. 'Go round to the front and make sure the ambulance knows where we are. There's another doctor on his way too.'

Kate looked up, wondering if he was sending her away, but he was talking to the policeman, who got to his feet, leaving quickly. They were on their own now, and Ethan was trusting her to help him.

It was quiet here. She watched as Ethan carefully probed the man's stomach, causing a weak moan to escape his lips.

'It's all right. Just hold on, the doctor's here…' She started to talk again, taking care to keep her fingers over the man's pulse. She saw Ethan nod, but the man seemed not to have heard her and was unresponsive again. All the same, she kept talking.

Then, sudden activity. One of the policemen was ushering a man in a high-visibility jacket towards them.

'Ethan.' The man set his bag down on the ground. He obviously knew Ethan, and Ethan's tight smile told Kate that this was the help that they so needed.

'John, thanks for coming. You have the REBOA kit?'

'Yes.' John knelt down next to Ethan, and Kate saw the identification flash on his jacket: 'Doctor'.

Ethan was quickly updating John about the man's condition and John was nodding. They seemed to be coming to a quick, unspoken agreement about what should happen next. 'You've done this more times than me, Ethan. You lead.'

*REBOA.... REBOA...?* Kate had heard those initials before, although they weren't a part of animal medicine. It was a last resort, something only available for treating people.

John opened his bag and Ethan turned to Kate. 'We'll need your help with this.'

'Yes. Just tell me what to do.'

There were plenty of people here who had basic medical training with the police and the mountain rescue team. Ethan must have anticipated this course of action, and he could have sent her away and chosen someone else. Kate had no doubt that he would have done, if it had been in his patient's best interests.

But, despite all her weakness, he'd chosen her. She wouldn't let him down, and she wouldn't let their patient down either.

Ethan was disinfecting his hands as best he could with wipes from the medical kit. John was laying out what they needed. Kate waited.

'Can you cut a little further across the leg of his jeans?' Ethan had already undone the waistband and zip to examine the man's stomach. 'I need access to the femoral artery—you know where that is?

'Yes, I know.' She could do this. Animal patients tended to wriggle a great deal more than human ones, and Kate could cut a dressing off almost anything. A pair of jeans was a piece of cake, but when Ethan handed her a pair of surgical scissors she cut as carefully as if she were doing this for the first time.

'That's great.' Ethan didn't look at her—he and

John were both busy with their own preparations—but his voice imputed that she really had done well. Kate breathed a sigh of relief.

She remembered what REBOA was now. A line was inserted into the femoral artery and a small balloon manoeuvred into place along the artery. When it was inflated, it would stem internal bleeding, in either the chest or the abdomen.

It was demanding work, and a technique of last resort even in controlled surroundings. Here it could only be contemplated if both doctors believed that their patient couldn't survive the ten-mile journey to the hospital without it.

Ethan was carefully inserting the catheter, the first part of the delicate process. His posture was relaxed, but his concentration was so focussed and intense that he probably wouldn't have noticed if the weather turned suddenly and it began to snow.

Ethan and John worked together, exchanging quiet instructions and updates. Kate kept her eyes on the blood-pressure monitor, praying that the falling stats might soon change. She held sterile lines clear of the ground, took pieces of equipment and then gave them back again exactly as instructed. If Ethan had told her to stop breathing, she would have done it.

'Nice.' John's one word as Ethan sat back on his heels was the only indicator of hope but Kate would take it.

Ethan was busying himself with the patient, and John shot her a smile. 'You did well. We can manage now if you want to go and change your T-shirt...'

Her T-shirt was spattered with blood. But Ethan had given her a job to do, and Kate wanted to see it through.

'May I just hold his hand, until the ambulance gets here? I won't get in the way.'

Ethan looked up suddenly. 'You've earned that.'

Kate took the young man's hand with trembling fingers. She'd earned her place here, and he was going to allow her to stay.

# CHAPTER NINE

WHEN THE TWO-MAN ambulance crew arrived, she was in the way, and she had to go. Not waiting for John or Ethan to tell her so, she stepped back, walking towards the policeman who was stationed at the corner of the hall, stopping anyone from approaching.

'Kate. Kate!' Mike was standing as close as he was allowed, holding a blanket and her zip-up sweatshirt. Kate ignored the blanket, zipping the sweatshirt around her and wriggling out of her T-shirt.

'Nice trick.' Mike grinned as she pulled the T-shirt over her head and threaded her arms into the sweatshirt. 'You're going to have to tell me how you do that.'

Kate smirked at him. 'Women's secrets.'

'Yeah. I'd figured that one out. How is he?'

'I don't really know, but it seems pretty bad. Ethan and the other doctor have done a surgical procedure.'

'Really.' Mike nodded. He'd been Kate's mentor when she'd first joined the mountain rescue team two years ago. He knew better than anyone that doctors waited to do surgery at hospital if it was at all possible. 'We'll just have to hope for the best then.'

'Is Sam still here?'

'No, his grandfather's taken him home. He had a bit of

a shock but once he was cleaned up he seemed all right. We gave him one of the kids' T-shirts.'

'That's nice.' They only had a few of those, and they'd been saving them. But Sam deserved one.

'One of the police dog handlers came over with a children's activity pack as well. We all made a bit of a fuss of him and he cheered up.'

Kate knew that the guys would have done their best to lift Sam's spirits. They all had children of their own, and knew that Ethan couldn't be there for his son. She wondered how he was going to feel about that, when this was all over.

'Is Ethan going to the hospital?' Mike broke into her thoughts.

'I don't know. Do you have another T-shirt? Ethan got the worst of the blood spillage.'

'Yep, no problem. Wait here, I'll bring it to you.'

She waited for five minutes, knowing that Ethan would come as soon as he could. He would want to know that Sam was all right. When he finally appeared, he made straight for her.

'He's still in a bad way, but you helped give him a chance, Kate.'

It took five seconds to say it. But it was five seconds in which Ethan could have asked about Sam, and he'd chosen to tell her what she needed to hear. She proffered the T-shirt with trembling hands.

'Sam's okay. Your dad cleaned him up and everyone made a big fuss of him. They've gone home.'

'Thanks.' Ethan stripped off his T-shirt, dropping it onto the ground.

Wow. The way Ethan filled a shirt, it had been impossible to conclude that he didn't have a good body.

The reality of it exceeded Kate's expectations. And she shouldn't be thinking that, because there were much more important things to concentrate on.

'You're going to the hospital?'

'Yes.' He pulled his phone from his jeans pocket and handed it to her. 'Would you be able to take my dad's number and call him, let him know? Tell him I'll be there as soon as I can and ask him to text me and let me know how Sam is.'

'Yes, of course.' He was trusting her with this, too.

'He's under "d"—for Dad.' One corner of Ethan's mouth twitched and Kate realised that she was staring at him. He took the clean T-shirt from her and pulled it over his head. Too late. Ethan wasn't someone you could un-see in a hurry.

He was looking over his shoulder, back to where John and the ambulance crew were carefully transferring the young man onto a stretcher. Kate found the number, transferring it into her own phone and checking it.

'Got to go...' For a moment, Ethan was still, his gaze locked onto her face. Then he turned and was gone.

The ambulance left, and she called George, letting him know where Ethan was, and receiving assurances that Sam was fine and that he'd text Ethan and let him know. And then there was nothing more for Kate to do. Mike shooed her away from the mountain rescue stand, which was rapidly being packed up and dismantled, telling her to go and get a cup of tea.

'You want a decent cup. Not a couple of mouthfuls.' The middle-aged woman who had been busy wrapping uneaten biscuits in cling-film ignored the cups and saucers that were still laid out on the tea table and reached underneath it, producing a mug.

'Thanks. You're a lifesaver.'

'From what I hear, you and Ethan Conway are lifesavers.' The woman smiled at her and Kate shivered. Hearing herself and Ethan mentioned in the same sentence was new, and oddly exciting. 'How is the young man?'

'I don't really know. He's on his way to hospital and Ethan's gone with him. He says that he has a chance.'

'Good.' The woman produced a hip flask from her pocket. 'Would you like some of this to go with it, love?'

'What is it?'

'Nice drop of brandy. Only, don't tell the vicar. Church premises....'

There was no particular reason why she should find it incongruous that the tea ladies were surreptitiously downing brandy in the church kitchen, but it made Kate smile all the same.

'I bet you can do with a drink after serving this many cups of tea.'

'That's for sure.' The woman reached for two teacups and poured a splash into the bottom of each, handing Kate one. 'I'm Pat. Here's to a happy ending.'

Kate grinned. 'Kate. To happy endings.'

They clinked their cups together, and Pat downed the contents of hers in one. Kate followed suit, almost choking as the astringent heat hit the back of her throat.

'Oh...!' Pat's eyes had filled with tears, and she blinked them away. 'I'm not used to this. But it's a bit of a tradition here, once we get the dishwasher stacked.'

Kate sat down with a bump on one of the chairs next to the tea table, her head swimming. 'Maybe I should have sipped it.'

'Me too. So much for bravado.' Pat reached for another mug and filled both with tea, pushing Kate's towards her.

'Here's to bravado, then.' Kate grinned, taking a welcome mouthful of tea.

'Yes, that's much better.' Pat sat down, looking at Kate speculatively. 'You know Ethan, then?'

'Yes. I'm a vet. I looked after his dog, Jeff.'

Pat nodded. 'Poor old Jeff. Great big thing but as gentle as they come. When Sam was little he used to sit himself down next to his pushchair, nudging anyone he didn't know away if they got too close. Jenna used to have to lean on him, to get him to move.'

'You knew Ethan's wife?' It seemed somehow presumptuous to use her name.

'Oh, yes, she came from around here. And she was often in the village. She used to bring Sam to see his grandparents. Such a shame. If there were ever two people that belonged together...'

Kate took a swallow of her tea. For a short time it had seemed that *she* and Ethan belonged together. But she knew so little about Ethan, and if the people he'd grown up with said he belonged with someone else then it must be true.

'Sam seems... He's got a great relationship with his dad.'

'Yes, he has. And Ethan's devoted to him. Chocolate biscuit?'

'Yes, please. Can I take it with me? I should get back to our stand. I'm sure there's something I can help with.' Kate managed a smile as Pat stripped the cling-film off one of the plates and wrapped three biscuits, putting them into her hand.

'There you go, my love.'

She wandered outside, sitting down on the steps outside the front of the hall. Her car was still in the garage, and Mike had said he'd drop her home, but he was nowhere to be seen.

Ethan had trusted her. It made her feel good...no, better than good. It had made her feel strong, as if his belief in her was worth more than anyone else's. But he'd gone now.

Of course he had. If he hadn't needed to go to the hospital, then he would have gone straight to Sam. They were priorities, and it would be unthinkable to expect anything different. And if she allowed herself to rely on him too much, then she would be just setting herself up for heartbreak.

She picked up her tea, wandering over to the empty mountain rescue tent. Sitting around drinking tea was all very well, but taking the tent down was the kind of problem she needed to distract her right now. At least that involved some possibility of success.

In the cramped space inside the ambulance, Ethan and John had managed to prevent their patient from bleeding out, or having a seizure, or a heart attack, or any one of a number of things that could have killed him before they reached the hospital.

Time had become an irrelevance, something that might be counted on a clock somewhere, but which didn't matter. An hour or a minute. It didn't make any difference as long as his patient was still alive and there was one more thing that he could do to keep him that way.

He'd made it to the resuscitation room. Then he'd made it past the concentrated activity which assessed his injuries and vital signs. He'd been stabilised, and Ethan had made the decision that he was ready for surgery. And then Ethan had finally looked at his watch.

He checked his phone and saw the text from his father, saying that Sam was all right. Then he spent ten minutes under the shower, knowing that he couldn't speak to Sam just yet. In a moment he'd be able to be a father again, instead of a doctor whose one aim was to keep the patient under his care alive.

'Hey, Sam. How are you doing?'

'You made the man better, Dad?'

'Yes, we did.' Surely he was allowed this one little lie, to reassure Sam?

'He had lots of blood on him.'

'Yes, I know. Were you frightened?'

'Yes.' Sam suddenly sounded subdued.

'I'll bet you were. It was a frightening thing to happen to you, and you were very brave to come and find us the way you did.'

'Did he have some blood left?'

'Yes, he had plenty of blood left. We gave him some extra as well. He's all right now.'

'Okay…'

Sam chattered on to him, and Ethan sat in the doctor's rest room, letting the tightly coiled spring in his chest loosen a little. Reminding himself that he'd made sure that Sam was well looked after.

He promised Sam that he'd be back soon, and then spoken briefly to his father. Then he called Kate.

'Ethan.' She sounded pleased that he'd called.

'Hi. I just wanted you to know that…he's made it into surgery.'

A puffed-out breath of relief. 'Thank you. That's really great. I suppose you don't know anything else yet?'

'No, but he's a fighter. That helps.' Kate would understand that. She was a fighter too.

'Well, that's good to know. Where are you?'

'At the hospital still. My dad's coming to pick me up
and I'll fetch my car and then go and get Sam.'

'I'd better let you go. Thanks so much for taking the
time to call.' She seemed about to hang up, now.

'Wait.' There was something more he had to say. And
even if there hadn't been he could still spare these few
moments, just to talk to her. 'I wanted to say that I'm
sorry. For rushing off like that.'

He heard her expel a sharp breath. 'Right. Because
there was nowhere you needed to go. Don't be crazy,
Ethan.'

'How about, sorry that I left you to find him.'

'No, that one doesn't wash either. You were making sure that Sam wasn't hurt. That's your first priority, Ethan.'

He'd been clinging to Sam, blinded to everything other
than the fact that he needed his son to be all right. Kate
had jerked him back out of that, and made him see what
he needed to do.

'I'm glad you think that I thought about it so ratio-
nally.'

'You're allowed to be irrational. Goes with the territory.'

Ethan chuckled. Just the sound of her voice was making him feel that somehow he'd managed to cover all the
bases. Look after Sam, be a doctor... Maybe even look
after Kate a little.

'Sam tells me he wants to be a mountain rescue volunteer when he grows up.'

'Does he? That's nice.'

'Yeah. And he wants to train his dog to shake hands.'

'That can be arranged. I'm an expert at getting dogs to shake hands.' She caught her breath suddenly, as if she'd said something she shouldn't. 'If you can't find anyone else, that is…'

The thought that maybe he should find someone else, someone who Sam wouldn't be tempted to accept as a mother figure, had occurred to Ethan. But right now he just wanted to feel life pumping in his veins, and Kate made him feel alive.

'Since you're the expert, it would be very bad manners to even think there was anyone else.'

She laughed and Ethan began to wish that he could touch her. Just to hold her for a moment and celebrate the warmth of life.

'You took a chance on me. When you asked me to help.' Her voice took on a note of tension, as if this was something that she'd been waiting to say.

'No, I didn't. You were as steady as a rock. I had no worries on that score. You know, don't you, that if I'd had any doubts I would have had no choice but to ask someone else to help.'

'Yes, I know. The patient's needs come first.' Her voice lightened a little, as if she half-believed what he'd just said.

'You're stronger than you think, Kate.'

'And how strong do you think I think I am? Or do you think that I think that you think—?'

Ethan's laugh cut her short. 'Stop. You lost me on the second "think". I'm going to go now, before you reduce my brain to mush.'

'Yes, you'd better. Give Sam a hug from me.'

Maybe he would. Just maybe…

* * *

Ethan went to check on the young man on Monday morning before he started work and then visited him every day after that. For the first three days he was in the intensive care ward. His mother had told Ethan that he was only nineteen, and that his name was Christopher but that his friends called him CK, because those were his initials.

On the fourth day, CK opened his eyes and focussed blearily on Ethan's face. Then, on day six, he told him that he'd climbed up on the roof for a bet, but that he'd learned his lesson. He remembered nothing of the incident or the minutes before it.

It would be a long journey for CK. He had significant internal injuries, and he would have to learn to walk again, after his leg had been shattered by the fence paling. But against all the odds he'd survived and was making a recovery. Ethan always tried to follow up on his patients and often the outcome wasn't such a good one. But somehow CK's hold on life seemed like a miracle.

# CHAPTER TEN

THE PART OF the week that Kate had occupied wasn't all that significant time-wise. Short phone calls to update her on CK's progress, and an hour one evening with Sam, taking him to see his puppy. But for all that, when his mind wasn't concentrated on work, Kate had occupied the greater part of Ethan's attention.

He had little enough to offer her—a scarred heart that still didn't know whether it was strong enough to love any more than it already had. Limited time and a schedule of early mornings that didn't fit in all that well with Kate's schedule at the veterinary surgery. He should keep in contact, try to be there for her if she needed him, but leave it at that.

Then, on Friday afternoon, he got a call. His father put Sam on the line, who explained that he had an important project on hand with Grandpa, and that he wanted to stay the night there. As soon as Ethan put his phone back down on his desk, he changed his mind and picked it up again, dialling Kate's number.

'I've got a free evening, as Sam's staying at my parents. I thought I might catch a film and wondered if you'd like to keep me company?' In other words, this wasn't a date.

'Yes, that sounds great. Do you know what's on?'

He'd forgotten to look. 'No.'

'Hang on a minute, let me get to my desk.' He heard the sound of Kate's footsteps, and then the chime as a computer was nudged into life. 'Here we are. There's a romance, but it's only got one star on the reviews. Gritty story of cops on the beat… Superheroes… Um…oh, and there's one in Chinese, with subtitles.'

None of that sounded particularly promising, but that wasn't really the point. 'What do you fancy?'

'I don't really know. What do you think?'

There was a short silence and they both laughed together. 'All right. I'll go first. I'm quite partial to superheroes, actually.'

Ethan chuckled. Why did that not surprise him? 'Me too. I heard that one was pretty good.'

'Yes it's got four-and-a-half stars. Unless you want to go and see it with Sam?'

'I think the one that's currently out is a bit grown up for Sam.'

'Oh, yes, so it is. What do you think, then? There are showings at eight, nine and half-past nine.'

'I'll pick you up at half-eight, then?'

The smell of popcorn and a woman standing next to him in the queue for tickets. Ethan hadn't done this for a while. But Kate was just a friend. They were two people, neither of whom had anyone to go to the cinema with, and who didn't want to go alone.

As they got to the head of the queue, her phone buzzed. Ethan selected the seats and was about to pay for them when suddenly Kate slammed her hand onto the debit-card reader.

'I'll get them.'

'No.' When he glanced across at her, Kate was frowning. This didn't seem like the usual squabble over who paid for tickets. She grabbed his arm, pulling him to one side, apologising to the woman behind the desk, who rolled her eyes.

'I've got a call out. Mountain rescue. Ethan, I'm sorry.'

That was usually his line—called away for an emergency somewhere. He knew just how bad Kate must be feeling at the moment, and was surprised to find that he wasn't angry in the least. He'd always assumed that other people's protestations, that it was all right and that he really must go, were just good manners.

'What's happened?' Ethan began to walk towards the exit doors.

'It's an old couple. Apparently they went to visit their daughter in the next village this afternoon and she saw them onto the bus home. But they never arrived. They searched everywhere and, when it began to get late, they called for help. The bus goes through...' She consulted her phone. 'How do you say that?'

'Coleswittam. The double "t" is sounded as "th".'

Kate raised her eyebrows. 'Right. That's sure to help a poor, confused Londoner find it. Do you know it?'

'Yes, it's to the west of here. Quite a tourist spot in the summer—hill-walking country with caves and a few waterfalls. It's very beautiful, but not the kind of place an elderly couple should be at night.'

Kate quirked the corners of her mouth down. 'It doesn't sound like it. I'm so sorry, Ethan.'

'Nonsense. Do you want a hand?'

She stopped so suddenly that Ethan almost bumped into her. 'Well...are you sure?'

'A doctor might come in useful.'

'Well, we hope not, but…' Kate started walking again. 'Let's go, then.'

Ethan drove to his house first, and Kate waited outside while he quickly found a pair of walking boots, stuffing them into a rucksack along with a waterproof jacket. He put his medical bag into the boot of the car and they drove to her cottage to pick up her gear. Then he took the short cut along a dirt track to Coleswittam.

'Is everyone at the Old Ford?'

'Yes, that's the meeting point.' The car got to the brow of a hill and she pointed ahead of them. 'There they are.'

The group of men and women seemed well organised. A sandy-haired man who was obviously in charge was splitting everyone up into search parties and showing them which area they should cover on the map. Kate walked towards him and he smiled.

'Thanks for coming.' His gaze flipped towards Ethan.

'This is Ethan Conway. He's a doctor. Ethan, this is Grant, our team leader.'

'Good to have you on board, Ethan.' Grant shook his hand firmly. 'Kate, I want you and Ethan to go with Mike. You should know that the husband has dementia, so he may have wandered off somewhere and got lost. His wife might be looking for him. We don't know. I want you to go up to the Kettle—Mike knows where that is—and maybe Maisie can get a scent there.'

The Kettle. Ethan had played there himself when he was a kid, and in the summer it was a great place to bathe, to explore the rocks and caves which surrounded the pool. At night, and with the weather closing in, it wasn't somewhere he'd want anyone to be lost and alone.

Kate nodded. 'I've got flashlights. Do you have a spare hard hat for Ethan, in case we need to go into the caves?'

'Back of my truck. We have a medical kit too.' Grant flashed a querying glance at Ethan.

'That's okay, I have my own in the car.'

'Great. Good luck, then. Keep in touch.'

'Will do.' Kate hurried over to the open back of an SUV, which bore the logo of the mountain rescue team, leaning in to find what she wanted. Then she joined Ethan as he transferred the contents of his medical bag into his rucksack. Mike joined them, leading Maisie, his dog, and Kate bent to greet the Border collie with a pat on the head.

'Maisie will find them if anyone can. She never gives up.'

Ethan was sure she was right. He knew that no one would stop looking until the elderly couple was found, but it was a matter of time, as well. An elderly couple might not survive a night out in these hills.

They walked away from the circle of car headlights into the gloom, only flashlights to light their way. After the heat of a summer's day the evening was cool and the spattering of rain on Ethan's face would have been refreshing if it wasn't another worry to add to all the others for the missing couple.

'Oh!' They'd walked in near silence for half an hour, concentrating on the uneven ground at their feet, and Kate's quiet exclamation as she stumbled sounded somehow louder.

'Okay?' He caught her arm, steadying her.

'Yes, thanks.' She stopped, shining the flashlight around her, and Mike bent to Maisie, taking a plastic bag out of his pocket which contained a folded item of clothing.

'No scent yet?' Kate's words were more of an observation than a question. They'd know when Maisie caught a scent of the old couple.

'Maybe she'll get one a little further on.' Mike fondled Maisie's head briefly and got to his feet.

'Another three quarters of an hour to the Kettle?' Ethan knew these hills well, but the darkness was disorientating.

'Yep. Bit less, maybe.' Mike pointed the beam of his flashlight in the direction they were going in and started walking.

'You know this area?' He heard Kate's quiet voice next to him.

'Yes. I spent half my time out here when I was a kid. It's a bit different at night though.'

At night. A thought struck him suddenly and he called to Mike. 'The couple we're looking for. They're local?'

'Yes, lived here all their lives.'

'Then they'll know the Kettle, right? We're headed for the east side, but on the west side...'

Mike stopped suddenly, scratching his head. 'Yeah. You're right. I'll call Grant and suggest we take the western approach.'

'What?' He could see Kate's eyes, wide in the darkness, looking up at him.

'Anyone who's lived here all their lives will know that the place for couples is the west side of the Kettle. The east side's a lot prettier, and that's where the walkers and tourists go. On the west side, there are caves and a bit more privacy.'

'And you think that they would go there—like a courting couple?'

'Maybe. Makes sense to me that they might. We used to come up here in the evenings all the time, when we were teenagers.'

Mike ended his call, putting his phone back into his pocket. 'Okay, Grant agrees. We'll go this way.' Mike shone his torch up an incline, and they made their way over the rough, stony ground.

'Surely they couldn't have managed this?' Kate was stumbling in the darkness, and Ethan took her hand to steady her. When she regained her balance she kept hold of him, her fingers warm in his.

'There's another way round, much flatter and easier to walk. If they knew where they were headed, then they could have taken that route.' Ethan remembered that there was a bus stop too, along the road on that side of the hill.

'You think they knew where they were headed? It must have been a long time since they did any courting.'

'For someone with dementia, those memories of their youth become more vivid, as the intervening memories fade. They often recreate their early memories, because they seem more real to them.'

'And *you* used to come here? Was it where you first kissed a girl?' It seemed that, despite the rugged terrain, Kate still had enough breath left to tease him.

'Yes. That was a very long time ago…'

Ethan heard Mike laugh and remembered suddenly that he and Kate weren't alone, however much it felt that she was the only other person in the world right now.

'Me and the wife used to go there, too. Her father didn't think too much of me.' Mike remarked.

There was no more possibility of talk as they toiled up the hill, but Kate kept her hand in Ethan's.

They were keeping up a punishing pace, uphill and in the darkness. But Ethan's dark presence beside her, his hand to guide her, was helping Kate keep up with the two men.

Then the terrain levelled out, onto what seemed to be a wide causeway. Easy to traverse, it seemed a lot more likely that an elderly couple might come this way.

A sudden bark from Maisie and a quiet exclamation from Mike. 'She's got the scent.'

Maisie ran ahead, the lead playing out behind her, and Mike quickened his pace to follow. Ethan broke into a jog and Kate followed him, keeping her eyes on the ground in front of them, which was lit by the beam of his torch.

'There. Up ahead....' Ethan grabbed her hand, switching off his torch, and in the darkness Kate could see... She wasn't quite sure what she saw. A faint glimmer, maybe, in the darkness.

'Yes! I see it.' Mike's voice. Maisie had disappeared ahead of him in the darkness, but Kate could hear her short, sharp barks indicating that she was following a scent.

The grass gave way to smooth rocks, and they scrambled across them. The light was becoming stronger now, yellowish, not white like the light from their torches. Mike was reeling in Maisie's lead and Ethan led Kate across the boulders in their way, into the mouth of a small cave, the rocks around them smooth and rounded.

Kate gasped. There was a fire, well-built and burning brightly. Beside it sat an old man, and on the other side a woman was lying, covered with a couple of coats. And the man was waving a burning brand from the fire, as if to fend them off.

Maisie trotted over to Mike, sitting at his feet, and he gave her a reward from his pocket. Ethan was suddenly still, holding on to Kate's arm to stop her from approaching the man.

'Hello. You must be Mr Fuller.' His voice was quiet,

without any of the urgency that all three of the searchers were feeling.

'What are you doing in my house? You're not my son.' Fred Fuller waved the branch ferociously, obviously confused and angry.

'No, I'm his friend. Ethan.'

'And is this your girl?' Fred pointed at Kate, seeming a little mollified by Ethan's words.

'Yes, that's right Mr Fuller.' Kate smiled, disengaging herself from Ethan's grip, and stepping forward. 'I'm Kate.'

'Let's take a look at you, then.' Fred lowered the branch, putting it down onto the rock floor of the cave.

She walked towards him, kneeling down beside him, and Fred peered at her face. Out of the corner of her eye, she saw Ethan behind her, quietly sliding the burning branch away from Fred's reach.

'You must be cold, Mr Fuller.' Fred was wearing a shirt and tie, with a V-necked sweater, but his coat was covering his wife. 'I've got a cup of tea.'

Fred brightened visibly. 'Yes, we could do with a cup of tea. Eh, Edie?'

'Is Mrs Fuller all right?' Edie Fuller seemed to be asleep, and Ethan was working his way round to take a look at her.

'She's...' Fred shrugged. 'What's he doing?'

'My...boyfriend's a doctor.' Kate kept the subterfuge up, feeling herself blush. 'He's going to see if Mrs Fuller's awake.'

'A doctor, eh?' Fred nodded in approval. 'You've done well for yourself, girl. Don't throw that fish back into the sea.'

Kate could feel her ears burning. But Ethan was taking advantage of Fred's sudden interest in her love life, and taking the opportunity gently to examine Edie.

'No, I won't.' She wriggled out of her backpack, opening it with one hand and pulling out the light thermal blanket. 'Here, would you like this around your shoulders?'

'What's that thing?' Fred looked at the shiny reflective blanket, pushing it away roughly. 'Where's my tea?'

'In my bag. I've got a thermos flask.'

Mike had stepped back, away from the mouth of the cave, and Kate could hear him on his phone, quietly calling their position in. There would be others here soon, but in the meantime they had to keep the old couple warm.

'I could do with a cuppa. I'm cold.' Fred's voice seemed suddenly thin and frail. Ethan turned for a moment, taking off his coat and leaving it on the ground beside him.

'What about this, then?' Kate reached forward, picking up the coat and wrapping it around Fred's shoulders. He seemed to like it a bit better than the blanket, and tried to push his arms awkwardly into the sleeves. Kate helped him, fastening the zip at the front.

'When he asks yer to marry him...' Fred leaned forward '...don't say no, now. You girls...you play hard to get and a man can get the wrong idea.'

Fred seemed to have no regard for the fact that Ethan must be able to hear every word of their conversation, and Kate wondered what he was thinking. Probably just the same as she was, that keeping Fred warm and quiet was the main thing right now.

'He hasn't asked me yet. I think he might, though.'

She pulled the flask out of her rucksack, hoping that tea might divert Fred's attention a little. Pouring a mouthful into the lid, she handed it to Fred, steadying it as he raised it to his lips.

'I can do it.' Fred glared at her but he drank his tea. 'Not much there. What are you going to say when he asks you?'

'Yes. I'll say yes. Here, have some more tea.' Kate poured another mouthful into the beaker and gave it to Fred, watching as he drank.

Ethan had his back to her. Edie wasn't moving.

# CHAPTER ELEVEN

THE SMALL FIRE in the cave was burning brightly and had been well tended. Fred was obviously intent on protecting his wife, and in his confused state he could so easily have jabbed the burning branch in Kate's direction.

But she hadn't faltered. She'd calmed Fred, her smile charming the old man into allowing her to tend to him while Ethan concentrated on Edie.

Fred had done a good job there, too. His memory might be patchy, but the details of how to make a warm bed had somehow stuck. Edie was lying on a makeshift bed of soft bracken and when Ethan felt her hand it was warm under the coats.

'Edie, Edie.' He spoke to her softly and Edie didn't respond. Her pulse was strong, though, and she was breathing steadily. In the torchlight, he could see that a dark bruise was forming on the side of her face and it looked as if she'd taken a fall. Ethan didn't dare move her.

Suddenly her eyes fluttered open. 'Fred?'

'It's all right, Edie. Fred's right here.' He smoothed her tousled hair back from her face, trying to give some comfort to the old lady. It was a wonder that she and Fred had got this far and she must be confused and in pain.

'I'm Ethan, and I'm a doctor. My friend Kate is with

Fred and he's okay.' Ethan wondered whether he should get his story straight with Kate's and call her his girlfriend. It was tempting. 'Are you in any pain, Edie?'

'My arm.' Edie looked up at him placidly.

'Okay, let's take a look.' He carefully moved the coats, looking at Edie's arm. It was bruised and swollen, almost certainly fractured. 'Anything else, my love?'

'No.' Edie tried to move and Ethan gently stilled her. Glancing quickly at her legs, he saw that she seemed to be able to move them without pain. That was a good sign.

'Can you do something for me? I just want you to lift your leg a little.' He put his hand gently under Edie's knee to support it. Edie obligingly lifted her leg an inch and he nodded. 'That's great. Perfect. Now the other one.'

No symptoms of a hip fracture. Edie was breathing and, when Ethan pulled his stethoscope out of his rucksack and listened to her heart, it was beating strongly.

'Are you bleeding anywhere?' The notes which Grant had handed him included a reference to Edie being on warfarin for a blood clot.

'No.' Edie's soft gaze found his. 'I know I mustn't bleed. I take warfarin, you know.'

It seemed that Edie was a lot more aware of her situation than Fred was. Ethan wondered what it might be like, knowing that they were stranded and alone and that her husband was unable to remember what they were doing here.

'Okay. I'm just going to check you over a bit. Make sure everything else is all right.'

'What about Fred?' Edie lowered her voice to a whisper. 'He can't remember, you know.'

'Yes, I know. And he's fine. Kate's looking after him. Just relax and let me look after you.'

Edie nodded, tears forming in her eyes. 'He just got off the bus and I followed him. He wanted to come here, and... I fell. He kept me warm.'

'Yeah, Fred did a good job, Edie. He looked after you really well.' Ethan turned quickly, tears blurring his eyes, and found Kate's gaze. In the flickering firelight he thought he saw her eyes bright with tears too.

'All right, Edie?' Fred was looking at his wife, his eyes tender now.

'Good enough, Fred.' Edie smiled towards her husband and he nodded, turning his attention back to the tea that Kate was holding.

'He always knows me.' Edie murmured the words quietly, and Ethan nodded, his fingers suddenly clumsy with emotion as he fumbled in his backpack for the inflatable splint.

Ethan had been so tender with Edie. He'd glanced back in Kate's direction more than once as he'd worked, a silent *'are you okay?'* and Kate had responded with a smile. Fred was confused, reacting sometimes to reality and sometimes to what was going on in his head, but he was calm now, watching Ethan tend to Edie.

'What's that?' The sound of a steady beat in the distance promised that the helicopter would be here soon.

'They're coming to take you to the hospital, Fred.' Kate wondered whether she should mention the intended mode of transport just yet.

'I want to go home. Tell them to take me home.' Fred frowned suddenly.

'Okay. But don't you think they ought to make sure that Edie's all right first?' She nodded over to where

Ethan was carefully putting Edie's arm into an inflatable splint.

'She's all right.' Fred turned to Edie. 'You're all right, aren't you, girl?'

'Yes, she's going to be all right. But she needs to go to the hospital so that they can look at her arm.' Ethan turned, speaking gently but firmly.

Fred turned his mouth down, as if he wasn't quite in agreement, but wasn't going to argue. 'They'll do well to get a car up here.'

'They're sending a helicopter for you.' Ethan grinned.

'Helicopter? Hear that, Edie? We're going in a helicopter.' Fred sounded almost excited.

The paramedics took over from Ethan and he helped Kate get Fred to his feet and out of the cave. The helicopter pilot climbed down, supervising as they guided Fred into the helicopter, and strapped him in securely. It was all quickly done but Kate saw Ethan find the time to jog up to Edie's stretcher, taking her outstretched hand and bending to exchange a few words with her.

Another party of mountain rescue volunteers, who had been combing the area next to theirs, arrived and Mike went over to talk to them briefly, before re-joining Kate and Ethan.

'You must be wanting to get back for Sam.' Mike spoke to Ethan. 'The others are going now. Why don't you go with them? I'll see to the fire in the cave.'

'Sam's with my parents. I doubt they'll appreciate my turning up in the middle of the night just to stare at him while he sleeps. I'll take care of the fire. I've got to go and pack my medical things up.' Ethan was pulling his coat back on, Fred having been persuaded to give it up.

Mike grinned. 'In that case, I might go home and stare at *my* kids. Do you know the way back? If you get lost, I'm not coming out again tonight.'

Ethan chuckled. 'I know the way. My memory's not that bad.'

He glanced at Kate. A silent question, the answer to which needed no thought at all. They were a team. They stayed together.

'Sounds good. Mike, I'll go with Ethan.'

'All right. If you're sure.'

She was sure. Leaving him now was unthinkable. She watched as Mike and the other volunteers disappeared into the darkness and then walked back to the cave, where Ethan was repacking his rucksack.

Kate stuffed the unused blanket back into her own rucksack. Suddenly, after feeling that there was so much that she had to say to him, she couldn't think of a single word to say it with.

'Hey…' He sat down, poking the fire with a stick, and it flared suddenly. 'Bit of a waste of a good fire.'

Kate laughed, sitting down next to him. She was not quite touching him, but somehow it felt as if she were. 'Fred made a good job of it.'

'Yes, he did. If he built it.'

'I don't imagine Edie did.'

'No, I don't imagine she did either. When I was a teenager, it was considered good form to collect up a few sticks and build a new fire when you left. Then, when you came back, someone else's fire would be there and you just lit it.'

'Ah. So there's no need to search around for something to burn while your girlfriend's sitting on a rock and shivering.' Kate grinned at him.

'That might be a consideration.' He stretched, holding his hands out to the warmth of the blaze. 'So. You're going to say yes, are you?'

He was teasing her, that was obvious. And if Kate denied it then it would only appear that she was protesting too much.

'I might. As Fred says, a doctor's a very good catch.'

Ethan chuckled. 'Long hours? Evenings on your own?'

'Never out of a job. Good pay scales.' Kate grinned up at him. 'I think Fred had an eye on the practical.'

'Having the time to be with someone *is* practical.'

There was a sudden catch in his voice. Ethan leaned forward, poking the fire with a stick so that it burned brightly, suddenly lost in his own thoughts, which seemed to be dancing among the flames.

'You seem very sure of that.'

He turned down the corners of his mouth. 'I am. I was working pretty hard when Jenna died. We'd just bought the house and she'd given up work when Sam was born. I wasn't around very much.'

Kate could see why that would matter to him, but it was something that a lot of people did. Buying houses, having kids. It all cost money. She wondered whether that was really the right thing to say to Ethan, and decided that this was one of those situations where there was no right thing to say. You just had to do your best.

'You were providing for your family.'

'Yeah, that's how we both looked at it. Jenna had been under the weather for a few days with a urinary infection. I'd given her a prescription for some antibiotics, and she said she was feeling better, so I went to work. I worked late that evening, and spent the night at the hospital. I called her and she said that she was okay.'

*I'm okay.* The very thing that she had said to Ethan. No wonder he'd refused to take her word for it, and had kept nagging away at her until she was honest with him. Kate swallowed hard. 'But she wasn't.'

'No. The infection spread to her kidney and she was sick...couldn't keep the antibiotics down. Then it got into her bloodstream and she developed sepsis. I got the call the following afternoon. My mother had gone over there to help her out with Sam and had called an ambulance.'

'But it was too late.' Kate knew that sepsis could kill quickly. The body's reaction to infection, it caused the vital organs to shut down, and once that happened it was difficult to reverse.

'Yes. She died two days later.'

'I'm so sorry, Ethan.'

He shook his head, staring into the fire. 'I've learned to live with it. But you see, a doctor who isn't around when his family needs him isn't as good a catch as Fred thinks.'

He blamed himself. 'But you can't think...'

'I don't think, I *know*. I wasn't there.'

'But...' This was crazy. No one could be there for someone all the time. And if Ethan was responsible, then so was his wife. Kate pressed her lips together. Maybe she shouldn't say that.

'But what?'

'I just think you can't be there for someone twenty-four hours a day. I tried to lock myself away from harm once, and it didn't work.'

'That's what you think—that it's like trying to lock them away from harm?'

Maybe she'd said too much. But Kate believed it, and she couldn't take it back now. 'Yes, it is.'

'Yeah, it's what I think too.' There was a note of resignation in his voice.

'But you don't feel it?'

'No, I don't.'

And no one could help him with that. Kate supposed that she wasn't the first person who'd told him that his wife's death wasn't his fault, and she probably wouldn't be the last. He'd grieved, and learned to move forward with his life. But he just couldn't get rid of the guilt.

'I really wish I had chocolate.' Kate puffed out a breath and heard Ethan chuckle quietly.

'What, you came out without chocolate? That was very remiss of you. Think you'll make it back?'

'Not for me, for you. It's a coping mechanism.'

'My coping mechanisms are just fine. But thank you for your concern.'

Kate shot him a look of disbelief but said nothing. Ethan had thought his coping mechanisms were working perfectly until he'd met Kate. He'd accepted that he was responsible for what had happened to Jenna and that what he needed to do from now on was to concentrate on taking care of Sam. That would be very easy if you removed Kate from the mix.

But he couldn't wish her away. He wouldn't do that, even if he knew that he was quite capable of failing her. He could call it selfish, or he could call it listening to what Kate had said and believing her.

Here, with Kate sitting so close, believing her seemed like a possibility. When he turned to look at her she was gazing at him, wide-eyed, hair the colour of the flames in front of them and just as unruly.

He stretched out his arm, putting it around her shoulders, and Kate nestled closer. They sat for a long time, watching the fire together, and then finally Ethan reached up, his fingers brushing her cheek.

If he took it slow, then she'd have the chance to stop him at any time. But then Kate pre-empted that by stretching up and planting a kiss on the side of his mouth.

So soft, so very sweet, yet with all the promise of something that might break the both of them if they gave in to it. Ethan wasn't someone who usually courted danger, but now the risk heightened the pleasure.

His hand moved to the back of her head and he did what he'd been wanting to do for a long time. He kissed her properly.

As soon as her lips touched his, Kate knew that this was a risk. But, despite all that, she wanted him to kiss her more than she wanted to breathe.

When he did, it was a wild voyage, discovering a forgotten pleasure. Finding that she'd been wrong when she'd thought that one kiss couldn't possibly send shimmers racing through her body, making her fingers tremble and her toes curl. It was breathless, heart-pounding, joy.

'I've been thinking about doing that for a while.' He whispered the words close to her ear, although even if he'd screamed them no one would have heard. Kate bunched the front of his jacket tight in her fingers.

'Tell me you're not planning on making me wait so long for the next one....'

His lips grazed her cheek, sending shivers through her. Maybe this was how it would be if he made love to her. Taking her right to the point of no return, and then slowing, just so that they could both feel the need.

She stretched up, kissing him, and felt Ethan's arm around her waist, pulling her onto his lap. He kissed her again, demanding this time, and she felt desire begin to pulse deep inside.

No... Too much. Too soon. Mind over matter was one thing, but she hadn't expected this. Kate drew back, pushing the feeling down before she lost control.

She could see it in his eyes too. The shocked acknowledgement that this wasn't just a kiss. Which was a problem, because Kate could barely handle just kissing him.

'I'm sorry, Kate.'

'It's all right. I started it.'

'We both started it, together. And perhaps we both have to end it now.' Ethan shrugged. 'I can't. I don't think of myself as having the right to do this.'

His guilt again. He'd grieved for his wife, and let that go, but he couldn't let go of the guilt. Ethan's world had somehow become smaller, leaving no room for him to move beyond just he and Sam.

'Maybe I'm not ready for it either.' These were stolen moments, only possible because tonight Sam happened to be with his grandparents. Kate needed someone to be there on a rather more permanent basis than that.

They were silent for a long time, both staring at the fire. That wasn't going to do any good. There weren't any answers there.

'The fire's burning down. We should go.'

'Yeah.' He got to his feet, helping her up, and then kicking at the fire to extinguish it. 'Perhaps we won't worry about rebuilding it.'

'No, we must. I can't break with tradition, not on my first time here.' She smiled awkwardly up at him.

Suddenly it was possible to think that they could be

just friends who had stumbled over the line by mistake in the darkness. They found bracken and twigs for the new fire, and Ethan built it while Kate watched.

'That'll do, I think.'

'Yes. It'll do very nicely.' Maybe the next couple who came up here and put a match to the fire that Ethan had left for them would have better luck and not discover that it had all been a mistake.

Kate took one last look around to make sure that they hadn't left anything behind and then followed Ethan out of the cave and onto the wide causeway for the long walk back to his car.

# CHAPTER TWELVE

NEITHER OF THEM had spoken much on their way back to Ethan's car and he hadn't heard from Kate the next day. That was probably for the best. He needed some distance, to get back into the routine of friendship, and he guessed that Kate did too.

All the same, he missed her. The slow meander of Sunday and the morning rush of Monday did nothing to erode the memory of how she'd kissed him. Even the careful, concentrated work of the day couldn't drive her completely from his thoughts.

He knew that going to see Edie before he left the hospital for the evening might involve bumping into Kate. But Ethan took the risk and the sudden thump in his chest when he saw her sitting at Edie's bedside told him that he couldn't just turn around and walk away. Watching from the entrance doors of the ward, he saw the two women carefully unpacking a cloth bag that Kate had laid on the bed. A packet of face wipes, some chocolate and some fruit. Small gifts, each one of which made Edie smile.

'Oh! Lavender water. Thank you, dear!' Ethan heard Edie's exclamation, and saw Kate reach forward, opening the bottle for Edie and tipping it so that she could dab a little onto Edie's wrist.

'Behind your ears?'

'Oh, yes, please. How thoughtful.'

It was thoughtful. A little luxury to chase away the smell of antiseptic. Ethan approached Edie's bed.

Kate jumped when she saw him and the thought that his presence was responsible for the sudden reddening of her cheeks sent a tingle down Ethan's spine. He shot Kate a smile and then turned his attention to Edie.

'How are you?'

'Much better, thank you. I've been a lot of trouble, haven't I? To a lot of people.' Edie twisted down the corners of her mouth.

'No one thinks that.' Kate patted Edie's hand. 'Everyone just wanted you to be safe and we're glad that you are.'

'I've made a decision.' Edie gave a firm little nod. 'My son found a really nice flat in a sheltered housing complex for us, but I said that I could manage Fred. I think it's time, though. We need a bit of help. And I'd be able to have a nurse in to look after him while I go out with my friends once in a while.'

'Where is Fred now?' Ethan knew that hospital was challenging for people with dementia and wondered if there was anything he could do to help.

'He's at home. My daughter's staying with him while I'm here.' Edie smiled, leaning towards Kate. 'Actually, it's rather nice. A bit of a rest.'

'Well, you'll have more help when you move into the sheltered accommodation.' Kate gave a little frown, obviously not sure how Edie might feel about having to move.

'Yes, I will. I'm rather looking forward to it, actually.'

\* \* \*

'Nice lady.' Ethan held the door of the ward open for Kate.

'Yes. I hope she'll be all right. It's a big step, moving into sheltered accommodation.'

'I don't see what else she can do. She can't manage Fred on her own any more.'

Kate nodded. 'That's clear enough. And I suppose that life will be much easier for her, once she has help to look after Fred properly. It's a big change for her, though.'

'Life's full of changes. We have to make them into new beginnings.' When he looked at Kate, Ethan had the courage to say it. Almost the faith to believe it.

'Yes. I hope Edie's new beginning is a good one.'

'She seems to think it will be.' The touch of Kate's lips echoed through his memory, leaving him trembling.

The thought that he'd decided never to love anyone again suddenly made him feel like a traitor. As if he'd turned his back on all the people who'd taught him how to love, telling them that love meant nothing.

'Would you like to go for coffee—something to eat, maybe?' Kate could be depended on to want something to eat.

'I'd like to, but...' She twisted her mouth in an expression of regret. 'I've got to get back to the surgery. I'm working this evening.'

'Too bad. Another time, maybe.'

She thought about it for a moment. 'How about the weekend? I'm pretty busy this week, as one of the other vets at the practice is on holiday and so everyone's filling in for her. It would be nice to do it some time when I don't have to rush away.'

Ethan smiled. Kate wanted to take time with him. He wanted that too. 'Why don't you come over on Friday eve-

ning and I'll cook? Sam's going over to my parents'. He
and my dad have a project they're working on together.
So I can cook something a bit different.'

The menu wasn't really the issue. Maybe being alone
with him would be, but Kate only hesitated for a moment.

'So we won't be having bangers and mash?'

'I was thinking maybe not.'

'Hmm. Shame. What time shall I come?'

One of the disadvantages of knowing Ethan was that
Kate had become obsessed by her own wardrobe. It was
no longer something that just got opened once or twice
a day, for long enough to pull out something which more
or less matched and was appropriate for the weather. It
had to be sorted through and studied carefully.

She puffed out a breath. She'd taken three perfectly
good summer dresses out and hung them over the tops of
the doors. One would be just as good as the other.

She held the red one up against her, looking in the
mirror. A bit short. She didn't want to look as if she was
trying to seduce him. When she did the same with the
green one, it was a bit long. Kate made a face at herself.

'They're just knees, for goodness' sakes. He's seen
lots of different knees before. He's a doctor.'

Kate puffed out another breath. The dark-blue one. It
fell just above the knee, slimline and a wrap-around at the
front. Before she could change her mind again, she put
the other two dresses back into the wardrobe and banged
the door shut. Her car was playing up and she had decided
that, rather than have it conk out on her again, it was best
to take it straight to the garage. If she was going to wash
her hair and blow dry it into something approximating a

style before the taxi arrived to take her to Ethan's house, then she'd better get moving.

Ethan had thought carefully about the menu for that evening. A couple of free-range steaks, done with peppercorn sauce and a salad. Nothing too fancy, but at least he could indulge his penchant for a medium-rare steak without Sam wrinkling his nose and telling him that his dinner was bleeding.

He made the salad and scrubbed some potatoes, taking the meat out of the fridge so that it went into the pan at room temperature. Then he set up the table in the conservatory, laying it carefully. A couple of candles didn't seem too far over the top.

Kate arrived at eight, blowing every rational thought from his head. She stood on the doorstep, wearing a blue dress, her hair tamed into a mass of curls at the back of her head. Ethan felt as if he was a teenager on a first date.

'Can I come in?' She was clearly unwilling to squeeze past him as he stood motionless, blocking the doorway.

'Uh…yes, of course.' Ethan remembered his manners and showed her through to the conservatory. A bottle of wine stood ready, and he poured a glass for her and a glass of sparkling water for himself.

He shooed her from the kitchen when she tried to help with cooking the steaks, reckoning that a steady hand was probably wise when dealing with a hot pan. He served the dinner, eating almost nothing in favour of watching her. It seemed that Kate, too, was on her best behaviour.

But dessert changed all that. When he set the two glass dishes on the table, she let out a little scream.

'Ethan!'

'I made it myself.'

'Home-made tiramisu! We can't possibly eat this here.' An impish smile spread across her face.

'Where do you want to eat it?' He followed the direction of her pointing spoon, and smiled. 'Good idea.'

He opened the doors of the conservatory, picking up a rug from one of the chairs and spreading it on the lawn, at the place where the lights from the house met the dark shadows at the end of the garden. Kate almost danced after him, holding the two dishes.

'So, you're not one of those doctors who gives a girl a hard time over dessert.' She plonked herself down on the rug, tucking her bare legs underneath her. The front of her dress gaped a little, giving him a view of one more delicious inch of flesh above her knee.

'Actually, I might be. Tonight I'll make an exception.'

She laughed, leaning towards him. 'Three-point-four.'

'Three-point-four, what?'

'My cholesterol level. Three-point-four.'

'Not bad.' Ethan chuckled at her outraged look. 'All right, then, it's pretty good. That's not all there is to it, though. But there's nothing wrong with something sweet from time to time, as long as you don't overdo it.'

She giggled, and Ethan's heart began to thump in his chest. Surely he could believe his own judgement. A little of Kate's sweetness…?

Ethan had ignored all her protests and insisted on driving her home. Kate hurried up her front path, aware that Ethan was watching her from his car, and waved to him before closing the front door. This evening had been lovely and she hadn't wanted it to end.

But all good things did come to an end. Maybe that was what made them good, leaving while you still wanted more and before the inevitable disappointment of real life set in. She automatically walked to the back door, hardly looking at it before she turned away to make her way upstairs, still lost in the dream that centred around Ethan.

The doorbell rang with pause between the 'ding' and the 'dong' as if someone had kept their finger on the bell for a little too long. Kate walked back downstairs, taking her phone from her bag as she went and stood in the hallway, staring at the front door.

'It's Ethan.'

His voice sounded muffled by the wooden barrier between them.

'Oh! What…what do you want?' She knew exactly what he wanted. Or rather she *hoped* she knew.

Kate opened the door and found him leaning against the entrance to the porch.

'I'd really like to come in.' His eyes were dark, his blond hair highlighted by the light from the hallway.

'I'd really like you to come in.'

For a moment they both hesitated and then Ethan stepped over the threshold, closing the door behind him. One of his hands drifted to her waist, his fingers brushing the fabric of her dress, and Kate felt her heart thump in her chest.

'Ethan, I… You know I get frightened at night sometimes. That's not why I want you here and—'

He put his finger across her lips. 'And I get lonely. That's not why I want to be here with you.'

'Why *do* you want to be here?'

He pulled her close in a sudden, powerful movement that left no room for doubt. Ethan wanted her and she wanted him back.

Kate pushed him back against the door in her eagerness to kiss him. Felt his chest move in a low sigh which sounded like the sudden release of everything that had kept them apart.

They were both trembling, with arousal and...something else that wasn't quite fear and wasn't quite shyness. It was the hesitancy of having been wounded. But Ethan's hands, his lips, gave her courage. Everything around them began to blur, leaving only him in sharp focus.

She broke away from him, backing towards the stairs, her finger crooked in an invitation to follow. 'Come upstairs...'

He moved fast, but not fast enough. Kate eluded his outstretched hand and ran up the stairs. He caught her at the top, backing her towards the bathroom.

'Wrong way.'

He grinned as Kate pulled him towards the bedroom door.

It seemed as if it were another lifetime when she'd last had a man in her bedroom. But, when Kate suddenly didn't know what to do, Ethan did. When he pulled his shirt over his head, the need to see and touch washed everything else away.

'You are beautiful.' He was broad-shouldered, skin the colour of honey. He was a perfect man, made even more perfect by the touch of the sun and hard physical work. She felt soft skin and the flex of muscle when she ran her fingers across his chest.

Ethan wrapped his arms around her, loosening the pins which held her hair back from her face. 'You have gorgeous hair...wonderful lips and...'

He tugged gently at the zip on the back of her dress. When Kate kissed him, he slowly drew it down. He made her *feel* beautiful—undressing her slowly, whispering his appreciation for every part of her body.

It would only take one more step—a few more scraps of clothing and then the delicious slide of his skin against hers. But it wasn't easy to take that step, for either of them. There was too much fear and too much pain. Too much wanting to be free of it and not knowing if they could.

Kate reached up, caressing his cheek. 'I can't think of one thing that could happen between us tonight that wouldn't be okay.'

'So you have no expectations? A guy could feel hurt.'

'I have expectations. I just want you to know that you tip my world upside down. And, if I falter, then it's not because anything's wrong. I'm just feeling my way.'

'Which makes us free. We can be whatever we want to be.' He brushed his lips against the lobe of her ear.

He understood. That was all she needed. She kissed him, her fingers touching his cheek, and he groaned, his body growing harder.

'I love the way I turn you on.' The thought that just her touch could arouse him so much make Kate's head spin.

'I'm not always this easy.' He chuckled, nipping the lobe of her ear.

'Just with me?'

'Seems that way.'

'I like that even better...' She caught her breath as he lifted her up, laying her down on the bed.

It occurred to Ethan, during the brief moments when he could think at all, that this dizzy, heady reaction was just the result of an instinctive craving to feel the touch of someone's skin against his. But he knew it wasn't. Only Kate could have made him turn his car around and do the unthinkable.

He'd thought that learning to love was a one-time thing. Done, then broken and now forgotten. But with Kate he knew that he could learn again.

And tonight was all about Kate, only about her—the way she moved, the light in her eyes and the softness of her skin. And, more than that, it was about her gentle nature—the way she made him feel that there was no fixed outcome for tonight, just a sweet exploration of possibilities.

They made love, staring into each other's eyes, feeling the warmth grow into an intoxicating heat. When she came it seemed almost as if it had taken her by surprise, something that hadn't been sought or worked for, but an expression of how she felt at that moment.

He felt a bead of sweat trickle down his back. One moment, just enough to kiss her as he felt the pulse of her body weaken again. Then feeling robbed him of any thought, other than the knowledge that when he cried out he called her name.

They clung together for a long time and then she moved away from him, curling up on her side of the bed, watching. When Ethan reached out to her, she twined her fingers through his.

Her brilliant smile told him all he needed to know. Drawing her close, he folded his arms around her.

# CHAPTER THIRTEEN

AT SOME POINT all the uncertainty had gone. How much Ethan was willing to give, and what he wanted to keep. When they'd curled up together, after that first time, it had been clear that he was ready to give everything.

'Favourite…food.' They'd already covered films, books and places, and now Ethan's lips twitched into a knowing smile.

'You heard my stomach rumble?'

'No. But, since you always seem to be hungry, it's a question that interests me.'

Kate thought for a moment. 'At the moment… Something cold.'

'Ice cream. Have you got any?'

She jabbed her finger against his shoulder. 'Do I have ice cream? I just made love with you. Don't make me think you don't know me at all.'

'I thought you might have eaten it all.' He laughed, pulling her close for a kiss. 'How many flavours?'

'Three.'

'Chocolate.' He brushed his lips against hers, and she felt a tingle run up her spine. This was actually far better than chocolate ice cream. 'Caramel?'

'You do know me, then.' It felt as if Ethan knew her better than anyone. 'Care to take a guess at the other one?'

'Passion fruit?' His innocent blue eyes suddenly turned wicked, and Kate felt his hand slide down her back. This was a new Ethan. One who didn't hesitate, but who trusted himself enough to take what he wanted. That was a good thought.

'No passion fruit. I have strawberry, though.'

'Just as good.'

He made it better than Kate could ever have imagined. A cold spoon trailed across her skin. Ethan's lips made her shiver and melt, all at the same time, and when he rolled her onto her side, running his tongue down her spine, she gasped.

'You like that?'

No need to answer. Kate felt him brush her hair forward, over one shoulder, exposing the back of her neck. Then his arms slid around her, one around her waist, the other hand cupping her breast. Heat engulfed her and she relaxed in his arms as he kissed the back of her neck.

'Not fair...' She wanted him to feel this trembling desire too.

'What isn't fair?'

'I can't touch you...' Her hands groped for something to hold on to and found only a pillow to grab. His hands moved, caressing her, and another jolt of pleasure made Kate squirm.

'And when you do?'

'I'll pay you back, Ethan.'

'Oh, yes? How, exactly?' He rolled her onto her back, covering her body with his. 'I want all the details.'

He loved this as much as she did. This long, slow burn, which turned the ache of wanting him into drawn-out pleasure. It ebbed and flowed between them, whispers and kisses, caresses. When finally Kate pushed him down onto the bed, reaching for the condoms on the bedside table, her shaking fingers fumbled with the foil packet and he took it from her.

He pulled her on top of him, a sharp sigh escaping his lips. 'Let me look at you. Just for a moment.'

His clear-eyed gaze said the words before he could speak. 'You're so beautiful, Kate.'

She believed it. Somehow making do with a glance in the mirror had slipped away, and she knew that in Ethan's eyes she *was* beautiful. And she trusted Ethan.

'And you are...perfect.' She ran her fingers across his chest. 'Just perfect.'

He moved beneath her and the slow burn began to turn into a fever. He *was* just perfect.

Well-made beds were over-rated. Cushions and pillows in complementary colours piled at the head were just an unnecessary complication and had found their way unheeded onto the floor. Just two crumpled sheets mapped out the course of their love-making last night and they were more than enough to make Ethan smile this morning.

He disentangled his foot from the corner of the sheet that covered them. *Almost* covered them. Kate looked like a Botticelli angel, white fabric draped around her body, her arms and legs bare. Ethan leaned over and kissed her, and she opened her eyes.

'Sorry to wake you this early. But I've got to go.'

She nodded sleepily. 'Sam?'

'Yes. It's a thing we have—breakfast.'

'It's a good thing. Go.'

He wished that he could have a breakfast thing with Kate as well. That he could stay here, raid her kitchen and make more than she could eat. It was a challenge, but one he would be more than willing to take on.

But, however hard he tried, he couldn't be in two places at once.

'Go.' Kate had seen his hesitation and was smiling. 'Here, take this with you.'

She pressed a kiss onto his lips and all the warmth of last night, everything they'd made together, flooded back into his senses. He felt her gaze follow him as he got out of bed, and gathered his clothes up from the floor. Instinctively his pace slowed a little.

'Watching you get dressed is almost as good as watching you get undressed.' Kate was propped up on her elbow, grinning broadly.

'Care to give me a hand?' One of the buttons of his shirt had been almost wrenched from its moorings, after he'd tugged impatiently at it last night. Even that small detail of a memory made him smile.

'No. I'm fine right here.'

She was better than fine. Sleepy-eyed and still half-wrapped in the sheet, she was gorgeous. Only one thing could stop him from tearing his clothes off and making love to her again.

'Stay right there. I'll call you later.' He bent over, planting his hands on the mattress on either side of her body.

'Video call?'

He grinned suddenly. 'In that case, I'll call earlier.'

She stretched lazily. 'Don't rush. I think I'll have a lie-in this morning.'

Ethan chuckled, dipping to kiss her forehead. He was

already mentally counting the minutes that it would take
to go home, shower, then get to his parents' house and
make breakfast for Sam. Then find a secluded spot in the
garden to make his call.

'Where's your phone?'

'Downstairs, I think. I took it with me when I went
to answer the door.'

Ethan found her phone on the hall table, switching it
on briefly to check it was charged. Then he brought it
upstairs and put it down on the empty pillow next to her.
One last kiss and then he tore himself away from her.

Kate's phone rang sooner than she'd expected. She jabbed
at the 'answer' icon, wishing she'd thought to get out of
bed and untangle some of the knots in her hair.

He was sitting in the morning sunlight, a neat garden in the background, grinning. 'Hey there, beautiful.'

Kate ran her hand across her unruly curls and he
chuckled.

'Don't! I've only just woken up again.'

'I can see that. It really suits you.'

She raised her eyebrows. 'What, my hair all over the
place?'

'Especially that.' The slight quirk of his lips told Kate
exactly what he was thinking. To be honest, she was
thinking the same right now. But last night was…last
night. Neither of them had said anything about this morning, and it was uncharted territory.

'You got back in time for Sam?' Kate decided to play
it safe.

'Yes. He's eating toast with my dad at the moment.
They're discussing their project.'

'What on earth is the project?' Whatever it was it

seemed to be taking a bit of time and energy. This was the second Saturday running that Sam had stayed at his grandparents'.

'They're making a space station for superheroes. It's in the field at the end of the garden.'

'Really? How big is it, then?'

'It's about the size of my conservatory, only the roof's not quite so high. Apparently, I'm surplus to requirements at this stage, but I might be needed later for some of the heavy work.'

Kate chuckled. 'Too bad.'

'Yeah. A year ago he thought I knew everything about everything. Now there are a whole range of things I don't know about.'

'Do you mind?' Kate settled back against the pillows. This was nice, warm and friendly, a different strand of intimacy from the one they'd had last night.

Ethan shrugged. 'Yeah, I mind. I'm trying not to, though, because I wouldn't have it any other way.'

He fell silent for a moment, his gaze fixed on her. If he asked her to lose the sheet that was currently wrapped tight around her, she'd do it in a heartbeat. But that would be less, somehow. It would break this new bond that was forming between them.

'So, what are you doing today?' Ethan seemed to understand that too, and his question made Kate smile. It had been a long time since anyone had been much interested in what she did on her days off.

'The usual. Shopping. Washing and ironing...' Maybe she'd leave the washing until tomorrow. One more night spent surrounded by Ethan's scent.

'You said that this weekend might be okay for us to pick up Sam's puppy.' There was a sudden tension in his voice. Kate had conveniently forgotten all about that, too afraid to suggest seeing Ethan again this weekend.

'Yes, I did. If you're ready to do that, then perhaps we could go over there tomorrow afternoon.'

Ethan nodded. 'I was thinking, if you'd like to come over tomorrow and have lunch with Sam and me, then we could go and fetch the puppy afterwards.'

Sunday lunch. It was a brave new inroad into territory that Kate had promised herself she wouldn't think about. Particularly not with Ethan.

'Yes. That sounds great, I'd love to. What time?'

He grinned. 'Any time after six am?'

'I'll come at twelve. Don't want to surprise you both in your racing car pyjamas' If Ethan wore pyjamas, Kate would eat the sheet she was currently wrapped in.

'Racing cars are so last year. He's got Ambigulon pyjamas now.'

'Ambigulon?'

'Yeah. Superhero stuff. Ambigulon has a glowing amber crystal which shoots power rays. They either heal a person or hurt them, depending on whether they have a pure heart.'

'Blimey! That's complicated.'

Ethan rolled his eyes. 'Trust me, it's just the tip of the iceberg. Superheroes are *very* complicated...'

Talking to Kate had been very complicated. However much Ethan wanted to tell himself that this was just two friends who happened to find each other attractive, it had been impossible to maintain the pretence. He'd found himself sharing his thoughts and feelings with her. The stories about Sam that he'd so often wished he could share with someone.

Ethan had told himself that asking her to lunch was a very obvious next step. Treating her as a friend. But everything he did seemed only to deepen the one role that he still wasn't sure he was capable of. A lover. Someone who protected and nurtured.

When the doorbell rang at exactly midday, Sam ran to meet Kate, aiming his Ambigulon crystal at the door, which stayed resolutely in place. Ethan herded him out of the way, getting rid of the obstruction in a more conventional manner.

'Hi. Am I too early?' Kate was standing on the doorstep, looking delicious. Ethan wondered whether, in common with Ambigulon's crystal, she had the power to divine whether a man's heart was pure or not. And what the outcome would be if his was put to the test.

'You're right on time. I'm running a little late. Sam, show Kate into the conservatory and I'll get on with lunch.' He flashed her a grin and she rewarded him with a brilliant smile.

Through the open door of the kitchen, Ethan could hear Sam chivvying her through into the conservatory and instructing her to sit down in a chair that he'd selected for her.

'Are we going to get the puppy now?' Sam reiterated the question that he'd been asking Ethan all morning, obviously keen on getting a second opinion.

'Not yet. After lunch.' Kate's voice was full of laughter and tenderness. 'Have you thought of a name for him yet?'

Ethan grinned down at the roast potatoes in the pan in front of him, wondering what she'd make of the answer.

'Sam. I'm calling him Sam.'

'Sam? But that's your name.' The rustle of skirts and

the faint creak of wicker as Kate moved in her seat. The sounds were almost unbearably erotic.

'How are you going to know whether your dad is calling to you or the puppy?' A short pause and then Kate laughed. 'Is that the point of calling him Sam—so you can pretend that you thought Dad was calling the puppy and not you?'

Sam sounded as if he was jumping up and down, laughing. 'Yessss!'

'Oh. So the puppy's going to get to eat all your ice cream?'

Ethan closed his eyes, silently begging Kate not to mention ice cream while he was in the room. He wasn't sure how long it would be before he could look at another tub of strawberry ice cream without thinking of last night.

'And is he going to wear your T-shirt?'

Silence. Sam was obviously thinking about the ramifications of his choice of names.

'Or... I can call him Ambigulon.'

Ethan shook his head. The idea of shouting, 'Ambigulon!' at the top of his voice to call the puppy back to heel didn't exactly appeal to him.

'That's a good name. But wouldn't it be a bit inconvenient if the puppy could reverse gravity?'

Ethan was sure he hadn't mentioned reversing gravity to Kate. The idea that she'd done her research on topics that would interest Sam was a novel one. She was clearly making an effort with him.

'I think... Arthur!'

Where had Sam got that from? It wasn't a family name and, as far as Ethan knew, it wasn't the name of anyone that Sam knew. But, actually, he could get used to Arthur.

'What does your dad think?'

Ethan decided to intervene. Popping his head out through the kitchen door, he saw Kate seated on the edge of one of the wicker chairs. Sam was leaning against her legs, smoothing the hem of her blue-and-white-striped summer dress with one hand. It was a curious reversal of roles. When Sam was around Ethan didn't get to touch her, but his son had none of those inhibitions.

'I think that Arthur's a very good name.' He mouthed a 'thank you' in Kate's direction and she flashed him a grin.

'So do I.' She smiled gravely down at Sam.

'Okay. Arthur.' Sam nodded, as if the matter was now closed. 'When are we going to get him?'

'After lunch.' Ethan found himself chorusing the words with Kate, and she looked up at him, blushing. Ethan chuckled, turning back to the kitchen.

Lunch was an exercise in Sam trying to eat as fast as he could and Ethan trying to slow him down. When the boy wriggled down from his seat, obviously ready to go, Ethan shot her a look of apology.

'Shall we have coffee when we get back?' She smiled at him, casually pushing her hand across the table towards Ethan, wondering whether he might respond.

'If you don't mind. I think he might burst if we make him wait any longer.'

Sam ran out of the conservatory and into the house and suddenly she felt Ethan's fingers around hers. As he raised them to his lips, his eyes seemed to flash a brighter blue.

'I don't want you to make any mistake over my intentions, Kate.'

She felt her cheeks redden. All her resolutions that needing Ethan in the heat of the night didn't mean she couldn't be independent the following morning seemed a little stupid right now. She needed him, but she didn't really know whether he even wanted her for more than a brief fling.

'We didn't have any intentions, did we?'

'I do now. If I ask whether we can take things slowly, one step at a time, then please don't think I'm not serious about wanting to make things work between us.'

Making things work. She wanted to make things work more than anything and she knew that both of them needed a little time to get used to the idea of doing that. 'Slow is good. I'd like to take things slowly too.'

'Slow it is, then.' His lips curved into the same smile that he'd had on his lips last night, when taking it slowly had been an exercise in everything that was delicious. He rose from his seat, bending to kiss her cheek before Sam scooted back into the room, dropping Ethan's car keys into his hand.

The afternoon was turning into the kind of sunny Sunday afternoon that seemed to have been lost irretrievably in Kate's childhood, when she'd felt that she could run barefoot in the grass, her dress swishing around her legs, without any danger of cutting her feet. When the sun couldn't burn her and she couldn't get wet in a sudden shower of rain. Where the only thing that could touch her was the look on Sam's face as he hugged his new puppy, the blue of Ethan's eyes and the sure feeling that whatever happened next couldn't disappoint her.

Sam seemed to know instinctively that Arthur was small and frightened. He coaxed him gently from the animal carrier, helping him to explore his new world.

After an afternoon of exploring, the two of them wore each other out at much the same time, curling up in one of the wicker chairs in the conservatory together and falling asleep.

Ethan had turned the chair slightly, so that its high back obscured Sam's view of the conservatory steps where he and Kate sat.

'No regrets?' Kate knew that he must have mixed feelings about this. Sam was growing up and beginning to be independent of him. And Ethan must still think about Jeff.

'None. Sam wanted this.'

'And you?'

'I'm…ready to move on too.' His tone was soft, but there was a finality about it. As if he'd thought about this and come to a conclusion. 'Did you see Sam's face when Arthur started playing with his dog toys?'

'It would have been difficult to miss.' Kate laughed quietly. 'Thank you for letting me be a part of it all.'

His arm was behind her. Not quite around her, but a tentative signal that it might be if she wanted it. Kate moved a little closer to him, and Ethan put his arm properly around her shoulders. That was better.

'Thank you for being here. And for making this afternoon happen.' He brushed a kiss against her hair. 'And for talking him out of calling the puppy Ambigulon.'

'That wasn't so difficult.'

'Sam can be very stubborn when he wants to be.' Ethan grinned.

'And you're not stubborn at all.' Kate smirked at him.

'Not even slightly. I'm always open to reason.'

'Of course you are.' Kate turned and kissed him. He

responded, pulling her tight against him. He was definitely open to that.

But even if Sam was sleeping, and wouldn't have been able to see them even if he woke, he was still there. Maybe that was a good thing. The loud voice which told her that everything was all right had got the upper hand this afternoon. But the doubts, the fear of losing herself and finding that he would let her down, were all still there.

'I'm sorry that…' He shrugged. 'Sam.'

'I know. It's okay. You have to put him first, always. I wouldn't like you very much if you didn't.'

He nodded. 'I wouldn't like myself very much. But there are times when I wish I could take the rest of the evening off. Right now, I do.'

'Another time.'

'Yes. I'd love that.'

He leaned over and kissed her. Warmly but with an echo of all that Ethan could do to her. It was enough, for now.

# CHAPTER FOURTEEN

YOU WERE SUPPOSED to look forward to Saturday night, weren't you? Kate couldn't remember having looked forward to one with such trembling anticipation before. Ethan called, saying that Sam would be staying with his grandparents again on Saturday. This time there was no pretence about happening to be alone and wanting some company. He asked her whether she might like to come out with him on a date.

Ethan took nothing for granted, his tone a little halting and formal. Kate accepted his invitation and she heard him laugh quietly.

'I'm glad you said yes.'

'I'm glad you called to ask.' She was grinning at the phone, wondering if he felt sixteen as well—that nervous thrill that accompanied a first date.

'Well, I have to go, now. I need to pop out into the garden for a moment and run round in circles, punching the air.'

Kate laughed. Even though they were both a little older and much wiser somehow, they'd both managed to put the intervening years aside and go back to the beginning. Could they really be sixteen again, unlearn everything they knew and start over?

'I have to go upstairs and fling my wardrobe doors open. Scream that I have nothing to wear...'

'What are you wearing now?' Ethan's tone took on a note of the hunger that she felt for him.

'Blue jeans. A red shirt.'

'You look beautiful. Come exactly as you are.'

Kate did just that, although she'd added a pair of high, strappy sandals and some jewellery which had taken her almost as long to decide on as selecting her whole outfit. When she answered the door to him, his face broke into a broad grin.

'You look far more gorgeous than I've been imagining you might. And that's a tough proposition.' He held out his arm and Kate felt herself thrill at the slightly stiff, old-fashioned gesture. Last weekend hadn't just been something that adults had done and then moved on from because it was much too complicated to contemplate anything else. Ethan had come a-courting. There was no mistaking it.

She stepped outside, locking the front door behind her, and took his arm. The two of them couldn't quite fit on the narrow front path and Ethan walked to one side on the grass.

'This is nice.' She smiled up at him as he opened the gate for her.

'I'm a little rusty. I haven't done this in a while.'

'If this is you being a little rusty, I can't wait to see what happens when you really get into your stride.' The thought was both exciting and terrifying. But Ethan was doing all the right things to calm her fears. Taking it slowly. Taking it tenderly.

'Thank you, ma'am. I'll do my best not to disappoint.'

He couldn't have disappointed her if he'd tried. She loved the way he'd drawn her hand up to his lips, looking into her eyes when he kissed her fingertips. She loved the quiet, country pub where the food was good and they could eat outside. Loved the way he was so interested in hearing about the things in her life—her job, her family, her childhood—and the way he told her about his.

'Come back with me.' He'd paid the bill and they were still sitting at their table, the lights around them beginning to glow bright in the gathering darkness.

'For coffee?' Ethan's smile told her that if it *was* just for coffee that would be fine with him.

'No. Not for coffee.' She leaned across the table towards him. 'Or don't you do that kind of thing on a first date?'

This was crazy. They'd already done *that kind of thing*. But Ethan understood. Last week had been one of those sweet things that had been unplanned, done to escape from the real world. Tonight *was* the real world and if they spent it together then it was a new and different hope for the future.

'There's nothing I'd like to do more...'

They made love by flickering candlelight, the open windows in her bedroom allowing what breeze there was in the still evening to caress their bodies. And, for every moment of it, Ethan was there with her. In the long, tender embraces when it felt as if he was making love to every inch of her. In the strong, passionate climaxes which came again and again, finally leaving them still, tangled together on the bed.

'Would you like some wine?' Kate stretched luxuriantly on the crumpled sheets. The bottle of wine and the ice-bucket had been ready in the kitchen and she'd fetched them on their way upstairs. She was glad now she'd remembered. Kate didn't want to be away from Ethan for even a moment.

'So...you had this all planned.' He reached for the corkscrew, his gaze flipping to the two glasses that sat on the bedside table.

'Yes, I did. Only, you didn't keep to the plan.'

He raised his eyebrows, taking the bottle from the half-melted ice and holding it to one side as he pulled the cork so that water didn't drip all over the bed. 'I hardly dare ask.'

'If I'd known you were going to take so long over it, I'd have left the ice-bucket in the fridge.'

'Too long...?' His smile told her that he knew darn well that wasn't the case. 'I could always hurry things up a bit, next time.'

'Don't you dare. I loved every moment of it. So... you're planning on a *next time*?' Kate pulled herself up on the pillows, taking the glass of wine from him. 'I'd be very disappointed if you weren't.'

'Yes. I'm planning on a *next time*.'

He clinked his glass against hers and took a sip, nodding in approval at her choice of wine. It was another pleasure, watching him here in the candlelight.

'This...is bliss. I could stay here for the next week.' Kate stretched lazily. It was impossible. She knew that. Ethan had to get back in the morning for Sam. They both had jobs to go to and, even if they hadn't, this was still new and there was still a lot for them to work through. But it was a nice fantasy.

'Me too.' He reached for her foot, propping it on his thigh, and Kate felt his thumb on her instep.

'That's nice.' The pressure grew a little harder, his thumb circling on the sensitive skin. The soles of her feet were about the only part of her body that Ethan hadn't already caressed and it seemed that he was intent on rectifying that omission now.

'You like it?'

'I love it.' Kate emptied her glass, sliding towards him. Ethan chuckled, taking the glass from her hand and putting it next to his on the bedside table.

'Oh…sorry.' Condensation had dribbled down onto the foot of the glass and he moved it, reaching to pick something up from underneath it.

He had her diary in his hand and was brushing the ring of moisture from the cover. Kate sat up suddenly, grabbing it from him. 'Don't.'

'There's no damage.' His body was suddenly taut, his eyes questioning. Kate clutched the diary, wishing that she'd just let him brush the water off and put it down again. He wouldn't have opened it. He would never have known that she'd mistakenly left it out in its usual place by the bedside.

'Sorry. It wouldn't matter if there was.' A ring on the cover of her diary. It would actually be quite appropriate. Something that Ethan had left here tonight, which couldn't be rubbed away.

But the spell had been broken. Ethan was clearly wondering why she was clutching the book tightly to her chest and no doubt he was about to ask.

'It's… Usha said it might help to write things down. It's my diary.'

'Was that the homework she gave you when she first saw you?' Ethan nodded slowly, his voice taking on that 'everything's all right' tone.

'Not quite. She suggested I make a dream diary, and I've done that. But I decided I wanted to write something every day as well.' Kate ran her finger along the piece of elastic fixed to the back cover and looped around the front, binding the book closed.

He nodded and then smiled suddenly. 'Put it away now. I want to ask, but if you want to share this with anyone it should be Usha.'

'I'm not sharing it with Usha. This is just for me. I might tell her about some of the things I've written but... not about you.' It seemed suddenly as if talking to someone else about what they'd shared would be a betrayal.

Ethan shrugged. 'It's okay. I'm not going to pretend that I'm not curious, but we both have things to work out. At the moment it's enough for me to know that you're doing it, and I hope that's enough for you too. It's important that you say whatever you need to say to Usha. That's how counselling works.'

'You don't mind?'

'I'd mind a lot more if you ever stopped reaching for the healing you need.' He stretched forward, touching the diary. Kate held on to it tightly, her fingers trembling.

'Trust me, Kate. Give it to me.'

He wouldn't look. Kate relinquished the book, watching as he opened the small drawer of the bedside table. His gaze never left her face as he slipped the book inside, closing the drawer.

What would he say if he read the parts about him? The parts where she'd confided her worries about how she'd fit in to Ethan and Sam's tight family unit. About what place she'd have there, the woman who could never replace Ethan's wife or Sam's mother. The parts where she'd said she wasn't sure she could ever trust any man, not even Ethan.

'I...I decided to write two things each day. The best thing that's happened and the worst.' This was something— an admission that the diary wasn't wholly out of bounds and that one day the things in it might be told.

'That sounds like a good idea. Is it working for you?'

'Yes, it is. I...' Kate shrugged helplessly. She just wasn't ready to tell him any more just yet. 'Thank you, Ethan.'

He nodded, a slow smile working its way across his face. He nodded at the clock that stood by the bed. 'As it's only eleven o'clock, I still have time to figure out something that might be the best thing for Saturday.'

'You're already the best thing that's happened to me today.' In so many ways. It wasn't just the sex, it was the way that Ethan understood her. The way he pushed her towards better things, but didn't ask any more of her than she could cope with.

He chuckled quietly. 'There's always something better.'

Moving towards her, his hand closed over the top of her foot and his thumb reached around to massage her instep once more, this time a little harder, more demanding of a reaction. Kate sighed and then caught her breath as she felt his lips against the inside of her leg, working up from the knee.

'Ethan...' She knew exactly where he was going with this. That delicious state, somewhere in between relaxation and tension which was beyond any words. He did it so well.

There was only now. Only his touch. Everything else faded into soft focus as he ran his tongue along the inside of her thigh.

\* \* \*

The bed rocked in response to urgent movement. Kate's eyes snapped open and then she squeezed them shut against the light. Ethan's warmth beside her had suddenly been snatched away and it felt as if he'd taken a part of her with it.

'I'm sorry.' She heard his voice, full of regret and panic. Opening her eyes, she focussed on the clock. She'd set the alarm for seven, and they must have both slept through it.

'I'm so sorry, sweetheart. I have to go.' Ethan had dressed in less time that it had taken her to realise what day it was.

She wanted to grab him, pull him back into bed with her. Tell him that Sam would be okay with his grandparents. Have Ethan make love to her for another hour. But that wasn't possible and, even if it had been, Kate wouldn't have done it. She'd known about this going in, and now was no time to complain.

'It's all right. I know.'

He was already making for the door, and she felt a tightness in her chest, the prelude to tears. At least he wouldn't see them. He'd be gone in a moment. But Ethan turned, striding back towards the bed.

'I wish I could stay.' He wrapped his arms around her, kissing her forehead.

'I wish you could stay too. But you have to go and get Sam. Go...'

All the tenderness, all the passion from last night, was still in his eyes. One last look, and then he stood. This time he didn't turn back.

Kate heard his footsteps on the stairs and the quiet

sound of the front door closing. Outside in the lane, a car engine burst into life.

She reached for her diary, flipping through to find the first blank page. She already knew the best and worst things that could possibly happen to her today.

*Best: making love with Ethan.*

Kate paused, wondering whether she should elaborate. But that pretty much said it all.

*Worst: when he left.*

She snapped the diary closed, throwing it down on the bed. Now that she was awake, she might as well get up and get on with the day.

# CHAPTER FIFTEEN

KATE LOOKED AT her phone. Ethan had called every day for the last four days, just to talk for half an hour after he'd put Sam to bed, and there was no reason why she shouldn't call him. It was half-past nine and he must be alone by now.

Her hands were shaking as she flipped through her contacts list. Maybe she could call Usha instead. But, although Usha had said she could call at any time, Kate didn't want to disturb her at this time in the evening.

'Ethan?'

'Hey there, beautiful. I was about to call you.'

'Sam's asleep?' Why was she whispering? Probably because Ethan was, but then he had to think about not waking Sam. Last night their whispered conversation had seemed delicious, but tonight it felt as if she was doing something wrong by calling him.

'Yes, finally.' There was a moment's silence on the line. 'Is anything the matter?'

How quickly things changed. On the night she'd been mugged, he'd tried to comfort her and she'd pushed him away. Tonight, she wanted him to hold her, but he couldn't.

'I fell asleep on the sofa. I...had a nightmare.'

'Sweetheart...' Ethan's voice seemed very far away. 'I wish I could be there.'

She wished that too. 'It's okay. I just wanted to hear your voice.'

'I'd rather...' He left the thought unfinished. Ethan knew as well as she did that there was no point in talking about what couldn't happen right now. 'You haven't had a nightmare in a while.'

'Not for a couple of weeks. I thought they'd gone, but this one...it was so real. Much more so than the others.'

'Sometimes it needs to be real. We need to get things out of our system before we can let go of them.'

'You think so?' Maybe she should tell him that she needed him and get that out of her system. But it wouldn't do any good. It would only make Ethan feel guilty for not being able to leave Sam, and Kate feel as if she was clinging to him when she had no business doing so.

'You should talk to Usha about this. But it seems to me that it's a good sign—you're ready to face what's happened to you and feel that fear.'

Kate wasn't so sure she was. 'Okay. Yes, I'll do that....'

'Are you going to be able to get back to sleep tonight?'

'Yes. I feel better for talking to you.'

'I wish I could hold you.'

The problem wasn't a practical one. She could get into her car and drive over to his place. But Ethan couldn't offer that. Tonight he was a father and he couldn't mix that with being her lover.

'We'll save that for when I see you. On Saturday.'

His quiet sigh told Kate that he was as unhappy about this as she was. She should face facts and make the best of them. There was no magic wand with which to wave the situation away.

'Yes. I miss you, Kate.'

That was a start. 'I miss you too. Let's talk about something else, eh?'

Kate hadn't remembered before now. It was as if she'd been pushed and then found herself at the bottom of the steps with nothing in between. But, in her dream, she'd felt herself falling. Felt the terror and the pain each time she hit the metal-edged steps on the way down.

Ethan had done his best to cheer her up, but only the warm presence of his body next to hers had the power to ward off the chill of her dreams. When she ended the call she felt even more alone than she had when she'd woken up from the nightmare.

She could deal with this. Kate stood up, walking to the mirror over the fireplace, staring at her reflection.

'You've done this before.' She saw her own face take on a stern look. 'Now's no different.'

But it *was* different. Knowing that Ethan was there, but that they couldn't be together, made all the difference. Kate turned away from the mirror, not wanting to get into an argument with her own reflection. Maybe writing it all down in the diary Usha had given her would get this feeling under control.

Ethan became aware that he was tapping his foot when the policeman behind the counter raised his eyebrows and glanced downwards.

'Sorry.' He made an effort to keep his feet still and resorted to staring at the ceiling tiles. Then he tried counting them, but fatigue made the rows swim in front of his eyes. It had been a busy week at work and he'd been up early with Sam. But he'd promised Kate that he'd be here.

Finally, after what seemed like an age, she appeared, holding a large brown manila envelope. She smiled at the officer behind the counter as he let her through and his rather forbidding demeanour brightened by several degrees.

She grabbed Ethan's arm, leading him through the doors and bundling him down the steps.

'Guess what?'

'I've no idea.' From the look on her face it was something good. 'You've won the police raffle?'

'Better than that.'

'They have some good prizes, you know.'

Kate dug her fingers into his ribs. 'Behave. The guy is pleading guilty.'

'Guilty. Really?' Ethan had kept in touch with Mags and there had been no hint that this might happen.

'Yes. It was unexpected, but apparently they found a load of stuff hidden in the loft at his mum's house. Once they had that, he admitted to all the charges. It's such a relief.'

Ethan smiled. Kate hadn't spoken of being worried about this morning's interview, but he knew it had been preying on her mind.

'What did Mags say? Did you see her?'

'Yes. I didn't expect to because she's so senior. She's nice, isn't she?'

'Yeah, she's very nice. Less so if you happen to break the law.'

'Well, she was very nice to me. She said she was very pleased for us.'

'Right.' He supposed that waiting downstairs for an

hour had been a bit of a giveaway and this time Mags had put two and two together and come up with the right answer.

'Did you tell her? About us?'

'No. She is a detective, though.' It might make Ethan feel slightly uneasy that everyone seemed to know about him and Kate, but it wasn't exactly a secret. They just didn't tell very many people about it.

'Anyway…listen!' Kate seemed too excited to bother about that at the moment. 'She explained it all to me and said that he's signed a statement and everything. They have him on more than one count of mugging and some other things as well. He's pleading guilty to everything, in the hope that he gets a more lenient sentence.'

'And how do you feel about that?' Ethan asked.

'Well, if it all goes the way it should, I won't have to testify. I wasn't looking forward to that.'

'True enough. You're sure you don't want your day in court, though?' Ethan knew that some people felt that was part of the healing process.

'No. I know what he did and everyone else knows it too. You know it, don't you?'

'I was there, remember? I know exactly what he did.'

'Then that's what I want. I want it over with, and for the courts to decide what happens to him.' Kate gave a firm little nod.

'Then I'm pleased you got what you wanted.'

Kate was practically skipping down the road and it was a joy to see her so happy. 'Oh, I nearly forgot. This is for Sam.'

'What is it?'

'It's for his show-and-tell at school.'

'His what?'

'It's where they stand up and tell the rest of the class about something.'

'Yes, I know what it is.' Ethan could feel a prickle of unease at the back of his neck. 'I just didn't know he was doing one.'

'You must have just forgotten. He asked me if I could get something from the police station when I came round this morning. So I asked Mags if she had anything suitable for his age group and she gave me this. I'm sure we can find something good amongst it all.'

Something gripped the pit of Ethan's stomach and twisted hard. It was entirely up to Sam if he wanted to ask Kate to get him something for school. But he'd rather his son had asked *him*. The realisation that he possibly had but Ethan had forgotten made him feel even worse. Looking after Sam was his responsibility—not Kate's.

'What?' she asked, taking in his expression. 'I thought you'd be pleased.'

'Yes, I am. Thanks very much.' His own voice echoed in his ears, not sounding very pleased at all.

'Did I overstep? I know I'm just a friend…' She was frowning now, and Ethan knew exactly what the unspoken end of the sentence contained. *I know I'm not his mother.*

'No. It's okay, really.' Ethan took the envelope, resolving to listen more carefully in future. Kate wasn't Sam's mother and she was always very careful never to try to be. This was his fault entirely.

But he couldn't let it go. Ethan had grown used to the juggling act that a demanding job and sole care of a five-year-old entailed and now, with his growing relationship with Kate… He was beginning to wonder if he hadn't stretched himself too thin and that he was in danger of dropping all the balls.

But Kate was too precious for him to give her up. He just had to hope that she'd understand that he couldn't always be there for her. That he couldn't rush to her side and kiss away her fears when she had a nightmare, however much it tore him in two not to.

'Look, I'm sorry, but I'm afraid I have to—'

She arched an eyebrow. 'Go?' she finished for him. 'You don't have to apologise for needing to be somewhere else. I assume that you do?'

Her understanding didn't make it any easier, because he knew that he was short-changing her. 'Yeah, I do. And I should probably be sorting Sam's show-and-tell out with him as well.'

'Okay. Good.' She smiled and Ethan wondered if she was just making the best of a bad job. 'At least that means I won't embarrass you by celebrating over a coffee with the most embarrassing combination of flavours I can think of.'

A stab of guilt slashed at Ethan's heart. 'You couldn't possibly embarrass me. Caramel, cream and a beautiful woman?'

Kate laughed, and this time she seemed truly happy. 'Go. We'll celebrate together later.'

Ethan watched her go, her step a little lighter as she negotiated her way along the crowded high street. It seemed that they still had a way to go before they could work out a way forward in their relationship, but he wanted to make that journey. All he could hope was that Kate would hang on in there with him while he found his way.

# CHAPTER SIXTEEN

WHEN ETHAN WAS there all Kate's doubts disappeared. They lay side by side on a blanket at the top of Summer Hill watching the sky darken. There were plenty of places they could have chosen to go on this balmy Saturday evening, but just being together was the most perfect.

'Are you cold?' Ethan's fingers were entwined with hers and he lifted her hand, pressing it to his lips.

'No. Are you tired?' Kate had noticed the dark rings under Ethan's eyes when she'd seen him that morning at the police station.

'Yep. You make me feel tired and happy, instead of just tired.'

'We'll go home. You can sleep.' Tomorrow seemed a long way away at the moment and all Kate could think about was ending today by curling up with Ethan.

'I don't want to sleep when I'm with you.'

Kate sat up, looking down into his face. 'I'll *make* you sleep.'

'And how are you going to do that?' Ethan grinned suddenly.

'Wait and see.'

'I don't have to get up so early tomorrow.' His lips

quirked downwards and Kate wondered what could possibly have got in the way of his morning hug for Sam.

'Is that…good?' The idea of being able to wake lazily with Ethan sounded wonderful.

'Yes, it's good.' He reached up, caressing her cheek. 'My mother's doing a "breakfast in bed" party for Sam. Apparently they'll be busy sitting around in their pyjamas and getting crumbs in the bedclothes until ten thirty. There are going to be games and Mum made it very clear that I'm not invited.'

'That's really sweet.' Kate had wondered whether everyone in his parents' village saw Ethan as just the grieving widower. It seemed that his mother, at least, was open to the idea that he might be ready to move on.

'Yeah. When I dropped Sam off this afternoon, she hustled me into the kitchen and gave me a piece of her mind.'

'And?' Whatever Ethan's mother had said, he was obviously thinking about it carefully. And clearly not entirely in agreement with her.

'She says I'm spreading myself too thin. That it would be better for Sam if I included him a little more in our friendship.' Ethan grinned. 'She's being tactful. She knows it's not just a friendship.'

It sounded like good sense. He *was* spreading himself too thin, trying to keep her in one box and Sam in another.

'What do you think?'

'I think that, if you agree… I'd promised to take Sam for pizza this week—maybe you could tag along with us?'

That wasn't what Kate had envisaged, and she doubted it was what his mother had meant either. 'Tagging along' for a pizza they'd already planned was a little different from Ethan deliberately incorporating her into their lives. But maybe that was asking too much of them both right now. It was her choice to be independent of him, just as much as his.

'Yes, I'd really like that.'

'I would too. And Sam will love it.' He sat up suddenly, as if the discussion had taken them as far as he wanted to go. 'You want to go home, now? I'm intrigued to find out exactly how you're going to send me to sleep...'

Pizza night came and went and it changed nothing. They met up in town, ate and then went their separate ways. But it was a start. Something to build on.

Exactly what was going to happen when Ethan's parents ran out of excuses for Sam to stay the night on Saturdays was anyone's guess. But the super-hero space station seemed some way away from completion still and Kate had almost convinced herself not to worry too much about it. Maybe George was stringing things out to give her and Ethan some time alone.

And now she was trembling with anticipation at the thought of another night with Ethan. She opened the front door, strolling out in the evening sunshine to greet him as he parked his car outside her house.

'Hey there, beautiful.' He put his arms around her shoulders.

'Hello, handsome.' She smiled up at him. Ethan always made her feel beautiful.

He turned a little, flipping the remote to lock his car, and then he frowned, looking at her car, which was parked in the driveway. 'What happened there?'

'Someone rear-ended me.'

'What, with you in the car? Are you all right?'

'Yes, I'm fine. He wasn't going all that fast.' Suddenly Ethan seemed more interested in the back of her car than he was in her, walking over to inspect the damage.

'You're sure? No headaches or anything?'

'No, I'm fine. It was just a bump; it looks a lot worse than it actually was. Come inside.' Kate didn't much want to talk about it.

'And you didn't think to call me?'

Yes, she'd thought about calling him. She'd really wanted to call him, but she'd known he'd be busy with Sam, and the thought of her asking and him not being able to come and fetch her was more than she'd been able to bear. It was better that she didn't venture into that territory at the moment.

'I was all right, Ethan. Someone called an ambulance for the guy in the car behind me, just in case, and the paramedics checked me over too. I was fine. I *am* fine.'

'And you won't let me be the judge of that?'

'No, actually.' Kate tried to brush the comment off. Ethan was just reacting from that part of him that still had the urge to protect. It surfaced from time to time, but he always got over it. '*I'm* the best judge of it.'

He turned away from her, bending down to inspect the damage on her car more closely. 'You really should think about getting a new one, Kate. This one's getting more and more unreliable.'

'Yes, I'm thinking about it. But I'm not entirely sure what that has to do with someone crashing into the back of me when I'm stopped at the lights.'

'No. I suppose not.' He shrugged. 'I'm sorry.'

Kate walked into the house and he followed, shutting the front door behind him. It should all be over and done with, but somehow it wasn't. There was more that Kate wanted to say, and from the looks of it more that Ethan had to say too. The unspoken words hung between them in the silence.

She made tea, taking it out into the garden. Kate plumped herself down at the table on the patio, frustration still simmering on a low boil.

'Look, Kate...' Ethan was making an obvious effort to control his exasperation, standing with his back to her, staring out into the garden. 'I can't do this. I care for you and, well, I know you don't want to hear this, but I can't help worrying about you.'

The aching feeling, wanting him to be there for her but too afraid to ask, was too much to bear. 'You have to trust me, Ethan. You can't be here all the time.'

'I can't help that.' He didn't look round.

'I know you can't. But until you can let me out of that box you have me in, you have to accept that I need to carry on with my life. I don't want to replace Sam's mother. I just want to be there for you both, and I'm prepared to wait for that, but until it happens you can't expect me to rely on you on a part-time basis. That's not how it works.'

He turned. The look of helplessness in his eyes was a death knell to all of Kate's hopes. She'd finally said the things she'd written in her diary and it didn't change anything.

'I know. But it's the way I want it to work.' He sighed.

'You want me to be safe, you want Sam to be safe... They're both good things, but you're stretching yourself too thin. You should concentrate on Sam and let me fend for myself for a while.'

This was what Kate knew how to do, fend for herself. She'd been mistaken in allowing herself to rely on Ethan.

He wanted to be the one she could depend on but it was too soon. Too hard for him.

'I don't know how to do that.' Something hardened in his eyes.

'You have to try. Ethan, you need to be with Sam and not me. I can deal with that. I just can't deal with your expectations because they make me want things that I can't have.'

Finally it was clear. They'd tried, but both of them had to change. And neither of them could do it quickly enough to stop them from tearing each other apart in the process.

It was such a small thing. A dent in the back of Kate's car shouldn't be able to wipe away everything they'd meant to each other in the last few months.

But Ethan knew that it wasn't the dent that was the problem. And Kate was right, she couldn't count on him, because he didn't know yet how to put aside his guilt and be the man she wanted him to be.

'You're right. I care about you, but that's not enough.'

'No, it's not. You have to change. *I* have to change.'

Ethan shook his head. He couldn't believe that he was about to say this, but it was the only thing that made any sense. The only thing that would allow her to heal. And maybe it would allow him to heal as well, but that didn't matter very much to Ethan at the moment.

'Don't ever change, Kate. Just find your strength.' He walked past her, trying not to look at her, but his gaze automatically found hers. 'I have to go.'

Her hand flew to her mouth and tears brimmed in her eyes. But she didn't stop him. Ethan walked back into the kitchen, hearing her footsteps behind him as he opened the front door.

'Ethan!' she called out to him and he turned. In that moment, he loved her enough to leave her.

'If you honestly think we can work this out, then tell me now.'

She stared at him wordlessly. She didn't need to say it. Her tears were eloquent enough.

'Then I'm sorry, Kate.'

He opened the front door without waiting for her answer. As he closed the door behind him and walked away, Ethan wished that somehow there could be an answer to all of this. But some things just didn't have an answer.

# CHAPTER SEVENTEEN

'WOULD YOU LIKE to take Arthur up to Summer Hill this morning?' Sam was sitting at the table in the conservatory, surreptitiously trying to feed some of his breakfast to the dog.

'Yesss!'

'Good. Well, you'd better make sure that you eat all your breakfast. And that Arthur eats all of his.'

It had been three months and Arthur was growing. The long days of summer had begun to to draw back in again, although the days were still warm. But it seemed to Ethan that he had hardly felt the sun on his face since the evening he'd walked out on Kate.

It was for the best. He'd told himself that so many times now, in an attempt to put the yearning for her back into perspective, that it wasn't necessary to repeat it once again. She was everything he wanted but there was one fatal flaw in their relationship—two, maybe. He was one of the flaws and she was the other.

The doorbell rang and he went to answer it. Sam scrambled down from his seat and followed him.

'What's that?' Sam eyed the parcel that the courier had just handed him.

'I don't know. Probably something from the hospital.'

Sam lost interest, running upstairs, and Ethan called after him. 'I'll be up in a minute.'

But he wasn't. The package contained a hard-bound notebook that he recognised immediately, with a sheet of notepaper slipped under the elastic closure. The world suddenly changed its focus.

Slowly he unfolded the paper. There wasn't much to read.

*Dear Ethan*
*I started this for myself, and now it's for you. You can do whatever you want with it—read it, keep it or destroy it. But I want you to know that you left me better than you found me.*
*Kate*

Ethan stared at the note, trying to divine the meaning behind her words. The writing wasn't Kate's usual ebullient scrawl, it was neat and careful. She'd obviously thought about what she wanted to say and said it in as few words as possible. And the ending said it all. Just *Kate* without any love or the usual hug and kisses.

If this was a goodbye, he didn't want to read it. They'd already done that and there was no point in opening old wounds. He put the book down on the hall table and then picked it up again, snapping the elastic back and opening it. Kate had sent this to him, wanting him to read it, and there was no way that he could deny her this one last thing.

The pages were closely written and as he flipped through them he saw that she'd almost filled the notebook. It would take a while to read all of this.

'Dad. Come *on*!' Sam's voice sounded from upstairs

and for a moment Ethan considered laying the book to one side until Sam was in bed tonight. Then he changed his mind.

'Okay. I'll race you. See who can get ready to go first!'

Getting Sam dressed, chivvying boy and puppy into the car and driving to Summer Hill took less than three quarters of an hour, but it felt like an eternity. Kate's notebook seemed to be burning a hole in the pocket of his jacket. Ethan trudged up the hill, Sam on his shoulders and Arthur trailing behind them on the lead.

Finally they were at the top. Ethan picked a spot where he could keep hold of Arthur's extending lead and Sam could run and play without straying out of sight. He sat down, taking the book from his pocket.

'Can we go to the stream?' Sam was cavorting around in the sunshine.

'Later, maybe. I have to read this…'

Sam puffed out a breath, laying his hand on Ethan's knee in a meditative gesture that seemed somehow older than his years. 'You're getting quite boring.'

Guilt stabbed at Ethan. Sam was right and he wished that he hadn't let his son see his unhappiness. He folded the boy in his arms, hugging him.

'I know. I'm sorry. Can you do something for me?'

'Okay.'

'Would you be able to play for a while, with Arthur, while I read this? I'll be as quick as I can. Then I promise you I'll do my best not to be boring any more.'

Sam nodded gravely. 'All right, then.'

It was so easy for Sam. He believed that his father could say something and then make it happen. As he watched the boy run over to Arthur, Ethan resolved that he *would* make it happen. He'd read what Kate had to say and then get on with his life.

The dates were entered at the top of each page, and underneath were the two entries for each date. Ethan flipped through the pages, stopping at one which contained only two sentences. He recognised the date. It was the day after the second night they'd spent together.

*Best: making love with Ethan.*
*Worst: when he left.*

Remorse stabbed at him. He remembered leaving in a hurry, and Kate must have written this then. He almost put the book aside, knowing that it would deal more blows than he could take, but he picked it up again. Kate wouldn't send him this out of spite. She wanted him to read it and he should start at the beginning.

The first pages were dated a few days after she'd started seeing Usha and the entries were hesitant. A cup of her favourite coffee, which made Ethan smile at the memory of Kate grinning and taking a sip. A long evening at the surgery, which had worn her out. But then the entries became more personal.

It was the story of their affair. Brief, shining, but dogged by doubt. And then the story of her life after that.

Seeing him from her car, heading towards the market in town with Sam on his shoulders. Ethan remembered that day, and wished that he'd turned to see Kate. A nightmare, where someone grabbed her and she fought for her life against a shadow in the night. He smiled at the entries for that day. The nightmare was the worst thing that had happened to her. The best was that it had been a whole month since she'd had that dream.

Being bitten by a dog. The everyday things that Kate had dealt with and then moved on from. There was the recurring theme of missing him, which echoed in Ethan's heart, because he'd been missing Kate too. And the mantra which he now realised that they'd shared for this last three months.

*It was for the best. It never would have worked.*

And then the tone began to change.

*Ethan's the best man I've ever known. He's the one I wanted to depend on, who I knew I could depend on if we'd just give it a chance. But our fears got in the way.*

*I'm learning to face my fears and I hope he can face his.*

He knew. It suddenly all seemed so simple that Ethan couldn't believe he hadn't seen it before. Perhaps he *had* seen it. He'd just been unable to trust enough to do anything about it. Ethan read to the last entry, written the day before yesterday.

*I hope that Ethan can understand. I believe he will.*

He shut the book with a snap and looked up to where Sam was sitting on the grass, deep in a rather one-sided conversation with Arthur. He understood. Finally, he understood exactly what he had to do.

'Sam. We've got to go.'

'Where?' Sam looked up at him. If his son could trust him to make things right, if Kate could trust him to understand, then what right had Ethan not to trust himself?

'We're going to see Kate. You remember Kate?'

'*I* remember Kate.' Sam shot him a look of reproach.

Ethan hadn't spoken about Kate for the last few months and he supposed he deserved that. 'Are we going now?'

'Yes. We're going now.'

Work was the only thing that quietened Kate's mind right now. Hard, physical work. She'd thought a lot about sending her diary to Ethan and in the end the decision had been all about putting an end to missing him and moving on.

But moving on wasn't just something you did whenever you decided to. Telling herself that she'd said all that she wanted to say and that was an end to it didn't stop the endless reworking in her mind. The endless other possibilities that she knew weren't going to happen.

The truth now was that she got on with her life. Maybe he'd send some kind of acknowledgement and maybe not, but knowing Ethan he'd think before he acted. Which meant that, if his reply was coming, it wouldn't be today. Or tomorrow, either.

Large, heavy rocks were just the thing. Maybe she should split a few in half, and add a ball and chain just to complete the effect. She wandered into the kitchen, surveying the pile of built-up earth at the end of the garden, which already boasted the four rocks at the corners which were the basis of her design.

Sweat trickled from the nape of her neck down to the top of her sleeveless vest. She took a bottle of lemonade from the fridge, pouring herself a glass. With any luck, this should take the whole weekend.

The doorbell rang and she dropped the glass in the sink. It smashed, sending shards flying across the draining board, and Kate cursed quietly to herself. When the work stopped, she was jumpier than she thought.

Drying her hands with a tea towel, she opened the door. For a moment, she thought she might be hallucinating.

Ethan was standing at the end of the path looking cool and incredibly handsome. Kate's hand automatically flew to her hair as she watched Sam run up the path towards her, arms outstretched in an impression of an aeroplane.

Shakily she bent down, unable to tear her gaze from Ethan's face. He wasn't smiling, but then again he wasn't *not* smiling. Maybe he felt as awkward as she did, but he certainly looked a lot better.

'What's this, Sam? Are you a plane?' She couldn't think of anything else to say.

'I'm a wing man.'

'Oh.' She was vaguely aware that Ethan was wincing in uneasy embarrassment. 'Do you know what a wing man is?'

'No.' Sam ran in a small circle, his arms outstretched. 'Someone with wings, I think.'

'That sounds about right.' She couldn't stop trembling. Ethan had come, and she didn't know what this meant. But if Sam was with him then surely it couldn't be anything other than a social visit? Maybe an attempt at friendship? Kate didn't quite know how she would respond to that yet.

'Go tell your dad to come here.' She smiled down at Sam, who obligingly veered back down the path, chanting the words at Ethan as he went. He nodded, walking up the path and stopping outside the porch, his fingers on Sam's shoulders.

'I got the book, Kate. And... I was going to come alone, maybe this evening, and then I thought that...' He shrugged. 'Sam and I come as a package. It's a "two for the price of one" deal.'

She didn't dare jump to any conclusions. But Ethan was here and maybe it was a chance to build a few bridges. Kate was covered in grime and sweat, but now was the time.

'Why don't you both come in?' She stood back from the doorway and Sam ran inside. Ethan followed him at a rather more deliberate pace.

'Why are you so dirty?' Sam looked up at her.

'I'm making something in my garden. Do you want to see?' She shepherded Sam through to the back door, looking out for any broken glass that might be on the floor and hoping that Ethan wouldn't notice the sink.

'Wow…it's a castle!'

'It's a rockery, Sam.' Ethan's voice came from behind her. 'Kate's going to plant flowers.'

Sam looked up at her questioningly. 'It's going to be a castle with flowers. What do you think?' Kate provided a compromise answer.

'They're *very* heavy.' Sam was looking at the pile of rocks which had been delivered last weekend.

'Yes, they are a bit.'

'We could give you a hand.'

'You can't, Dad. You've got your best shirt on.' Sam reprimanded him and then looked up at Kate. 'We had to go home so he could put his best shirt on.'

Ethan laughed suddenly as if, faced by an immovable force, he'd decided to give in gracefully. 'What would I do without my wing man to keep me honest?'

Sam shrugged, clearly more interested in the castle than a conversation that he didn't quite understand. He ran across the lawn to inspect Kate's handiwork and Ethan turned to her.

'Kate, I heard what you said. I'm hoping that some of your courage might rub off on me.'

'You mean...?' Suddenly she knew what he meant. It was in the deep-blue gaze that she'd been trying to avoid.

'We both thought we couldn't make things work because we didn't trust ourselves to change. But you've done it and I want to show you that I can too. If you'll give me the chance.'

'You think my good intentions will rub off?' She allowed herself a smile at the thought.

'I think they will. Kate, I love you. I want us all to be together—you, me and Sam. If you'll take us.' He shrugged. 'Personally, I'd advise anyone against it. But I'm hoping that you're that reckless.'

She loved him. More than she had before. However successful she'd been in denying it, this had all been for Ethan. For herself as well, but in her darkest moments, when she'd woken frightened in the night, it had been him she'd thought about.

'I love you too, Ethan. I want to give this another try.'

He nodded. His hand wandered to her arm, his fingers leaving a trail of goose bumps. He glanced out at Sam, who was exploring the end of the garden, and then pulled her towards him.

'We'll take care of each other. That has to be enough, doesn't it?'

'It's more than enough. It's everything.' Kate kissed him. It wasn't the deepest of kisses, or the warmest of embraces, but she could feel the shock of sudden pleasure run through him, just as it raced through her.

'You just changed my whole world, Kate. Tipped it upside down.' He didn't seem to mind that she'd get his best shirt dirty if they went on like this. Holding her close now, he kissed her again.

'Sam...' Kate came to her senses, digging Ethan hard in the ribs. Sam was still exploring the garden, but any moment now he was going to be running back to the house, wanting to share something with his dad.

'I'll explain things to him.' Ethan kept hold of her hand, as if it belonged to him now, and he wasn't going to give it up. 'Or *we'll* explain things. I dare say he'll have a few questions.'

A bright belief in a future that could be different. One that might hold a few problems, but problems were there to be solved.

'And I dare say we can answer them.'

'I think we can. And, in the meantime, it looks as if you have *two* volunteers to help with your new castle.' Ethan nodded towards Sam, who was collecting small stones from the flower beds and piling them up around the larger ones.

'That's good. I could do with the help.'

Ethan had stripped off his shirt, and Sam had followed suit, draping his shirt over his father's. The twitch of Ethan's eyebrow made Kate shiver at the thought that later he might strip off *her* shirt.

They moved the larger rocks together, Ethan issuing a stern instruction to Sam to stand back. He was stronger than she was, but there was equal effort from both of them. Each played their part, instead of Ethan insisting that Kate join Sam and watch.

She was working now because she couldn't stay still. By the end of the day, the rockery was looking more or less as she'd imagined it would, with the added bonus of a few additions of carefully piled pebbles from Sam.

'Chinese?' Ethan straightened up, surveying their handiwork.

'Yes!' Sam liked the idea and Kate grinned.

'Sounds good. I'll get cleaned up.'

He caught her arm, stopping her. Over the course of the afternoon, they'd touched often, but always as a result of heaving rocks or digging holes. Now his fingers on her arm were electric.

'Would you like to come over to mine? Bring a change of clothes. You can clean up there.'

He mouthed one silent word. *Stay.* Kate nodded.

Yes. Whatever the future decided to throw at them, she'd stay.

Blind trust had been Ethan's only weapon against the fears that today had brought into sharp focus. What if Kate didn't want him? What if it was all too late and her diary really was a sign that she'd moved on? As soon as that fear had been assuaged, two new ones had replaced it.

What if Sam didn't understand? And what if Ethan was in too deep and he couldn't do what he'd promised and change?

Sam had turned out to be the least of his problems. He'd sat down with him after dinner, told him that he loved him and that he'd always be his wing man. And that Daddy and Kate wanted to go out together. Sam had nodded sagely.

'I know about boyfriends and girlfriends. You want to kiss her, don't you?'

Ethan wondered vaguely what else Sam knew and decided to leave that one for another time. 'Yes. I do.'

Sam turned the corners of his mouth down and Ethan's

heart thumped, wondering what was going on in Sam's head. Then he slithered down from Ethan's lap, running over to Kate.

'Can we have ice cream—in the castle again?' When the afternoon had been at its warmest, Kate had predictably resorted to ice cream, eaten perched on the rocks in the rockery.

'Yes, of course. In fact, that's one of the rules. We can have ice cream in the castle whenever you want.'

Ethan decided not to intervene. Kate's idea of ice cream whenever you wanted was tempered by a balanced diet in between times, while Sam's wasn't. That was a minor detail that could be sorted out later. Sam's smile was the one thing that could make things complete at the moment.

And he did smile. Kate hugged him and he clambered up onto her lap. 'Do you know the story?'

Her gaze flipped to Ethan's face, and he grinned. Surely happiness couldn't be *this* easy? 'I'll fetch the book. Would you like Kate to read your bedtime story?'

Sam nodded, and Kate hugged him tight, her face shining. 'Get the book, Ethan.'

When they'd both kissed Sam goodnight and Ethan had put him to bed, the second fear resurfaced. He and Kate were alone now and he had to live up to all he'd promised. He almost didn't dare touch her.

'I meant what I said, Kate. I'm going to let go of the guilt. I'm going to be there when you need me.' How he was going to do that was a question that still baffled Ethan. But he *would* do it.

'I trust that you will be.' She stepped into his arms and Ethan felt his heart thump in his chest. 'And I'll be there for you and Sam.'

It felt so good to hear her say that. The suspicion that Kate might just have the answer for everything occurred to him.

'And if I start falling back into my old ways, you'll tell me?'

'I'll do a lot more than tell you...' She jabbed him in the ribs.

'Always?'

'Yes, always.'

Always was more than he deserved, and more than he'd ever thought possible. Ethan would take it.

'Come to bed.' He wanted Kate in his arms more than anything now.

'I thought you'd never ask...'

# EPILOGUE

*Six months later.*

THEY'D SEEN THE last of the hot summer days and the beginning of autumn, the sparkle of Christmas and bright new hope for the coming year.

Things hadn't always been easy. Kate had worked hard to make Sam feel that she wasn't taking his father from him and that she wasn't trying to replace his mother. But Sam, already secure in the knowledge that his father loved him, had come up with his own answer. His mother was 'Mummy' and, after a few months, he'd started to call Kate 'Mum'. When Kate had taken him to buy a Christmas present for Ethan, Sam had revelled in having a secret to keep and someone else to keep it with.

The evening she'd come home late from work and found Ethan pacing the sitting room had brought back all Kate's old fears. The silence between them had lasted for a while and then Ethan had simply walked up to her and hugged her. She'd felt his tears, wet against her face, and they'd talked for hours. His darkest fears and hers were finally seeing the light of day, where they could at last be calmed.

When she'd moved into Ethan's house, she'd kept most

of the boxes she'd brought with her packed, not wanting to disturb anything that Jenna might have done. Her cottage was closed up, all the furniture under dust sheets, because Kate could quite bring herself to rent it out yet. Ethan had said nothing for a week and then, when Kate had returned home from a shopping trip with his mother, she'd found that everything had been moved. Cutlery was in a different drawer, plates were in a different cupboard. The furniture was in a different place in their bedroom and Kate's things had been neatly packed away in drawers and cabinets. The relief was tempered by neither of them being able to find anything for weeks.

Ethan had organised a surprise, a visit to London with a stay in a luxurious hotel. Just the two of them, while Sam stayed with Ethan's parents. They had breakfast in the huge bed and then a walk in the crisp, winter morning.

'Is this the place?' He stopped suddenly, right next to the statue of Boudicca that looked out over the Thames.

'You remembered!' Kate smiled up at him.

'Your second-favourite place.' He wrapped his arms around her. They were both secure in the knowledge that being in each other's arms was their shared favourite place.

'Yes. Even in winter I like it.'

He was looking up at the statue. 'Think Boudicca had red hair—like you?'

Kate laughed. 'I have absolutely no idea. I wouldn't mind the chariot, though.'

'Sam and I could take a look at your car. I'm sure we could do something with it.' Ethan grinned, shoving his hands in the pockets of his coat, his breath pluming in front of him in the cold air.

'Is this…was there something you wanted to mention?' Kate was going to wait, and pretend she knew nothing about any surprise, but he seemed so on edge all of a sudden and it seemed downright cruel not to put Ethan out of his misery.

He winced. 'Sam told you, didn't he?'

'No, he didn't. When you were taking his things inside at your parents' house he sat in the car, looking at me with his hands over his mouth. I asked him if anything was the matter, and he said that he'd promised you not to tell. He says that, now that he's six, he's grown up enough to keep a secret.'

Ethan laughed. 'Do you mind? That he's in on it?'

'Of course not. He's your wing man, isn't he?'

They'd talked about going away somewhere for Easter and Kate had come to the conclusion that Ethan must have tickets in his pocket.

'Yes. I might have to have a word with him about strategy…' Ethan wound his arms around her shoulders, kissing her.

'Mmm. Lovely. Can we go now? I'm getting cold,' she teased him.

'No, stay right there. Don't move an inch.'

He dropped to one knee in front of her and Kate's hand flew to her mouth. *This* she hadn't expected.

'What…? Ethan!' She was trembling all over now, hardly able to stand. 'I thought you'd booked a weekend away.'

He smiled. 'I want more than a weekend. I'm aiming for the rest of our lives. Will you marry me, Kate?'

She might not have expected the question, but she had her answer ready. 'Yes. Yes, I will!'

He got to his feet and kissed her. Kate was dimly

aware of the city going about its business around her. That a few people had stopped when they'd seen Ethan down on one knee and that when he'd kissed her there was a murmur of approval. A woman's voice came from somewhere, wishing her happiness. She nodded blindly. Ethan was the only thing she could see right now.

'You'll be relieved to hear that I didn't take any of my wing man's advice on choosing the ring.'

'You have a *ring*?' Here in his arms, that hardly mattered. All that mattered was that Ethan wanted to spend his life with her, and she wanted so much to spend the rest of her life with him.

'Of course I do. I've got a plan.' He took a small box from his pocket, opening it and showing Kate the contents. 'Do you like it?'

It was a square-cut canary-yellow diamond on a plain white-gold band. Kate caught her breath. 'It's beautiful, Ethan.'

'Let's see whether it fits. Hold still. Stop jumping around.'

'I can't help it!' Kate's feet seemed to be doing a little dance of excitement, quite of their own volition and without any input from her.

He slid the ring onto her finger, pushing it carefully over the knuckle. It was a perfect fit and Ethan nodded in satisfaction. 'Not so bad. I was hoping that I'd got it right.'

'It's perfect, Ethan. Beautiful... How *did* you get it right?'

'I measured your finger while you were asleep. Ticklish business. I was hoping you weren't going to wake up and catch me doing it.'

Kate laughed with delight. 'It was a beautiful plan,

Ethan. Thank you so much.' She flung her arms around his neck, hugging him.

'There's more.'

'I don't care. This is enough, and nothing you could possibly do could be any better.'

He laughed, a low rumble of complete contentment. 'Try this…'

He handed her an envelope and Kate opened it. It was a letter from a firm of land surveyors. She scanned the words, too excited to read them the first time, and tried again.

He'd made an offer on the land adjacent to her cottage. One acre, with planning permission to build. Kate flipped over to the next page and saw a plan. The land included the old orchard that she could see from her back window, and extended to the side right up to the curve in the lane.

'This is… But aren't we going to rent the cottage? What does it mean?'

'It means that, if we want to, we can take your cottage off the rental listings and extend it. Very considerably, actually, as the planning permission allows us to double the frontage and go back to form an L-shape. It would give us three times the space you have now.' He turned the page in front of her and Kate saw a plan of the new building, which ran along the side of her cottage, reaching almost to the end of the garden. 'The planning authorities say that the frontage would have to be in a complementary style, but then I think we might want that anyway.'

'But we can't afford this, can we? Have we won the lottery or something?'

Ethan chuckled. 'No. We'll sell my house.'

'No… Ethan, how things are at the moment is fine. You don't have to sell up.'

'It's just a house, Kate. I like it, but this would be something that we'd built together. There's a great little school in the village for Sam. And we'd have space.'

'For Sam to grow. And…more children?' Kate put her arms around his waist.

He smiled broadly. 'That possibility hadn't escaped me. Along with Arthur, and a few cats and dogs, and whatever else you bring back from the surgery needing a temporary home. You'll keep your garden, and I can grow apple trees.'

'You've got this all worked out, haven't you?'

'It's nothing without you, Kate. If this isn't what you want, then we'll do something else. I have a week to sign the documents on the land, but if I do it's ours.'

'You're sure this is what you want?' It sounded like heaven, but if Ethan wanted to live in a shack she'd be fine with that too.

He took her hand, kissing it, and the ring flashed in the winter sunlight. 'You've got your own Ambigulon stone. You could try it out.'

'Is that what Sam said?'

'Yeah. Although that wasn't anywhere on the list of priorities when I chose it.'

'Might come in handy, though…' She held her hand over his heart. 'I see… Ah. It's all good.'

Ethan chuckled. 'You can't stop there. What *do* you see?'

'I see an honest heart that loves me as much as I love you, Ethan. I think your plan is just perfect.'

'I'm glad you like it.' He put his arm around her and started walking. He was holding her tight, guiding her steps, because Kate wasn't looking where she was going.

All she could see was the ring on her finger and the man she was going to marry.

'It'll keep us busy. A wedding and a house. Children…'

'They'll keep us very busy. But there are a few other things in the plan as well.'

'Hot chocolate?' She grinned up at him and he nodded. 'Happy for the rest of our lives?'

'Yes. The first is about ten minutes' walk away. The second starts right now.'

\* \* \* \* \*

# A CHILD
# TO HEAL THEM

LOUISA HEATON

MILLS & BOON

For the real Tasha, Bonnie and Lucy.

# CHAPTER ONE

SHE COULDN'T SEE the road. There were too many people criss-crossing in front of her. This way. That. Seemingly with no order to their lives.

Women were heading home from the market with goods balanced in baskets atop their heads, babies strapped to their backs in swathes of fabric. Cattle chewed the cud at the side of the road, as if bored with life, idling alongside market traders who were much more vibrant, calling out, selling their goods—brightly patterned fabrics, spices and vegetables—whilst loud pop music blared from speakers she couldn't see.

Her nose was filled with the scents of food—fresh fish, caught that day, being the strongest.

Tasha Kincaid urged her off-roader forward, sounding the horn as much as she could. Thick, choking dust was being kicked up from the tyres as she revved the engine, desperate to get through the crowds, anxious to get back to the *Serendipity*, on the far side of town, because of her passenger, lying on the back seat, unmoving.

Children were not meant to be this still. This quiet.

The *Serendipity* had anchored just two days ago. She'd taken the children in her class to see it. The vast vessel, a floating hospital ship, sat there in the waters of the

Mozambique Channel, waiting to give aid to those who needed it for free.

The children in her class had drawn pictures of the boat, and she'd used the lesson to teach them about kindness and giving. About helping others. They'd even been able to go on board briefly and talk to one or two of the nurses, who had generously given their time.

Maria and Rob were from Ireland and were volunteers, helping out on board for six months before returning to their paying jobs back home.

Back in class, she had pinned the children's pictures to the peeling walls of the classroom, instantly brightening up the place with their happy colours. That had been the day she'd first found herself worrying about Abeje.

Abeje was Tasha's star pupil. She tried not to have favourites. All the orphaned children in her class were special, brilliant and curious. But Abeje was different.

She had been orphaned at a young age after both her parents had died, and the only home she'd ever known was the Sunshine Children's Centre. She'd never had a proper family, but she was bright and intelligent. A deep thinker. A philosopher. And she wanted to be a doctor.

The similarities between them had struck Tasha hard. She recognised that gleam in her eyes. That yearning and thirst for knowledge. To do well. She wanted to let Abeje know that she could be anything she chose to be—that Tasha would help give her that chance. That the whole world could be hers as long as she pursued a passion.

But on the day they'd visited the *Serendipity*—the day that Tasha would have expected Abeje to be at her most attentive, her most intrigued and excited—Abeje had seemed somehow *off.* A little listless. A little tired, and complaining of a headache.

All children got sick. It was inevitable. So when Abeje hadn't come to school the next day Tasha had figured she was probably just taking a day to recuperate. Knowing that Abeje had no mother or father to soothe her brow, she'd thought it might be a nice gesture to go to the children's centre and check on her, take her some pretty flowers to brighten her room. Just to let her know that she was being thought of and worried about.

But the second she'd seen Abeje, semi-conscious and sweating, Tasha had known that there was something to be worried about. With the matron's blessing, she'd scooped Abeje up into her car and had screeched away in a trail of thick red dust in an effort to get to the hospital ship.

The vehicle hit a pothole and Abeje moaned as the car bounced them around in their seats. Tasha risked a quick glance. The poor girl was drenched through with sweat and the sun was glaring down at them, burning everything it cast its gaze upon.

'Not far now, sweetie! We're nearly there…just stay with me!'

Horrible thoughts were rushing through her head—meningitis, encephalitis. Maybe a waterborne infection? A slideshow of horrific images passed through her brain, courtesy of the books she'd once studied.

She could smell the docks as they inched closer. The heat, the brine, the dust. The fish caught during that morning's outing were only now being brought back to port. Fruit, meat, chickens in cages were all piled high, the chickens squawking and flapping, the busy trade causing human traffic that she had to struggle to get through.

She cursed quietly, biting her lip, hitting the horn in

frustration as the giant sides of the ship loomed over her—so near and yet so far. The car was surrounded by a thick crowd of people and she was making minimum progress.

Growling, she stopped the car, put her keys in her pocket, scooped Abeje into her arms and began to push her way through the throngs of people.

'Excuse me! Sorry! Can I just squeeze through?'

Suddenly she was at the gangplank, Abeje heavy in her arms.

She ran up it, panting in the heat, sweat prickling her underarms, her back. The coolness of the ship's interior was welcoming. The air-conditioning a blessing. For her, at least.

Desperately she tried to remember her way around the ship from the brief tour they'd taken a few days ago. The emergency clinic was down this corridor.

Hefting Abeje into a firmer grip, she ran down it and burst through the double doors into the clinic, where there was a twenty-bed ward. 'I need help!' she yelled at Maria and Rob, who were making up a bed with new sheets.

Tasha ran to a spare bed and laid Abeje down upon it as gently as she could. The two nurses moved towards the bed.

'She's sick! I don't know what's wrong, but I think it's serious! Please help her!'

She stepped back as the two nurses rushed forward. It was hard to fight the urge to do something herself. To let go. To give her precious charge up into a stranger's hands.

'What's going on?'

The male voice instantly cut through the haste. Authoritative. English. The sort of voice that made you turn around and pay attention to the speaker.

It was a voice she'd heard before. One that took her right back to her childhood.

*To that moment.*

*Him.*

*It can't be...*

Surely she was wrong? Memories were fickle, and she'd done her level best to forget his very existence. How he looked. How he *sounded*. The voice that she had once closed her eyes to listen to.

Tasha glanced over her shoulder...

At the man that had once torn her heart in two.

Only now her heart was galloping, her head was pounding with incredulity and her mouth was dry, clogged with all the dust from the road. She was aware of sweat drenching her skin.

*How can it be him?*

*How is he here? In this place?*

They'd been children. She just thirteen years old. Him three years older. And it might have been an adolescent crush, something silly, but she remembered the pain and the humiliation all too well, even now. It was like being that teenage girl all over again.

'*Quinn?*'

The doctor frowned at her briefly, clearly wondering how she knew his name, but then his attention was returned to Abeje, who lay still on the bed. 'Tell me her symptoms. When it began.'

Tasha blinked hard, still not quite believing that he was *here*. Of all the places in the world he might have gone he was *here*. On *this* ship.

As if from a world away, unable to tear her gaze from his face, she began to relay Abeje's symptoms, stunned into numbness and a creeping sense of hurt. The box she'd put him in, and all her feelings about him—the box that she'd locked and hidden away for all these years—was finally beginning to crack open, creating a canyon of a scar upon her heart.

There was something about the tall blonde who had just appeared in his clinic. Something weirdly familiar. But he didn't have time to place her. He'd thought he knew most of the English people here in Ntembe, but obviously not.

Perhaps she was new? She had corkscrew honeyed curls, deep blue eyes and a mask of sun-kissed freckles across her nose. Cute.

But he didn't have time to think about her, much as he would like to. She wasn't the important one. The most important female at this point in time was the semi-conscious one lying on the bed—not the one who somehow knew his name.

Quinn examined the young girl, his stethoscope already in his ears, the metal diaphragm at its end already upon her clammy chest. She was about six years old, a little underweight, but not so much that it concerned him. She had a temperature of nearly one hundred and three degrees, sweats and chills. Drowsy. Flu-like symptoms.

His first concern was malaria. 'Has she been vomiting?'

The blonde shook her head, curls shimmering. She looked terrified. Almost as if she were afraid to look at the little girl on the bed. As if she was shutting herself down.

'I don't know.'

'Any family history I should know about?'

She shook her head, looking at him in apology, cheeks colouring.

'I don't know.'

'Has she been given anything?'

There was a pained expression in those blue eyes of hers.

'I don't know. I'm sorry. I'm just her teacher.'

He listened to her heart. It sounded good, if a little rapid. Her chest was clear at the moment. Checking her eyes and the palms of her hands, he saw she seemed pale, and the possibility of anaemia assured him that malaria was probably the case here.

'Let's get her on an intravenous drip and get some blood drawn so we can do a rapid diagnostic test. She's probably going to need anti-malarials.'

'You think this is malaria?' the woman asked, heart-break in her voice.

'It looks like it. The bloods will let us know for sure. You're her teacher?'

She looked frightened. On edge. Her arms were wrapped around herself protectively, making her look smaller.

'Yes.'

'Are any of your other students sick?'

She shook her head. 'I didn't think... I'm sorry. I don't know.'

It seemed there was a lot she didn't know. But he didn't want to get frustrated with her. This wasn't the first time a patient had turned up at the ship with no one knowing anything about them. Sometimes they'd get dumped there. Abandoned.

'Can I sit with her?'

'You've taken anti-malaria tablets before coming over here?'

She nodded.

'Good. Then you can stay.'

There was something about those eyes of hers. Something familiar. Oceanic blue and just as deep. Thick, dark lashes enveloping them. Where had he seen them before?

He held out his hand, determined to find out. 'Dr Quinn Shapiro.'

Hesitantly she took his hand, as if she'd been asked to touch a live, hissing and spitting cobra. 'Tasha Kincaid.'

*Tasha Kincaid.* The name didn't ring a bell. Perhaps he was mistaken about her being familiar somehow? Some people just had that type of face...

*Though she seems to know me...*

'Nice to meet you.'

She looked at him strangely. Questioningly. Surprised. *Relieved?*

'Likewise.'

Nice to meet him? Quinn Shapiro? Here on the *Serendipity*? Of all the hospital ships in all the world, he had to be on *this one*? Off the coast of Africa? What were the chances?

She didn't want to think about what he'd done. What he'd said. About how he'd made her feel. *So small. So unimportant. So ugly.* Those feelings she'd stamped down on long ago, determined not to let them affect her self-confidence.

It had been a struggle for a while, especially because she'd been at such a vulnerable, impressionable age, but she'd done it. The only way she'd been able to carry on had been to pretend it had never happened.

Tasha sat by Abeje's bed, holding her student's hand. Abeje was sleeping now, her face restful in repose, her chapped lips slightly parted. Her skin was hot to the touch—boiling. Her small body was fighting a battle that had no definite outcome. The rapid test, which had given a result within minutes of their arrival, had shown that it *was* malaria.

'Don't you die on me,' she whispered to her small charge, hoping that her just saying those words would make some higher power hear them and infuse the little girl with a fighting spirit. 'Do you hear me? You've got to pull through this. You've got to fight it. You can't give in.'

'How's she doing?'

Quinn's voice behind her had Tasha leaping to her feet, her heart thundering like galloping horses, her cheeks flushing red. She turned around, stared at him, resisting the urge to start yelling at him. To humiliate him. To embarrass him the way he had once done her.

Trying her best to hold the bitterness back, she said, 'She's sleeping.'

'That's good. Her body needs rest.'

Yes, it did. So did she. But her own tiredness, her own endless, exhausting fear, was something she had to dismiss right now. Her body was once again thrumming to the presence of Quinn Shapiro, apparently having forgotten that years ago she'd made a decision never to be attracted to him ever again.

Who knew the human body could be so treacherous? It apparently had a mind of its own…was reacting to him in ways she couldn't control.

He clearly didn't recognise her. The last time she'd seen him she'd been thirteen years old, chubby and grubby, and he'd been sixteen. Just three years older, but seemingly so worldly-wise, so mature, so stunning. And so handsome. With a dazzling smile that had made her heart go pitter-pat.

Her newly teenaged little heart hadn't stood a chance when Quinn had first appeared on her radar. Tall and rangy, with a blond quiff, captain of his school's rugby team, he'd had an easy charm and boy band good-looks. She, on the other hand, had found comfort in food and books, and her wild mass of unconquered curls had earned her the nickname Nit-Nat. Just because she'd once caught nits and spread them to the other kids in the children's home.

She'd never thought that was fair. It could have happened to any of them. Every time she'd itched and scratched, her fingers buried in the mass of her thick curls, the other kids would run away from her, laughing. She'd spent many hours in front of the matron, painfully enduring the process of the nit comb that kept getting stuck in the knots of her hair. They'd even used a special shampoo, but it had stunk, earning her even more nicknames.

Her misery had been punctuated with happiness at Quinn's visits. She had been regularly ensnared by Quinn's smiles and friendly open manner to the other kids at the home when he'd visited to pick up his best mate Dexter.

Her crush on Quinn had been absolute! She'd drawn hearts in her notebooks and put her initials and his inside them with a little arrow. Signed her name with his surname—*Natasha Shapiro.* It had looked so exotic, so stylish, so grown-up. Everything she had not been, but aspired to be.

She'd try to chat with Dexter, as casually as she could, trying to get information. Quinn wanted to travel the world. To be a doctor. To change people's lives.

Could he have been any dreamier?

His dreams she had decided to make hers. She'd always enjoyed medical dramas on the television. Always liked to try and guess what was wrong with people and sometimes would get it right. So she had decided that she, too, would go to medical school when she was older. She would travel the world and treat people and make them better and everyone she tended to would be just so grateful to her. Thankful to her for saving their lives. She would be adored. Loved at last. No one would look down on her ever again...

But it hadn't worked out that way. Following someone else's dreams had only brought her nightmares.

'I wonder if you could do me a favour?' Quinn asked.

Once upon a time she would have jumped to do any favour he'd asked of her. But now she felt cautious. Wary of getting hurt again. Wary of awakening that mean streak he'd once unleashed upon her.

'What is it?'

'I need you to check on the other children in your class and at the children's home. Could you do that for me? Report back if any of them are sick?'

She thought about his request. Was it possible that the others might be sick? She hadn't even considered the idea. Once she'd seen the state Abeje was in her only thought had been to get *her* help.

'You think they might be?'

'It's a possibility. The bloods show we're dealing with the parasite plasmodium falciparum. It's an aggressive strain. We're treating with chloroquine and ACTs.'

Tasha frowned. 'Because some falciparum parasites are immune to the chloroquine?'

He raised a single eyebrow. 'That's right. How did you know?'

She shrugged. 'Oh, I…er… I think I read that some-where. Before I came over here.'

'Well, it's just as a back-up.'

She thought about having to leave the ship. Leave Abeje behind. 'I don't want to leave her alone.'

'She's in safe hands.'

Of course. Of *course* he would say that. *He* still be-lieved in medicine and his skill to save this little girl's life. Her own belief was a little more battered. But then, as his words began to have more potency the longer they lingered in her brain, she thought about the other children in her class—Machupa, Tabia, Claudette, Habib and the others—all those little faces, all those little people she had come to care so much about. She knew she had to do the right thing and go and check on them.

'Of course. You're right. I'll go right now.'

She had to get away from him. Needed some breath-ing room. Some time to think.

'Wait.' He held up his hand as she moved to slink past him. 'I think maybe I ought to come with you—and you need to have a drink first. It's the middle of the day and you've had nothing since your arrival. You need to hy-drate.'

Her stomach was churning. How would she be able to drink anything? He wanted to go *with her*.

'I can do it by myself,' she said quietly.

*What's happening to me? How has he turned me into a mouse again?*

'I insist. Abeje doesn't need her teacher collapsing on her as well, does she?'

Tasha sat down in her chair and looked at the sleep-ing girl. So young and already fighting for her life. How much more bad luck did she need to experience at such a young age? There was no one else to sit by her bedside. Just Tasha. And, yes, she *did* need to look after herself. No one else would do it for her. But she felt herself bristling at his suggestion. Ordering her about. Telling her what was best for her. Even more so because he was right.

*I'm going to have to deal with it.*

If the other kids were sick, wouldn't it be better to have a *real* doctor by her side?

'Okay.'

'How do you like it?'

She blinked. 'What?'

'Your tea.'

He smiled, and the devastating power of it—the familiarity, the punch-in-the-gut strength of it— almost winded her. Those teeth… That dimple in his right cheek…

*Remember what he did to you.*

'Er…milk. One sugar.'

His eyes creased as he smiled again, bookending the corners with lines that had never been there before, but that just increased his attraction. How did the nurses get any work done around him? How did anyone concentrate? Were they immune? Had they had some sort of vaccination? Because if they had then she damn well wanted one for herself!

She'd worked *so hard* to forget this man. And she'd thought she'd been successful. It had just been a crush, as a child—so what? He'd broken her heart badly—but who cared? It had been years ago. *Years.*

And it turned out he didn't even recognise her.

Or remember her.

If she was so forgettable, then she wanted to make sure he meant just as little to her now.

She did not need his help or advice. She knew what

she was looking out for. And the idea of spending more time with him when she wasn't prepared for this unexpected onslaught only made her feel sick.

He was not the man she wanted by her side.

Quinn hauled himself into the passenger seat as Tasha gunned the engine. There seemed to be fewer people about now, the morning market trade dissipating, so she was able to reverse easily and begin the drive back to the Sunshine Children's Centre.

Her nerves were on edge. She felt prickly. Uncomfortable. He still hadn't recognised her and she was in two minds about telling him who she was.

If Abeje recovered quickly, perhaps there would be no need to tell him anything? But her gut reaction was that Abeje was in for a long fight and that it would take some time before they saw any signs of recovery. Malaria was an aggressive disease in this part of the world still, and she'd racked her brains to try and remember what she knew about the condition.

A single mosquito bite was all it took to get infected, and most people showed symptoms within a couple of weeks of being bitten. The terrible thing was that it could be fatal if treatment was delayed. She could only hope that they had got to Abeje in time. A combination of drugs was slowly being dripped into Abeje's system through an IV. She hoped it was enough.

'What made you come to Africa to teach?'

So he wanted to do small talk? Though she wasn't sure if *any* talk with him would ever be small for her.

'I just did.'

The desire to keep her life away from his scrutiny was strong. He'd already ridiculed her once. It might have been years ago, but that didn't mean the pain was any less. Being with him now made her feel raw again. Unguarded. The wound in her heart, open to infection.

'You've always taught English?'

'No.'

'What did you do before?'

She glared at him as she drove, before turning back to keep an eye on the road. It was none of his business.

'This and that.'

'Mystery woman, huh?'

Without looking at him, she knew he was smiling. She heard it in his voice. He really had no idea, did he?

*So two-faced! Trying to charm a woman you once thought so little of.*

'What made *you* take a post on the ship?'

There was a pause before he answered, allowing time for the potholes in the road to bounce them around, so that their shoulders bashed into each other briefly before the car was righted again.

'I needed a change. I'd spent some time working in British hospitals, but I felt like stretching my wings. I didn't want to become stale, you know? Complacent. I needed a new challenge.'

'Well, Africa certainly does that to you.'

He nodded. 'It does.' He turned to look at her. 'Did you come out here for a challenge?'

What could she tell him? That she'd come here on pure instinct? That teaching at schools in the UK had worn down her spirit?

Such long, gruelling hours, weighed down by the gazillions of reports and lesson plans and resources she'd had to create. Hours spent on assessments and figure-juggling that would never see the light of day but had to be there in case the inspectors turned up. Weeks spent worrying about work politics and staffroom gossip and pressure from the senior management team to be constantly at the top of her game.

She'd just wanted to teach. She'd wanted to forget all the rest and get back to what she enjoyed. Seeing the face of a child light up with understanding. Being with children who were *eager* to learn. She'd wanted to get back to grass roots. Find her joy again. Her spirit.

Africa had always seemed to her an exotic place— both beautiful and dangerous at the same time—and after going to a seminar in which the speaker had talked about her time teaching in Senegal she'd found an agency and signed right up. She'd needed to get away from the everyday. She'd needed to find something special.

And she had. It had brightened her heart, coming here. Given her exactly what she'd needed.

'I came out here to make a difference.'

He nodded in understanding. 'I know what you mean.'

She doubted it. She imagined that Quinn's life had always been rosy. Nothing too horrendous or upsetting for *him*. Surely he must have cruised through life? Privileged and well off?

Tasha drove on through the hot, dusty streets of Ntembe. She was glad that Quinn had made her drink that tea. She *had* needed it. And now she was hungry, too, but that would have to wait. They had children to check up on.

She parked the vehicle outside the centre.

The Sunshine Children's Centre was a long, low building, with a corrugated tin roof and a hand-painted sign made by the children. There was a bright yellow sun in one corner, its rays stretching across the sign, behind the words, and in another corner, if you looked hard enough, beyond the accumulation of dust, there was a child's face with a big, happy smile.

'This is it.'

'How many children live here?'

'Fifty-three. Most of them girls.'

They got out of the car and dusted themselves down. 'How many of them are your students?'

'Ten—though others go to the same school. They're just in different classes.'

'We should check them all—hand out anti-malarials just in case.'

She nodded. Yes, it was best to err on the side of caution. Preventative medicine was better than reactive medicine.

'Okay. I'll introduce you to the house matron—her name's Jamila.'

'Lead the way.'

She led him into the interior, explained the situation to Jamila and told her what they wanted to do to check on the children. Permission was given for them to treat them.

Tasha was glad it wasn't a school day, so the children were all at the centre, though some of the boys were out at the back, playing football. All seemed to be in good health. None of them were showing signs of illness or fever.

'Looks like Abeje was the unlucky one.'

Jamila stepped forward. 'Abeje travelled with an aunt back to her village two weeks ago.'

'With Ada?' Tasha asked.

'Yes. The village is about a two-hour drive from here. Do you think she could have got infected there?'

Tasha looked at Quinn and he nodded. It was a distinct possibility.

'I wonder if anyone is sick at the village? Is it remote? Do they have any medical facilities nearby?'

Jamila shook her head. 'The *Serendipity* is the closest they have.'

Quinn frowned. 'They might feel they're too sick to travel. Perhaps we ought to go out there? Check on everyone?'

'Do you have enough medication?'

'We'll have to go back and restock. Maybe get a nurse to come along, too. You'll come, Tasha, won't you?'

At one stage in her life she would have jumped at the opportunity. But this was different. She didn't need to go if Quinn and a nurse were going. As far as they knew she was just a teacher. They didn't need her. Besides, she wanted to stay here and keep an eye on Abeje. Taking a trip with Quinn was her idea of hell!

'You won't need me.'

'Nonsense! As Abeje's teacher you'll be able to explain why we have to do this. Introduce us to the aunt. Talk to the villagers.'

'I barely know Ada. I've met her maybe once. Perhaps twice.'

'More times than any of us.'

The way he was looking at her was dangerous. As if he *needed* her. *Wanted* her. Desperately. And it was doing strange things to her insides. Confusing things.

Okay, so more hands on deck might help get the medication distributed more quickly, and she couldn't expect him to take many medical personnel from the ship to help. Some of them needed to stay behind. To look after Abeje, for one thing.

She could feel her resolve weakening and she hated that. Just like before, she was being pulled deeper and deeper into Quinn's world.

'Fine. Okay.' She nodded quickly, hating herself for giving in. Imagining already how difficult it would be to spend so much time in his company.

'Great.' He beamed. 'And whilst we're getting there you can tell me how you know me—because I sure as hell can't place where you're from.'

She froze as he walked back outside.

So there *was* something, then. He recognised her as being familiar, but couldn't *place* her.

How would he react when he realised she was *Nit-Nat?* How would he feel? Would he have forgotten what he did? What he'd said? Who she was? How he'd destroyed her little heart in a matter of minutes?

She wanted him to suffer. To feel uncomfortable. To apologise and grovel for her forgiveness…

Part of her wondered if it was better just to pretend she didn't know what he was talking about. To insist that they'd never met before. But a stronger part of her wanted to let him know their connection. Their history. To surprise him and have him see how she had changed. She was no longer a chubby, nit-infested, braces-wearing girl in secondhand clothes.

She had not changed for *him.* She'd just grown up and been battered by life in so many ways. Life had given her plenty of challenges—killing her parents when she was young, making her grow up in a children's home, having Quinn humiliate her, her job destroy her and her marriage break down. And yet she had come through it all. Was still standing. Still able to find joy in her life. To enjoy it. To feel worthwhile.

Was fate, or karma, or whatever it was called, finished messing with her life?

She hoped so. But the fact that she was here and Quinn was here and they were together made her suspect that fate hadn't finished putting her through the wringer just yet.

Tasha stepped out into the sunshine, shielding her eyes from the worst of the sun's rays. She climbed into the vehicle, started the engine and turned to look at him, butterflies somersaulting in her stomach, her mouth dry.

It was time. She had to say it.

*Just say it. Get it out there.*

'You do know me. I'm Tasha Kincaid now—but you might know me by my former name, Natasha Drummond.'

She saw him frown, think, and then his eyebrows rose in surprise as his eyes widened.

'That's right. You're in a car with Nit-Nat.'

# CHAPTER TWO

*NIT-NAT? SHE* WAS *NIT-NAT?*

When she'd first said her name his mind had gone blank. Natasha Drummond? Nit-Nat? He hadn't recognised those names at all. And then a small tickle of a memory had suggested itself. A sense of something appalling. Something he couldn't quite grasp, slippery and evasive. Something about that name being familiar. Something about that name being unpleasant.

Then he'd realised. It was something shameful. A memory he had tried to suppress... And then the memory had become stronger, fiercer, until it was roaring loudly, like a lion, right up in his face, and the hot breath of fetid shame was washing over him as he remembered what he'd once done.

He'd been fifteen years old the first time he'd become aware of her. Although perhaps 'aware' was the wrong word. She'd just been one of the many background faces at the children's home where his best friend Dex had lived.

He'd always been fascinated by them each time he went to the children's home, simply because of what they represented. He was one parent away from being there himself, having been raised by his ex-Marine father be-

cause his mother had walked out on them. The children
at the home had been a bright example of what his life
might have been like if his father had left, too.

He'd gone there for Dex, so that they could play footie,
or rugby, or cricket. Or simply just go for a wander, try
to hook up with girls. He'd never paid much attention to
the other kids at the home, but there had been one stand-
out girl there. But she'd stood out for the wrong reasons.

Overweight, always a bit sweaty-looking, she'd had a
thick mass of hair that had never looked combed. Metal
braces on her teeth.

And the worst thing...? She'd had a crush on him.

Dex had told him.

'Nit-Nat's got the hots for you, mate! You're in trouble!'

'Why do you call her Nit-Nat?'

'She's got bloody nits! They're all caught up in that
mop she calls her hair! They can't escape! I reckon it's
one massive nest!'

He'd wrinkled his nose in disgust. Nits? They were always sending letters from school to parents telling them
to be vigilant against nits. He'd remembered having them
himself once, when he was about seven or eight—not that
he'd been about to tell Dex that.

Dex had had great fun teasing him about Nit-Nat fan-
cying him. It had been a running joke that never seemed
to go away. Quinn had hated it. He'd worked so hard to
perfect his image amongst his friends. He'd wanted to be
known for going with the hottest girls of his year—not
for the disgusting crush Nit-Nat had on him!

He'd tried to laugh it off, tried to ignore it, and he'd
even once got angry with Dex for going on about it. In the
end he'd let it wash over him, pretending to play along,

pretending to be mortified so that the joke wasn't on *him* but on poor, misguided Nit-Nat.

The crush had become more and more obvious each time he'd visited Dex—almost to the point that he hadn't wanted to go there any more and had asked Dex to meet him somewhere else. That had worked for a while. He'd stayed away for a good six months. And then, when even *he* had forgotten about it, he'd made the mistake of calling in on Dex at the children's home.

She hadn't changed. In fact she'd seemed thrilled to see him.

*'Quinn! You're back!'*

She'd beamed a smile, revealing all that metal.

He'd been appalled. *It wasn't over.*

*'Hi.'*

*'You here for Dexter?'*

*'Yep.'*

He hadn't wanted to give her anything. It had been embarrassing, the way she'd stood there—thirteen years old, her hair a frizzy mess and her round body forced into a dress that was at least one size too small. Those buttons had looked as if they were about to burst apart.

*'Haven't seen you for a while.'*

*'I've been busy.'*

*'What with?'*

*'This and that.'*

*'Did you know there's going to be a party this Friday?'*

*'Nope.'*

*'It's for Lexi. She's sixteen. We all get to bring a friend.'*

*'That's nice.'*

*'Would you come as my friend?'*

He'd stared at her in horror, and realised her invitation had been timed perfectly to coincide with Dex's arrival down the stairs.

Quinn had looked at his friend, hoping he hadn't heard, but it had been plain by the look of awesome amusement on Dex's face that he had heard *every word*.

He'd been embarrassed, not at all happy that she'd had shamed him this way again when he'd been trying to be so cool and standoffish. He'd had to make it stop. Had to make that crush of hers end. And the only way he'd known how to do that at the time was to be brutally blunt.

Only it had somehow tipped over into cruelty.

He'd grimaced, walked right up to her.

*'You realise you're ugly, right? And fat? And that there are so many things living in your hair they could do a nature documentary over five seasons?'*

He'd looked her up and down, unaware that loads of the other kids in the home had gathered round to see what all the shouting was about.

*'If you were the last girl on earth I'd probably kill myself!'*

He'd seen the look of horror on her face. The way her cheeks had flushed bright red. The way tears had welled up in her eyes and had begun to run roughly down her ruddy cheeks. And he'd hated what he'd said, but hadn't been able to stop himself.

*'The only boyfriend you could ever get would be a blind one.'*

And then he'd grabbed the gaping, gawking, laughing Dex.

*'Let's go.'*

Dex had ripped into him for hours after that, and he'd spent days feeling angry and ashamed that he'd treated someone like that, made her feel small just so he could maintain his street cred with a friend.

He'd not been brought up to be that way. His dad had raised him to be respectful of women, despite the way his own wife had treated him. He'd been taught never to bring another person down, but instead to make yourself better. Despite his mother walking out on them, he had *never* heard his father badmouth his wife.

And what had he done? Believed his reputation to be more important. Believed that being 'one of the boys' was more important.

He'd never gone back to the children's home after that. He'd not wanted to see the hurt in Nit-Nat's eyes. Not wanted to be reminded of what he'd done. And the only way he'd been able to cope had been to push it to the back of his mind, pretend it had never happened and bury the shame beneath mountains of other stuff. Fighting the urge to go and apologise the way he knew he should.

He hadn't thought about her *for years*. Why would he? He'd been just sixteen when it had happened. She had been thirteen. It was ancient history. So much had happened since then. Other stuff had taken precedence, as was wont to happen in life.

Until now.

He'd never believed they would ever be face to face again. The world was a big place to get lost in.

Quinn sucked in a breath, his heart pounding in his chest, the shame from all those years ago flooding him like a tsunami of regret. He knew what he ought to say. Right now.

*I'm sorry I hurt you. I apologise. I never meant to do it. I hated myself for it.*

'Tasha, I—'

'You know, I *know* we were just kids, but I was thirteen years old. *Thirteen!* You were my first love. The first boy I lost my heart to. Now I know why they call it a crush. Because when you're rejected and humiliated in front of everyone it *feels* like you're being crushed. That's what you did. That's how you made me feel. Tiny. Inconsequential. Stamped on from a great height. You could have just said *No, thanks.* I would have understood.'

He watched as she gunned the engine, put her hand on the gearstick to shove it into first gear.

Quinn laid his hand upon hers. He didn't want her to start driving yet. He had to tell her. Had to let her know.

'I'm so sorry. I behaved appallingly. I know I did. You won't believe me, but I was incredibly ashamed of what I said to you. It haunted me. I wasn't raised to act like that and yet I did, out of some misguided belief that my credibility with my friend was more important than your heart. I felt guilty for ages.'

She yanked her hand out from under his. 'Good. I'm glad.'

'I really am sorry, Tasha. I should never have hurt you.'

'Well, you did.'

She stared at him for a moment, those eyes of hers welling up once again. As the first tear dripped onto her cheek she revved the engine.

'Let's get back to the ship.'

And then she was driving.

He sat in the passenger seat beside her and gazed at her profile as she concentrated on the road. The curls had been tamed and glinted golden in the hot African sun. She had a soft caramel tan and her blue eyes were steely and determined. The set of her jaw showed she meant business and wouldn't take any crap from anyone.

He knew he had to make it up to her. Make up for all the years of hurt and anger she must have carried inside because of him.

Tasha Kincaid—once Natasha Drummond—had certainly grown up. The puppy fat of youth had disappeared with the braces and she'd emerged as a beautiful young woman. A gazelle—long-limbed and graceful. He'd seen the possibility in her back then. But kids were kids and anyone different—fat, bespectacled, red-haired—was an object for their attempts at humour.

He vowed that he would show her the way a woman *deserved* to be treated. That he would be charming, caring and kind. He would build her up and replace her harsh memories of him with something more wonderful.

He hoped he could do that.

He'd originally asked her to go with him to introduce them to Ada and the villagers because he'd wanted to spend more time with this enigmatic woman who knew his name and somehow seemed familiar.

He didn't regret asking her. Because now he knew it was important that she came with them. Because he needed more time with her.

Time to put things right.

Before Quinn's humiliation of her they'd once gone on a trip together. Years ago—when they were children and Tasha's home had organised a visit to the zoo. Everyone had gone along, and somehow Dexter had wangled a place for Quinn on the bus.

The boys had sat at the back, loud and vocal, but Tasha had been at the front, very aware that Quinn was there.

She'd worn her best dress—a pale blue number, with tiny daisies on it—white ankle socks and scuffed patent leather shoes. Hours had been spent in front of the mirror, trying to tame her hair, but the more she'd combed it the frizzier the curls had become, so in the end she'd tied it back with a red bow, wanting to look her best for Quinn. She'd practised her smile in front of the mirror before they left, trying to work out the best way to do it so her braces didn't show too much.

She'd said hi to him when he'd arrived in the morning, barely getting a nod of acknowledgement in return, but that hadn't mattered. She'd offered him a drink and fetched him a glass of juice from the kitchen. He'd taken it, smiled at her and said, *'Thanks, Nit-Nat.'*

Her little teenage heart had almost exploded with excitement. This dashing, handsome, blond-haired young stud had smiled at her! Said her name!

And then he'd said, *'You look nice today.'*

It was the only thing he'd got to say to her before they'd left but she'd dined out on that compliment for days. It had warmed her. Had made her feel good. All gooey inside and yet shy. He'd liked her dress. Liked what she'd done to her hair. She vowed to do her hair like that all the time if he liked it that way.

She'd wanted to turn and smile at him on the bus but she hadn't, knowing that Dexter would wind her up about it, so she'd spent the trip staring out of the window, intently listening to everything she could—hoping that he might be talking about her in a nice way.

He never had been.

Her day had been spent half looking at the giraffes and the wolves and the lions and monkeys, and half sneaking glances at Quinn and having little hopeful dreams about their future together. She'd wished she had a camera, so she could take his picture and put it in her bedroom.

He'd wanted to be a doctor and so had she. She'd imagined them working together at the same hospital. They would save lives! He would look at her after a long day together and thank her, and give her a hug, and then they would go home together, because of course they would be married. And at home it would be even more blissful than at work. She would have beautiful little blonde-haired children, with big blue eyes, and they would take them with them on their many trips around the globe.

None of that had ever happened, of course.

But here they were today. Together again. In Africa. Hopefully off to save some lives.

Maybe all she'd ever needed to do was wait?

It didn't take him long to inform the personnel on the ship of what they were doing. The staff seemed excited about the idea of a road trip, and as they busied themselves in preparation for a possible mass vaccination Tasha found a moment to check on Abeje.

She was asleep. Sweat beaded her brow and pooled in the dip at the base of her throat. Her breathing was rapid.

Tasha laid a hand against the little girl's skin and winced at the heat. *Poor thing.* She let out a breath and took a moment to centre herself. She could remember being poorly as a young child herself, with no one to sit by her bed, to soothe her brow or just to give her cuddles and goodnight kisses. It had been so lonely.

Quinn knew who she was now. It was an even playing field. And, though she'd been worried about telling him who she was, now that it was out in the open she felt glad. He had a lot of making up to do if he was ever going to be in her good books again. He'd apologised, but that was too little, too late.

*You should never have hurt me in the first place.*

He deserved to spend some time wriggling on the end of her hook. She knew she ought to be gracious and allow him to show her who he was *now*. They *had* both been children. But…

He'd always said he was going to be a doctor. Always said he was going to travel the world. And here he was, doing just that. She liked it that he had stuck to his grand plan and was doing something worthwhile and noble. It showed her he wasn't still that cruel teenage boy he had once been. That there was more to him now.

It would have been so easy for him to have stayed working in a hospital in the UK, with modern equipment and civilisation and technology all around him, but no. He had come out here. To treat the needy, to give aid to those who had none.

That was a good thing to do, wasn't it? Heroic?

*So you get some Brownie points, Quinn. I get that you're not all bad.*

Tasha reached for Abeje's hand as a nurse, Rowan, came up to her.

'She's doing okay. I know it looks like nothing is happening, but we have to wait for the medications to work.'

Her Irish accent was lilting and musical. Even reassuring in a homely way.

'How long should that take?'

'It depends how long she'd been sick for, before we got the meds on board. The parasite she has in her system is quite an aggressive one.'

'It could kill her.' It wasn't a question. Tasha knew the risks of this parasite.

'We need to hope for the best.'

Rowan was not saying yes or no. Not promising that everything would be all right.

Tasha knew how to do that. She'd done it herself. But she'd never realised just how frustrating it sounded when she was on the receiving end of it. When you were worried sick about someone you needed someone in charge to tell you it would be okay. That they wouldn't die. This vagueness, the non-promise, was devastating, but as a doctor she'd always assumed her vague answer would be comforting. Would give hope.

'Will you keep an eye on her whilst I'm gone?' she asked Rowan.

'Of course. There won't be any change for a while, so it's probably best that you're out there doing something else. It'll help keep your mind off it.'

Tasha wasn't sure that was true. She was hardly going to forget Abeje. The little girl was almost like a daughter. Not that she'd ever had one. But she definitely wanted children some day, and this was how she imagined it to be—worrying constantly. Fearing for their wellbeing.

'You'll contact me on the radio if there's any change?'

'Of course I will. It's a good thing you're doing. Going to help those villagers.'

Tasha nodded and Rowan walked away. It felt strange to her that she was going out with a medical team. It had been such a long time since she'd walked in their shoes, and it felt a little terrifying to be returning to it.

The last time she'd made a field trip with a hospital team had been out to the London bombings, back in 2005. There had been carnage. Injured people lying in the streets. Blood. Screams. She shuddered just remembering it.

What would they find in Mosa? A whole village wiped out? One or two people ill? Everyone healthy?

She hoped for the latter. Steepling her hands, she closed her eyes and began to pray to whatever god might be listening.

The *Serendipity* had a truck. Quinn and Tasha sat up front and two of the ship's nurses sat in the back, along with all the medical equipment and drugs they might need. It was a two-hour drive to the village from Ntembe, and if they got out there by mid-afternoon they could have everyone vaccinated by late evening—in time to drive home again. If people were sick they'd brought tents to stay in overnight.

Quinn was driving, his muscular forearms wrestling with the wheel as it reacted to the rough road surface.

'So, tell me something good.'

Tasha looked across at him. Something *good*? Sure. She could do that. In fact she yearned to make him see that she was happy and successful. That what he'd done had not had any profound effect on her life. That it had not left her scrambling for any scraps of self-esteem she might have had left. Yes, he'd torn her down, but she had rebuilt herself and done so in spite of him.

'Qualifying as a teacher was a good day.'

He smiled, nodding. 'That's great! Which uni did you go to?'

'I did my PGCE at Kingston.'

'Fantastic! You must have felt very proud when you passed.'

She had. But not as proud as she had been when she'd qualified as a doctor. That had been after many years of hard work—not just one. But he didn't know that teaching had been her second choice. Her fall-back position.

'It was a lot of hard work. Lots of essays.'

'Universities *do* like those essays and dissertations.' He smiled again. 'Tell me what it felt like the first time you had to stand in front of a class of kids.'

She sighed, thinking back to her first placement. The one that had almost made her quit. The out-of-control kids, their jeering and taunts. It had reminded her of how she'd felt once before.

'The first one was awful. They send you out on two-week placements during training. It was like putting a kitten in front of a pack of baying, rabid dogs. The students were awful. Teenage boys. Laughing and disrespectful. On my first day I ended up running from the room in tears.'

She didn't add that she'd felt particularly raw to teasing from teenage boys. Surely he must understand that? That she'd been weakened by him from the get-go and had never stood a chance? How it had made her feel like she was Nit-Nat all over again.

'I'm sorry.'

'It wasn't your fault, was it?'

But maybe it was? Maybe he'd made her ripe for the picking? Those boys had sensed her nerves. Her weakness. One of her first lecturers had talked about *showing no fear*. Said that some kids were like packs of hyenas, looking to wear a newbie teacher down.

'No, but…'

'My second placement was much better. Great kids—attentive. Determined to do well. The contrast in the two places really surprised me, but it was a lesson for me to persevere. I could so easily have given up after that first experience, but I think, in a way, that you toughened me up. I was determined to carry on and succeed. Lippy teenage boys weren't going to ruin my life.'

He nodded. Smiled. 'Lippy teenage boys are mostly cowards. Perhaps the only way they knew to deal with someone better than them, was to try and tear them down.'

She smiled back. 'Well, they failed.'

'I'm very glad to hear it.' He was solemn.

'What was it like the first time you had to treat a patient?'

He laughed, clearly relieved that the conversation had taken a brighter turn. 'Awful! I took the patient's history okay, but then I had to take a blood sample. Something I'd done in practice many times, that I thought I was good at, but I couldn't find a vein. The guy was like a voodoo doll by the time I'd finished with him.'

She smiled, imagining it. Remembering the first time *she'd* taken blood from a real, live patient. She'd actually done okay, even though her hands had been shaking with nerves. And her patient, a wonderful old lady, had been so kind to her. *'Everyone has to learn, ducky,'* she'd said.

'Ever lost someone?'

The question just came out, and the second it did—the second she realised what she'd said out loud—her cheeks flamed hot. Why had she said that? Why had she asked? Of *course* he was going to say yes. *Every* doctor had had someone die on them.

'Too many,' he answered politically. Non-specific. No details. Answering but not telling her anything. 'It's hard. You tell yourself you're ready. Your lecturers and mentors try to prepare you. But...'

Tasha stared at the road ahead, terracotta sand and

rocks, scrubby bushes and thorny trees. A chorus of insects could be heard faintly above the roar of the engine.

'You can never be ready for loss.'

She looked at him. At the rigid set of his bristled jaw. His knuckles tight upon the steering wheel. He'd been the one who had first introduced her to loss. To pain and grief. She'd thought she'd known what that was, not having parents. But he'd provided her with insight into another kind with his hurtful words.

Perhaps he was right? Perhaps he *had* been a coward? Afraid to let his friend Dex see him as someone else.

'No,' she answered. 'You can't.'

The village of Mosa hoved into view just after four in the afternoon. It wasn't big—twenty or thirty homes at the most. Large brown cattle grazed by the side of the dirt road and the villagers working in the fields stopped their work to stare at the truck as they drove past. They probably didn't get a lot of visitors.

Quinn parked the truck and they all got out gladly, pleased to stretch their legs and work the kinks from their muscles. It hadn't been a long drive, but it had been a hot one, with the air-conditioning in the truck temperamental.

Tasha smiled at one of the villagers. 'Hello. My name is Tasha, and this is Dr Shapiro and his two nurses. We're looking for Ada Balewa.'

The villager stared at her for a moment, and then silently pointed to a hut further down.

She beamed a smile. 'Thank you.'

Together they walked down the track, towards the primitive hut that had been indicated.

'Ada Balewa?' she called out.

A small woman emerged from the depths of the hut, wrapped in a brown dress, frowning. 'Yes? Ah! Miss Tasha!'

Tasha smiled and greeted Ada with a hug. 'You're looking well.'

The other woman frowned again. 'Yes, I am, but I do not think that is why you are here.'

This was the part that Tasha had been dreading.

'Abeje is poorly. She was bitten by a mosquito and now she's sick with malaria. We have her in a hospital ship, but we thought maybe there might be some other people sick here. Can you tell us if anyone has a fever?'

Ada nodded. 'Yes. A boy and a girl.'

'Could we see them? We've brought medicine.'

'I will take you to them.'

They followed Ada—Tasha, Quinn and the two nurses, Maria and Rob. As they walked Ada asked about Abeje. Tasha told her what she could. That everything was being done for her.

'I wish I could see her.'

'If there's room we could take you back with us.'

'I have my own children here. Crops to tend. I cannot leave.'

'Then try not to worry. We'll do our best for her.'

'Thank you.'

The boy and girl that Ada had spoken of were brother and sister. The boy twelve, the younger girl nine. They were sweating and had been sick.

Quinn was quickly by their side. 'Let's do the rapid tests—double-check this is what we think it is. In the meantime let's get them on IVs so they don't dehydrate.'

Tasha stood back and watched him work. He was a true professional. She'd seen it before with Abeje and now she saw it again as he cared for these two siblings side by side. They were conscious, so he spoke to them, keeping his words simple in case their English wasn't good. He smiled. Explained what he was doing. Told them not to be afraid.

Even if they didn't understand his words they would at least understand his kind, caring tone. His unthreatening behaviour. His empathy and desire to help. It was good for her to see it. This side of him. It gave her hope.

She wished she could do more. Instead she silently watched as he worked, anticipating and expecting his every move. His care of the two siblings was exactly what she would have done herself. It was hard to stand back and do nothing.

The rapid tests confirmed malaria so he started the anti-malarials. When he'd done, he turned back to Ada. 'Is anyone else sick?'

'No.'

'I really don't want to leave these children here. They need urgent care. Would you allow me to take them back to the ship?'

Ada nodded. 'I will speak to their parents.'

She disappeared from the hut.

Tasha stood in the doorway, afraid to stay, afraid to leave. 'Is it wise to move them right now?'

He frowned. 'We won't do it straight away. I'd like them to get fluids on board first. We might have to stay here the night. Give them time to rest...get them stable before we move them.'

She'd known it might be a possibility when she came, but she'd hoped they'd be lucky enough to escape with a quick visit. Now she would have to spend the night out here with Quinn.

Tasha gave him a nervous smile. 'I'll go and tell Rob. Maybe get started on setting up those tents?'

She went to find the nurse. Rob was standing by the truck with Maria. It looked as if they were counting the medicines.

'There's more than enough here to inoculate the entire village.'

Tasha smiled. 'Anything I can do to help?'

'It's probably best if we gather everyone in the same spot to explain what we want to do. Then we can set up a line and treat everyone.'

She nodded. It did seem the best idea. 'I told Quinn we'd get the tents set up for an overnight stay, too.'

'Good idea. Perhaps we all ought to get something to eat, as well,' Maria added.

The tents went up easily—even though Tasha had never put one up in her life. Rob was clear on the instructions and they worked well together as a team. Tasha cracked open some bottles of water, so they could hydrate underneath the hot African sun. Even though it was evening, and everything was a little cooler, they still poured with sweat.

She looked out over the horizon at the vast emptiness, the grey, stony mountains in the distance. It was so different here from in Ntembe. At the port city there was always a sea breeze blowing in—there always seemed to be air and noise and life. Here in Mosa it seemed more solitary, more empty. Quieter. She missed the busyness of people. The safety of numbers.

As she hugged her arms to herself Quinn came to stand alongside.

'You all right?'

'I've only ever known Ntembe. I thought I knew more. Thought I knew Africa. But I don't.'

'It's a place that can always surprise you. Its capacity to inspire, to fear, to amaze, will always keep you on your toes.'

She looked at him. 'How are the children doing?'

'As well as can be expected. I think they were infected earlier than Abeje. They're sicker.'

Fear welled in her gut. 'Are they going to die?'

'Not if I can help it.'

He stared at her, determination in every feature.

The inoculation line was long, but each and every villager had turned up to receive medication. Tasha could see that Quinn was very happy about that. Neither of them would have liked to leave anyone out, and Ada had been instrumental in speaking to the villagers *en masse* and getting their understanding and trust, translating to those who didn't understand English very well.

They sat around a small campfire later in the evening, drinking coffee with Maria and Rob, who soon disappeared for an early night, leaving Tasha and Quinn alone.

'They're a couple,' Quinn explained after the two nurses had left to share a tent.

That left one other tent. One *small* tent. For Quinn and Tasha to share.

She hadn't realised the two nurses were together. When she'd seen two tents in the back of the truck and then erected them she'd figured that the two men would share one and she and Maria the other. But obviously that wasn't going to be happening, and she felt apprehensive about being in such a small space with him.

'Oh. You knew we would have to share?'

'Yes. But I can sleep in the truck if that's a problem. I promise you I can be perfectly trusted to keep my hands to myself.'

He poked at the fire with a stick, creating sparks, unaware of the physical ones he was sparking within her.

The idea of Quinn Shapiro letting his hands roam over her body made her feel infinitely hotter than the African sun could ever do. Right now she needed less of a fire and more like a bucket of ice water. She was imagining him looking intently into her eyes as they both lay on the ground, facing each other...

*Oh, dear Lord...*

She took a sip of scalding coffee and winced.

Beyond the light of the fire the nocturnal noises of the bush had begun—insects, hyenas, and she even thought she heard the roar of an elephant from somewhere. Miles away, but instantly recognisable.

She was surrounded by primal beasts. There could be tigers out there, lions, predators of all shapes and sizes. But she was only afraid of the man opposite her.

*Okay, maybe not afraid of him. But afraid of how he's making me feel.*

Her teenage self would have screamed with glee at the idea of spending a night with Quinn Shapiro in a tiny tent. But her adult self was more cautious. So many years had passed since she'd last known him and she knew that *she'd* filled in the intervening years with a lot of baggage. Had he? Apart from his childhood, she hardly knew anything about him. He could still be a jerk, for all she knew. Just because he *said* he wasn't, it was hardly a guarantee.

'So, what did you get up to after we lost touch?' she asked, determined to maintain eye contact, to see if he got shifty, or lied, or tried to evade her question.

But he looked straight back at her. 'School, college, medical training—all the usual suspects.'

'Ever get married?' Her pulse was thrumming like jungle drums in her ears, sweat beading her upper lip.

*We've got to share a tent.*

He blinked, the twinkle in his eyes fading as a shadow passed over his soul. 'I did. You?'

*So...there* is *something you're not telling me...*

'I did too.'

She thought back to the day she'd stood in that small register office and made her vows to Simon. They'd been so happy. Or at least *she* had, believing their vows would tie them together for ever. But the only vow Simon had truly honoured was his Hippocratic Oath.

'Well, I think we both tried to skip past that answer as quickly as we could, didn't we?' He grimaced, poking at the fire once again.

'Do you want to talk about it?'

'Do you?'

No, she did not. She did *not* want to tell Quinn about how her marriage had failed and destroy the image she was trying to create for herself. Successful, happy, teacher Natasha. That was what she wanted him to see and believe.

She'd always told herself that if she ever did run into Quinn Shapiro again she would make him see her as wonderful, glamorous and successful. Happy and content. She did not want to go down the road that had led to her marriage going down the pan.

'I think I'll get some rest. It's been a long, eventful day,' she said.

He smiled, not challenging her answer. 'It has. Get some sleep. Goodnight, Tasha.'

'Goodnight, Quinn.'

And she headed for the tent, hoping and praying she'd be fast asleep before he turned in.

Quinn hadn't got much sleep. He'd got up in the night a couple of times to check on the two children and change their IVs for fresh ones. Each time he had sneaked back into the tent and just lain there, thinking about his wife, Hannah.

He tried not to, as a rule. Thinking about Hannah made him feel unstable. Rage and grief would bubble up, making him feel angry and vengeful. He didn't like the feeling that thinking of her could make him lose control at any minute. He didn't like the chaos inside him when he thought about Hannah.

So he did what he'd been taught to do by his father—pushed it all inside. Stamped it down.

*'Boys don't cry!'* his father had said. *'You stay strong—like a man.'*

Being strong. Gritting his teeth, thinking of other things, had worked. In fact his job had helped him the most. There were always sick people needing help. There were always lives he *could* save, even if he hadn't been able to save hers.

*Theirs.*

He swallowed and looked away from Tasha, not allowing himself to think of his wife and child. How odd that he had come all this way and found Nit-Nat. It had all started with this girl. The rules he had set down for his life had all begun with her.

*Don't hurt anyone.*

*Always heal.*

*Always save life.*

*Saving the many could save you.*

And Tasha lay beside him, unaware of just how much she had affected him back then.

She probably believed that he had been nonchalant about what he'd said. That he'd just walked off with Dex and forgotten about it, or bragged about it. *Laughed* about it. But he hadn't. He'd brooded on it for days, weeks, months.

He'd hated the terrible feelings he'd had inside—feelings that he'd caused through his own callous, unthinking behaviour. He'd wished he could apologise, but when he'd finally got up the strength to go back there, to face her and tell her he was sorry for what he'd said that day, Dex had told him that she'd been fostered out.

She'd never come back after that. His chance had been gone. And so he'd sat outside that home on a brick wall, underneath the window that had been hers, and he had vowed, out loud, that he would never hurt a living soul ever again. He had hoped, somehow, that she would *feel* the sense of his vow. That his earnest feelings would somehow carry across the world, through time and space to wherever she was, and somehow make her feel better.

Now she was by his side. Asleep, her face in repose, those curls spread out on the red ground sheet, her pale freckles masking her nose and eyes, her nose upturned at the end in a gentle slope, her lips full and parted...

The urge to kiss her came out of the blue.

He sat up abruptly, startled by the feeling. He crawled from the tent and stood outside, stretching, sucking in the morning air, and decided the best thing for him and Tasha was to have a little space between them. If he'd kissed her she would have been startled, for one, but would she also have thought that he was somehow pitying her, or something? Making up for those years lost in a childhood crush?

*Whatever. It's crazy whichever way I think about it.*

But as he marched across the campsite, towards the hut that contained the two ill children, his mind wrestled with images of her face in serene sleep. How much it meant to him to have her by his side. To have a chance to put right the things that had haunted him.

And to know just what it might feel like to take her in his arms…

# CHAPTER THREE

TASHA WAS IMPRESSED with the speed at which Quinn worked. Watching him was fascinating. Almost hypnotic.

They'd set up two small cots on the flatbed of the truck, rearranging their equipment and medicines so that there was room for the two children, their parents and the two nurses. Then they stood and said goodbye to those that had gathered.

'We've done what we can, Ada. We'll try and get this family back to Mosa as quickly as possible.'

'Thank you so much. Please hug Abeje for me. She is very precious. My sister's only child.'

'Of course.' Tasha gave the woman a hug and then they all got back into the truck so they could head back to the ship. They leaned out of the windows and waved as Quinn turned the truck in the opposite direction and began to drive.

He seemed different this morning. More work-focused, if that were possible. When she'd woken he'd been gone, and she'd fought with feelings of relief and disappointment.

There'd been some anxiety in her about what waking up with Quinn might be like. Would it be awkward? Would he tell her that she snored and talked in her sleep, as Simon had always complained? But then opening her eyes and finding him gone had been sad, too. Part of her had wanted to wake up and see his face on the pillow next to hers. She'd wanted the chance to lie there and study his face, to look at the man Quinn had become. So many years had passed...

The road was as bumpy as she remembered, and for the first few miles she said nothing, just stared ahead through the windscreen, occasionally looking out and spotting gazelles, or scavenger birds whirling in the sky, soaring on the morning thermals. But the silence in the truck was wearing her down. Yesterday he'd asked her lots of questions. Today he was like a monk who had taken a vow of silence. What had changed?

'Did you...er...sleep okay?'

He shrugged. 'A bit. I got up a few times to check on the children. Changed their IVs. I got a few hours.'

'I can drive if you want the chance to get some more shut-eye.'

'Thanks, but I'm okay. It's only two hours to Ntembe.'

'And when we get back you'll have a long work-day. You'll be exhausted.'

'Awake enough to look after my patients—don't worry.' He smiled. 'Doctors have survived on less sleep than this.'

Survived, yes. Thought clearly? No.

'And that's when accidents happen.'

She didn't want to think about her own mistake. The sequence of events that had led to her quitting medicine. It was exactly this kind of ill-advised bravado that Quinn was gushing that caused tragedies in the first place. She should know. And they were returning to the boat, where he would have to look after not only Abeje but the two children currently in the back of this truck.

'Stop the truck and let me drive.'

'Honestly, I'm fine.'

'Quinn! Stop the damned truck!'

He frowned, turning to look at her. 'Are you okay?'

'I'll be better knowing that you've had some decent rest before we get back to that ship.'

'If you're worried about my ability to look after Abeje, I can reassure you—'

'Reassurances mean nothing, Quinn. They're just words. Would you *please* put my mind at rest and allow me to drive?'

He thought about it for a moment. Checked his watch. Looked at the road ahead. Then he gave her one last look. 'You're sure?'

'I'm *very* sure.'

Quinn pulled the truck to a stop, the brakes screeching in protest.

Tasha had taken over the driving, but he felt a little confused by how angry she'd got. He sat in the passenger seat, frowning, wondering if she thought he would be a danger to Abeje.

'What was that all about?'

'Nothing. I was just being safety conscious, that's all.'

'So that was just you being a teacher and doing... what...a risk assessment for the trip?'

'Not just the trip, no. I want you on good form and well rested when you get back to the *Serendipity.*'

'You don't think I'll look after Abeje well enough?'

She let out a sigh. 'I'm sure you will, but doctors work long hours and push themselves when they really ought to take a break, and exhaustion can have an effect on their decision-making skills. If anyone's health suddenly took a turn for the worst I'd want your brain firing on all cylinders and not just one or two because you think you're Super Doc.'

'I can assure you I never think of myself as that.'

He turned away and closed his eyes, welcoming the opportunity to get the rest she was offering him. It *had* been a long night and he had lied. He hadn't got one or two hours' sleep at all. He'd barely got forty winks. He'd been up and down, checking on his patients, and in between staring at Tasha as she slept, trying to work out how she made him feel. How much he needed to do to repair their past.

'Good. So do me a favour and shut up and sleep.'

He smiled sleepily, feeling exhaustion slowly claim him. The warmth of the day, the rocking of the vehicle, the hum of the engine...all served to lull him into unconsciousness.

He didn't wake until the screech of the brakes woke him again, and they were portside to the *Serendipity*.

No one could have been more happy to see the *Serendipity* than Tasha was. She wanted to see Abeje, and she wanted to know the two children in the truck would be in a hospital, where they ought to be. She was also exhausted herself. It had been a long two days. She was tired, hungry and thirsty. And she was covered in dirt from the road. She needed a shower. She must look a sight.

Next to her, Quinn yawned and stretched.

'Wake up, sleepyhead. We're back.'

He smiled, rolling his shoulders, working out the kinks. 'You got us back here in one piece, then?'

'I *can* drive a truck. Does that surprise you?'

'No. I'm sure you have all kinds of skills I know nothing about.'

Tasha looked down at her hands.

*You'd be surprised.*

'I'd like to come on board and see Abeje before I head off to work. Is that okay?'

'Sure. We've got staff showers you can use if you want to freshen up.'

She ran her hands through her hair and her curls released a spray of red dust around her in a halo. 'I think that's probably a good idea. I must look a sight.'

'You look absolutely fine.'

Fine? *Fine?* That was almost as bad as *You look nice.* Damning with faint praise. But what else was he going to say to her? That she looked gorgeous? Beautiful? Stunning?

'Thanks.'

But she flinched backwards as he leant in towards her, his hand reaching out. *What is he doing?* She could feel herself begin to panic. Her breathing increased, her heart pounded, her mouth went painfully dry.

His fingertip swiped a line of red dust from the slope of her nose.

He wiped the dust on his shirt and grinned at her, opening the truck door to get out. 'You've got half the road on you.'

And then he disappeared out of her sight to go to the back of the truck.

Tasha sat there for a moment, steadying her breathing, wondering just what the hell was going on in her insides.

He just had to look at her, smile at her, touch the tip of her nose and her body went into overdrive!

What was *that* all about? Was her body still remembering the crush she'd had on him? Or was this something new? Something infinitely more powerful? More primal?

Perhaps it was something she ought to be afraid of…

Tasha's shower made her feel more human. She stood under the cool spray and let the water run off her body, revelling in the refreshing flow until she suddenly remembered she had a class to teach today and there was no time for standing around.

She towel-dried her hair, wincing at the wildness of her curls, and then headed off to check on Abeje.

There'd been no change. Not for the better, anyway. Abeje was sleeping, so Tasha went to check on the other two children.

'How are they doing?' she asked Quinn, patting down her hair, hoping it wasn't going crazy and wild in the heat.

'They're stable.'

*Stable.* Another one of those medical terms that was so politically correct. Neither giving hope nor taking it away. So no one could be blamed.

'Have you done the bloods?'

'Yes. We've just sent them off to the path lab.'

'They're on the chloroquine and ACTs?'

He nodded, looking at her strangely.

She folded her arms, a surge of frustration flooding her body at not being able to do anything to help except watch and wait as Quinn took the children's observations, marking them on a chart.

Temperature. Blood pressure. Heart-rate. Respirations. Oxygen saturations.

Numbers. Always numbers deciding someone's chances. Numbers and statistics had ruled her life at the children's home, too—the chances of being adopted as a teenager, the likelihood of girls being preferred to boys, the fact that the longer you stayed in a home, the less chance you'd have of being adopted.

The day she'd turned thirteen her hopes of being adopted had plummeted. No one would take her. No one had wanted her in all these years—why would they take on an unruly teenager? Each day had added to the fact, depressing her, and only her crush on Quinn had brightened her day.

Looking at him now, just on the other side of the bed from her, reminded her of what it had been like to watch him as a young girl. He'd always seemed so out of reach. So unattainable.

'I'd better get back. I've got a full day of teaching.'

'Well, you're welcome to come and check on your young charge whenever you've got a spare moment.'

'I'll come round straight after I finish—later today.'

'Great. Maybe we could have a coffee or something?'

She flushed. She couldn't help it. Years ago she would have bitten his hand off in excitement. Now she was more wary, worried about what it might mean.

'A coffee?'

'No strings. Just two old friends spending time together after a long day.'

'I don't know…'

'Come on, Tash. We've both changed. We're both different now. We've moved on. Let's not dwell on the past.'

'The past is what's made me who I am today.'

He smiled. 'And I'd love to know more about who you *are* today. Give me the chance.'

That smile… That smile of his was powerful. Did he realise what it did to her insides? She could still see that sixteen-year-old boy in that smile, but there was also the man too—and boy, oh, boy, that man had a come-to-bed smile.

She was scared. Her entire body felt his pull, but the logical part of her mind was desperately trying to remind her of how cruel he had once been. How much he had hurt her.

But didn't he deserve a chance to show her that he was different?

She nodded quickly, before she could change her mind. 'Okay. Coffee.'

He smiled. 'Great. I'll see you later.'

As she walked away all she could think of was *him*. The time they'd spent together so far. The way their pasts bound them. All that had gone before…all that was still unwritten.

Her feelings for him were strong, but what *were* they, exactly? Friendship? Attraction?

It was hard to ignore the fact that she still felt attracted to Quinn. Because she'd rather hoped that all these years of thinking of him as the bad guy would have wiped out the teenage crush that had begun all those many moons ago.

Was this a bad idea? Was agreeing to coffee the wrong thing to do? Their relationship was from the past—perhaps it was best to leave it there? Undisturbed.

*I think it's too late.*

She was already involved. She was already *disturbed*. She couldn't help it.

She was drawn to him, wanting to know more about him, about what he'd done in all these years. If he'd ever thought about her, the things he'd accomplished, his dreams for the future. And she realised, as she sat at home with a cup of tea, that she wanted to share the details of her life with him, too. She wanted to talk to him about stuff. Things she'd done, things she'd seen, places she'd gone to.

He was her only connection to childhood. Her strongest memory.

He felt like home.

Abeje was awake when Tasha returned to the ship in the evening, and even managed to give her a small smile.

'Oh, you're awake! Hi, you. How are you feeling? You really had me worried.' She bent over and gave her a small kiss on the cheek.

'I'm tired, Miss Tasha.'

Tasha stroked the hair back from her face. Abeje's skin still felt hot to the touch, but not as bad as it had yesterday.

'Of course you are, sweetpea. But you've been getting some good medicine. You know where you are?'

'The ship.'

'That's right.'

She felt so much relief that Abeje was awake and talking. That her eyes looked clear and bright and that the anti-malarials Quinn had given her seemed to be working. She knew they weren't out of the woods yet, but maybe they'd got to Abeje early and stopped the parasites in their tracks?

'We did some creative writing today in class. Everyone wrote stories. They were really wonderful. You'd have liked that.'

Abeje smiled and then closed her eyes. When she was

sure she'd gone to sleep Tasha got up from her bedside and pulled the curtain around her to give the little girl some peace and quiet.

The ward was quite busy. They had the three children in this ward, and next door they'd had some new patients come in, to whom Quinn had been called.

She figured if they were going to get a coffee it was certainly going to be a late one. Perhaps it would be best if she just left him to it? They could grab a coffee another day.

Reluctantly, she headed off the boat, and was thinking about going home and grabbing something to eat when she heard her name being called.

Quinn was waving to her from the deck. 'You bailing on me, Tasha Kincaid?'

She face lit up without her realising it. 'Not at all! I just thought you were busy.'

'I'm done! Hold fire and I'll be down in a minute.' He disappeared from view and she stood there like a young girl again, feeling all silly and excited, waiting for a boy.

*The* boy. Quinn Shapiro.

*What am I doing?*

She tried to remind herself that she was a grown woman, with a lot of water under the bridge. She tucked a stray curl behind her ears and sat on a wooden crate beside the dock as she waited.

Soon enough Quinn joined her, wearing a fresh blue linen shirt and khaki trousers. 'Hi. Ready to grab a coffee?'

'Actually, I'm starving. Could we get something to eat, too?'

'I wouldn't say no to that.' He smiled and took her arm, guiding her towards a small dusty and rusty car.

'This is yours?'

'Well, we're not stealing it.' He grinned, holding the door for her to get in.

It looked old. Dilapidated. As if he'd picked it up from a scrapyard rather than a dealership. Foam was bursting out of the torn seats.

'Does it work?'

'Like a dream. The aesthetic helps to deter thieves.'

Hesitantly, she got in, reluctant to touch anything in case it came off in her hand.

He got in beside her and started the engine. It fired first time.

Tasha looked out of the window and smiled.

*What am I doing?* she thought again.

Quinn drove them through Ntembe, occasionally having to sound his horn to clear the way, sometimes sticking his arm out of the window to wave and say hello to people he knew. He seemed popular.

'How long have you been here?' she asked.

'Only a couple of days.'

'But the entire port seems to know you.'

'We've docked here many times.'

Which meant he'd left many times, too. 'How long are you here for?'

'A month.'

A month! So in a few weeks he'd be gone again?

She wasn't ready for the onslaught of disappointment that hit her like a freak wave.

*People always leave me.*

'Where will you go next?'

'Madagascar is our next port of call.'

'Oh.'

He looked at her. 'Will you miss me?'

She looked away from him, out of the window at the passing streets, still filled with people on their way home from long working days.

'I haven't been with you long enough to miss you.'

The atmosphere in the car had changed. She appreciated that he was trying to be bright and perky, friendly and amiable, but she wasn't sure if she could cope with that from him yet.

'Maybe we should just stick with coffee,' she said.

Quinn quickly pulled over.

She turned to look at him and ask why. 'What are you doing?'

'I want to know what's wrong.'

'Nothing's wrong.'

'So why do you want only coffee now?'

Exasperated, she undid her seat belt and got out of the car. He'd stopped by a small field of what looked like sweetcorn. Between her and the field was a small irrigation ditch that smelt quite dank and dirty. It made her think about mosquitoes and malaria and sick children. About Abeje lying in her hospital bed, weak and feeble, whilst she was out gallivanting with a man who, by rights, she really ought not to be talking to.

And then there were thoughts of another child. A child she hadn't been able to save. She hugged her arms around her body, haunted by the past.

She heard Quinn get out, too and then he was by her side. 'What's wrong? Come on, Nit-Nat, you can tell me,' he said in a soft voice.

Tasha shook her head, angry. 'Don't call me that.'

'Tasha.' He stood in front of her, forcing eye contact.

'I don't know. I don't *know* what's wrong! I'm on a rollercoaster with you, Quinn! There's no straight and steady…it's all ups and downs! We shouldn't be here. We should be back with those children. Healing them.'

He considered her for a moment. 'There's nothing we can do at the moment but wait.'

'It's not enough. There must be more we can do! I hate feeling helpless. Useless. It feels horrible.'

'Hey…' He lifted her chin with his finger, wiped away the tear that had begun to trickle down her cheek. 'It's okay.'

She had to ignore the sensation of his soft thumb sweeping across her skin. 'Is it? How do we know we're doing enough?'

'Because I *know* we are. You have to trust me.'

She stared back at him, confusion, hurt and anger blustering through her with the force of a storm. Buffeted by emotions she didn't want to feel. 'That's what it all comes down to, isn't it? Whether I trust you.'

He stared back at her. 'Well, *do* you?'

'I don't know. I want to, but…'

'Well, that's a start. It wasn't a no.' He smiled. 'Give me a chance—that's all I ask. A chance to prove to you that you can trust me.'

She looked up into his face. Into the face that had haunted her dreams for years. A face that seemed open and kind. The face of the man she so wanted to believe in.

She'd really like to close the door upon her pain. It had hurt for too long. Here was a chance. A chance to change that hurt into something positive. If it went wrong, what would she have lost? Nothing. But if it went right...

'Okay. One chance.'

He smiled. Nodded. 'That's all I need.'

They found a little café that neither of them had been to before and went in. The Coffee Bean was small and intimate, but it offered hot food, and it was open till late, so they decided to chance it. The tables were old Formica, their surfaces indented with scratches, but the flowers on each table were real, their scent competing with the aroma of the food. Somewhere amongst the din music played from a radio.

Quinn and Tasha sat by the open door, so they could feel the evening breeze.

'So...what *really* made you come to Africa, Quinn? What made you think, *Okay, I'm going to leave the UK and head out on a hospital ship*?'

He laughed, but it wasn't a happy, genuine one. She watched his face carefully, wondering what nerve she'd just hit and how he was going to answer. It would have to be the truth. She would know if it wasn't.

'I needed a change. A challenge.'

'You were an A&E doctor?' That hadn't been her specialty. She'd trained in paediatrics. Thinking that caring for kids would add some joy to her day.

Quinn nodded.

'I would have thought A&E was challenging enough.'

'It was. I just...' His voice drifted away and his fingers fidgeted with the condiment pots on the table. 'English schools not enough of a challenge for *you*?'

She nodded. 'They were...'

'But...?'

Tasha smiled. 'But we were talking about *you*. You asked me to give you a chance and I am. I need to know more about you. What makes you tick.'

'I was married, as I said before,' he replied, looking directly at her. 'And it didn't end well and I... I just needed to get away.'

'How long did it last?'

Quinn let out a sigh. 'Eighteen months.'

*One and a half years? I wonder what happened?*

'I'm sorry.'

She sensed there was more, but he obviously wasn't ready to tell her just yet. Maybe if he knew something about *her*...?

'I was married to Simon. He was a doctor,' she explained, leaving out the fact that she'd been one, too. 'We had a whirlwind relationship, which initially started with a whole lot of lust and secret assignations in linen cupboards. We got caught once, which was embarrassing, by a nurse who'd come to fetch some clean pillowcases.'

Quinn smiled at her.

'We both seemed to want the same things. It was exciting, and thrilling, and so when he asked me to marry him I said yes and we went to our nearest registry office and did the deed, with two witnesses off the street.'

'Wow.'

'Was I impulsive? Crazy? Probably. It all went downhill once we'd signed the marriage certificate. It changed things between us. Subtly at first, but then more noticeably.'

'In what ways?'

She sighed. 'The *fun* seemed to go. We were official. Man and wife. We weren't those horny young people any more, looking for a thrill. I think he began to see me differently. I know I did the same to him. We were married. I wanted to plan our future, I wanted us to be serious. But getting married had somehow poured water on our fire. And then I discovered he was having an affair.'

Quinn frowned. 'I'm sorry…'

'We'd drifted apart. He thought the fun in linen cupboards would continue and I wanted a serious relationship. To have a family of my own.'

He grimaced. 'How long did *your* marriage last?'

'A year.' She laughed, then, realising the irony. 'Aren't we a great pair?'

He nodded, just as the server brought them their food. They'd ordered *poulet yassa*—chicken marinated overnight in peanut oil, lemon juice, onion, vinegar and spices—which was served with couscous and roasted plantain. The aroma was mouth-wateringly good and they tucked in with gusto.

'What was your wife's name?' she asked, her fingers dripping with the marinade.

'Hannah.'

She smiled. 'Why do you think we both failed so badly at marriage?'

He shrugged. 'I don't think we *failed*. I'm sure we both fought as hard as we could to save our marriages.'

There was something he wasn't telling her. But she didn't feel she could push because she knew damn well there was lots *she* wasn't telling *him*. But they'd made a good start. They'd begun to open up to one another. What they had would take time. Trust didn't happen overnight. And though she needed to trust him, he also needed to feel he could trust *her*.

'You're right. I didn't want it to fail, but Simon was the one who gave up on us. He didn't even try.'

Quinn swallowed a mouthful of chicken and nodded thoughtfully. 'There's nothing you can do if the other partner just gives up.'

Tasha raised her mug of coffee and held it towards him to make a toast. 'To friends that don't give up.'

He raised his mug and smiled.

'To friends that don't give up.'

Quinn drove her home. He was so very pleased that he'd met up with Tasha again. What he'd done to her in the past had always been a stain on his memories—one that he hoped he was now beginning to rectify.

It had been a little difficult to start with, but since sharing a meal and some conversation at The Coffee Bean he really felt that his friendship with Tasha was heading in a great new direction.

All he had to do was keep her as a friend and not ruin it by wanting more.

He always expected other people to give their all. Ever since Hannah had died—since *they* had died—he'd wanted other people to give everything. Not to give up when things got hard or painful.

Hannah had tried to protect him. She hadn't told him how bad her pain was. Insisted they were making the right choice in holding off treatment. He would never have gone along with it if he'd known how much pain she was in each day. But she'd been so determined to give their unborn son life.

Their deaths had almost destroyed him. His wife's doctors—people he'd once thought of as friends— had also known the truth, and he hadn't been able to be around them again. Hadn't been able to walk in the same corridors and wards he once had. His workplace as much as his home had become tainted by lies and deceit.

He'd felt angry. Had wanted to lash out at everyone. And afterwards Hannah's family had blamed him. Blamed him for not doing more to save her. Their own guilt had been eating them alive, and they'd turned that pain on him.

It had been the safest thing for all of them for him to get away. To start afresh. To go somewhere there would be no memory of his wife at all.

The vacancy on the hospital ship had arrived at the perfect time and he'd jumped at it, determined to secure the post and get away from everything that reminded him of his loss.

He was glad he'd met up with Tasha. He'd been able to shine a light on one of the dark spots in his past. He could rectify that in a way he couldn't with his wife or child. He was making it better and it made him feel good.

But *she* made him feel good, too. Being with Tasha was like breathing again after being in a vacuum. She made him feel brighter. Lighter. Unburdened. Her smile could light up the room. He didn't know exactly what it was, just that being in her presence made him believe that life could possibly be good again. And he liked that feeling. He wanted more of it.

More of *her*.

Who'd have thought that the freckle-faced curly-haired girl he'd humiliated in his long-lost past, might just be his saviour?

Quinn was determined to spend as much time with Tasha Kincaid as he could.

He was hungry for the healing warmth of her friendship and trust after being out in the cold for so very long.

# CHAPTER FOUR

ABEJE WAS SHOWING signs of jaundice. A nurse called Quinn during the night and he got up to inspect the little girl. She had the shakes and was complaining of muscle pain and tiredness. The lack of red blood cells was causing it, but she was still producing urine so her kidneys hadn't been affected yet. He prescribed treatment, including a transfusion to aid her platelet count, and then went to check on the other patients in the clinic.

The two children they'd brought back from Mosa were sleeping soundly and reacting well to their medications, despite having received them after Abeje. There was a woman with a serious case of mastitis, and they were doing their best to help her work out the blockage in her milk ducts so she could continue to feed her baby. There was a middle-aged farmer with a suspected stroke, but they hoped to discharge him soon, and a patient awaiting surgery on a large goitre in his neck.

A mish-mash of cases, but he liked the variety in his work. The only cases he didn't deal with were obstetric. Maternity and pregnancy was a big no-no for him. Thankfully there were other doctors on board who *did* specialise, so he was able to hand over to them, but he did his best to stay away if he could.

He didn't like it. He had made an oath to treat all people needing help. So if there weren't any of those other doctors around he did it, because he had to, but inwardly he hated every second. And that hate came from fear. Fear that he would fail another mother-to-be. Fear that he would lose two patients in one.

It was too close to home. Cancer he could deal with. But pregnant mothers...? All he saw was Hannah.

Hannah with her burgeoning belly, sitting up in bed, smiling at him, holding his hand, despite the pain she was going through. The sickness. She'd refused chemotherapy to give their baby a chance at life, but the pancreatic cancer had been aggressive and had spread rapidly throughout her body. And she'd died before the baby could be saved.

Their son had been just twenty-two weeks in gestation, and though they'd tried to deliver him when his wife's system had gone into mass organ failure he'd not been strong enough to live. The steroids they'd injected her with to strengthen his lungs hadn't been enough. He'd been tiny. Almost see-through. A fragile body no bigger than his hand.

His son had struggled to live for a matter of hours.

He'd watched his wife die slowly, whilst she'd tried to keep their son safe and give him a chance. And then he'd had to watch his son die.

They'd let him hold him at the end. He'd unbuttoned his shirt and slipped his son's baby bird body onto his chest, barely registering his weight, tenderly cradling him. His son's minutely thin fingers had held one of his, and tears had dripped from his eyes, down his cheeks and onto his son's failing body.

He'd never felt so helpless. So impotent as a doctor.

He'd felt his son's last ragged, struggling breaths and he'd raged against a world that could let this thing happen to such an innocent young life.

Quinn had sat in that hospital chair, gazing at his son's face, memorising the shape of his eyes, his tiny button nose, his small mouth invaded by a tube, his little body covered in fine downy hair, and told him over and over for hours how much he loved him, how much his mother had loved him. How precious he was. How brave. And that it was okay to stop fighting.

He could let go.

He could stop.

The last juddering breath had come with a sigh, and when his chest had moved no more he'd held him for a long time, until his tears had run dry. The nurses had taken pictures for him and he had those now, in his wallet, never far from him at all.

If he'd lived he would be a little boy by now—Abeje's age—learning through play, making friends, laughing and having fun.

But instead his son was just a memory. A powerful memory that drove Quinn on, that gave him the courage to get through life. Because if he could survive losing his wife and son he could survive anything.

What could life do to him now? It had brought him Tasha and she was a *good* thing. He knew that.

They'd have a month together. Four weeks in which they could consolidate their friendship. Twenty-eight days after which he knew he would have to sail away from her, knowing that each time he returned to Ntembe she would be here. A reassuring presence. A smiling face to welcome him.

In the privacy of his office he took out his wallet and looked at the photo he treasured most.

He was a father. A father without a child. A husband without a wife. He'd had the most precious people taken away from him already.

He wasn't going to lose Tasha's friendship.

Not now he'd been given this second chance.

But as he stared at the photo, as he was reminded of his loss and the pain he had gone through, he felt hesitation. Hesitation about getting close to someone again, even if it was just as friends. Would he and Tasha ever be *just friends*? She'd had such strong feelings for him once. Had loved him. And he didn't want to be responsible for hurting anyone ever again.

He'd taken an oath not to.

The classroom wasn't the same without Abeje. Tasha really missed her presence, her bright, smiling face, her eagerness to learn. Her empty seat was a painful reminder that whilst the rest of them were there, learning about adverbs and adjectives, Abeje was lying in a hospital bed, fighting for her life.

It was hard for Tasha to stand there and concentrate when all her instincts were telling her she needed to be back on the ship. When all she wanted to do was sit by Abeje's bedside and whisper words of encouragement.

Malaria was a killer. Nearly half a million children died from it each year, most of them in Africa. It was a horrific number and she wished she hadn't looked it up on the internet last night, when she'd been searching for details on the disease, but she'd not been able to help it.

She'd known when she chose to come here that it was a country rife with it, but she'd naively believed that she wouldn't have to face it. That she would stand in a schoolroom, by a blackboard, chalk in hand, and the most pressing thing on her mind would be whether the children understood the rules of grammar.

She couldn't make a difference as a doctor any more, so she wanted to make a difference as a teacher. She needed to change someone's life for the better. She *had* to! Because what was it all about, otherwise?

She told her class that it was time to go out and play, and when they'd all filed out and the classroom was quiet Tasha went over to Abeje's chair and sat down on it. Lifting the lid on her desk, she looked inside and saw Abeje's books, all neatly lined up. She picked up the top one and looked inside. She saw Abeje's progress, from hardly being able to write to almost being fluent. Her mastery of the English language was evident in her sentences and stories.

Abeje was clever and special, and Tasha didn't know what it was, but she *felt* something for the little girl. A need to do more for her. A need to give her a greater chance in life. But how?

She put the book down and closed the lid, smoothing her hands over the old wood. She would go to visit her tonight. Straight after work. And perhaps she would see Quinn, too…

Just thinking about him lightened the feeling of burden that was upon her shoulders and in her heart. Last night they'd had a lovely time together. Just talking, sharing stories, laughing, enjoying being in each other's company. It was the start of a beautiful friendship. She knew that. They got on well together. Despite the past. She was glad she had chosen to be brave and give him the chance he needed.

This afternoon all the children were going to write letters to Abeje. Letters that would form a book. Letters that might make their friend fight to get better and come back. That would let her know that everyone was worrying about her.

It was something she herself would have loved when she'd been sick as a child. She'd once contracted the flu and had been stuck in bed for almost two weeks. Apart from one 'Get Well' card, Tasha had barely seen the others at all.

She'd been so alone. Frightened. Desperate for love.

She didn't want anyone else to feel that way.

'Abeje?' Tasha sat by the little girl's bed, holding her hand. She'd been alarmed when she arrived, to see how yellow her eyes looked. Jaundice was caused by a build-up of bilirubin in the blood and tissues, which in turn was caused by the breakdown of red blood cells. It wasn't a good sign, and her research last night was fuelling the fires of her worry. It might lead to coma. Kidney failure.

Death.

That kind of thought made her blood run cold.

'*Abeje?* It's Miss Tasha.'

'She's sleeping. She was awake a fair bit during the night,' Quinn interjected from behind her.

She hadn't known he was there.

'Was she bad?'

He took her arm and walked her away from the bed. 'I was called about the jaundice and we began treatment, but she had chills and shakes for a while, which kept her awake until they settled in the early hours.'

Tasha looked back at her. She looked so small in the hospital bed. Too tiny to be fighting a major disease such as this one. 'Alone…?'

'I stayed with her. She was never alone.'

*Oh. That was kind of him.* She smiled her thanks.

'She's getting the best treatment. We just have to give it time to work.'

'I know.'

She knew all about time and how important that was. She needed to be patient, but she wasn't very good at that any more.

'I feel so helpless. I read last night that the treatment for the falciparum parasite should be different according to geographical location. Are you sure she's on the right medicine?'

'I'm sure.'

'She has complicated malaria, though. Jaundice, anaemia, impaired consciousness…'

'She's okay.'

'But she's *not* okay! What made you choose the chloroquine and ACTs? She's under eight—she could have had the quinine-based regimen or clindamycin.'

He frowned. 'Hey, don't *do* this. You'll drive yourself insane. I appreciate that you care, and you're worried, but you have to trust me as a doctor as well as a man.'

But her faith in medicine had been weakened.

'I can't just sit here. Watching her. Waiting for her to die.'

He blinked. Stared back at her. 'She's not there yet. You need to find hope. Like the rest of us.'

She sighed. 'How do you do that?'

'You dig deep inside. You find the strength. You think you've got it tough? Well, it's harder for the patients. And they need you to be there for them. To hold their hand and tell them it's okay.'

She heard something in his voice. A little hitch. He'd been through something. Lost someone close. She could tell.

'How do you know so much?' She appreciated that he was a doctor, and doctors saw death all the time, but this was different. *Personal*.

'I just do. I wish I didn't, but...'

She laid her hand upon his arm, empathising with his pain. He looked so forlorn, so haunted by whatever the memory was. He'd been through something terrible. Perhaps he *did* know what he was talking about?

'I'm sorry.'

'What for?'

'For whoever you lost.'

'It was a long time ago. Besides, you haven't lost anyone yet. We're nowhere near that. There's still hope. And time. You have to give the medicines time to work.'

Tasha let out a heavy sigh and turned back to look at her small charge, all the way across the room. 'Okay. You're right. *Again*.'

'And next time you feel the urge to consult Dr Internet, perhaps you might like to consult with me first?'

She crossed her heart. 'I promise.'

'Good.'


He was glad to go into surgery to assist in the removal of the goitre. He needed that intensity of concentration, the focus that only surgery could bring, after that moment with Tasha earlier on.

He'd had to reassure her, but he'd been worried, too. There'd been tears forming in her eyes and he hadn't wanted to see her cry. Not because crying women made him uncomfortable—he just didn't want to see *Tasha* cry.

He cared about her. Especially now that he'd been

given a second chance to put things right in her life. And seeing her upset had upset him, too. It had felt as if it was *his* fault. That somehow he needed to put things right.

Having her stand before him with tears in her eyes and her bottom lip trembling had been like a flashback to all those years ago.

He couldn't have that. He *wouldn't*.

Now he had to think. Had to concentrate on the surgery. Make sure that he and his colleague both safely avoided the two laryngeal nerves which affected the vocal cords as they removed this goitre. They didn't want to paralyse this man's voice or his ability to breathe.

*He'd* felt paralysed. Briefly. Seeing her standing there, almost in tears. The surge of desire to make everything better for Tasha had startled him, and had made him realise just how much Tasha was beginning to mean to him already.

And that worried him. It had only been a few years since he had lost his wife and child. Was he having feelings he shouldn't have for another woman already?

Or was Tasha *just a friend*? As he kept telling himself she was.

*This is all so complicated!*

How many of his feelings were tied up in the past? His past with Tasha? Was it because he felt he owed her a debt? That he had to put things right? Or was this something different?

He felt her pull. She was a very beautiful woman. He'd done a double-take the first time she'd run onto his ward, then he'd spent hours staring at her face during that night in the tent in Mosa and wondered what it might be like to kiss her. The time they'd spent together since had been wonderful. Warm and refreshing. He looked forward to seeing her every day. Wanted to spend even more time with her. Wanted to be *with her*.

*Guilt. That's what I'm feeling. Guilt that I might be moving on.*

But it didn't mean he would forget Hannah, or his son. Of course he wouldn't. But was he ready for such a relationship? Was he reading too much into this in the first place?

He was sure Tasha felt something for him, too. They were both just afraid. Afraid to put themselves out there and commit to it. Held back by fear.

He didn't want their relationship to be complicated, even if it was just as friends. He wanted—*needed*—this to be easy. Light. Enjoyable.

Quinn would never forget his wife and child, but if he wanted Tasha to be more open with him then he had to find the strength he had inside to let her know that she would be safe with him.

But she was so concerned about Abeje. So worried about her. Clearly she loved the child, and it was even clearer that they wouldn't stand a chance together unless Abeje lived.

He *had* to make her live.

He couldn't lose her.

Because if he did then he'd lose Tasha Kincaid as well.

Tasha spent the next couple of days teaching all day and going to visit Abeje in the evenings. The little girl looked so frail and small in her bed, her breathing sometimes ragged, sometimes not. She'd taken along the book of letters that the class had made and she spent each evening reading them out, convinced that even if Abeje wasn't conscious she would still absorb the positivity of the words, the good intentions, and that somehow they would help power her through this difficult battle.

Quinn often stopped by to speak to her, to update her on Abeje's condition and progress. He told her everything he could and she appreciated it that he didn't shield her from anything that might be construed as negative. He was open and forthcoming. Keen to make her understand his medical decisions and treatments, which she also appreciated.

When the end of that first week drew near, and the weekend stretched out ahead of them, he asked her if she'd like to go with him on a second trip to Mosa to check on the villagers and make sure that no one else had got sick.

She really wanted to go, but she glanced at Abeje in the bed. 'What about her? I don't like leaving her.'

'She's stable. We'll only be gone for the day. No overnight stay in a tent.'

'Are you taking the other two children back?'

'They're not ready yet. They're still sick.'

'Oh…' She wasn't sure if she really needed to go. What could she do? She wasn't a doctor here, or a nurse. And she'd only gone on that first trip because she knew Abeje's aunt. But then she thought about how nice it might be to get out of Ntembe and spend some more time with Quinn.

It had been nice that time they'd gone out for dinner, and she was enjoying their little chats each night, but he was always busy in the clinic and they didn't get to talk as much as she would have liked. Spending the day with him travelling to Mosa would be an opportunity to get to know him more.

She smiled. 'Okay. I will.'

'That's great!' He seemed really pleased. 'Maria and Rob will come too. I think it's important that the villagers see the same faces.'

The next day arrived quickly, and Tasha arrived portside to join the others in the truck to Mosa. She got into the back of the truck with Quinn, as they'd offered to let Maria and Rob have the comfy seats this time. There was some equipment on the floor of the truck, along with boxes of tests and medications just in case, but Quinn was hopeful they wouldn't need any of it.

He banged his hand a couple of times on the back of the truck to indicate to Rob, who was driving, that they were ready to go, and the truck began to pull away from the dock.

It was weird, at first, being in the back of the truck with Quinn. They only had each other to look at. That or the road behind them, covered as they were by a khaki-green material hood.

He kept looking at her and smiling.

'What are you doing?'

'Looking at you.'

She felt her cheeks heat with colour. 'Why?'

She still felt it. The disbelief that he might be interested in her. That Quinn Shapiro would look at her with any interest that wasn't full of ridicule. Her young girl insecurities were still there, trying to hold her back.

'I'm just trying to decide if you'd agree to come out on a date with me.'

*A date?* Her heart raced at the idea. Thrilled that he'd suggested it, but also wary, she was unable to meet his gaze as her mind raced over possible outcomes at a mile a minute.

*This man hurt you once! Don't you forget that!*

Yes, he had, but that had been so long ago. They'd been children! A part of her really wanted to say yes... but what he had done before hadn't just hurt her for a short while. It had devastated her. Floored her for weeks, months.

She'd made a lot of her life choices because of this man. Choosing to become a doctor because she'd wanted the same things as him. Choosing to be *like him* because if she couldn't go out with him then she'd at least be experiencing the same world and hopes and dreams.

She couldn't just forget all that. It was such a huge part of her childhood. And choosing to be a doctor had led to one of the most disturbing episodes of her life— one that had overshadowed the humiliation he had put her through. She had questioned who she was. Whether she needed to be punished. She had had to change her entire life.

Besides, what if she did give in to his suggestion and it all went wrong and they ruined this friendship they were building? What if they had a great big falling-out and he devastated her again? And what was the point in dating him when he was going to leave in three weeks' time?

*I'm always being left behind.*

Her parents, Quinn, Simon.

She wanted to say yes, she *would* go on a date with him. She wanted to with all her heart. But they had a timeline working against them.

'Is that such a good idea?'

He sighed. 'I know...but don't you feel it? Our connection? It's more than just our history. I'm sure of it.'

The truck rattled them around as the tyres hit divots and potholes, but no matter how hard it shook them they still maintained eye contact.

'I'd be a liar if I said no.'

'So I'm not imagining it?'

Tasha smiled. 'No. You're not.'

'You can call us crazy, if you want. I don't mind. But I'd really like to spend more time with you, Tasha. Time that's meant for you and me. For *us*.'

She wanted it. She dearly wanted it. But *was* it crazy to do such a thing? Reckless? He would leave in three weeks. She would be left behind. Again! He'd sail off to Madagascar and not come back for months. She was only contracted for four more months in Ntembe. She could be gone by the time the *Serendipity* sailed back into port.

She was *so* tempted. Something about this man pulled her in. She couldn't help it any more than a moth could prevent itself from flying into the light. She knew it would probably all end in tears—mostly hers—but she still felt she wanted to take that chance. Just to see what would happen between them.

She felt helpless. As if she had no strength to resist him.

*I loved him so much once...*

He'd broken her heart before. Could she get involved with him knowing it might happen again? Or perhaps knowing there was a time limit on the relationship would help her cope with it better? Make her grateful for the magic times they might have? Cherish the memories of three weeks?

This was her opportunity to see if her childhood wishes were a possibility! A chance to see if she and Quinn would *work*. She wasn't a tearful thirteen-year-old any more. She was a grown woman, with life experience, and so far she'd survived all that life had thrown at her.

Why not this?

Why not have fun?

She'd survive again, wouldn't she…?

'No.'

His hopeful face dropped. 'No?'

She nodded. 'I want to… I do. It's just…'

He frowned. 'Just what?'

'Just that I think it's best we see each other as friends. Go out as friends and nothing more. There's too much water under the bridge.'

He looked disappointed. He leant forward, his elbows on his knees, and stared out through the back of the truck.

Tasha watched him, feeling terrible but knowing she had done the right thing. The right thing to protect her heart.

The people of Mosa cheered to see them return. They wanted news on the two children who had been taken back to the ship, so Quinn filled them in on that. Then they gave the villagers a secondary check-up and no one else had succumbed to a bite from a mosquito, so it looked as if the villagers were in the clear.

Ada and some of the other women banded together and presented them with a meal of *bobotie*—spiced minced lamb with an egg topping.

And later, as Tasha was helping pack up the truck, Quinn came over to her and draped something around her neck. She stopped to look at it. It was a necklace, made with string and small pebbles that had been painted in bright rainbow colours. It was beautiful.

'Oh! That's gorgeous, thank you.'

She was surprised. After she'd turned him down in the truck he had barely said a word. So the fact that he had brought her something so beautiful made her see just how much he valued her despite her saying no.

'Ada said that the people here give each other these necklaces as a sign of friendship. To show that they will always be friends, no matter what.'

She fingered the small stones. They were tiny. Such work must have gone into each one to bore a hole for the string and then paint them in the array of colours...

'I love it, thank you.' She looked up at him, smiling, glad that her refusal had not made everything awkward. And he stood in front of her, close, their bodies almost touching. He stared at her for a long moment and her pulse raced under his close scrutiny.

She gazed at his mouth. His lips. She looked back into his eyes. She'd once dreamed of that first kiss. What it would feel like. His lips touching hers.

He reached up to tuck a stray curl behind her ear and she had to look away. Embarrassed and hot with the attention.

'Are you two gonna help? Or stare into each other's eyes all day?' joked Rob, interrupting their moment as he dropped a crate of meds back into the truck.

Quinn smiled at her, and then stepped back to get out of Rob's way. 'We'll help.'

She could breathe again!

She stepped back too, feeling her heart thudding, her pulse racing, her face burning with heat and desire.

*These next three weeks are going to be intense.*

Back in Ntembe, Tasha found she was living on her nerves. But in a good way. She looked forward to going to the ship to visit Abeje, knowing that Quinn would be there, too, exchanging glances and secret smiles with her. She might have agreed to just friendship, but it was a friendship unlike any she had ever experienced before.

There was heat between them. She felt it. She knew he did, too. But he was respecting her choice, which she was glad about—even if she *did* keep dreaming about being in his arms at night.

It was like being thirteen again. But this time Quinn's reactions to her weren't just in her imagination. They were real.

And then on one of her visits he asked if she would like to go out for dinner.

'Just friends.' He smiled.

She nodded, almost too shy to speak, her heart thudding away like a thousand stampeding wildebeests. Dinner with Quinn would be very nice. And probably safe, too. Her on one side of a table, him on the other. Good food. Maybe some wine. Conversation. Moonlight.

He turned up at her door dressed in casual dark trousers and a white shirt that showed his tan to perfection. In his hand was a small posy of flowers. Where he'd got them from, she had no idea, but they were very beautiful.

'Are they *wild* flowers?'

He nodded, smiling.

'How did you get them?' She lifted them to her nose to inhale their scent—sweet and fragrant.

'You'd be amazed at what you can buy at a busy port.'

She raised an eyebrow. 'I'm sure.'

Quinn laughed. 'Are you ready?'

'Where are we going? You didn't say.'

'Somewhere special. Trust me.' He looked her up and down. 'You look very beautiful.'

She blushed, inordinately pleased at his compliment. But she told herself to put it into perspective. He was just being kind and polite. What man *didn't* say a woman looked nice when they'd both made an effort to go out somewhere together? Just because Quinn had said it, it didn't mean anything. They were just friends.

*Me and Quinn....friends. I would never have believed it.*

He escorted her out to his car, which looked like a jigsaw: different coloured panels everywhere. Nothing matching. A real rust-bucket.

'I know it's not a stretch limousine...'

She smiled. 'You couldn't buy one of those at the port?' she joked.

'They were all sold out.'

He opened the passenger door for her and she looked in at the familiar bursts of foam sticking out of the seat covers. It seemed such a long time ago that he'd taken her out to The Coffee Bean that night.

She'd not felt this happy for a long time, and she touched the pebble necklace at her throat with nerves. She'd wanted to wear it tonight. For him. To show that she appreciated his gesture. That they were both trying, here.

She laughed when the engine didn't start. 'Should I call for a mechanic?'

He looked at her a little bemused. 'Give it one more chance. All she needs is a little love and patience.'

'Don't we all?'

And then, on the fifth attempt, the engine roared into life, sounding as if it might conk out again at any moment.

'Are you sure we're going to make it home later?'

'I'll give you a piggy-back if I have to.'

Putting the car into first gear, he drove them away from Ntembe, kangarooing every now and again, before steering them down the main road and then taking a dusty side track that led them up a hill, signposted 'The Heights'.

The road was long and winding, skimming the edge of the mountain, providing them with terrifically scary views, and just before the top, where it levelled out, there was a small building, lit with dangling white lamps, with a small terrace that gave great views out to the sea.

She'd never known about this. Never seen it before. 'What *is* this place?'

'The Heights restaurant. An ex-patient owns it.'

'Wow!' It was all she could say.

The terrace was filled with intimate little tables for two, white tablecloths covering each one. There were candles and lamps, small potted plants, and on each table a single flower in a tall, thin glass vase.

Quinn got out and opened the car door for her, and she heard guitar music playing from speakers as she stepped out in her long maxi-dress.

The maître d'—a young, well-presented man in a black shirt and bow tie—escorted them to a table on the terrace.

'Thank you.' She sat down, smiling, and accepted the menu that he proffered. It was printed in the most elegant script, and it surprised her to find a place of such class and distinction in a part of Africa she'd always believed to be deprived.

'Tonight's specials are the *liboké de poisson* and our fishball stew.'

She frowned. 'What was the first one?'

The maître d' smiled. 'The *liboké de poisson* is our fish of the day, wrapped in banana leaves and baked.'

*Mmm. Sounds wonderful.*

Tasha thanked him and, as if he could read their minds and knew that they needed to chat and discuss life before choosing their food, the maître d' slunk away almost as if by magic.

She smiled at Quinn over her menu. 'How did you find this place?'

'I actually discovered it on one of my first trips here. One of the doctors who'd volunteered on the ship was retiring, and we all came here in a group of about forty. We took over the whole restaurant, and I remember it because the food and the views were just so amazing. Later the guy who owns it came to us for a procedure.'

'Is everyone on the *Serendipity* a volunteer?'

'A lot of them, yes.'

'Are you?'

'No, I've been there too long.' He smiled. 'What would you like to drink?'

'I'll have a dry white wine, please.'

'Sounds great. I'll join you.'

The maître d' appeared and Quinn gave their order, and they both soon had their glasses filled with the house special.

The staff came and went like culinary ghosts.

'It's just so beautiful up here,' she said, gazing out at the bay far below, where vessels bobbed on the water like rubber ducks.

It wasn't chilly. The night was perfect. They could see the *Serendipity*, and all the other boats and ships docked in port. There were the lights of Ntembe, and beyond that the port, and the vast stretch of water that was the Mozambique Channel. All glittering in the moonlight.

'It's peaceful up here, too. Makes you feel that you have no hardships. That there's nothing to worry about.

It's hard to imagine that there are hundreds of people down there, all living their lives, going about their business, unaware that we're looking down on them from above.'

A waiter came and took their food order.

'It's important to get away from things sometimes,' Quinn said. 'The pressures of life and living. Escapism is good every now and again.'

Tasha knew about escaping. She'd done it to survive. But there was a difference between escaping physically and escaping mentally. Once something was inside your head—fear, guilt, shame—you couldn't escape that no matter where you went. You took it with you.

Escaping to a different place, going for a nice meal, like tonight, or going on holiday to Bali or Bora Bora, or wherever, was just window dressing. Wherever you chose to go it wouldn't help at all unless you got everything right in your head. You could choose to try not to think about something for a while—read a book, watch a movie, have time out with friends or a loved one—but it would always be waiting for you. Lurking in the dark recesses of your mind. Ready to cause trouble and anguish once again.

'It is. Sometimes we need to pretend that everything's okay and that we have nothing to worry about.'

He smiled and raised his glass to her in a toast. 'Here's to having nothing to worry about.'

She clinked his glass with her own and took a sip of wine. It was deliciously fruity. 'And here's to Abeje getting better.'

He clinked her glass. 'To Abeje. And every other patient on the ship tonight.'

'We never do stop worrying, though, do we? You have

patients you must think about constantly, and I have students who are never far from my mind.'

Quinn nodded. 'Are there *any* jobs, do you think, in which people can truly switch off from work the second they leave?'

She thought about it for a moment, her mind reaching for possibilities before throwing them away. 'I really don't know.'

He smiled at her. 'It's just human nature, I guess.'

'But working with children, like you and I both do, isn't that the hardest?'

She wondered if he'd ever experienced what she had. If he'd ever had to make a choice over someone's life, Decided who to treat first, knowing that the one you left till second might die because of that decision?

'It can be. There have been times when I have truly not wanted to be a doctor. The knowledge it gives you is powerful, but when there's nothing to be done it can be… At times like that I wish I could walk away. But I made an oath and I meant it.'

She'd made that oath, too.

Once.

And she *had* walked away.

*What does that make me? Am I a coward? Or should I just never have been a doctor in the first place?*

She gazed down at the sheer white tablecloth, adjusted her cutlery slightly. Sipped her wine. Remembering.

Remembering what she'd done.

# CHAPTER FIVE

THEIR WAITER BROUGHT them a platter of seafood—oysters, crab, shrimp, calamari—served with scalloped potatoes, fresh crusty bread and curls of butter, the aromas of which, caused their mouths to salivate in anticipation.

As other guests arrived and the restaurant began to fill up they chatted pleasantly over their meal.

Tasha was aware that as it got darker Quinn's eyes looked even more devilish, twinkling in the low lantern light. He smiled a lot, and he was a good listener as she told him some of her teaching stories.

'So, how long have you been a teacher?' he asked.

'Oh, not that long,' she answered without thinking, his easy-going nature having made her let down her guard.

'So what did you do when you left school?'

*Oh.*

She shrugged. 'This and that. I kind of drifted,' she lied, hating herself for telling him untruths, but not sure she could tell him everything.

How would he look at her if she did? She'd *quit* being a doctor! She'd made that oath that was so important to him and then she'd walked away. She'd lost a child. A whole *life*. Because of making the wrong choice. Could she tell him *that*?

No. Not when she was enjoying spending time with him. He would look at her differently. View her differently. Here he was in Africa, saving lives, giving medicine to those who had none.

He gave his all here. She could see that. Even if she *did* get frustrated at the level of response Abeje was showing. And she liked being a success in his eyes. It was an image she wanted to maintain—especially with him.

That earlier part of her life was something that she found shameful, and she didn't feel comfortable enough with him yet to tell him the truth. She would have to keep that to herself until he left. And each and every time she saw him after that. If they got the chance.

'What about you? Did you keep in touch with Dexter?'

He smiled at the name. 'Dexter Green…now *that's* a name I haven't thought of for a while. I did for a bit. But he went off to one uni and I went off to another. You know how it is—you lose touch, sometimes.'

'I wonder what he ended up doing?'

'I think he was a sports journalist, last I heard.' He patted his mouth with a napkin. 'Do you keep in touch with any of the kids from the children's home?'

She shook her head. 'No. The day I left I cut every tie.'

'You must have been lonely.'

'I had a new foster family to get to know.'

He frowned and reached out to take her hand, gave it a reassuring squeeze. 'I'm sorry you didn't have a great start in life. But look at you now. In Africa, doing a job that you love, living the dream…'

She smiled back, aware of the sensations as he touched her. Stroked the back of her hand with his thumb. It was a simple gesture, but intimate. One that was sending fireworks of frenzy zipping around her body, making her high on adrenaline. She couldn't help but stare at their hands interlocked upon the tablecloth.

'Are you finished with your plates?'

Their waiter had come to take the platter away. They thanked him, told him it had been delicious, and he magicked away their used crockery with a smile of satisfaction upon his face.

'It *is* your dream? Teaching?' He was looking at her carefully. Trying to read the emotions rushing across her face.

'Of course. It's just…'

'What?'

'Abeje getting so sick…it's thrown me.'

'Children get sick.' His eyes darkened.

'Yes, but if we were back in England she'd have a cold or tonsillitis. This is *malaria*. It could kill her.'

He squeezed her fingers more reassuringly.

Then their waiter came back to their table. 'Excuse me, sir. You're Dr Shapiro?'

'Yes?'

'There's an urgent telephone call for you inside.'

*An urgent call.* Was it Abeje? Suddenly the food in Tasha's stomach sat heavily. Sickeningly.

Quinn glanced at her apologetically. 'Excuse me.' He dabbed his mouth once again with the napkin and got up.

She watched him go, weaving his way through the tables, following the waiter to the phone.

When he was gone she pulled her hand back towards herself and thought about what she was feeling. Quinn was making her question herself and she was feeling very disconcerted. *Was* she living her dream? Or was she just in her fall-back position of teaching?

She *missed* medicine, but she wasn't certain she was

strong enough to go back to doing it. Perhaps there was a branch of medicine she could be in that wouldn't be so upsetting? Dermatology? Ear, nose and throat? But she knew instinctively that any of these options also carried risks. No matter where she went or what she chose she would always face heartbreaking cases.

And now she was here. With Quinn. Closer to him than she had ever believed possible.

He wasn't gone long. Just a few minutes. He came back into view, striding to their table, his face sombre.

He stood by her side. 'I'm sorry to cut our date short, but we have to go.'

She stood up, feeling nauseous and suspecting she already knew the answer to her question but having to ask anyway. 'Is something wrong?'

He nodded, and looked as if he was deciding about whether to tell her the next part or not.

'It's Abeje. She's taken a turn for the worse.'

Quinn got them back to the ship in less than twenty minutes, but it was the longest twenty minutes of Tasha's life so far. All she could imagine was getting on board and hearing those terrible words. The words she couldn't bear to hear.

During the drive back she'd bombarded Quinn with questions.

'What did they say, exactly?'

'That she's spiked a high fever and that her urine output has slowed.'

'How high a fever?'

'They didn't say.'

'Well, was it over a hundred?'

'He didn't say.'

'Well, when he said her output had slowed, did he say how much? How many millilitres an hour is she producing? How full was her bag?'

'He didn't say.'

She'd got so frustrated with him! So angry.

'When did she last have a kidney function test?'

'A few hours ago.'

'What were the results?'

'I wasn't there. I was seeing to other patients, It'll be in her notes.'

If the kidneys failed it would be a slippery slope from there. All her organs would shut down. She'd fall into a coma.

She might die.

She'd seen it happen before. The kidneys were often the barometer of the body. You watched the kidneys like a hawk.

Not being able to see Abeje's most recent notes, not to have them in her hands...

*Why did I agree to this date? If I hadn't said yes we'd be there right now!*

Tasha had felt as if she wanted to throw up. Adrenaline firing, her heart hammering, her throat feeling tight and closed. She had even shivered as Quinn raced them back down that hill towards Ntembe port.

*I can't lose her! She can't die!*

She had to lift up her skirt to run up the gangplank after Quinn, whose massive stride seemed to take no effort at all, and they burst into the clinic together and headed straight for Abeje's bedside.

She looked listless and clammy, her breathing irregular.

'Let's get her on oxygen right now, and I want a full

blood screen, asap!' Quinn ordered, grabbing the stethoscope from Rob's neck and listening to Abeje's breathing and heartbeat. 'Heart sounds strong.'

Tasha grabbed the notes from the end of the bed and ran her gaze over all the figures, interpreting what she saw. The kidney function tests seemed okay. The bottom end of normal, but still within the normal range.

*Why* had Quinn not double-checked this? *Why* hadn't he been concerned?

'Heart-rate's good.'

She had to grab on to any strands of hope she could.

She tried to keep out of the way, but the desire to rush forward and grab the stethoscope from his hands, push him out of the way and tend to Abeje herself, was overwhelming. Instead she hung the notes back on the edge of the bed and backed off, grabbing the counter, grounding herself and telling herself that she couldn't do that. She had no right to practice medicine.

All she could do was hold that counter, concentrate on the feel of it in her hands, as Quinn and Rob tended to Abeje.

The oxygen seemed to be helping.

'SATs are back up to ninety-five.'

'Respirations are at twenty-two.'

Quinn ordered medication and wrote down all his observations on Abeje's chart.

'What's happening now?' Tasha asked.

'We've got to wait and see if her fever comes down.'

'That's *it*? Wait and see?'

Surely there was more they could do? Not that she could think of anything herself.

'It's all we *can* do. I've given her meds and full oxygen. We've taken bloods to check the status of her levels. Until those results come back there's nothing more we can do.'

'There must be *something*!' She raced to the side of Abeje's bed and grabbed the little girl's hand. 'We can't just leave her to…'

'To what?' Quinn looked at her strangely.

She stared at Abeje's face. So serene. So peaceful. She almost looked as she was…

Tasha closed her eyes, wincing. She couldn't think that. She *couldn't*! 'I can't lose her.'

'We're not at that point. No way near.' He laid a hand on her shoulder, then knelt by her side and made her look at him. 'Hey, she's okay at the moment. Stable.'

'But critical. That's the bit you're not saying, isn't it? I read the notes.'

He looked away, guiltily.

She turned back to Abeje. Thinking of how far she'd come. Of all that she had survived. 'Do you know what her name means?'

'Abeje? No. I don't.'

'It means *We asked to have this child*.' Tasha turned to Quinn, tears in her eyes. 'She was wanted, Quinn. She was *wanted*! A precious first child! She wasn't meant to be an orphan! She wasn't meant to be in a children's home, all alone with no one to care for her.'

'But she *does* have people caring for her. She has us. She has *you.*'

Tasha wiped away a tear that had escaped her eye and trickled down her cheek in a lonely waterfall. 'What if I'm not strong enough?'

He frowned, lines furrowing his brow. 'Why wouldn't you be strong enough?'

She gazed at him, tears blurring her vision. 'I'm not. I'm *not*!'

She began to cry. Big, snotty sobs—proper, ugly crying—as she thought about all that Abeje had been through and *still* had to go through. Life was unfair. Seemingly all the *good* people—her, Abeje—who deserved to have a *good* life, were given traumatic ones instead. Their lives filled with heartache and pain.

Abeje wasn't even a teenager yet and she'd had both parents die, ended up in an orphanage with almost no hope of being adopted and now she was fighting for her life! Tasha thought *she'd* had it bad as a child, but it was nothing compared to this! She'd never been struck down by a terrible illness. The worst she'd had was the flu.

Why? It made no sense to her at all.

Quinn slipped his hand into hers. 'Come with me.'

'What? No. I can't leave her.'

'Tasha. Come with me. Please.'

She looked up at him, sniffing, not caring how she looked, wondering why he wanted her to go with him. 'But, Abeje—'

'Abeje will be fine for a moment. Please. Come with me.'

He looked so determined. So certain. So sure.

Feeling the need to latch on to someone strong, she got up and allowed him to lead her out of the ward and along another corridor. They went down a flight of stairs and he led them to what looked like a maternity ward. There were about five women on the ward. All new mothers. Two of them had their babies in their arms and were breastfeeding.

Tasha frowned, confused. 'What are we doing here?'

'I want you to look at these women. At these mothers.'

She frowned. 'Why?'

'Because you need to know how strong you are.'

She shook her head. 'I don't get it...'

He took her hand and gestured at the women on the ward.

'Each of these women thought that they weren't strong enough to carry on. They were exhausted and spent. And each time they thought they couldn't handle another second, another contraction, we told them that they had to. Because they did. If they didn't find that strength— if they chose to stop—something terrible might have happened. So they pushed. And pushed. And when they thought they couldn't push any more we told them to hang in there. That they could. That they were strong. They kept on because those babies in their arms, those children in their care, are the most important thing in the world and they *had* to do it. Tasha, you're a remarkable young woman. You overcame a difficult start in life and you're here, alone, in a developing country, fighting to improve the lives of children. Don't you *see* how strong you are?'

'I'm not a mother.'

'Mothers aren't necessarily the women who give birth to a child, but those who love them.'

She frowned, thinking. 'Like the woman who fostered me?'

He nodded. 'Yes. She didn't give birth to you, but I bet she loved and cared for you like she had.'

It was true. Tasha had even called her 'Mum'. Still did to this day. It had been one of the most surprising events of her life, finding a home. People to care for her. Love her. She'd thought all her chances were gone.

'You're telling me I can *do* this?'

His voice was soft and gentle. 'I'm telling you, you can do this.'

He reached up to stroke her face, the backs of his fingers tracing the line of her jaw, his gaze focused on her lips.

She smiled hesitantly, feeling his arms come around her body and hold her close. She soaked up his strength. His belief in her.

Staring at him, this close, she could almost barely breathe. Time stopped. The air felt thick with tension. She looked at his mouth. The mouth she had once dreamed of kissing. The mouth that belonged to the man she had once loved so much her heart had almost broken in two. She could feel it. Wanted to belong to him again.

He lowered his head towards hers.

He was going to kiss her.

She could protest. She could pull away. She could tell him no.

But she didn't want to.

Tasha closed her eyes and allowed her lips to meet his.

Quinn wished they could stay like that for hours. Tasha in his arms, her body against his. The feel of her, the scent of her hair, her perfume... It was a heady mix.

He hated the fact that she'd got so upset. He'd felt it. Her pain. Her fear of losing the child. And he'd known he had to give her hope. Because there still *was* hope. For both of them.

What he'd said was true. Women *were* infinitely stronger than men—mentally, physically and emotionally. They had greater depths to dig from.

Look at Hannah and the way she'd coped with everything thrown at her. She'd had cancer and she had done her level best to protect him from the pain she was in as she strove to grow their child, tried to give him life.

She'd tried to protect him as well as their son, whilst ignoring her own welfare. Had tried to carry on with life as if everything was normal. She had even made plans for their future, as if she'd believed she had one.

And he'd gone along with it—hoping and praying that she would be there with him to change nappies and do midnight feeds and watch their child take his first steps. Had he blinded himself? Deliberately made himself naïve to what was going on?

Desperate people made desperate decisions.

Hannah had fought till the bitter end, knowing that every minute their son stayed in the womb was an extra chance that he would survive. She had been utterly un-selfish, staying alive for their son for as long as she could, fighting for every breath just as he had done.

And now he found himself with yet another strong woman.

Tasha had no idea of the depths of her strength. She was frightened, and he understood that, but once she pushed past that fear she would realise just how much she had inside her still, in order to fight and to keep on fighting.

That was why he had brought her down to this ward. Because being here helped him. Reminded him of what life was all about. Because it wasn't about death. It was about life. And living.

Being here also hurt him. Seeing these mothers holding their babies in a way Hannah had never got the chance to do. Seeing these full-term babies when his own had been so small. But he could push past that pain because Tasha was worth it. She needed to see. Needed to understand.

And now had stood there kissing her.

Kissing a woman who wasn't his wife.

It should have felt awful. Treasonous. An act of betrayal.

And it did.

But it also felt amazing and right. And something about Tasha being in his arms, about Tasha being the woman he was kissing, seemed to be a full circle completing itself.

He hadn't kissed her because he felt he owed it to her. He hadn't kissed her to make up for what he had done to her as a teenager. He'd kissed her because he'd needed to. Wanted to.

And the crevasse in his heart was beginning to close.

No one had ever said life was going to be easy. He'd been through the worst thing anyone could ever experience—the loss of his wife and his baby—and yet he was still here. Still breathing. Still putting one foot in front of the other.

He knew Tasha could do it, too. Even if he had to hold her hand.

He liked doing that. Touching her. Holding her. He drew comfort from it—a comfort that he hadn't realised he'd been missing.

Tasha gave him a strength that he'd forgotten about. Gave him the need to care about someone. The need to be close to another human being.

It was not just about friendship, though that was very nice. It was about having that special connection. Something deeper, more primal than friendship. A vulnerability. That was what you got when you opened up your heart and let someone in.

'Are you ready to go back up?' he asked her, staring into her deep blue eyes.

'One more minute,' she replied, and laid her head soothingly against his chest.

Tasha sat beside Abeje's bed, straight of back and rigid of jaw, telling herself sternly that she could *do* this. Quinn believed in her. All she had to do was believe in herself. Sit by Abeje's bedside and not freak out.

Abeje was still breathing. Still alive.

The worst had not happened. And it might never happen. She had to believe that.

She cast her mind back to how she'd freaked out like that once before. That day she'd quit being a doctor. She'd sunk to the hospital floor, knowing she was responsible for the death of a child, staring at the tiles, wondering how on earth she was going to be able to call the parents in the middle of the night and tell them they needed to come in.

Her hands had visibly shaken as she'd picked up the phone, she'd even misdialled twice, her fingers had trembled so much, and then there had been that awful moment when she'd heard the mother, at the other end of the line, picking up even before the second ring and saying hello.

Her mouth had gone so dry. Her heart had thudded dully in her chest—an ever-present reminder that even though *her* heart could still beat, this woman's daughter's could not. Did not.

This woman's daughter was lying in a secluded bay, a white sheet pulled over her face.

*How could she speak? How could she find the words that must be said?*

The mother had begun to sound panicked.

*'Hello? Is there anyone there?'*

There was just a blank after that. She wasn't sure what
she'd done in the time from that phone call to the time
the parents arrived, dishevelled and red-eyed, at just after
three a.m.

The Family Room had been small. Two sofas, facing
each other. A small table in between with a vase of fake
flowers and a box of man-sized tissues. There'd been
an odd stain on one of the cushions and a frankly pallid
painting of a beach scene on the wall.

The parents had looked at her anxiously, wringing
their hands, their faces pale.

*'What's happened? How's Maddie?'*

*'I'm sorry...'* she'd begun, and the parents had collapsed in on themselves even before she'd got to the end
of her sentence.

It had been horrific to witness.

She'd delivered news like that before and had always
managed to maintain a professional distance. Stating
the facts clearly, telling the family that she was sorry
and then leaving them to have some privacy whilst they
mourned. Going back in later, after a respectable amount
of time, to ask if they'd like to see their loved one?

But not that time.

The rawness of those parents' grief, the keening sound
of the mother as she'd collapsed against her husband,
the guilt that she'd felt, had ripped Tasha's heart in two.

*I did this. It's my fault. Maddie shouldn't have died.*

She'd fled the room, pulled off her lanyard and thrown
it to the floor. Stalked to her locker, taken her things and
walked out. Never to return.

Her mobile phone had rung almost non-stop, Simon's
name flashing up constantly. Her email inbox had over-
flowed, but she'd answered nothing.

There'd been an investigation—of course there had. And the coroner had said that no one was to blame for the tragedy—certainly not Dr Tasha Kincaid, who'd had to make an agonising decision in the middle of a busy nightshift on call. But that hadn't made her feel any better. She'd still felt to blame and the sound of Maddie's mother's crying and wailing had woken her most nights.

Was Quinn right? *Did* she have the strength to get through this?

*Abeje's still alive. That's what I have to cling on to.*

But the insidious thought remained that the tables might soon be turned. That Tasha would not be the doctor delivering the bad news but instead the person taken into a family room and having Quinn in front of her saying, *I'm sorry...*

Quinn—whom she'd kissed. And not as a friend.

What did it all mean?

She stared hard at Abeje in her hospital bed, willing her to get better.

'I've brought you some tea and toast.'

Tasha had slept in the chair next to Abeje's bed all night, and now it was morning. The fever had come down, and the child's condition was stable once again. But Tasha looked crumpled and exhausted.

She took it from him, her face smiling with gratitude. 'Thanks.'

'You stayed?'

'I did.'

'We have temporary cots, you know. I could have brought you one so that you didn't have to sleep in a chair.'

'Well, maybe next time.'

'She's improved a little. I think you might make it home tonight.'

'I have to teach today,' she said, stretching and wincing at a pain in her shoulder.

'Here—let me.' And he stood behind her and began to massage the knots out of her muscles.

She gave a little groan of pleasure and he tried his hardest not to replay that sound in his head. But he couldn't help it. His mind made him wonder what it would be like to hear her make different noises of pleasure.

Quickly he admonished himself. *Be a professional, Quinn! You're still at work.*

'That feels good,' she said. 'Were you up all night?'

'I got forty winks in the on-call room.'

'Lucky you.'

*She could have joined me.*

His body stirred at the thought of that, and he had to let go of her shoulders and walk round to the other side of the bed to create some distance, hoping she didn't notice that he might look a little flushed.

Where were all these thoughts coming from? Okay, so they'd kissed once. And it had been amazing. But what had it really meant? Had he just been comforting her? Or had he truly allowed his desires to take over? He'd begun to believe he would never desire another woman ever again, so what was happening to him?

She smiled her thanks and then picked up a triangle of buttered toast. 'Mmm. Lovely.'

'Abeje's doing well. Her fever broke during the night. And the two kids from Mosa are doing well, too.'

'That's great. Have you got to work today?'

He nodded.

'Shame. I would have liked to be able to show you my class of kids and how wonderful they are.'

'Maybe I could come over during my lunch break?'

She beamed. 'That would be great! Look, thanks for this, but I'd better get back and change. Have a quick shower.'

'Of course. I'll see you later?'

'I'll look forward to it.'

She took a quick sip of her tea and then bolted, and when she'd gone, leaving sweet perfume in her wake, he realised just how much he was missing her already.

He liked having her around. She was sweet and caring and loving. Tasha had a big heart. She always had. She fell in love easily.

Was he capable of the same thing?

He woke with a start, the lingering effects of his bad dream ebbing from his mind as he blinked his eyes to clear them of sleep and tried to slow his racing heart.

He'd only meant to have a power nap, and normally he didn't dream—or if he did he didn't remember. But this one had been fierce in its imagery.

He'd been with his wife, Hannah. She'd been lying in bed, her hands protectively wrapped around her stomach. He'd been kneeling beside her, talking to the baby in her belly, telling him about how much he was already loved. But when he'd finished—when he'd looked up to smile at Hannah—it wasn't her any more but Tasha, and she'd been holding Abeje in her arms, crying, screaming at him to save her!

*'Save my child! You have to save my child!'*

Quinn rubbed at his eyes and stood up from the bed in the on-call room, stretching. The dream had unsettled him. But for what reason he wasn't sure. Because Hannah had become Tasha? Because he was worrying about Abeje? Or was it more to do with how connected to Abeje Tasha was?

He knew he shouldn't be worrying about this. He was impressed by her dedication as Abeje's teacher. Clearly she cared for the children in her class. and that was a good thing. But…

*But what?*

*What if it all goes wrong and I can't save her?*

No doctor liked to think the worst, but sometimes you had to consider your course of action. Malaria was contentious. Tricky. You never knew how people were going to react to the meds. Sometimes it came down to how well they'd been *before* they'd got infected, but they'd done a full work-up on Abeje and hadn't found anything else wrong.

Quinn ran his fingers through his hair and then quickly brushed his teeth. It was nearly time for him to go and see Tasha. He said he'd pop down to the school to meet the other kids.

But maybe he shouldn't? Maybe he was getting too deeply involved here?

He liked Tasha. Immensely. He couldn't deny it and he'd like their relationship to go further. But…

*Perhaps I'm getting cold feet?*

Did he really want to get into another relationship? Another relationship in which the welfare of a child was of primary significance? Did he need that complication? No one could know if Abeje would survive this and he feared Tasha's reaction if she didn't.

Tasha needed to get some space. She needed to take a

step back. She wasn't Abeje's mother—she'd said it herself. Perhaps he needed to help her decide just who she was to the child? She could go either way, but then he'd know. Know what he was up against.

He hated not knowing—the blind naivety that believed everything should be all right as long as they remained positive.

His reflection stared back at him from the small shaving mirror and he let out a sigh, feeling terrible for the thoughts he was having. Who was *he* to say who she should care for?

But he'd experienced the loss of a child and Tasha hadn't, and she had no idea of what it could do to a person. He needed to warn her, somehow. He needed to make her let go—because if she didn't she just might be devastated, and he wasn't sure he could deal with that, with being the cause of her pain once again.

Because he *would* be the cause, wouldn't he? If Abeje died then Tasha would think it was because *he* hadn't been able to save her, and he didn't want the blame.

He'd been blamed for a death before. Hannah's family, in their guilt, their grief, had taken it out on him, telling him that as a doctor he should have saved her. Should have fought to make her take the chemo and have a baby later!

*'You should have made her take the chemo, Quinn! What kind of a husband are you?'*

The accusation of their voices was still bitter in his mind.

He'd lost patients before—of course he had. All doctors had. But this case was different. Was personal because of Tasha. And he wasn't ready for that. Wasn't ready for the intense emotions that were already playing out between them.

He would fight and do his best for every patient, but Abeje had become a VIP. It was vital he didn't lose her.

Because he wasn't sure he could be witness to Tasha's collapse.

And to her blame.

It was scorching away from the air-conditioning of the boat. An oppressive heat that weighed as heavy as his fears. Despite it, he decided to walk to the school where Tasha taught. He felt he needed it—a little time to gain perspective on all that was happening. A little time to think of what he needed to say to her. That maybe he was rushing into a relationship he hadn't thought through properly. That maybe they ought to put the brakes on for a while—at least whilst Abeje was still sick.

*I'm too close. I need to be Abeje's doctor, but I can't do that properly if I'm involved with Tasha.*

*All* his patients deserved his utmost care, but he was beginning to feel as if Abeje should have *more*, somehow. His decisions and choices were being clouded by his feelings for her.

It felt good to walk through the port, where the fishermen were offloading their catches and wares. It was busy and vibrant and full of noisy life. A good reminder that outside of the confines of the boat, where he was generally surrounded by sick people, there were others living their lives as best they could.

There was happiness here, and warmth and community. People *knew* one another, and as he passed through the crowds he was greeted often and frequently by broad, smiling faces.

He loved these people. He really did. They filled him with an energy and a purpose that he had never found elsewhere—not since Hannah, anyway. They were people with a genuine need…not like some of the people who would sometimes wander into A&E back home, complaining of a broken acrylic nail or a splinter, or something equally stupid.

Medical care here wasn't abused at all.

*Perhaps I should have pushed Hannah more.*

He'd kept his emotions contained after Hannah had died. And then, when he'd lost his son hours later, he'd bottled them up. It had been easier to retreat into a numbed state. His father, an ex-Marine, had raised him to believe that if he was to grow into a big, strong man then he would have to get control of the wobbly emotions he had inside him. That crying was for the weak.

Quinn wasn't sure that was true any more. He wished he *could* cry sometimes. It might help to let the lid off the pressure cooker.

As he neared the school he could hear the children inside one class reading aloud from a book as one. He recognised the names of the characters and smiled, imagining Tasha standing at the front of the class, holding her book about wizards.

She must have seen him through a window, because suddenly she was leaning out of one, smiling happily and waving him over. 'Quinn! Come on in and I'll introduce you!'

He felt his heart lift at the sight of her beautiful face and gorgeous smile, and he smiled back and waved in return, feeling a cold lump inside his gut. He knew that he was about to hurt her. To do something he'd vowed not to do again. But he was doing it in the best interests of his patient and she would want that.

At least that was what he tried to tell himself.

She was energised. He could see that. She had to be a great teacher if she smiled like that all day long. Tasha was in a job that she loved and he could understand that. She made a perfect teacher. And she cared.

Inside, a sea of smiling faces awaited him.

'Everyone, I want you to say hello to Dr Shapiro, who works on the *Serendipity*—the hospital ship we visited a few days ago. Dr Shapiro is looking after Abeje.'

'Hi, Dr Shapiro!' the children all intoned, one or two waving from the front row.

'It's great to meet you all,' he said, smiling. 'Miss Tasha has told me all about you.'

They seemed happy about that, and Tasha stood beside him, beaming. 'We were reading, Quinn. Would you like to finish off the chapter before they all go out to lunch?'

'I'd love to!'

*Anything to delay the inevitable.*

He took the book from her and she pointed out where they'd got to. Her fingers brushed his and he felt that frisson he always felt when she touched him. He swallowed—hard.

'Okay, let's see how this goes...'

He began to read and the class listened intently.

Something special seemed to wrap itself around him as he stood reading at the front of the class. It was the way everyone was listening and reading along with him. The silence of their expectation as he tried to do special voices and vary his tone, giving it everything he could. It felt so good he wanted it to last for ever.

He had them all in the palm of his hand...rapt. And when he came to the end of the chapter and closed the book the classroom of children all looked up at him and began to clap appreciatively. He stood there, gave a slight bow, and looked at Tasha—who was also clapping.

Was this what it was like for her every day? To have *this*? He could see why she loved it. He'd adored every second.

'Okay, everyone. Put your books away and then I want you to line up by the door for lunch.'

The children all did as they were told and quietly, one by one, they lined up as instructed. Tasha stood by the door, waiting patiently for the last stragglers, and then she let them out, saying something kind to each one, thanking all the children for their efforts that morning.

When they were gone she closed the door and turned to him. 'Wow. I didn't know you could read like that!'

'Neither did I. It just...*happened*.'

'Well, I'm sure they'd love you to read to them from now on. I'll be out of a job!'

'No fear. I wouldn't have a clue what to do. I think I'll stick with doctoring.'

She smiled. 'I'm starving. Want to grab a bite to eat?'

'Sure.'

'Great!' She grabbed her bag from the back of her chair. 'And whilst we're queuing up for lunch you can tell me how Abeje is doing.'

They both purchased a small portion of stew that had been made with lamb and a variety of vegetables, served with some kind of wonderfully light dumpling that he'd never tasted before. He hadn't realised how hungry he was until the food was in front of him.

'How has she got on this morning?' asked Tasha.

'Pretty much the same, I have to say.'

Tasha sighed. 'It seems to be taking so *long*. I can't bear it—the not knowing.'

'She has one of the most aggressive strains of parasitical infection.'

'I know, but you gave her treatment for that. The two children from Mosa seem to be doing better than she is.' She let out a sigh. 'I'll come and sit with her again tonight. Look at her chart…see if there's something we haven't thought of.'

Quinn frowned, confused. 'Have you been researching on the internet again? I told you not to do that.'

She coloured slightly, stirred her stew. 'I couldn't help it.'

He stirred his own stew with his spoon, his appetite disappearing as he thought of how to voice his next words.

'Maybe you shouldn't come to the ship again.'

She looked up at him, questioning. 'Why?' A frown lined her brow.

'You need a break. You'll exhaust yourself this way. Teaching for long hours, then spending all night by Abeje's bedside. You've got to look after yourself.'

'I'm not the one who's sick. She *needs* me. I have to be there for her. She has no one else fighting in her corner.'

He felt a little affronted by that. '*Doesn't* she? My team are doing everything they can. *I'm* doing everything I can. Can't you see that?'

'I know that—but it's not the same as having someone by your bed, holding your hand. Like a mother.'

'You're *not* her mother, though.'

Tasha put down her spoon and frowned at him. '*What?* One minute you're taking me to the maternity ward and showing me mothers, telling me that I'm *like* a mother, and now this about-face? Why are you being like this?'

Perhaps he *was* giving her mixed messages, but his thoughts about the situation were all over the place right now. He didn't want to have to give Tasha bad news. He didn't want to be that doctor who had to stand in front of someone and tell them their loved one had died. He couldn't do that to her.

'I'm just trying to look out for you.'

'Well, you don't have to. *I'm* not your concern. Abeje is.'

'But this isn't just about Abeje, is it? It's about *you*. You see yourself in her so you're trying to save her.'

'What's wrong with that?'

'An abandoned kid in a children's home—'

'Lots of my students are from the children's home.'

'But *they're* not the ones you can't tear yourself away from!' He looked away, feeling an anger that he hadn't known he had rising inside him. 'You need to take a step back.'

He could feel the pressure coming from her. The demand that he did not allow Abeje to deteriorate.

'You need to remember you're just her teacher. If anyone can save her it's me, not you, and you've got to allow me to do my job!'

Tasha stood up abruptly, her spoon clattering to the floor as she threw her napkin on the table. 'I can't believe you're saying this.'

Then she grabbed her bag, threw it over her shoulder and stormed away. Everyone else in the small dining room stared at him, wondering what he'd said to upset their favourite teacher. He hated the fact he'd made her angry. Hated the fact that he couldn't make his mind up about what he wanted her to be. Who she needed to be. How she was making him feel.

Were those thoughts more about *his* feelings than *hers*?

He patted his mouth with a napkin and pushed his plate away.

# CHAPTER SIX

TASHA STOOD OUTSIDE the school building fuming. How *dared* he say such things to her? What right did he have? He didn't *know* her. Not really. He had no idea of all that she'd been through. Or what she was capable of.

*You're not her mother....*

No. She wasn't. But mothers weren't just the women that gave birth to a child. *He'd* been the one to tell her that! Mothers were created through love. Created by the bond of a woman who cared for a child as if it were their own. Which was how she felt about Abeje.

Abeje had no one else.

Tasha couldn't help but recall those long, lonely nights, sitting in her bed at the children's home, wondering if life would ever get better. Her back against the wall, her knees tucked up against her chest, she had stared out of her open curtains and wondered if there was anyone out there who would care and love for her the way she wanted. With the intensity of love that would make them take a bullet for her. If there might be someone out there who would love her so much that they would be devastated if anything happened to her.

*She'd* had no one else.

She'd felt surplus to requirements. An overspill in a

children's home already fit to bursting with lost children. But she'd grown up, and now she'd come here, and she'd met all these kids, and Abeje had found a way into her heart.

Abeje wanted to be a doctor, too. They were so similar! She couldn't help that any more than she could help her need to breathe. *She* could make that girl feel someone cared. And having Quinn tell her to back off was just way out of line!

She couldn't tell her heart just to switch off. Because if she could she'd probably still be a doctor. She wouldn't have nightmares. She wouldn't be feeling all sorts of emotions that she didn't want.

She'd be happy.

Not standing here with tears in her eyes.

She looked up as the school door opened and Quinn stepped out, his magnificent form filling the doorway. He scanned the play area, looking for her.

Wiping her eyes, she began to walk away.

'Tasha! Wait!'

'I don't want to talk to you, Quinn!' She tried to run, but the strappy sandals she was wearing weren't built for that. Agitated, she started walking fast.

She thought she'd got away. She thought he'd understood her message and maybe headed back to the ship, But when she slowed down she felt a hand on her arm.

'Tasha, please.'

He looked dismayed to see she was crying, and tried to pull her into his arms. 'Hey, I'm sorry.'

'Don't, Quinn! Just...*don't*.'

She pulled her arms free of his grasp and stood there in front of him, feeling like a child, her arms hugging her body. It was like being thirteen all over again. He'd hurt her. The way he'd sat there and told her she wasn't enough. *Again!* He'd *promised*. He'd promised to show her who he really was and perhaps he still really was that bully from all those years ago?

'I should never have said anything. I was…projecting. I was trying to stop you from getting hurt. I…'

She looked up into his face. 'You were projecting *what*?' She felt confused. What did he mean?

*You're not her mother.*

*You need to take a step back.*

*I was trying to stop you from getting hurt.*

'I'm not just another case for you to worry about. I'm not a patient.'

'I know.'

'How close I am to Abeje shouldn't be a concern to you. It should be a cause for *celebration*. That someone out there in this huge, cruel world actually *cares* about her!'

'I know.'

'So why did you say such horrible things to me? I don't understand.'

He was looking at her strangely, as if he were deciding what to say. If he should say anything at all.

His mouth moved silently, as if he were trying words for size. Trying to build his explanation in his mind first, before speaking the words out loud.

He sucked in a breath. 'I told you about Hannah.'

*His wife?* What did *she* have to do with this? She remembered him saying their marriage hadn't lasted very long.

'Yes?'

'We didn't get divorced. I know I made it sound like a failed marriage, but Hannah and I were very happy.

We married on impulse, but everything was great between us.'

Tasha shifted, looking up at him, wondering what he was going to say next. He'd implied that his marriage was over, but if they hadn't divorced, then that meant...

'She had one or two bad days when she didn't feel great. But she was a strong woman. She believed in soldiering on. It was nothing that concerned either of us to start with. We both worked hard, we were both exhausted, and when she learned that she was pregnant... we put it down to morning sickness.'

He looked at Tasha uncertainly.

Clearly he had never said those words out loud before. This wasn't a well-practised anecdote. This was something intensely private. And painful.

What was he about to tell her?

What did this have to do with her taking a step back from Abeje?

And Hannah had been *pregnant*. They had been about to have a baby.

Tasha could imagine the sort of father Quinn would be—funny, sporty, involved, loving, adoring. She tried to imagine a baby in his arms and her womb actually *ached*.

'You were going to be a dad?'

'Yeah. But she began to suffer terribly—sickness, weight loss, pains, jaundice, exhaustion. We were both doctors, and we both knew that something else was going on.'

Tasha ran the symptom list through her head, trying to work out what they might indicate. Sickness and exhaustion might have been from the pregnancy, but weight loss? Jaundice? Pain? None of those were good.

'What was it?'

'They diagnosed her with stage four aggressive pancreatic cancer. They did a scan and found metastases in her lungs, liver, spine and brain.'

'Oh, Quinn...'

Stage four cancer meant that it had already spread, as Quinn had said, to other organs. Typically, that would have meant the lungs or the liver, but the aggressive nature of Hannah's cancer had clearly caused a spread to her bones and brain, too. Which she knew meant incurable. Terminal.

'What were the treatment options?'

'They told her that she needed palliative surgery to remove the larger tumours, palliative pain treatment and an immediate chemotherapy. So we would have to abort the baby if we wanted Hannah to have a chance to live.'

Tasha stared in horror. She'd thought his life had been a breeze. Had imagined that the golden-haired, blue-eyed boy from her youth had just sailed through his life pain-free.

Imagine him being faced with that news. Knowing that even whilst his wife's body was being riddled by a killer disease it had still created the miracle of life.

'What did you do?'

'I told her I'd support her choice. That we could always have another baby, but I couldn't have another *her*. That I wanted her to fight it and to live as long as she could. The idea of losing her...'

He ran his hands through his hair and sank down against the school wall until he was crouched by her feet.

Tasha sat down next to him, empathising with the pain he must have gone through. The joy and the ecstasy of discovering he was going to be a parent and then the crashing diagnosis of his wife's cancer. The knowledge that if they wanted her to live they would have to kill. To go against all they held dear.

'She'd always wanted to be a mum. After being a doctor that was her dream. And she believed in the Hippocratic Oath so much—about not doing harm—that she couldn't terminate our child. So she chose to defer treatment until after the baby was born.'

Tasha didn't know what to say, so she reached out to lay her hand on his, grasping his fingers and giving them a squeeze. 'Oh, Quinn…'

'I didn't know what to feel. The fact that she was putting off chemo, putting herself at risk, made me angry beyond belief… But then I thought of that baby inside her, who had found a way to live and survive in a body that was under assault from a deadly disease. I wanted our child—of course I did—but I wanted her more. I also knew it was *her* body. *Her* life. And at the end of the day it had to be her decision.'

'It must have been terrible for you both.'

'They operated to remove one of the larger tumours, but when they opened her up they could see it was hopeless. She tried to keep as much of her pain from me as she could…pretended she was okay so she could give our son the best chance at life.'

'It was a boy?'

He nodded. 'But the cancer was too aggressive and she went into multiple organ failure at twenty-one weeks. They kept her going on a life support machine for a few hours, but then her parents and I decided to turn it off. They delivered our little boy, but…' He swallowed. 'He wasn't strong enough to survive.'

Tears were dripping from her eyes, just from trying to imagine his pain and grief. She'd got him *so* wrong.

She'd never imagined this pain, this grief, for him. Once again she had spun a fantasy of sunshine and rainbows regarding his life, believing everything had been golden for him.

'I'm so sorry. Truly, I am.'

'I held him in my arms, against my chest. Kangaroo care, they call it. You hear those stories of babies who are dying somehow coming back to life after a parent does that. I hoped for the same. But it was a vain hope. He was tiny. So fragile I thought he would break! His little hands…his fingers so small! He barely weighed anything. I sat in a chair with him on me and felt his every breath. Including the last one.'

He reached for his wallet and pulled out a photo, passed it to her.

It was well-worn. Obviously it had been held a lot. Looked at a lot. And there she saw Quinn, sitting in a chair, his shirt open, his tiny son—no bigger than his hand—resting against his chest. His son wore a tiny knitted bonnet in a pale blue. Quinn was cradling him. Holding him so gently. His face full of grief and despair.

She'd seen faces like that before. The faces of Maddie's parents. The faces of all those family members she had delivered bad news to.

She watched as tears trickled down his face and then she laid her head against his shoulder, giving him the time he needed.

He had not been afraid to share those emotions with her. She was proud of him for that. For sharing them with her.

She heard him sniff, felt him wipe his face, and then he turned to look at her.

'I've lost someone I love. I've watched my child die.

Felt it. It was the most horrific thing in the world. I sat there, concentrating on each breath that he struggled to make, begging him to just take one more. To keep on. To fight through. And it was selfish! *I* wanted him to carry on, because *I* didn't want to face the future without him! I knew that *I'd* be the one to fall to pieces, because watching a child die—it tears you in two. I mean it. It's pain unlike any other.'

She knew. *She knew*! Should she tell him? Should she just get it all out in the open? The way he had opened up to her?

He carried on talking. 'I said those things earlier because…because I've *been* there. I've been the person by the bedside. I've been the one holding the hand of the one I love, watching the last few breaths ebb from exhausted lungs, and you don't want to see that. You *don't*! It's horrible and it takes ages to get past it— weeks, months, *years*! The thought of *you* having to go through that… It almost destroyed me. I left everything to come and work on a hospital ship on the other side of the world because it was the only thing that didn't remind me of home. I'm trying to protect you by saying you need to take a step back. Because—believe me, Tasha—you *don't* want to witness the death of a child. And I don't know if I'm strong enough to help you through it.'

She looked at him now, her face pale, the shadows under her eyes dark. 'You think Abeje's going to die?'

He gave her a look that told her he didn't know. 'Malaria is a killer—I know that. I'm doing everything to save her, but I'm warning you that I might not be able to.'

She laid her head against his broad shoulder again, comforted by the feel of him next to her. 'Thank you for telling me what happened. I know it must have taken a lot for you to tell me.'

'I care about you. Maybe too much. It's muddling my thinking.'

'And I care about *you*.'

She swallowed hard, thinking about what he'd just said. *'I care about you. Maybe too much.'*

Well, if he cared about her then he deserved to hear the whole truth. No matter how painful. She had to tell him. She *had* to! Even if he then saw her for what she truly was. A failed doctor.

'You can't protect me from something that's already happened,' she whispered.

He shifted to look at her better. He was frowning. Not understanding. 'What?'

'I didn't just watch a child die, Quinn.' She looked down at the ground. Away from him. Away from any judgement she might see in her eyes. 'I killed one.'

Quinn blinked. Once. Twice. A third time. Still he couldn't stop looking at her face. Her tear-stained, red-eyed face.

She'd killed a child?

*No! That can't be! She has to be wrong!*

'What do you mean?'

She gave a shake of her head and then got to her feet, wiping the dust from the back of her skirt.

He got up too, rubbed his eyes and then stood, hands on hips, waiting for her to explain. She *couldn't* have killed a child! She wouldn't be allowed to be a teacher, for a start.

She turned to face him, eyes red.

'I've only been a teacher for a couple of years. I implied that I'd had a variety of jobs after leaving school before doing my teacher training, but that was a lie. I lied to you.'

She'd lied? Only people with something to hide lied.

'But you're telling me the truth now?'

'Yes.'

He believed her. Maybe he shouldn't, but he did.

'I'm listening.'

He couldn't imagine harming someone. He was a *doctor*! He *healed*. He tried to make things better. Taking a life…? He couldn't imagine how that must feel, even though he'd contemplated it to save his wife. But he hadn't had to go through with it. Neither of them had. They had fought for *life*.

'I went to medical school.'

Tasha smiled at him. A sorry smile. A *sorry-I-lied-to-you* smile. Short. Brief. Sad.

'I trained to become a doctor. It was all I'd ever wanted to do after meeting you. After falling in love with you when I was just thirteen and hearing the way you talked about how you were going to change people's lives…'

Her voice almost trickled into a whisper.

'You *did*?'

He couldn't believe it! *A doctor? Tasha?*

'I wanted *my* life to change. Back then I wasn't *living*, Quinn. I was just existing. I had no idea of what to do and no one steering me in any direction. I thought I'd probably end up in some dead-end job, but then Dexter brought you into my world and you talked about all the wonderful things you were going to accomplish as a doctor—delivering babies, saving lives, transplanting hearts, living with a purpose! I wanted that for myself. You made it sound so good. So valuable and important.

And I loved you so much I thought you might notice me if I wanted the same things as you.'

He was blown away. 'Tasha, I—'

'It's okay. We were just kids. You never understood how I felt about you. How could you? You'd never experienced my world. You'd never been without love.'

He looked down at the ground, realising just how terrible her life must have been. He hadn't ever thought about it. He'd just been a stupid kid with a stupid ego and he'd almost ruined her life because of it.

'I qualified. I took the oath. I began practising in a large hospital. It was hard. Exhausting. Night after night on call, in an understaffed department, unable to get a toilet break or even to eat sometimes. Some nights I survived on coffee. But I carried on because I knew that what I was doing was noble and worthwhile. And suddenly, for the first time in my life, I felt *important*. Valued. Wanted. *Needed.*'

'You were always important,' he said.

'I didn't know that back then. Like you said, we were kids.'

'What happened?'

He almost didn't want to hear, knowing that as soon as he did her words might make him think less of her. He didn't want to feel that way.

But he knew junior doctors screwed up sometimes. She was right. They were overworked and exhausted sometimes. But they got through it—because if they didn't then people died.

'It was a night shift, and I was the doctor on call. I'd worked two days straight, with barely any sleep, and I'd been beeped to this girl—Maddie—a couple of times already. She had pneumonia, and her SATs kept going really low and she would struggle to breathe, but every time I got to her and gave her some treatment she recovered. Then there was a huge input of casualties into A&E, and I was called to tend to a pregnant woman who was threatening to deliver after abdominal trauma.'

Quinn swallowed, imagining her fear of having to treat that pregnant woman.

'As I rushed to A&E my beeper went off again for Maddie. I stood there in the corridor, staring at it, trying to make a judgement call. The pregnant lady? Or Maddie? Two lives? Or one? I knew Maddie had kept on recovering with the treatment I'd ordered previously, so I called in my instructions for Maddie and chose to go to A&E.'

'I would have made the same choice.'

She gave that smile again. Quick. Brief. A thank-you.

'I was in A&E for a good two hours. The time went so quickly—you know what it's like when you've got to think fast, make immediate decisions, do everything at a running pace?'

He nodded.

'I delivered the baby. It was a boy, and he went up to SCBU until his mum could come out of Theatre. I headed up to Paediatrics to see Maddie as soon as I could, but...'

She faltered, fresh tears dripping down her cheeks.

'Maddie was in respiratory arrest. They'd been paging me but I couldn't answer them. They were frantically trying to get her back. They were doing CPR when I arrived on the ward. I pushed the nurse out of the way to do it myself. I was completely shocked that she'd deteriorated so quickly. Had I missed the signs? Had I misdiagnosed her earlier? Given the wrong treatment? I felt her ribs break. Puncturing lungs that were already damaged and filled with fluid.'

Tasha began to cry with heaving sobs, hiccupping her way through the story.

'I couldn't get her back! I tried! I tried everything. But she just slipped away! She died because of *me*. I had to tell her parents that I'd done my best, but *had* I?'

'Tasha...'

'I walked out of the hospital that night. After I'd told the parents their little girl was dead I walked out. I didn't go back. I couldn't. I knew I couldn't be put in that position again, where I had to make a choice over who lived and who died. Who was *I* to decide such things?'

'It wasn't your fault, Tash. It sounds like you did everything you could.'

'You weren't there! How could you *know*?'

'Because I know you. Because I know what it's like in a hospital when you're on call. I've listened to every word you've just said and I know it's the truth. Because I've seen inside your heart and there's not one shred of darkness there. You did your best. You were put in an impossible position to choose between two lives and I would have done the same as you.'

'But she *died*, Quinn. Because of *me*.'

He took her hands in his and pulled her close, hugged her against his chest. 'No. *Not* because of you.'

She sobbed against his chest. Hot, wet tears soaked into his shirt and he hated it that she was feeling so much pain. All this time he'd been trying to protect her from such devastation but she'd already been through it. And she felt responsible!

He knew that kind of guilt all too well. He'd questioned every decision he'd made after Hannah and his son had died. Especially when Hannah's parents had blamed him for not healing her. For not making a better-informed decision. For not forcing her to have a termination so she could have had the cancer treatment more quickly.

He'd almost been torn apart by guilt, and he'd found himself in a very dark place after the funeral.

Now he understood why Tasha cared so much. Now he understood why she had such a strong attachment to Abeje. It was love. Plain and simple. She had adopted this child in her heart and she was now being faced with losing her if she didn't do the right thing.

'You did everything right,' he murmured, stroking her hair. 'You did everything *right.'*

Soon her crying stopped. Became just gentle sniffs. And they stood there holding one another, leaning on each other for support.

But it was more than just physical strength. It was emotional strength, too.

She needed him.

*And I need her.*

He'd had to leave her at the school. She had lessons to teach that afternoon and he needed to come back to work, too.

He stood at the end of Abeje's bed, wondering why she wasn't getting better. Why it was taking so long.

*Am I just being impatient? Or am I afraid of the pressure I feel to cure her?*

Tasha had completely sideswiped him with her confession. She'd been a doctor. *A doctor!* All this time she'd been on the hospital ship and not said a word. He hated it that she'd kept things from him. Such important things, too. Hiding her pain the way Hannah had. They'd talked about their pasts and he'd hoped that she'd feel she could tell him the truth.

*Like I told her everything?*

No wonder he hadn't had to explain anything medical to her. All those times she'd sounded knowledgeable, explaining it as internet research. Most friends or family members of patients wanted the doctors to explain the treatments and the medications—what they were, what they did—but she *hadn't.* Because she knew already.

And she was carrying around that guilt born from the death of a child, even though it sounded as if she'd made the right call and done all she could.

But he knew how exhaustion felt when you were just a registrar. Those long hours with barely any sleep or proper nutrition. Soldiering on because you had to...because there was no one else to do it.

How many nights had he stayed up trying to find cures for Hannah? How many medical trials had he hunted down, trying to extend her life?

He'd been there. *All* doctors had been there. And it was awful.

No wonder she was worrying about Abeje so much. She knew what could go wrong! She knew that it was taking a long time to see improvement. When she sat by Abeje's bedside did she see Maddie's face? Was *that* what was scaring her?

But the thing that frightened him most was that he could see a lot of Hannah in Tasha. They were both the same. Both trying to give a child the chance of life more than anything else, even to their own detriment. How many nights had Tasha sat by Abeje's bed without food or rest for herself?

Rob came over. He looked weary, too, and handed Quinn a chart for him to sign off on some medication.

'The two kids from Mosa are doing well. They managed some real food earlier.'

'That's good,' Quinn said, staring at Abeje and wondering why she wasn't recovering just as quickly.

She was so little. Smaller than the others. Perhaps her immune system wasn't as strong? What if there was something else going on in her system?

'I'd like another round of bloods taken for Abeje, Rob. A full work-up. Everything.'

'Sure thing. I'll get right on it.'

'And I'd like a full scan done. Just to check that there's nothing else going on that's preventing her recovery.'

'Okay, I'll schedule it.'

All children were precious. But the pressure to save Abeje was high. Higher than it had ever been. He would do everything in his power to save her—to stop Tasha having to lose another precious little girl. A girl she saw herself in.

If Tasha felt she couldn't save her, what would it do to her?

Abeje deserved to live. She deserved to fight another day.

He *had* to save her.

He had to save them both.

It felt different boarding the ship that evening. Tasha had laid herself bare to Quinn. She'd told him everything. And that vulnerability felt strange. As if she had nothing left guarding her. Nothing shielding her from harm any more. She was glad she'd told him. That he knew everything.

Outwardly, he hadn't reacted badly.

But had it changed his opinion of her?

He knew who she was and who she had been before. And she'd told him just how much he had influenced her life's choices—how somehow he had always been in her life.

It was almost embarrassing. That a childhood crush had formed her career decisions and she had failed so miserably at it.

Perhaps she'd never been meant to be a doctor? That had been *his* choice, not hers. Perhaps she should have been something else? A sales assistant somewhere. She'd always liked shoes. She could have done something with that.

She'd not been made of stern stuff—hadn't had any of the weapons that doctors needed in their arsenal. She'd never been able to separate herself from the pain and hurt that her patients went through. Had always faltered with the professional distance doctors ought to establish. Had always wanted to comfort grieving relatives. Put an arm around their shoulders. Give them a hug. And then, in solitude, she would cry herself.

She'd been a taut, raw nerve.

Tasha quietly entered the ward, hoping no one would notice her sitting beside Abeje's bed. But Quinn saw her the second she sat down and came over.

She sucked in a steadying breath. No doubt he would think differently of her now. Perhaps he would consider her a coward. And if that was the case then so be it. He'd never felt much for her before, when they were kids, she could cope with that again. It didn't matter any more. What mattered, she told herself, was this gorgeous little girl in the bed beside her.

'Hey.'

'Quinn.' She smiled.

'How did your afternoon go?'

'It was very nice, thank you.'

'What were you teaching this afternoon?'

'How to write instructions.'

'Oh.' He nodded, as if he recalled a similar lesson himself.

Her gaze drifted over to the two siblings from Mosa, who were both sitting up in bed. 'How are the other children doing?'

'Good. They ate today and kept it down. Always a good sign.'

Yes, it was. But it was just another piece of evidence that said Abeje wasn't eating yet. She wasn't keeping food down. She was being fed through a tube still. She wasn't improving. The worst might still happen.

Tasha shifted in her seat. 'That's great.'

She couldn't meet his eyes. Those beautiful eyes of his that just a short while ago she'd stared into on that mountaintop terrace. How did life change so quickly? So brutally?

'We took some more bloods today. And we did a scan. Hopefully when the results come in they'll give us some good news.'

She nodded. 'Thanks for letting me know.'

'Tash, could I—?'

She held up her hand. 'It's okay. I'm all right.' She retrieved a book from her bag. 'I thought I'd carry on reading to her. It helps, I think.'

He stood there for a moment longer, not sure whether to stay or go. She hoped he wasn't going to ask about earlier. She'd told him the truth, but she wasn't sure she was ready to go into it again. Not this soon. Having Quinn reject her wasn't something she wanted to cope with right now.

He walked away to tend to his other patients and she let out a strained breath. Then she opened the book and began to read, trying to lose herself in a story where nobody died and everyone got their heart's desire.

But she couldn't do it. Her eyes kept leaving the page and looking up to see where Quinn was. For one moment she stopped reading for about three minutes, just staring at him, watching him as he diligently worked on his patients.

*You'd have made a great father, Quinn.*

Her heart ached for all that he'd been through. What he must have suffered. The picture of him cradling his son had seared itself into her memory. She'd always thought he'd lived such a golden life. He'd had a wonderful childhood home. A family with loving parents. Had known what he wanted to be and done it. Even believing his marriage had ended after only eighteen months hadn't made her think otherwise. She'd believed that he and his wife had obviously been wrong for each other, because he was still here—still smiling.

But there'd been heartache behind his words. Things he'd kept to himself. She couldn't imagine the pain that he and Hannah must have gone through, and then, after losing the love of his life, he'd had to watch his son die just hours later?

She'd thought the loss of Maddie was hard. The fear of losing Abeje was hard. But Quinn had been through real trauma. Real heartbreak. How dared she even *think* that her pain compared?

How did anyone recover from that? How was he still upright?

Why were some people's lives so distressing? When was it their turn to have a little happiness?

\* \* \*

She couldn't sleep. It had been a long evening on the hospital ship. She'd read a good four chapters to Abeje before the doors to the ward had burst open and a man had come limping in, with blood running down his leg and a large spike of metal in his thigh.

She'd leapt to her feet, thinking she needed to run over to him, to help him to a bed in order to study the wound and work out how best to remove the spike, but then she had remembered that it wasn't her job any more.

She had sunk back down into her chair as Quinn and his team had leapt into immediate action. Then, knowing that they would be busy, would probably have to go into surgery, she'd slipped away unnoticed.

Now she was at home, sitting with her back against the wall, her knees hunched up to her chest, staring out of her bedroom window as she often did. Trying to decide if anything Quinn had said was the right thing. Whether she ought to take a step back.

She had allowed herself to get close again. She had opened up her heart and that was dangerous. Look at how she was feeling right now. Maybe she should be contemplating leaving Ntembe and going somewhere else? Perhaps it had been wrong of her to let Abeje get inside her heart like this? She never wanted to feel the way she'd felt about Maddie ever again.

Was this what it was like for people who had families? She'd never really had one. She didn't know.

But she couldn't imagine walking away. Not now.

*I'm not going to be a coward.*

She loved little Abeje. She couldn't leave her behind. What sort of person would *do* such a thing? It would be cruel. And if—*when*—Abeje recovered, Tasha wanted to be there to hug her tightly and let her know that she was loved.

Because she was. And it was important for an individual to know that. They could draw strength from it. They could stop feeling alone.

The moon glowed brightly in the inky sky above, and she could see one or two stars.

*Even the moon isn't alone.*

Sighing, she slumped down into her bed and pulled a thin sheet over her in an attempt to go to sleep. But the second her head had touched the pillow she heard a knock at her front door.

*Who's that?*

Her heart thudded loudly in her chest.

She wasn't sure she wanted to open the door in this neighbourhood, this late at night. It could be anyone! She lay there, trying to think about what was best to do. Perhaps if she ignored it the person would go away?

But they didn't. They knocked again. Harder this time.

'Tasha?'

*Quinn?*

Tasha slipped from her bed and pulled on a thin dressing gown, tying it around her waist. She had a peephole she could look through, and she laid her hands against the door as she pressed her face closer to it.

His hair was ruffled and he looked a little flushed. What was he doing here?

*Maybe something's wrong with Abeje!*

Tasha undid the lock and yanked the door open. 'What's going on? Why are you here?'

He looked at her, almost as if he was surprised that

she'd actually opened the door. But then he took a step towards her, put his hands either side of her face and pulled her towards his lips for a kiss.

# CHAPTER SEVEN

*OH, MY. WHAT'S HAPPENING? Why is he...? Oh!*

She stopped thinking for a moment. Stopped worrying. This moment that she'd first dreamt about at the age of thirteen was actually *happening*! Their kiss outside the maternity wing had been one of comfort. But this... This was one of pure need—desire.

She had always wondered how it would feel.

And now she knew.

It felt wonderful. In his arms. Pressed close.

The feel of him was magical. The feel of him wanting *her*. After all this time. Kissing her, tasting her, breathing her in. It was a heady mix of excitement and elation.

She slipped her hands around his waist and sank into him.

He felt good. Broad and strong. Solid.

It was impossible to think straight.

And then—as quickly as it had begun, as quickly as she had been surprised by the kiss—he ended it, stepping away, looking uncertain. Regretful.

'I'm sorry. I shouldn't have done that.'

Bewildered, stunned, unable to speak because she was still lost in the wonder of that kiss, she simply looked at him, her fingers touching her lips where his had been.

'I had to… You were shutting me out. I didn't like it.'

'I…'

'We were getting close. Becoming good friends. And then you said all that stuff about what had happened to you and suddenly everything changed. *You* changed. It was like you retreated into yourself and took yourself away from me.'

She stared at him. At the way he'd retreated from *her*. He was standing as far away from her as he could, his back against the wall, his hands pressed against it— as if by doing so he would stop himself reaching out to her again.

*I want him to kiss me again. This time I'll be ready for it.*

'I thought you'd think differently of me. Knowing I'd given up being a doctor,' she said.

He looked confused. 'Why would I do that?' Lines furrowed his brow and then suddenly he looked up at her, realisation dawning. 'Because *he* did—didn't he? Your husband? Simon.'

The pain of that moment from her past flared into being once again. Simon coming home from work the day she'd lost Maddie and asking her why she'd walked out of work… At first he'd been understanding. Knowing what it felt like to lose a patient and how that could affect someone. He had listened as she'd told him how horrifying it had been to take Maddie's parents into that sad little family room and tell them the worst news of their lives.

*'We've all been there, Tash. It'll be okay.'*

*'No, it won't!'*

*'You just need time—'*

*'I'm not going back ever again!'*

*'What?'*

*'I quit!'*

Simon had taken a step back from her, released her, and looked at her with incredulity.

*'You can't quit!'*

*'Watch me.'*

And then he'd started staying at work longer than normal. Saying he was working longer shifts. But she'd known what was happening. Eventually a friend had called to let her know what he was up to, and the smell of a perfume that wasn't hers had been a big clue.

*'You're having an affair, aren't you?'*

*'No.'*

*'Don't lie to me, Simon!'*

He'd admitted it. Said he couldn't change who he was—that he needed that release and that she'd changed since their marriage. Had stopped being the fun Tasha he'd always known.

The divorce had gone through quickly—thankfully.

Tasha looked at Quinn, feeling that old hurt—the betrayal, the pain—still in her heart. That feeling she'd carried her whole life.

*I'm not good enough. I wasn't good enough for my parents to keep me and my husband discarded me, too.*

'That bastard!' The vehemence with which Quinn spoke the word was startling.

Tasha's eyes widened in surprise, and he must have realised that he'd scared her slightly.

'I'm sorry. It's none of my business, of course.'

'It's okay.'

'No. It's not. Look, I'd better go. I just came round to check that you were okay and to…'

His gaze dropped to her mouth and she felt heat rise up within her body as her heart pounded in its cage. Her fingertips were tingling with millions of pins and needles, feeling the desire to reach out and touch him once again. But she didn't. Something was stopping her.

*I'm not good enough. He didn't mean to kiss me. It was a mistake. Like everything else. We shouldn't have...*

'Quinn?' She said his name as he stepped back outside and began to walk away from her door.

He turned in the street, his eyes twinkling in the dark. 'Yes?'

She didn't want him to go. Didn't want him to leave her. Not again.

She felt her throat and her tongue tighten with all the stuff she couldn't say. Wouldn't allow herself to say. Her feelings for him.

'Goodnight,' she managed.

In the darkness she saw his smile. His shoulders dropped.

'Goodnight, Tasha. I'll see you tomorrow.'

She nodded and watched him walk away. She kept watching until the darkness swallowed him up, then slowly, reluctantly, closed her front door.

The taste of her was still on his lips. What had come over him? He'd gone there because he hadn't been able to stand the awkwardness that had been there between them earlier. He'd felt her pulling away, the same way Hannah had tried to protect him, to make things less painful when the end came.

He couldn't have that happen now—with Tasha. He needed her. More than he'd realised. He'd gone round to tell her that—to just *say* it, straight out, let her know how he felt, that her past didn't matter—but the second she'd opened her door, looking all ruffled and curious as to why he was at her door in the middle of the night, he'd not been able to stop himself.

He hadn't gone there to kiss her.

He'd been trying desperately to forget the way it had felt to have Tasha in his arms outside the maternity wing.

But tonight...tonight had been startling. Kissing her had been... He shook his head, trying to clear his thoughts, but in doing so he lost his balance. He reached out to grab something to hold him upright, but there was a divot in the path and he went straight over, landing on his left arm.

He heard something break. Felt pain radiate like a burning star in his shoulder and chest. Throbbing. Lightning-bright. Intense. He struggled to his feet, supporting his left arm with his right.

*Dammit! I'll need an X-ray.*

He'd heard of falling head over heels—but tripping over a hole in the middle of a street? He ought to have known better. Ought to have brought a torch. This wasn't like England, where there were streetlamps every few metres. The blackness was absolute out here. With just the moon and the stars for illumination.

His shoulder hurt. And his arm, feeling like a giant lead weight, was pulling it down even more.

He trudged on. Imagined how he was going to explain this to the rest of his team.

When he got to the *Serendipity* he'd totally beaten himself up over how stupid he'd been. He should never have gone racing round to Tasha's...he should never have kissed her...he should have waited until he'd got his thoughts and feelings under control before he'd acted impulsively.

But he'd needed to go. Had had to make his feelings clear. It was the only way.

And if he hadn't then he wouldn't be sitting on a plastic chair, looking at an X-ray showing a broken collarbone, of all things.

Maria had smiled at him as she'd put his arm into a sling. 'I don't know why you don't just tell her you love her.'

He'd frowned. 'What?'

'Tasha! It's perfectly clear to me and to everyone else around here that you two are attracted. It was clear the first day she ran in here, with that poorly little girl. The look on your face!'

'I didn't know who she was back then.'

'No, maybe not. But there was a little something in you that switched on. The light came on behind your eyes. First time I've ever seen it since I've been working with you, Dr Shapiro!'

'It's complicated, Maria.'

'When *isn't* it? Nobody ever said life was easy.'

'We're completely different people. She lives *here*. We'll be leaving in a week or so.'

'You've never heard of long-distance relationships?'

He smiled. 'Yes, but I'm not sure I want to be in one.'

'She could come with us. Volunteer on the boat.'

'She would never leave Abeje.'

Maria sat down opposite him. 'She's close to that little girl, isn't she?'

He nodded, looking across to Abeje, who was restless in her bed.

'Why doesn't she adopt her?'

'I don't know.'

But he *did* know. She was scared to. Tasha was scared of most things. He could see it in her. Scared to commit. Scared to get too involved. Scared to care too much in case it hurt. She thought she could get through this remotely. From a distance. But it was impossible. The world was filled with people, and people made you care.

'I think they'd make a grand pair, those two. If the little tyke pulls through, of course.'

'How has she been since I've been out?'

'Restless. Her fever's building again. We've been trying to keep it down as much as we can, but I think this is her turning point.'

Quinn looked at Maria. Met her gaze.

He felt immense pressure to get this right. The blood results that had come back earlier were good. Abeje's scan was clear. There wasn't anything else going on in her system. She was just a young kid battling a deadly disease. Every patient responded differently.

'Let's see which way she turns, then,' he said.

'What happened to your arm?'

He'd been by Abeje's bed, monitoring her progress as best he could with one hand, balancing her notes on his lap as he wrote with his pen.

Tasha had crept up on him unawares.

Hearing her voice, he instantly stood up, and Abeje's notes, on their clipboard, went clattering to the floor.

Tasha picked them up, scanned what he'd written and looked up at him, frowning.

'She has another fever?' She bent over the girl to rest her hand against the girl's brow.

'We're doing everything we can to make her comfortable.'

'Have you given her acetaminophen?'

'Of course.'

'Has she been seizing?'

'No. She's stable at the moment. Her condition has neither worsened nor got better over the last few hours.'

'You should have called me.'

'You wouldn't have been able to do anything.'

She shook her head. 'I could have *been* here.' She took a seat beside Abeje and took the little girl's hand. It felt clammy.

'Your arm? You never said how you hurt it.'

'My arm's fine. It's my collarbone that's broken.'

Her face filled with concern. 'How did *that* happen?'

'I tripped in a hole in the road.'

'Last night?'

He nodded.

Tasha could see he was still wearing the same clothes from yesterday. He didn't look as if he'd washed yet, or rested, and she wondered just how on earth he was going to manage any of those things with just one arm.

'I'm not teaching today. I'll stay and help you out.'

'You don't need to.'

'When did you last get any sleep? Have a shower? Eat some proper food? Look, I'm *here*, I've got two hands and, to be honest, if I just sit by Abeje's bed all day I'm going to go mad! Let me look after you for a bit, and we'll both be here if her condition changes.'

The thought of Tasha being around and looking after him was appealing. He *liked* having her around, and he *had* been struggling with his arm in the sling. He'd taken painkillers, but the injury still hurt. The slightest movement seemed to set it off—like a smouldering fire beneath his skin.

And if he was going to feel *any* smouldering heat he'd prefer it to be another kind. Even if that *did* make him feel guilty for thinking about a woman who wasn't Hannah.

'Okay. Thank you.'

'When are you off shift?'

'As of eight hours ago.'

She smiled, understanding immediately. Of course she would. She'd used to be a doctor. You couldn't just switch off when your shift ended. Sometimes you stayed. You carried on to see a patient through. Sometimes you found it hard to let go.

'Right. Let's get you sorted, then.' She stood up, slipping her arm through his good one. 'Show me where your cabin is.'

It was larger than she'd expected. Whenever she'd pictured what the crew's cabins were like she'd imagined tiny rooms, big enough for just a single bed and a sink. Maybe with a small portable television up high on one wall. A small cupboard with a rail to hang clothes. Not much else.

But Quinn's room was a decent size. There was a single bed, neatly made, with a porthole just above it looking out onto the Ntembe docks. Beside it was a small two-seater sofa, a small desk and chair, and opposite a floor-to-ceiling wardrobe for his clothes and a door that led to an en-suite bathroom with a shower and toilet.

He'd made it homely. There was a bed runner in traditional African fabric. A couple of cushions on the couch covered in the same material. And on the desk was a framed photograph of Quinn and a woman who could only be his wife. Hannah.

She picked it up. 'This is Hannah? She was very beautiful.'

'She was. Inside and out.'

Tasha put the picture down and turned to him. He was

standing close and she could feel her body responding to that proximity.

'When did you last eat?'

He shook his head. 'I don't remember.'

'Typical doctor.'

He looked down at the floor, smiling, and her heart just melted. She felt it happen. That simple gesture of his—smiling, looking down—let her see that he knew he was being caught out in how badly he was looking after himself. She felt like liquid. Her body was going to pieces over this man.

'You can't look after patients if you don't look after yourself.'

He continued to smile at her. He had no defence.

'I'll go and get you something to eat from the canteen.'

He nodded, and she sidestepped him and closed the cabin door behind her, letting out a heavy breath, feeling relief flooding through her.

She had to be careful. She couldn't get carried away just because he'd kissed her. He'd told her he hadn't meant to do it. Clearly he regretted what he'd done. But there was something more between them now. She could feel it.

A heat. An intensity. And it was stronger than any silly crush she'd experienced as a teenage girl. This was different. More potent.

More real.

It wasn't a fantasy any more. It wasn't a crush.

She and Quinn had kissed and she could imagine a whole lot more. What she had to do now was keep control of herself, stay logical and remind herself that he would be leaving soon and there was no future for them.

They would both have to keep their hands to themselves.

She found her way to the ship's canteen by following

her nose, and returned with a tray filled with scrambled eggs, bacon and toast. She'd also brought two mugs of tea and a small fruit salad.

Holding the tray with one hand, she gave a gentle knock on his door, saying quietly, 'It's me.' And then she went in.

Quinn was lying on the bed, still dressed, his eyes closed. Fast asleep.

She stood and watched him for a moment, gazing at his face, smiling. Feeling a warmth inside her that was making her feel dreamy.

*What am I doing? This has no future.*

She put down the tray, as quietly as she could and settled on the sofa opposite. There was a book on his desk—some tale of spies and espionage—and she picked it up, intending to read. But once she'd flicked through the first pages—the dedication, the acknowledgements, the first paragraph—she let her gaze return to Quinn. Knowing she could look at him without being caught. Without being judged.

Her feelings for him were growing. Exponentially. But should she be getting involved with another guy? Look how badly it had always worked out for her with men.

It had been such a long time since she'd been in a relationship she was craving it. That closeness. That intimacy. There'd been no one since she'd broken up with Simon. And she'd had a wall of solitude around her for so long that now it was coming down, and she wanted to let him in so badly!

But it was *Quinn*. And her feelings for him had always been muddled since day one. And he'd be leaving soon…

*Perhaps I'm just scared? Finding reasons to walk away because I've never been given a reason to stay?*

Tasha let out a heavy sigh. She stared at Quinn, taking in every detail of his face, until her eyelids began to droop and she, too, fell fast asleep.

She woke with a start some time later. Quinn was still sleeping and she checked her watch—three hours had passed! *Three!* Okay, so she hadn't got much sleep last night after Quinn had kissed her and then walked away, but she hadn't realised just how tired she was.

Stretching, she got up to work out the kinks in her muscles, and as she stretched her arms high and wide she heard Quinn stir behind her.

'What time is it?'

Blushing, she turned around and sat on the couch. 'Midday. Lunchtime. I brought you breakfast, but you'd fallen asleep by the time I got back.'

'I was beat. But, thanks.'

He tried to pull himself up into a sitting position, but seemed to struggle with just one arm, so she got up to help pull him upright. He pulled the tray towards him and began to eat the cold bacon and eggs.

'I can go and get you something fresh.'

He gave her a thumbs-up sign. 'This is fine.'

She sat down again and watched him eat, but then she felt self-conscious and got up, trying to give him some space. It had been such a long time since she had been close to a man. She couldn't believe she was finding it so difficult to be with him.

When he'd finished eating he swallowed down the cold tea and then began to fiddle with the buttons of his shirt.

'What are you doing?'

'I need to have a wash.'

'Oh.' She watched him struggle for a moment more,

but it was painful seeing him fail to undo his buttons with just one hand.

'Here—let me.'

She reached for his last two buttons near his waist, trying not to look at the expanse of chest that had been revealed already. It was making her have palpitations just thinking of what he might look like with no top on.

She went to stand behind him, so she could pull each sleeve off carefully. It was a bit fiddly. She had to release the sling to get the shirt off, but when she did she realised she was staring.

He was beautiful. Not overly muscular, but she could tell he looked after himself. He was trim, with a neat, flat waist, his shoulders were broad and strong, his skin suntanned and golden. When he turned to face her she saw his chest had a smattering of hair in the centre, sun-kissed and barely there.

The urge to trail her fingertips across his skin with a feather-light touch was strong. His nipples were taut and she had to yank her imagination back from the fantasy of wanting to do things to them.

'I shouldn't get this sling wet, so I'll just have a flannel wash. Could you fill me a bowl of water?'

'Sure.'

Colouring, she hurried into the bathroom and smiled broadly at her reflection, shaking her head at all the wicked thoughts that were running rampant through her mind.

*I'm a very naughty girl...*

She put a bar of soap in the water and let out a big breath before she carried the bowl and a flannel back to him, realising that if anyone was going to wash him down it was going to have to be her.

'I can do my front…but if you could do my back?' he asked, an eyebrow raised.

'Sure.' Did her voice sound as wobbly as it felt?

Tasha watched him wash his chest. He obviously had no idea how erotic it was. Watching him squeeze the flannel with one hand to get all the water out, wiping soap all over his skin, leaving white smears and bubbles that he then smoothed away with the flannel, his skin glistening in the sunlight from the porthole as the fabric brushed over muscle and sinew, his nipples peaking.

He did his chest, his stomach, his face. But he'd need her to do the rest.

She jumped up like a shot.

'Okay. I'll…er…start on your back.'

Her hands were trembling. He couldn't see it, but *she* could. Standing behind him, she looked at his skin, at the line and curve of his spine that she could imagine tracing with her tongue. His broad shoulder blades.

*I can't have shaky hands.*

She tried to stop it from happening. She ran the soap over his back, biting her bottom lip, trying not to think of this as a sexual act. Then she used the flannel, feeling the ripple of his muscles under his skin, trying to be tender over his left arm and near his broken collarbone. She wanted it to last for ever.

'I think you're done.'

She didn't want it to be done.

'Shall I get you a towel?'

'No. It's nice to air-dry in this heat.' He looked at her uncertainly. 'I'll…er…do my legs myself. I can reach those. But I'll need a change of clothes. Could you get me something?'

She nodded and turned to open the wardrobe, surprised to see a neat, orderly pile of items, some shirts and trousers on hangers, shoes paired and lined up at the bottom.

'If you wouldn't mind carrying the bowl back into the bathroom for me, I'll finish up in there.'

'Of course.' She smiled, feeling her cheeks blush and thanking whatever god was listening that she hadn't had to soap down his thighs, because if she'd had to do that...

She blew her fringe from her face. Was it hot in there?

In the bathroom, he looked at her uncertainly. 'Er... could you do the button on my...?'

He looked down. At his trousers.

*Right. Yes.*

She stood in front of him, her hands on the waistband of his trousers, undoing the button, telling herself inwardly over and over, *Don't touch the zip. Don't touch the zip!*

But all she could think of was slowly drawing down the zip and letting her hand slip inside.

When she was done Tasha backed away, closing the door behind her, and sank down into the chair.

*What the hell...?*

That was probably the most erotic thing she'd done in a long time. How terrible was *that*? That she'd somehow, in all of this, forgotten she was a woman with needs. She'd been so busy shutting everyone out she'd forgotten about who she was under there. Hidden in the dark recesses of her mind. Being alone was all well and good for the majority of the time, but there were other times when she just needed...

She swallowed. Trying not to think of what she needed right now.

She'd been on autopilot for so long now. Cruising

through life at thirty miles an hour because it was safe.
Becoming a teacher because it was safe. Staying single
because it was safe. Shutting down her sexual drive because it was safe.

But now she was in a danger zone. And she didn't
know what to do. Or how to react to Quinn. No. She knew
*how* she was reacting, but was she going to do anything
about that reaction? Was she going to act on it?

From the bathroom she heard a small thump and a
small, 'Ow!'

'You okay?'

'Yeah.'

'Well, just holler if you need help.'

He came out wearing fresh trousers, but he held the
shirt in his hands. 'Can you help me get this on and but-
toned up?'

She nodded, feeling heat surge into her cheeks. 'Sure.'

She stood up and took the shirt, gliding it over his left
arm first, so they could get it back into its sling, and then
the easier, right arm. Then she stood in front of him to
do up the buttons.

*Don't look at his face!*

The last time they'd stood this close he'd been kissing
her. She could feel the heat radiating from his body. He
smelled fresh. Manly. A primal scent that she couldn't
help but react to as the memory of his perfect chest and
body stayed at the forefront of her mind.

'All done.'

'Thanks. I couldn't have done it without you.'

She looked up. Wanted to stare into his eyes for eternity. 'Quinn, I…'

He stared back. 'Yes?'

His voice was thick. Guttural. Had he been affected

as much as she? Had he been awakened by the feel of her washing him? Running the flannel over his skin? Having her fingers slip into the waistband of his trousers?

Having her stand *so close*?

His eyes were like pools. She could drown in them happily. She wanted to touch him. To hold him in her arms, if only just for a moment.

But she knew he wouldn't act first. He'd already done that once, when he'd come to her place in the middle of the night and kissed her, and then he'd backed away.

Would kissing him now be a mistake?

Would she be muddling everything they had?

*But I want to so much! Perhaps he needs the first move to come from me? Perhaps he feels that by acting first he was taking advantage?*

She reached up to touch his face. To run her fingers down his jawline, over his slightly bristled skin. His lips parted and she couldn't help but focus on his mouth. A mouth that had kissed her and could do so again.

She stood up on tiptoe and brought his face down to hers. Unable to fight her doubts for a second longer.

His lips met hers. Delicately. Hesitantly. But then, as if a dam had broken, their lust for one another powered through and Quinn was pushing her back against the wardrobe as her fingers reached for the buttons of his shirt once more—only this time she wouldn't be removing it so gently.

He reached out for the lock on his cabin door.

And she allowed herself to submit to her basest desires.

Back on the ward, they found the parents of the two children from Mosa busy packing up their things. The children sat in their beds, smiling, talking quietly to each other, obviously pleased to be going home.

Tasha stared hard and then turned to look at Quinn, surprised. 'They're going home?'

She couldn't believe this! It was great for them—of course it was—but why hadn't he told her?

The passion they'd just shared was forgotten as she watched the two children get ready to leave while Abeje still lay in her bed, sick.

'Their parents were keen to take them home. They're much better—we think they'll be fine.'

'But...'

Exasperated, she couldn't think of anything to say. Her lips, her body, were still on fire from the intensity of their lovemaking, but the shock of seeing that the siblings from Mosa were about to leave was slowly numbing her once again. It was a clear reminder that whilst she had been cavorting in Quinn's cabin Abeje had still been ill.

*I can't believe I did that! What kind of person am I?*

She felt hot. Sick. Ashamed of what she'd done.

She went straight over to Abeje's bed, her legs trembling, feeling weak. She would *never* leave Abeje's side again.

*It's good that the children are going home. People do recover from malaria.*

It didn't always have to destroy and decimate.

She saw Quinn give them a small bag of medication as Maria translated to the parents how and when to give the meds. The parents listened, and before Tasha knew it the staff were waving them all goodbye.

Tasha had no doubt that this family would be absolutely fine. They were lucky. It was all working out for them and they deserved this moment as they walked out through the ward's double doors.

She looked down at the floor, sick with regret. Her moment with Quinn had been everything she had dreamed it would be. He was an amazing lover. The need they'd felt for the other had been overwhelming. But...

His gaze locked with hers and she felt heat rise to her cheeks before she looked away. Abeje had been fighting her fever and yet she had gone to Quinn's cabin to look after him and somehow ended up in his bed!

How could she have done that when Abeje was so poorly? How could she have slept with Quinn when this darling little girl was still fighting and needed her by her side?

*I abandoned her...like I abandoned Maddie.*

What if something had gone wrong? What if she had got worse? Deteriorated all alone while she had so selfishly sought comfort from a man. From Abeje's doctor!

*I could never have forgiven myself. I already owe the debt of one life. I can't afford to lose another.*

Tasha vowed to herself there and then that no matter what happened she would not leave Abeje's side again until she was walking out of this hospital ship to go home.

Quinn had felt elated. For about a minute afterwards. And then the guilt had come tumbling down upon him.

He'd slept with Tasha. The first woman he'd slept with since Hannah. It felt wrong to have done so. And he hated the shame he felt inside.

He'd been the one to get out of bed first, to try and dress himself, but he'd had to stand there whilst she helped him with his buttons again. He'd done his best not to look at her, but when he'd had to he'd tried to smile, hoping she wouldn't see the shame he felt.

When they'd got to the treatment deck and Tasha had seen the Mosa kids were leaving she had bolted for Abeje and he'd been glad for the distance. Glad to involve himself with the kids' departure, ensuring they had everything they needed. When they'd gone he'd turned to look at her, trying to decide what to do, but she'd not been looking at him—for which he was grateful.

*I feel I've been unfaithful to my wife.*

Logically, he knew that was ridiculous. Hannah was dead. Had been for years. And he was bound to feel this way the first time he was intimate with someone.

Should it have been Tasha?

A woman he'd already hurt?

A woman he felt responsible for?

*The woman I...*

He couldn't say the last word. Not even to himself. If he said that—if he thought it—it would be like admitting that he might lose another mother and her child.

*I don't know if I can do that again.*

He'd jumped out the frying pan and straight into the fire.

And sparks were flying.


'Miss Tasha?'

Gasping, she looked up, her eyes locking onto Abeje's in an instant. The little girl's eyes were open and she was trying to smile.

*'Abeje!'*

She held her tightly, trying not to squeeze her, but feeling such elation that she was awake and talking. She lay

Abeje back against the pillow and pressed her fingers to her lips for a kiss, then put those fingers on Abeje's cheek.

'You've had me so worried! How are you feeling?'

'I'm thirsty.' She coughed. 'Can I have some water?'

'Of course! Of course you can!' She turned to Maria, who was standing close by. 'Can you get her some?'

'Of course!'

Tasha turned back to the little girl in the bed. 'Everyone has been missing you so much! You have no idea.'

The corners of her mouth curled upwards, just slightly.

'I've been reading to you. And there's a special book of letters the class wrote. When you've got a bit more strength I'll show it to you.'

'I'd like that.' Abeje blinked slowly. 'I am tired.'

'Of course you are. You've been battling hard.'

She laid her hand against Abeje's forehead. Her fever was down. She'd broken it. Beat it. She was going to be all right. Relief flooded her system in such waves that she thought she might easily be knocked off her feet.

Maria brought over a small jug of water and poured some into a cup. As she did so the ship filled with the sound of an alarm—distant, from another floor.

'Excuse me.'

Maria rushed off the floor. No doubt to an emergency.

Tasha held the cup to Abeje's mouth, supporting her head so that it didn't spill everywhere.

'You're going to be all right.'

# CHAPTER EIGHT

ABEJE WAS COUGHING a bit. Sounding chesty. He had to listen in. Just to check. Her lungs were a bit crackly, and he wanted to do something about that.

The pressure to heal Abeje had been weighing heavy on his shoulders. He did not want to feel responsible for ripping Tasha's tender heart in two. He'd not been able to bear imagining Tasha at Abeje's bedside, feeling hopeless as she watched another child die, and to be honest he didn't think he'd have been able to do it either.

He'd feel as if he were to blame. He knew he would. And he couldn't carry the burden of another death on his shoulders.

If he wanted to be with Tasha then she came with Abeje. He knew that. And that was risky for him. He wasn't sure he could allow himself to care for another child like that. So intensely. With his whole heart. She seemed a sweet girl, and Tasha had told him lots about her, but he didn't *know* her.

He wanted to believe that he could. He wanted to believe that maybe he could be happy once again. Be settled, have a family. But...

He watched Tasha as she laughed and smiled and

chatted with Abeje. They were so good together. *Belonged* together.

Perhaps it was best if he just walked away?

Sailed away to Madagascar and didn't look back?

Cursing, he draped his stethoscope around his neck and wrote on her chart.

'I'm going to order an X-ray of her chest.'

'You think she's got an infection?'

Tasha's eyes were wide with fresh fear. With the worry of yet another complication in Abeje's recovery. He saw it clearly. Felt it like a punch in his gut.

*Heal this child.*

'I think she might be developing one.'

'Then we need to get her on antibiotics.'

'We need the films first.'

'But we should start them anyway. What harm would it do?'

He didn't like the way she kept trying to interfere with the treatment. Yes, she might once have been a doctor, but she wasn't one right now, was she?

*Dammit, I'm allowing my fear to become anger. At her. For putting me in this position.*

'Fine. But I'm still ordering an X-ray. It might take a while. That alarm we just heard will be occupying all available staff.'

It was just him, Tasha and Abeje on this floor at the moment. He'd not been able to attend the emergency call. A doctor had to remain on each ward at all times. He couldn't leave. No matter how much he might want to.

'Do you think it might be pneumonia?'

He didn't want to guess. But it was a good assumption.

'I don't know.'

'Pneumonia's bad.'

'You think I don't *know* that?'

She looked hurt. 'Why are you getting angry at *me*?'

'I'm not! I'm just...' He sighed. 'Let me order the X-ray.'

And he stalked over to his desk to phone the order through. Hopefully the X-ray bay would be clear and they could take her straight down.

Only it wasn't. They had someone in there from another floor. Could he give them thirty minutes?

*Sure.*

He sat at his desk, staring over at Tasha, wondering what in the world he was going to do.

His shoulder hurt. Quinn took a couple of painkillers and flexed and stretched his fingers. Having his left arm in a sling was a real obstacle. He hadn't realised for how many things you needed both hands. Simple things. Like doing up buttons. Closing the zip on his trousers. Trying to make a cup of tea. Putting on a fresh bandage. Setting up an IV. Trying to take bloods.

He frequently had to get one of the nurses to assist him.

He felt hobbled, and he didn't like it. It reminded him of the time when he was eighteen and had broken his ankle playing football. Being on crutches for weeks had seriously impaired his mood. That feeling of being somehow *less* than he normally was had been incredibly uncomfortable.

He tried to imagine how Abeje felt, lying in her bed, weak and feeble. Not at full strength. He tried to imagine how Tasha must feel, not being a doctor any more.

*I'd miss it! Way too much!*

He could never stop being a doctor. He could never leave this ship. Well, he didn't think he could. Though he supposed there *were* other medical jobs he could do in Ntembe. Maybe he'd set up his own clinic? That way he could be with Tasha properly and the people here would never be without medical aid. Currently, if *Serendipity* wasn't in dock, they had to walk for days to find it.

*But that would be a big step to take.*

In fact it would be a giant step! They'd both admitted they had feelings for each other, but he had no idea of the *strength* of her feelings. If he jumped ship to stay behind with her, that would make a pretty big statement, wouldn't it?

'Penny for them?' Rob slumped into a chair next to Quinn.

He looked at his good friend and considered admitting everything. But he wasn't a great talker. If his dad had taught him one thing, it was to button up all emotions. You kept them hidden so you weren't thought of as weak.

'You and Maria...you get on, right?'

Rob grinned. 'Yeah, we do.'

'Working together? Living together on this boat?'

'Yeah.'

'And it's going well?'

'Well, we're engaged, so I'd have to say yes.' Rob smiled and chewed on the end of his pen. 'You and Tasha thinking of making it serious?'

Quinn shook his head. 'I don't know. It's complicated.'

'When *isn't* it?'

'It doesn't look complicated for you guys,' he said.

'Are you kidding me?' Rob leaned in to whisper. 'When I met Maria she was with some other guy. A yahoo paramedic who went base-jumping and bungee-jumping and all that other adrenaline junkie crap. Her family *loved* him. Thought he was a real man. Someone who lived life to the full.'

'What happened?'

'To him? Nothing. He's probably still throwing himself out of aeroplanes. But the thing is she fell in love with *me*, and I worked on this ship, and that meant I was going to be taking her away from her family—which the other guy hadn't done—so they hated my guts. Told her that a *real* man would be a doctor, not a nurse, and that she had to break it off with me.'

'I had no idea.'

'They told her it was me or them. That if she came away with me they'd have nothing to do with her. Can you imagine that kind of pressure?'

Quinn shook his head.

'She left with me. And though we're happy, and very much in love—as you can tell—she has this constant battle with vicious emails and telephone calls from her family.'

'She sacrificed love for love?'

He nodded. 'Yeah. And I'm thankful for it every day. I know what it took for her to be here with me.'

'Tasha has sacrificed a lot, too.'

Rob leant forward. 'Look. If you want to be with Tasha, then *be* with her. If you love her, if you have feelings for her, if you can't imagine your life without her, then do it.'

*Could* he imagine life without her now? He thought about sailing off to Madagascar, unable to see her again for a few months. Waving to her from the ship as she remained in port, holding the hand of the little girl she loved so much.

Tasha would bring a ready-made family. She'd come with Abeje—no doubt about that now.

Could he get involved with a mother and child? Put his heart on the line once again?

'She lives *here*.'

'It's gotta be your choice, man. You can save lives anywhere. But your heart stays with one woman.'

'You trying to get rid of me, Rob?' he joked, trying to make the atmosphere less strained.

'No way! You're the kind of guy I'd want in my corner if I ever got sick. But I see how you look at her. How she looks at you when you're not watching. You've got something special. Don't waste it. You have no idea if it'll ever come along again.'

Quinn stared down at the desk. Then he looked up, saw the way Tasha stared at Abeje, with intensity in her searing gaze, desperate for the little girl to get better but fearing a new complication. A new battle to fight for such a small body.

He heard Abeje cough again. It didn't sound good. Alarm bells were sounding in his mind.

Sometimes he found it hard to switch that off—constantly assessing people. Counting respirations. Looking at the sclera of someone's eyes, checking for jaundice.

A million things could give you many clues about a person. A lump low in the throat could be a thyroid problem. A rash could be any number of things from innocent to deadly. Sneezing. Coughing. The sound of someone's breathing. How many breaths they took in a single minute. The way their fingernails looked. The way they walked.

There were always signs a doctor saw, discarded, or became concerned about.

Abeje tried to sit up a bit, so Tasha reached forward to help adjust her pillows. Sitting upright would help her breathing. But she didn't look great.

'Thanks, Rob. I'll…er…have to think about it.'

He wanted to listen in to Abeje's chest again. Maybe start wheeling her down to X-ray. They could wait in the corridor if they weren't ready for them, but it was better to be safe than sorry.

He stepped up to the bed. 'Just whilst you're sitting up, can I have another listen?'

He placed a SATs monitor on Abeje's finger to check her oxygen saturations. It read ninety-four. Which was lower than he'd like. Just to be on the safe side he placed a nasal cannula into her nostrils to give her extra oxygen, tucking the thin tube behind her ears and then tightening the clasp just under her chin before listening in with his stethoscope.

Tasha looked at him, one eyebrow raised, but she sat and took hold of Abeje's hand.

'Now, I don't want you to worry about the work you've missed in class. I'll help you catch up when you're much better.' She smiled. 'I took some photos on my phone of the class. Let me show you what we've been up to.'

Tasha leaned in and turned her phone so Abeje could see.

'This is one of everyone showing their acrostic poems, using the letters of their names. Habib's one was *very* funny! Just wait till you hear it—he's going to grow up to be a comedian!'

Quinn stood beside them, grateful that she was trying to keep Abeje's spirits lifted. He wrote her SATs into her medical notes, but the monitor on her finger was still there and he could see that even with the nasal cannula her SATs were falling.

'Tasha...'

'Look at this one of Claudette. Oh, she was so proud of this painting! Can you tell what it is?'

Tasha hadn't heard the note of warning in his voice. The concern. She was just thrilled to be showing her pictures to Abeje.

The oxygen saturations continued to fall. Ninety-one. Ninety. Eighty-eight.

'Okay, Abeje, I don't think that position is a good one for you to be in. I'm going to give you some full-flow oxygen.' He leant forward to remove the cannula and place the mask over her face.

Tasha sat back as if he'd shocked her with electricity, her face draining of colour. 'What's happening?'

'Her SATs are dropping.'

'What's going on?' There was a note of panic in her voice now.

'I'm not sure.'

He met Tasha's gaze then, and read the question in her eyes. The question she didn't want to speak out loud in case it frightened the little girl.

*Is she going into respiratory arrest?*

That was *his* fear.

He looked for Rob. He'd been there a moment ago—where had he gone? It was just him and Tasha.

Abeje's eyes closed and her face went slack.

'Oh, my God!' Tasha leapt back, startled, dropping her phone to the deck.

Quinn smacked the emergency button behind the bed and the alarm sounded. He needed to remove the pillows from behind Abeje's head, but he needed both hands—

one to remove the pillows and another to steady Abeje's neck. But he was hobbled…one arm strapped to his chest.

'Tasha, remove the pillows. I'll hold her head.'

'Quinn…'

He looked at her. She was terrified. Her worst fears were coming true—so much so that she had frozen, unable to do anything.

But he needed her. Needed her desperately to help him.

'Tasha! Look at me. *Look. At. Me!*'

Her terrified gaze shifted to his face. 'I need you to help me. I need you to do CPR. She's stopped breathing. I need you to help her.'

'I…' Tasha looked down at little Abeje, who lay lifeless and non-responsive on the bed. 'I can't!'

'Yes, you can! I can't do it like this. *Quickly!* Please! If you don't help her now…' He didn't want to finish his sentence. He didn't want to say the words.

*Then she'll definitely die.*

*She* was the one who had to do this. He could maybe attempt chest compressions with one hand, but they needed her lying flat. They needed to remove those pillows. Get a backboard so that the chest compressions would have a decent effect.

He grabbed hold of the pillows and yanked. Abeje's head flopped onto the mattress. He couldn't open up her airway with one hand—he needed Tasha!

And suddenly she was there. Her hands crossed over each other, in the centre of Abeje's chest, doing compressions, her face a mask of agony, her tortured voice counting out to thirty as tears streamed down her face.

'I'll get the backboard.'

He ran over to the side of the room, grabbed it off the

wall, where it hung in case of emergencies such as this one, and then came running back.

'Help me slide it under.'

He had no idea what had suddenly caused the little girl to go into respiratory distress. It had just happened. But he saw this all the time, and he hated it that he'd known something like this might still happen. She'd taken so long to get better, and she'd always seemed so weak. He'd sensed this. Suspected that something might still go wrong, that she wasn't out of the woods yet.

*If she dies...*

He couldn't think about that right now. Ifs. Whats. Maybes. All that mattered was following life-saving protocols. Nothing else.

Kids frequently went into respiratory distress. It was more common for that to happen than a cardiac arrest. But it could *lead* to a cardiac event.

He checked her pulse.

It was absent.

'I'm going to get the crash cart—keep going!'

Tasha was giving her two breaths as he rushed away for the cart, which was on the far side of the ward, and when he returned she was back doing compressions.

'Fifteen...sixteen...seventeen...'

'You're doing great, Tash.'

He reached for the pads, but they were in a pack that needed to be torn open. He couldn't do that with one hand.

'Open these.'

Using the heel of his right hand he continued to do compressions whilst Tasha fumbled with the pack, ripping it open audibly. And he continued to pump up and down as Tasha placed the pads—one near the right shoulder, just under the collarbone, the second just below Abeje's left breast.

*Analysing.*

The machine paused to read Abeje's heart trace, if any.

*Shock required. Stand clear.*

Tasha checked to make sure he'd stepped away from the bed, and then she pressed the button with the little red lightning flash on it.

'Shocking!' she yelled.

At the moment the charge was delivered the ward door swung open, smacking the wall behind it, and in ran Rob. He took one look and then ran to them instantly to take over compressions.

*Maintain CPR.*

Quinn stepped back, exhausted and spent, his injured shoulder raging with pain, but that didn't matter. All that mattered was the little girl.

*Analysing.*
*No shock required.*

Rob checked her pulse. 'She's back. I've got a pulse!'

They gave her full-flow oxygen again and Rob rolled her into the recovery position, constantly monitoring her breathing.

Abeje began to moan as she came to.

Quinn let out a long breath, relief flooding through him as he looked at Tasha. She stood there white as the bedsheet, horror in her eyes, staring at her hands. At what they'd had to do.

'Tasha? You okay?'

She looked at him. A startled rabbit in the headlights. It was as if she'd just seen something in him that she'd never seen before.

Turning, she bolted from the ward.

He couldn't go after her. He had to stay and help Rob in case Abeje went into arrest again.

She wasn't in the clear yet.

*What had just happened?*

Tasha couldn't believe it. One minute they'd been smiling and looking at pictures, and the next...

It had turned into a nightmare.

*A nightmare!*

Her worst fears...

She'd been depending upon Quinn to keep Abeje safe. Trusting him with her, trusting the medication, trusting in his care, and it had been hard for her. The worst thing she'd ever had to do because...

Because she'd tried to save Maddie and she had failed. But she had tried to save Abeje and she had started breathing again. They'd got her back.

Her belief in her own abilities was changing, and she'd realised something as she'd pumped up and down on Abeje's chest. Something that had become quite clear as she'd tried to save the little girl's life.

She *needed* Abeje to survive—not just because it would be awful if she died, but also because she was beginning to believe she could have a family. Beginning to believe that she could love again. Beginning to believe that she was worth caring for.

*And she couldn't lose her family.*

Not just Abeje, but Quinn too.

She'd been through some tough times in the last few years, but she was still here. Still upright. Still trying to live and love.

She already loved Abeje, but she wanted to love Quinn, too.

He'd helped her to get Abeje back. They'd done it together. And she'd seen in his face, in his eyes, in the depth of his soul that he was trying everything he could, trying his utmost to bring Abeje back to her. One of her most precious loves.

It wasn't shock at the realisation that Abeje had survived—it was shock at the realisation that she'd put herself out there again…for him. To give him her heart…to give him her trust, her love.

*Only he didn't want it, did he?*

She'd seen the regret in his eyes after they'd made love. The guilt he'd felt. The shame? She had almost felt him backpedalling away from what they'd done when he'd got out of bed and asked her to help him put his shirt back on. He'd barely been able to look at her.

But the life or death crisis over Abeje had cleared the veil from her eyes. Her heart beat for *him*. It always had. It was probably in sync with his, both beating like hearts in a mirror.

And he was discarding her once again. Discarding her as her parents had. As Simon had. As he had when they were teenagers. Only back then she hadn't slept with him. Now she had, and that hurt even more.

Abeje's crisis had made her see her own.

She couldn't look at him.

Couldn't bear the idea of meeting his gaze.

That was why she'd run away, needing fresh air, needing space to get some perspective on what she would have to do.

*Abeje will want me by her bedside.*

But still she couldn't go in.

*I don't need to see the goodbye in his eyes.*

She'd cared.

Loved.

Had given her heart to him.

And now it hurt. Hurt as if someone had reached inside her chest, ripped her still-beating heart from it and then crushed it right before her eyes.

A low, keening groan escaped her lips as she bent double, almost unable to breathe.

*This was it.*

This was what the pain felt like when you lost everything.

She couldn't go back.

She couldn't face anyone.

Not Abeje, not Rob, Maria.

Not Quinn.

None of them.

Because she was a failure. Everyone else had always known it but her, it seemed.

She couldn't do this.

She didn't have the strength.

Now Quinn would see her for what she really was.

*A coward.*

And he would leave her—just like everyone else in her life had already done.

* * *

Quinn wiped the clammy sweat from his brow and sat down, exhausted. His shoulder burned like nothing he had ever experienced before. A white-hot ball of fire. But it was nothing to the pain of the emptiness he felt inside.

Tasha had scared him. The way she'd stood there frightened, frozen in fear, when he'd needed her to help him. Needed her to help save Abeje! He'd not been able to do it alone, he'd needed her help. When she had just stood there like a statue for one terrible moment he'd thought he'd have to try and do it alone, and if he'd had to do that, with just one arm, try to do CPR and apply pads and provide breaths, he knew he would have failed.

Abeje would have died. His worst fear would have been realised.

Thankfully Tasha had leapt into action—but that pause, that hesitation, that inability to move had terrified him. He'd not been ready to lose that little girl and he'd certainly not been ready to give in. *He couldn't have.*

Because he'd known if he had to wrap his arms around Tasha one more time to stop himself seeing her heart torn asunder he would be lost.

He'd be hers.

Totally and utterly.

And that scared the hell out of him.

He'd loved a woman and a child before. He'd made them his everything. And when he'd lost everything he had known how absolutely soul-destroying it could be. There was no way he wanted to go through *that* again.

But they'd been lucky. They'd worked as a team, they'd saved her life, and then Rob had arrived to provide relief and there had been more hands, and Abeje had been breathing again, and...

She was stable for now. They'd done a scan and discovered that Abeje had fluid in her lungs—he wasn't sure if it was a result of the parasitical infection or not at this moment, but they were treating her now. She was awake, her face covered by a high-flow oxygen mask, and she was talking. Sore, but talking.

Quinn was sure that she would be okay. It had been tricky there for a while, but he believed her crisis was over.

And Tasha was nowhere to be seen.

Abeje was asking for her. Missing her. They'd grown close, those two, like mother and daughter, and Abeje wanted her 'mum'—like all kids when they're sick. Tasha was the closest thing to a mum that Abeje would ever have.

Well, if she couldn't have her mum...

He slipped into the chair at the side of Abeje's bed and took her hand in his, cradling it as if it was a jewel. Stroking it. Trying to convey with the power of touch his concern, his love.

'Miss Tasha's just getting some fresh air. You know you scared us?'

Abeje nodded. 'I was scared, too.'

'I bet.' His heart bled for her. She was so strong—so brave! So...

And that was when he realised. He didn't just care for Abeje because she was part of Tasha's package—he cared for Abeje because he really *cared* about her! He didn't want her to be hurt. He didn't want her to feel frightened and alone and now he had stepped in. Stepped over the mark that doctors should not cross and taken up the mantle of a *father*.

It shocked him.

Scared him.

But, although the shock of adrenaline that hit his system made his legs feel weak, he also realised something else about himself.

*It's okay. I can do this.*

He *wanted* to do it! Wanted to expose himself in that way to the terrifying reality of being a parent again—but he wanted to do it with Tasha. She was his beating heart. His soul. His life. He couldn't live without her. Even now, with her gone, it was unbearable!

Sure, he'd felt guilty after they'd made love—but wasn't that to be expected? It had been his first time with a woman since his wife.

He didn't want to leave either of them.

He needed to let Tasha know how he truly felt.

'I'm going to get Tasha. Bring her back to the boat,' he told Rob as he came to Abeje's bedside to adjust her drip.

'All right, mate.'

It was like an oven outside as he strode out of the cool air-conditioned ship and into the heat of the African sun. His painkillers were just starting to take the edge off his pain, but they weren't touching the pain he felt in his heart at the thought that he might not get her to come back.

He expected to have to go all the way to her house, but as he stomped down the gangplank he saw her at the bottom, sitting on the bonnet of his rusty car.

She looked up. Saw him coming and then madly wiped her eyes and got up to walk away. 'Please go away. I don't want to see you.'

'We need to talk.'

She spun round, glaring at him, her eyes watering. 'How's Abeje?'

'Stable. Asking for you.'

'I can't go in looking like this. Tell her I'll be in soon.'

'You look amazing.'

'*Don't!* Just…don't. None of your pity, please. I know how you feel and you don't have to tell me twice. I'm used to rejection, and I'm particularly used to rejection from *you*!'

'I love you, Tasha Kincaid.'

It felt good to say it. To say it out loud. And proud. He didn't have to hide from those feelings any more.

'*What?*' she looked at him, incredulous, through blurred red eyes.

'I love you. From the top of your curls all the way to your toes. I love you and I want to be with you.'

She blinked. Confused. Shook her head. 'But after we…'

'I was frightened. I felt guilty about Hannah. I hadn't been with anyone since she passed away. You were my first. I was shocked by how it made me feel. But what we just did—we saved a life! Saved *Abeje's* life! It's made me see just what I don't want to lose. I've always tried to avoid this. Mothers and their children. And for the most part I've been successful. But you, Tasha, you came into my life like an explosion of feelings I wasn't ready for. You confused me. Made me second-guess myself. I wasn't sure what I was doing half the time. But then we saved Abeje, and, I held her hand, and I realised that I was ready. Ready to love again. Ready to be a partner. A husband. A father. I can do it. But only if I have you by my side.'

She wrapped her arms around her waist. 'People I love always leave me.'

He stepped up to her, unpeeled her arms and took her hands in his. 'Not me. *Not me.*'

She looked at him uncertainly. 'You mean this? It isn't a joke? One last joke on Nit-Nat? Because if it is then you're being very cruel.'

He kissed her hands. 'I mean it.'

'What if I'm not good enough? What if you realise that after all this time I really am just Nit-Nat? The girl you despised.'

'I never despised you. *Never.* There was nothing wrong with you, Tash. That was all *me*, being stupid. Like I've been stupid these last few days, allowing fear and shame to control me as it did all those years ago. But you make me strong. If I have you then we can get through anything together, and I just know—if we let it—we could have a great future.'

'But you're leaving soon.'

'No. I'm not. I'll stay here. What if…? What if we build a clinic together? So the people we love here can have medical care when they need it—not after a two-day walk in forty-degree heat, or after waiting for a ship to pull into port? We can build our dreams *here*, Tash. Together. What do you say?'

She seemed to be thinking about it. Keeping him in agony until a small smile began to build upon her face.

'Tell me you love me again.'

He let out a breath and beamed her his best smile.

'I love you, Tasha Kincaid. Now, tell me you feel the same.'

'You always were the root of my problems, Quinn Shapiro.'

'But…?'

A smile broke across her face. 'But I love you.'

He scooped her up and whirled her round, then put her down only to cradle her face and kiss her.

'Right. We can celebrate later. Right now there's a young girl that wants to see you.'

He took her hand and began to pull her up the gang-plank.

'Quinn?'

'Yes?'

'Thank you. For everything.'

He smiled.

# EPILOGUE

'WE DON'T WANT to be late. Have you got your shoes on?'

Tasha popped her head into Abeje's bedroom and saw her daughter fastening the buckles on her sandals.

She held out her hand. 'Come on.'

Wearing sunhats and their finest dresses, they left the house hand in hand.

'Will Daddy be at the clinic?'

'Yes. He had to get there early. He wanted to do one last check on the place before we open it up to the public.'

'And I get to cut the ribbon?'

She smiled. 'You get to cut the ribbon.'

Abeje was so excited about being the one to open the clinic. But it seemed right. They'd thought about getting the town leader to do it, but they wanted someone close to them to do it. They'd adopted Ntembe as their home, and Abeje as their daughter, so it seemed only right. It wasn't favouritism, or nepotism. This was her home. Her city. She'd lived here before they had.

The long dark days of malaria were behind them. Abeje had grown big and tall, thriving in the warmth of a loving family. The day the adoption papers had gone through had been the happiest of their lives. Their next dream? To open this clinic!

A crowd had gathered outside, and it took them some time to work their way through it to the front. There were so many people Tasha knew now, and they all wanted to stop her, say hello, shake her hand or kiss her on the cheek. Thank her for what they were doing for their community.

Tasha was incredibly excited, nerves tumbling around in her stomach. She couldn't wait to see Quinn. Couldn't wait to stand by his side.

And then she saw him, dressed in a white shirt and khaki trousers, ensuring that the yellow ribbon stretched across the entrance was fixed securely for the grand opening.

'Quinn!' she called, beaming when he turned round and smiled at both of them.

He held out his arms and Abeje went running into them. He scooped her up, hoisting her onto his hip.

'You're getting a bit big for this now.'

'Never!' Abeje laughed.

'Well, when my back gives out we'll stop, okay?'

'Okay.'

He kissed her on the cheek and then put her down, reaching out to embrace Tasha.

She sank into his arms happily.

Today was a great day.

They'd had many great days together. The day Abeje had left the hospital…waving goodbye to the *Serendipity* as it sailed out of port, leaving Quinn by her side… moving in together…getting married…adopting Abeje.

And now this day. The opening of their clinic. Their dream.

It meant so much, what they would be able to do—not only for this community but those around it. Cutting down treatment times, getting healthcare to those who desperately needed it. And they'd even got a small team of trucks to use as mobile hospitals, after remembering the trips they'd taken out to Mosa and the more remote villages.

Many lives were about to change for the better.

As were theirs.

Tasha kissed Quinn, revelling, as she always did, in holding him close, feeling the strength of his love for her.

The intensity of their love for each other was overwhelmingly wonderful. She'd never felt anything like it. She had a family of her own. Was this what other people had? This happiness? This *belonging*?

'I'd better make a start, then.' Quinn said.

'Good luck.'

She let go of his hand as he stepped up onto a small podium and the assembled crowd grew quiet. A sea of expectant happy faces looked up at him.

Tasha handed Abeje the pair of scissors she was to use for the ceremony. 'Stay with me. Wait for Daddy to finish.'

'Hello, everyone! Welcome to the Ntembe Clinic! It's good to see so many of you here today. So many familiar faces.'

Tasha could see Maria and Rob in the front row. They stood holding hands, beaming smiles up at their old colleagues. It was good to see them here. They'd taken leave from the *Serendipity*—just for a month for their honeymoon—and they'd promised to be here, despite no doubt having many more important things to be getting on with!

'My wife Tasha and I have long held a dream to open up a clinic here. To serve you—our friends, our family, all the people we have come to know and love here. We hope it will become a vital site—not just for healing, but for education and support for everyone.'

They certainly had grand plans. They wanted to teach here. Teach communities about safe sex, about immunisation, about first aid practices and how to do CPR. They wanted to run a volunteer centre here, a blood clinic, a midwifery centre, and most of all they wanted to accept medical students—to give them the education and experience they would need to advance in the medical world. It wasn't just going to be a clinic to patch people up and send them on their way.

'So, without further ado, I would like to invite my daughter, Abeje, to do the honours and open up the Ntembe Clinic!'

He stepped down from the dais and moved back so that everyone would be able to see her cut the ribbon.

Shyly Abeje stepped forward, and held the ribbon. She looked up at her father and he nodded encouragingly. Then she took the scissors with both hands and with a huge smile cut through it. The two pieces fluttered to each side as everyone behind her cheered and clapped their approval.

'Well done, sweetpea!' Tasha took her hand and together they stepped into the clinic. Their brand-new, clean-as-a-whistle clinic, with the crowd following in behind them.

She felt a hand slip into hers. Quinn.

'This is it. The start of everything.'

She smiled, looking back at him. 'It is.'

'Was my speech too short, do you think?'

'It was perfect. It's too hot to stand out there listening when everyone wants to be inside to see it for themselves.'

'You're right. As ever.' He kissed her cheek.

They stood there, accepting congratulations from everyone who passed. They shook countless hands, thanked hundreds of people, it seemed, and spent hours explaining what each room was for, what services they'd offer, and said that everyone was welcome—whether they could afford to pay or not.

And when the crowds were gone, and the last person had said goodbye, the three of them stood in what would be the waiting room of the clinic and looked about them.

'Can you believe we did it?' asked Quinn.

'Yes,' she said. 'Because we did it together.'

He stroked her cheek. 'I couldn't have done it without you, Dr Shapiro.'

'Well, in a few months you might have to,' she answered, her cheeks flushing as her hand went to her belly and she began to tell him the secret she had held inside her since discovering the good news just a few short days ago.

He frowned. Then his eyes widened. 'You're pregnant?'

She nodded. 'About ten weeks.'

He pulled her into his arms and hugged her tight.

She was so happy that he was thrilled. She'd been dying to tell him, but had thought that telling him today would be the best thing. She'd wanted to be sure. And it had taken a few days for it to sink in with her, too.

Her own baby. Her own flesh and blood. She'd never had that.

Tasha kissed him, looking into his eyes, and then she knelt down, beaming at Abeje.

'You're going to be a big sister!'

* * * * *

# MILLS & BOON

## Coming next month

### BOUND BY THEIR BABIES
Caroline Anderson

People joked all the time about sex-crazed widows, and there was no way—*no way*—she was turning into one! This was *Jake*, for heaven's sake! Her friend. Not her lover. Not her boyfriend. And certainly not someone for a casual one-nighter.

Although they'd almost gone there that once, and the memory of the awkwardness that had followed when they'd come to their senses and pulled away from the brink had never left her, although it had long been buried.

Until now...

Emily heard the stairs creak again, and pressed down the plunger and slid the pot towards him as he came into the room.

'Here, your coffee.'

'Aren't you having any?'

She shook her head, but she couldn't quite meet his eyes, and she realised he wasn't looking at her, either. 'I'll go back up in case Zach cries and wakes Matilda. Don't forget to ring me when you've seen Brie.'

'OK. Thanks for making the coffee.'

'You're welcome. Have a good day.'

She tiptoed up the stairs, listened for the sound of the front door closing and watched him from his bedroom window as he walked briskly down the road towards the hospital, travel mug in hand.

He turned the corner and went out of sight, and she sat down on the edge of his bed, her fingers knotting in a handful of rumpled bedding. *What was she doing?* With a stifled scream of frustration, she fell sideways onto the mattress and buried her face in his duvet.

Mistake. She could smell the scent of him on the sheets, warm and familiar and strangely exciting, could picture that glorious nakedness stretched out against the stark white linen, a beautiful specimen of masculinity in its prime—

She jack-knifed to her feet. This was crazy. What on earth had happened to her? They'd been friends for years, and now all of a sudden this uncontrollable urge to sniff his sheets?

They had to keep this platonic. So much was riding on it—their mutual careers, if nothing else!

And the children—they had to make this work for the children, especially Matilda. The last thing she needed—any of them needed—was this fragile status quo disrupted for anything as trivial as primitive, adolescent lust.

It wasn't fair on any of them, and she'd embarrassed herself enough fifteen years ago. She wasn't doing it again.

No way.

Continue reading
**BOUND BY THEIR BABIES**
Caroline Anderson

*Available next month*
www.millsandboon.co.uk

# LET'S TALK
## *Romance*

For exclusive extracts, competitions
and special offers, find us online:

Or get in touch on 0844 844 1351*

For all the latest titles coming soon, visit
millsandboon.co.uk/nextmonth

*Calls cost 7p per minute plus your phone company's price per minute access charg

# Want even more
# ROMANCE?

## Join our bookclub today!

'Mills & Boon books, the perfect way to escape for an hour or so.'

Miss W. Dyer

'Excellent service, promptly delivered and very good subscription choices.'

Miss A. Pearson

'You get fantastic special offers and the chance to get books before they hit the shops'

Mrs V. Hall

**Visit millsandbook.co.uk/Bookclub**
**and save on brand new books.**

## MILLS & BOON